33204

#3.75

Critical acclaim for the novels of Vonda N. McIntyre

TRANSITION

"*Transition* is a m[...]
extrapolati[...]

"A fin[...]
—Greg Bear

METAPHASE

"The best Starfarer novel to date."
—*Booklist*

"With this third novel, *Starfarers* clearly becomes
the most important series in science fiction . . .
the most exciting and satisfying science fiction
I have read this year."
—Ursula K. Le Guin

DREAMSNAKE

"[*Dreamsnake*] is filled with scenes as suspenseful
as anyone could wish . . . but most of all it addresses
the humanity of all of us."
—*The Seattle Times*

"[*Dreamsnake*] is an exciting future-dream
with real characters, a believable mythos and,
what's more important, an excellent, readable story."
—Frank Herbert, author of the *Dune* series

Agora Books
228 - 7 Avenue S.W., Calgary, Alberta Canada T2P 0W8
403-294-1449

Bantam Books by Vonda N. McIntyre

The Starfarers Series
STARFARERS
TRANSITION
METAPHASE
NAUTILUS

DREAMSNAKE

And coming in November in hardcover
Star Wars®: THE CRYSTAL STAR

STARFARERS

Vonda N. McIntyre

BANTAM BOOKS
NEW YORK · TORONTO · LONDON · SYDNEY · AUCKLAND

This edition contains the complete text
of the original edition.
NOT ONE WORD HAS BEEN OMITTED.

STARFARERS
A Bantam Spectra Book/by arrangement with the author

PUBLISHING HISTORY
Ace edition published/April 1989
Bantam edition/October 1994

SPECTRA and the portrayal of a boxed "s" are trademarks of Bantam Books,
a division of Bantam Doubleday Dell Publishing Group, Inc.

All rights reserved.
Copyright © 1989 by Vonda N. McIntyre.
Cover art copyright © 1994 by Michael Herring.
No part of this book may be reproduced or transmitted in any
form or by any means, electronic or mechanical, including
photocopying, recording, or by any information storage and
retrieval system, without permission in writing from the publisher.
For information address: Bantam Books.

ISBN 0-553-56341-6

Published simultaneously in the United States and Canada

Bantam Books are published by Bantam Books, a division of Bantam
Doubleday Dell Publishing Group, Inc. Its trademark, consisting of
the words "Bantam Books" and the portrayal of a rooster, is Registered
in U.S. Patent and Trademark Office and in other countries. Marca Reg-
istrada. Bantam Books, 1540 Broadway, New York, New York 10036.

PRINTED IN THE UNITED STATES OF AMERICA

OPM   0 9 8 7 6 5 4 3 2 1

*To Michael, Holly, Terry, Leroy, Sue,
for believing in the starship before it existed;
To Ryan for the video and Steve for the t-shirts;
and, of course,
To Majel & Gene for encouragement at the
airport*

For two books in a row, I've drawn on the work of Dr. Gerard K. O'Neill, the founder of the Space Studies Institute. His speculations on the ways human beings might live and work and thrive in space added immeasurably to the background of my novel and to the structure of *Starfarer*.

Dr. John G. Cramer, nuclear physicist and sf novelist in his own right, the author of *Twistor*, once again offered his expertise and advice. I'm grateful for his help with *Starfarer*'s propulsion systems, among other things, and glad that he is still willing to speak to me despite my fascination with faster-than-light starship drives.

A conversation with Howard Davidson gave me the idea for sensory artists.

The organizers of Orycon, Portland's sf convention, gave *Starfarers* programming time for several years running, until the members of the starship's alien contact department took over and demanded that I write their story.

Only I can be held responsible for the wilder social, political, or biological speculations of *Starfarers*.

Nervous and excited and rushed and late, J. D. Sauvage hurried down the corridor of the terminal. The satchel carrying her personal allowance thumped against her hip. The other passengers had already begun to board the spaceplane.

"J.D.!"

Victoria Fraser MacKenzie strode toward her. J.D. was aware of the attention of the other people in the waiting area, surely recognizing Victoria, perhaps also wondering who the heavy-set, sunburned newcomer might be. Victoria was the sort of person one noticed. Though she was small and compact, she had a powerful presence. Everything about her was intense: her energy, her eyes, the black of her hair, her passionate defense of the deep space expedition. She had been much in the news lately.

She extended her hand. J.D. took it. The contrast of Victoria's hand, dark and smooth, the nails well groomed, to her own, the skin roughened by exposure to wind and sea, the nails pared down as short as they could get, made J.D. wish she had had more time to prepare for this trip.

"I'm glad to see you," Victoria said.

"Were you afraid I'd changed my mind again?"

"No. Not once you agreed. J.D. . . . I know how important your research is to you. But the expedition is unique. The orcas will still be here when we get back. The divers, too."

I hope so, J.D. thought, but she did not say it aloud.

"Come on," Victoria said. "We'd better hurry."

They walked into the entry tunnel and joined the end of the line.

"This is your first trip up, eh?" Victoria said. "Is there anything you want to know that they didn't cover at the orientation?"

"Um . . . I missed the orientation."

"You *missed* it?"

"I was down at cargo. It took longer than I expected."

"Was there a problem?"

"They didn't want to load my equipment."

"Whyever not?"

"Because it didn't look like equipment to them. They tried to redefine it as personal and make me take only what I could fit in my allowance."

"What kind of equipment is it?"

"Information, mostly."

"Why didn't you put it on the web? Arachne can always give it back to you."

"Most of it is books, and most of the books I have aren't in any databases."

"You could have had them scanned."

"Some of them are unique, though, and they get so beat up when you send them out for scanning. I didn't have time to do it myself."

"What kind of books are you talking about?"

"Old ones. You won't understand until you see them."

"How many did you bring?"

"Three hundred fifty-seven kilos."

"Good lord."

"That isn't really very much, when you're talking about books."

"And it isn't half what any experimental physicist would bring. As for a geneticist—" Victoria laughed. "Considering all the stuff Stephen Thomas brought, you'd think he was single-handedly in charge of diversity and cloning."

"Is he?"

"No, that's his boss, Professor Thanthavong."

"I'm really looking forward to meeting her," J.D. said. "Do you think I'll get a chance to?"

"Sure. She's not standoffish at all. The more you can forget she's famous, the better you'll get along with her, eh? Anyway, Stephen Thomas still does some bioelectronics, though that's pretty much been taken over by the developers. He's branched out into theories of non-nucleic-acid inheritance. Exogenetics. One of our celebrated 'nonexistent' disciplines. The equipment he needs is pretty standard lab stuff, but when he came up, he brought a lot of extraneous things."

"How did he talk it all through cargo?"

Victoria made a strange little motion of her shoulders, a gesture of amused disbelief. J.D. wondered why she did not simply shake her head. Maybe it had something to do with her being Canadian. J.D. had studied a number of different cultures, but had never looked past the superficial resemblance of Canadian culture to the majority culture of the U.S. She decided not to admit that to Victoria.

"If you ask Arachne for the definition of 'charm,' " Victoria said, "it gives you back a picture of Stephen Thomas Gregory."

J.D. followed Victoria to their places. Victoria helped her transfer her allowance into a string bag, then showed her how to strap in against the upright lounge. It held her in a position with her hips and knees slightly flexed.

"Where are the controls for this thing?" J.D. looked for the way to turn the lounge into a chair. "How do you sit down?"

"You don't," Victoria said. "It takes a lot of energy to keep your body in a sitting position in microgravity. It's much easier to lie nearly flat. Or stand, depending on how you look at it."

J.D. thought about how it would feel to sit and stand and lie stretched out in space, comparing it to her diving experience.

"Okay," she said. "I see. That makes sense." She grasped the armrests. Fright tinged her excitement, not unpleasantly. Her fingers trembled. Victoria noticed her nervousness and patted her hand. The sound patterns changed as the spaceplane readied itself for takeoff. J.D. would have sworn that like a bird or a dolphin she could feel the increase in the magnetic field, the shift and slide of it as it oriented itself to thrust the spaceplane down the long rails. Of course that was absurd.

Victoria finished transferring her own allowance from the carrier to the compartment. She had several acceleration-resistant packages, but most of her allowance consisted of fancy clothes, similar to what she was wearing.

"Victoria," J.D. said hesitantly, "do people dress, um, more formally on board than they would back here?"

Victoria was wearing an embroidered shirt and wide suede trousers caught at her ankles with feathered ties.

"Hmm?" Victoria closed the compartment and gave J.D.'s satchel to the artificial stupid waiting to take them off the plane. Getting out of earth's gravity well was too expensive to spend the acceleration on suitcases. The AS buzzed away.

"I couldn't help but notice what you're wearing. I didn't bring anything like that, if that's what's called for on the ship."

Victoria glanced at her, then chuckled. J.D. shifted uncomfortably. She had thrown away most of her beat-up old clothes, and ordered new ones that she packed without trying on. She had not had time even to consider buying anything formal.

"I'm not laughing at you," Victoria said quickly. "Just imagining going to the lab in this outfit. We're pretty casual on campus. But sometimes I get tired of casual. I always fill up the extra corners of my personal allowance with silly clothes. You can get necessities back home. It's the things you can do without that you start to miss."

"I see," J.D. said, relieved.

"Don't worry, you'll fit right in. There's no dress code, and the environment is moderate. Too moderate, I think. We don't have weather, we have climate. I wouldn't mind some snow, or a thunderstorm. Satoshi thinks it's too cold, but he's spoiled—he grew up in Hawaii."

Victoria leaned against her couch and fastened the straps. "*I'm* ready," she said. "So let's get going."

"I should tell you something," J.D. said.

"Oh?"

The careful neutrality in Victoria's tone told J.D. that her own original decision—to turn down the invitation to join *Starfarer's* alien contact department—had had an effect that would take time to overcome.

"I resigned from the Department of State," J.D. said. "And turned back my grant."

"Did you? I'm glad. I'm sorry I snapped at you about having such close ties to your government. But these days you never know when they might slap 'classified' all over your research." Suddenly Victoria grinned. "Though if you were still an ambassador, that would put you higher on the protocol list than the chancellor, eh?"

"I was more on the level of special attaché, and anyway the orcas don't use titles. They don't even understand them, as far as I could ever tell. It's one of those human concepts like ownership or jealousy that if you finally get through a hint of what it means, they just think it's funny. We're pretty funny to them in general. I used to wonder if they let me hang around for my entertainment value."

"What made you decide to quit?" Victoria asked bluntly.

"I thought about what you said, about the arguments between the U.S. government and EarthSpace. I worried."

"As do we all."

"I didn't want divided loyalties." J.D. felt guilty for making two true statements and implying a direct connection between them. For the moment, though, she could not explain to Victoria, to anyone, her real reasons for all her decisions of the last few days.

She stared out the window at the mountain slope, the treeline a few hundred meters below, the peaks receding to blue in the distance.

"Don't worry," Victoria said, mistaking her distraction. "The acceleration isn't bad at all."

"I'm sure I'll be fine."

The plane jolted slightly as it released itself from the gate. J.D. gasped and clutched Victoria's hand.

Victoria smiled and let J.D. hold on as the plane slid forward.

Victoria loved riding the spaceplane. She enjoyed the landings, but she liked the takeoffs even better.

The plane accelerated, racing over its magnetic rails, its delta-vee increasing, pressing Victoria against her couch. The plane reached the bottom of the long fast slope and pulsed forward along the magnetic lines of force, driven faster and faster by a great roller coaster with a single unending rise.

The magnetic rail flung the plane off its end and into the air. The acceleration ceased abruptly: heart-fall hit.

"Wow," J.D. said, breathless.

"What do you think?"

"That's the first time I ever rode a roller coaster that I liked."

Victoria felt the slight pressure of her body against the seat belts as, in weightlessness, gravity no longer held her against her couch. Beside her, J.D. peered eagerly through the roof window as the blue sky gave way to a deep indigo that gradually faded to starry black.

"It's just beautiful."

"It is, isn't it?"

The spaceplane rotated around its long axis and the earth came into view through the roof window. Despite the lack of gravity, the arrangement of the couches made the window feel like "up." Earth appeared to loom above her. For her first few trips into space, Victoria had tried to cultivate an attitude of nonchalance about the sight of earth spinning slowly before her. Gradually, though, she realized that even the veterans of space travel never lost their awe, never grew hardened. No matter how matter-of-fact they acted about the dangers or the hardships of the early days, they never pretended to have the same cool indifference to earth, vulnerable and without boundaries, whole in their sight, a sphere they could cup in their hands.

Victoria glanced at J.D., who stared up through the window with her mouth slightly open. Her short lank hair stood out from her head as if she were underwater.

"I never thought . . . I've imagined this, I've seen it in pictures and on film, even on sensory recording. I thought I'd know what it felt like. But it's different, seeing it for real."

"It is," Victoria said. "It's always different, seeing it for real."

The earth fell behind. The spaceplane slid smoothly into an orbit to catch up and dock with the transport to *Starfarer*.

"What's it like to swim with the orcas?" Victoria said.

"It's like this," J.D. said.

"Like space travel?"

"Uh-huh. Looking at earth from space is the nearest thing I've ever felt to being underwater and suddenly realizing that the light at the limit of your vision is the white patch on an orca's side. Then when they come closer . . .

They're magical. Until now I thought that if I could find the right words, I'd be able to explain it to everyone. But no one ever found the right words to explain—to me, anyway—how it feels to look at earth from space. Maybe no one can explain either."

"Damn," Victoria said. "I wish we'd had this conversation a couple of days ago."

"Why?"

"Because I'd have stolen your line, when I talked to the premier last night. And I wish I'd thought of saying that to your Mr. Distler, when I testified last year."

"*I* didn't vote for him," J.D. said. "Not for senator—I don't even come from the same state—or when he ran for president. Never mind, I know what you mean."

"That's what I should have told him—that he couldn't understand why we wanted to be here unless he came and saw it for himself." Victoria made herself relax, balancing her body between the contour couch and the seat belts. She sighed. "Probably even that wouldn't have helped."

"The orcas are interested in *Starfarer*," J.D. said.

"The orcas? The divers, you mean?"

"There's a diver who's interested, yes. But I mean the orcas themselves discussed applying to the expedition."

"Outlandish," Victoria said.

"Why do you say that?" J.D. asked mildly.

"I can't imagine a cetacean on board a starship."

"That's the trouble," J.D. said. "Nobody imagined it when they designed the cylinders. The ecosystem was evolved around salt marshes, but there isn't much deep water."

"Would you have proposed transporting an orca to *Starfarer* if there was deep water?"

"Not one—several. They're social beings, even more so than us. They get bored and slowly go crazy and die, all alone. They don't like to be confined, either, but they pointed out that when humans used to catch them they lived in much smaller places than the largest bodies of water on *Starfarer*, for longer than the expedition is planned to last."

"Then you think it's a good idea."

"I think it would be wonderful to have two different kinds of intelligent beings along on the expedition. I love the orcas, though. I love their freedom. They would have been willing to risk it, and I think they could have survived. But I wonder if they would have been happy?"

J.D. gazed out at space, at earth, where the oceans dominated. A weather system had just passed over the Pacific Northwest, leaving the area clearly visible.

The clicks and squeals and stutters of the orcas echoed across the inlet. The cold, clear water moved with a gentle, irresistible power, rolling fist-sized stones one against the other on the rocky shore, creating a rumble of counterpoint to the calling of the whales.

J.D. swam. The artificial lung, nestled against her back, absorbed oxygen from the sea and transferred it to her mask.

Kelp waved below. A bright orange nudibranch swam past, propelled by its frilly mantle. At the limit of J.D.'s vision, a salmon flashed silver-blue in the filtered light.

She shivered. Her metabolic enhancer could produce only so much heat. She could have worn a wet suit, but it limited her contact with the sea.

Soon she would have to swim away from the mouth of the inlet and return to shore. She stroked upward and broke the surface of the clear green water. Before her, the inlet opened out into a part of Puget Sound where no one could go without an invitation. Apparently the divers would not invite J.D. into the wilderness today.

The orcas remained out of sight around the headland. She could imagine them playing, oblivious to the cold, their

sleek black and white bodies cutting the swells. By morning
they would be gone. They could swim a hundred kilometers
between one dawn and the next. Orcas never stayed in one
place for long.

The sun on her face made the water feel even colder.
J.D. turned and swam toward shore. Her cabin stood back
among the Douglas firs that grew to the edge of the stony
beach.

Just offshore, she stopped at the anchored deck. She
teased the artificial lung from her back and tethered it beneath
the planks, where it would feed and breathe and rest and
pump seawater through itself until she needed it again. She
dove from the deck and swam easily home. Without the lung,
she no longer felt a part of the sea.

Barefoot, she picked her way among the beach stones.
It was getting on toward evening. In the shade of the trees
it was cool, and inside her cabin it was chilly. She plunged
into the shower. The sun-warmed water splashed over her.
After a few minutes she stopped shivering.

Toweling her short straight hair, she turned the heat on
under the kettle for a warm drink.

"J.D.?"

She started and wrapped the towel around her.

"Zev, you're so quiet. You scared me."

"I never meant to." The diver stood in the doorway. Fine
white-gold hair clothed his mahogany body in a translucent
sheen. He looked awkward, seeking her out on land. She felt
awkward, talking to him when she did not have any clothes
on. That was strange, because she swam naked with him and
his family, divers and orcas alike.

"Sit down, excuse me a minute." She turned her back
and took a last swipe with the towel beneath her heavy
breasts, then pulled on a shirt and a pair of baggy black
pants.

"I thought to find you in the sea," Zev said.

J.D. deliberately finished tying the drawstring. "I hoped to find you there. But I can't stay in the water forever."

"We were talking," he said. He lowered his gaze and glanced at her sideways, with an expression both mischievous and shy. "We sometimes talk for a long time."

"I've noticed that." On the solar stove, the kettle steamed. Being in a wilderness area, the cabin had to be rustic. It contained no electronics beyond her web link. Nothing operated by voice activation. Now that she knew how everything worked, it amused her to remember how long it took her to figure out all the mechanical switches. But it had not been very funny at the time.

"Do you want a hot drink? I'm cold, and my fingers and toes are shriveled up like prunes."

Zev looked at his own hands, turning them over, spreading his fingers, stretching out the translucent swimming webs.

"My fingers never do that," he said. "Why not?"

"I haven't the faintest idea," J.D. said. "Physiology isn't one of my specialties. Don't you know?"

"We are different," he said.

"That's for sure." The kettle hissed. "What did you decide? Do you want some tea, or maybe some cocoa?"

"Some ice cream?" he said.

J.D. laughed. "Sure."

He perched on the window seat, his knees pulled up, his feet apart, completely unconscious of his nakedness. When she first met him she wondered about his gender, for he had no external genitals. His people had engineered their basically human bodies into a more streamlined form: male genitals drawn inside, female breasts small and flat. Both genders possessed a layer of subcutaneous fat that burned away during any long underwater exertion, leaving the individual ethereal and with an appetite like a shark. Zev always amazed her with how much he could eat. She made herself some tea, gave him a dish of ice cream, and sat on the rag rug in a patch of sunlight. She still felt cold. She sipped her tea, glad of its sweet spicy warmth.

"What was your family talking about?" she said.

"Oh," he said. "You, of course. That was why we did not invite you out today."

"I don't see that it would have made much difference," she said, "since I can't understand your language yet."

"You will never begin to understand true speech, as you are." He spoke quite matter-of-factly. "I will never understand it completely, either. But the next generation will."

If there is one, J.D. thought, but she kept her silence. She found the idea intolerable, that the divers might be permitted—or encouraged—to die out. It was all too possible, if the new administration acted on its prejudice against genetic engineering.

"Besides," Zev said, "it is rude to talk about someone in front of them when they cannot understand. Is that right?"

"That's right. Some people would say it's rude to talk about someone behind her back, though, too."

"Oh. We did not know. We did not mean to be rude." He hesitated. "J.D.?"

"Yes?"

"When *is* it polite to talk about someone?"

"Good question," she said. "Anytime they don't know it, I guess."

"That is strange."

"Yes, it is," J.D. said. "But never mind. Everybody does it, anyway. What did you say about me? Or can you tell me?"

"No one said I should not. But perhaps you would rather have a surprise."

"I'd rather know."

"It is all right, then." He put down the empty ice cream bowl. "We played and talked. Some said you were strange, swimming masked against the sea."

I might as well have stayed in the city, J.D. thought. The divers aren't the only people who think I'm strange.

"But I said you felt the sea as well as any diver, and would feel it more deeply when you could dispense with your machines."

Zev moved his hands like waves. Underwater the divers communicated by sound, and by touch when they were close enough. On land they retained the very human quality of adding to their speech with gestures.

"We are aware that we know things you would like to understand. And we all agreed that you know a large number of things about which we have fallen into ignorance."

"Thank you for the compliment," J.D. said.

"My family thinks it is too bad that you are still entirely human. Many of us wonder if you have considered changing your nature."

J.D. clenched her hands around the mug of tea, oblivious to its heat.

"J.D.?" Zev said. "I *have* surprised you. I did not mean to. Are you angry?"

"Not angry," she said. "Stunned. Zev . . . all I ever hoped for was that you'd invite me to stay in the open water—that you'd give me permission to bring my boat so I wouldn't have to come back to the cabin every evening. What you've asked me is more than I dreamed. Is it possible?"

"Of course," he said. "You have visited our lab. We know what to do. We were never born from human and orca, as some say. Nor did people throw little children into the ocean and say, 'Swim, grow fins and extra lungs!' We chose our creation, like all changelings."

"I know where divers came from—but no one's gone from human to diver in a generation," J.D. said. "Where are you going to get the biotechs?"

"My family has resources."

J.D. blew on her tea and sipped from the cooling surface, taking time to think.

What Zev offered her was attractive. It was also illegal. Even before becoming U.S. president last fall, Senator Distler had repeatedly sponsored a bill to force the divers to change back into ordinary humans. J.D. feared that now, as president, he might be able to force the bill through Congress. The divers had few vocal supporters, and they employed no lobbyists. It would be terrible public relations for the government if it rounded them up and forced them to undergo reversion against their will. That might be the divers' only protection. After all, any individual could decide to revert at any time. The divers chose to remain as they were.

As far as Distler and his supporters were concerned, preventing genetic diseases was one thing, changing the human species something quite different. The enthusiasm for human engineering had peaked and faded rapidly, leaving a sizable group of divers and a few other changelings. Only the divers had increased their numbers.

"How will you decide?" Zev asked.

"I don't know," J.D. said slowly. "I feel like saying yes without even thinking about it. But I should think about it."

"But *how* will you decide? With divers, the whole family plays and talks. Then we decide. Will you go to your family and talk with them? Will you play? You should play more, J.D."

She laughed, though Zev's was a perfectly serious comment.

"My family—" She started to describe her family, half-siblings, half-parents, step-siblings, step-parents, dispersed and recombined. It was an unusual family even in these modern times.

"My family never swims together," she said, and left it at that. "This is a decision I'll have to make by myself. May I have some time?"

"My mother will talk to you tomorrow," Zev said. "That will be the real invitation. But I think . . . you will have to decide quickly."

That was the last thing she had expected Zev to say. She had never known the divers to make an important decision in haste.

"Why?"

"I cannot tell you," Zev said. He scooped up the melted ice cream on the bottom of the bowl with his finger and licked the chocolate from his knuckle and from the swimming web. He stood up. "Thank you for the ice cream."

"You're welcome."

He crossed to her and hugged her, holding her close. He was shorter than she. He laid his head on her shoulder, and the curls of his pale hair tickled her skin just below the hollow of her throat. J.D. put her arms around Zev, giving him a big-sisterly pat on the shoulder. On land the heat of his body was even more noticeable than in the water.

He sighed deeply and stroked her breast. Startled, she put her hand on his, moved his fingers, and drew away.

"What is wrong?"

"You shouldn't do that."

"But why? We touch each other when we're swimming."

"It's different on land, Zev. In the sea it's just playing. On land, touching is more serious."

"Oh," he said. "You see? We need you, to tell us these things we have forgotten, so we will not forget everything about living on land."

His semi-retractile claws clicked on the linoleum, then his feet scrunched in the gravel of the beach. He moved with a languorous grace, as if he were already in the water. He waded through the gentle surf. The water rose around his legs. When it reached his hips he breaststroked forward and vanished. The waves obliterated the ripple he left behind.

Each wave reached a handsbreadth higher on the beach. J.D. watched the tide come in. Her tea grew cold.

The invitation gave her more than one decision to make. Accepting it would completely change her life. She would be able to resurrect her career, though she would have to restrict its focus to a single blended society. The story of the integration of the divers with the orcas deserved to be told. If she accepted, she would be in a position to tell it.

I should have accepted on the spot, J.D. thought.

She could not come up with a single good reason to refuse—aside, of course, from the fact that she could be put in jail for becoming a changeling. This frightened her more than she cared to admit. She had been raised to obey authority, not defy it.

This is the best chance you're ever going to have to practice your profession, she told herself. *If your application to* Starfarer *hadn't been rejected, things might be different. But you were turned down. And, anyway, why should human contact with aliens off the earth be more important than human contact with the beings that live on the same world, and still are alien to us?*

The change in her life would include her form. She would become not only a chronicler of the divers, but a diver herself. Somewhere, somehow, the divers would obtain the sensitizing virus, and the changing viruses; they would inoculate her with the one, then with the others. As the changing viruses spread through her body and integrated themselves into her genes, she would begin to change.

She imagined her lungs enlarging, altering, the tissue of one lobe of each transmuting into a substance like the artificial lung. In that respect the divers differed from other marine mammals: they *could* breathe underwater, absorbing oxygen directly from the sea.

She would dispense with the metabolic enhancer, because her body would gain the ability to accelerate into a more efficient state. Spreading her strong square hands, she imagined swimming webs between her fingers. She imagined her light complexion darkening to protect her from exposure to the sun, and wondered if her brown hair would pale to gold or red.

She curled her toes to feel phantom claws extending, scratching the floor. Her breasts were heavier and her hips wider than any diver's, and her imagination failed when she tried to think of her body changing to resemble their sleek shape. She wondered if her breasts would shrink and flatten, if her hips would narrow, if the changing virus could alter even a person's bone structure.

The idea of the change both frightened and intrigued her.

She wondered what her family would say. They would not object. Her dad might make one of his offhand remarks, so dry that J.D. often found herself laughing before she realized what was funny, so offbeat she could not imagine what it would be.

The shadows of the Douglas firs lengthened across the beach and pierced the water with their tips. The breeze freshened. J.D. felt cold again, as if she had never really been warm.

She had to give herself time before deciding. So many factors came into the mix. The opportunity of joining a group of beings that she loved, of telling their story, had to be balanced against the possibility—indeed the probability— that academic colleagues would no longer take seriously the work of a researcher who had, in the old-fashioned phrase, gone native.

And she had to face the legal question of making the change.

Perhaps a few years ago it would not have mattered. It was possible that even now, no one would notice. But if they did, the current fashion of despising science and technology would cause her a great deal of trouble. And that did worry her.

So did Zev's uncharacteristic reluctance to tell her why she would have to make her choice so quickly.

The sun set. Darkness crept into the cabin.

Needing the familiarity of simple actions, J.D. put her teacup in the sink, puttered around straightening up the cabin, and, for the first time all day, asked her web link for mail and messages and the day's report.

It reported.

Victoria's invitation to join the alien contact team suddenly made her life even more complicated.

Victoria watched J.D. as she gazed back at earth. She was glad the contact specialist had agreed to join the expedition on such short notice, after Nakamura quit.

It must have been hard on her, Victoria thought, to be turned down and then invited again. It takes a lot of guts to put aside hurt feelings.

Nevertheless, she wished she knew all the reasons J.D. had changed her mind about staying with the divers. Victoria felt certain that she did not yet have the whole story.

"J.D.?"

J.D. continued to stare out the window for a moment. When she turned to Victoria, her expression was wistful, lonely.

"Time to board the transport."

In low earth orbit, the spaceplane docked with the EarthSpace transport, an ungainly-looking but efficient craft, one of the trucks that ferried cargo and passengers from low earth orbit to the O'Neill colonies and the labs, to lunar orbit, and to *Starfarer*.

As Victoria helped J.D. negotiate the zero-g path from the plane to the transport, she glanced over the passengers sharing the journey. The spaceplane, which should have been full with a waiting list, was half-empty. These days, too few people traveled out to *Starfarer*. Far too many traveled away, recalled by their governments, or, like Nakamura, giving up in despair.

While the plane resembled a regular jetliner, with well-maintained upholstery and paint, the transport looked more like a tramp freighter. Its workings hung out in plain sight, exposed, growing shabby with age and use.

"Quite a difference," J.D. said, glancing around. She held the net bags stuffed with her and Victoria's personal allowances. Her possessions were drab next to the bright colors and textures that showed through the mesh of Victoria's bag.

"There's one new transport," Victoria said. Towing J.D. by one hand, she pushed off down a corridor. "They always schedule it so it's the one that picks up the VIPs on their junkets. I never have figured that out. If we let them see the old equipment, we might get enough money to keep it properly maintained."

"Can I try this myself?" J.D. said.

"Sure." Victoria took the two mesh bags. "Remember that even though you haven't got any weight, you still have mass and momentum."

J.D. planted her feet, kicked, and headed for the far wall too fast and too hard. Victoria winced and pushed off after her, but somehow J.D. managed to turn in midair, catch herself on her toes against the bulkhead, and bounce back, awkward but safe. Victoria used her arms and legs as springs to give all her momentum to the metal surface. She floated beside J.D., who hung upside down nearby, laughing. Her hair, short and limply dry from exposure, flew around her head.

"Even better than diving," she said. "And you don't need half as much force to get you where you're going. I'll learn to compensate. I thought maybe I'd let my hair grow, but I think I'll keep it short."

They found their closet-sized cubicles, where they could rest during the trip to the starship.

"One of Satoshi's department members says the transport reminds him of his college days," Victoria said. "He used to travel cross-country in a bus. But I think of the transport as the China Clipper. Crossing space like a prop plane crossing the Pacific." The transport was less luxurious but safer, not as unbearably romantic.

"The middle of the Pacific is scarier," J.D. said.

The transport freed itself from the spaceplane with a low clang and a vibration that trembled through the ship. J.D. started, then flushed with excitement when the gentle acceleration provided microgravity.

"We're really on our way, aren't we?"

"We really are," Victoria said.

Starfarer lay in the far distance, barely visible to the naked eye. Charge-coupled binoculars brought the ship into view, its dual cylinders spinning, the mirrors lined with light, the sailhouse an eerie glow floating among the cables, and beyond it all a silver line that soon would unfold into a tremendous solar sail.

Each house in the campus cylinder of *Starfarer* lay underground, partly hidden by a low hill, daylit by one whole wall of floor-to-ceiling windows. In the house where Victoria lived, her partner Satoshi Lono trudged into the main room, looking for coffee, anticipating its smell. Grass mats rustled under his bare feet. He yawned. He had stayed late at a lab meeting, with no solution in sight to the problem of one of his graduate students. Fox could not apply for a permanent position on the expedition because her twenty-first birthday fell six months after the starship's departure.

When the meeting ended, knowing he would not be able to sleep, he had spent several more hours on the web, analyzing map complexes. When he finally slept, he dreamed those maps. Bright images of stacks of contour descriptions still filled his mind.

He stopped.

A weird piece of equipment stood in the middle of

the main room. The AS that cleaned the house circled the contraption, like a cat stalking a gigantic insect. The AS rolled forward, its antenna outstretched. It backed off and circled again.

The piece of equipment, complicated in form but primitive in design, consisted of twisted glass tubes fastened together and supported by a metal rack. The feet of the rack dug into one of Satoshi's better grass mats.

The AS, hovering, tapped the glass tubes again.

"It's all right," Satoshi said. "Look at it and remember it and leave it alone." The AS hesitated, assimilated the information, then rotated and rolled away. When the partnership first got it, it had had the same reaction to, and the same instructions about, the shirts Stephen Thomas stored on the floor. Satoshi wondered how Stephen Thomas so often contrived to leave things lying around that the cleaner could not figure out what to do with. Satoshi liked living in a neat environment. It irritated him to be put in the position of having the urge to pick up after one of his partners.

"It's too early for this," Satoshi muttered. Deciding to assimilate his own advice, he detoured around the mess in the middle of the main room and stopped in the kitchen nook, wondering what had happened to his coffee.

He was not at his best in the morning.

Everything did not always go exactly as planned on *Starfarer*. The campus was rough and new, the equipment at the shakedown stage. But the kitchen nook was hardly leading-edge technology. It should have had his coffee ready for him. Instead, the pot stood on the counter, half full of cold, malodorous dregs. He poured it out and started over.

Stephen Thomas strolled into the main room, put his arms around Satoshi from behind, and rested his chin on Satoshi's shoulder. His long blond hair tickled Satoshi's neck.

"Good morning."

"Did you drink my coffee?"

"Huh? I drank some last night when I got in, why?"

"Dammit—!" Satoshi woke up enough to be irritated. "You could have left it the way you found it."

"I didn't think of it. It was late and I was tired."

"It's early and I'm still asleep!"

"God, all right, I'm sorry. I'll make you some."

"It's done now." Satoshi took the cup to the table and sat in a patch of sunlight by the sliding windows. He deliberately ignored the contortion of glass tubing.

For the thousandth or the millionth time, he missed Merit. Times like these reminded him of before the accident, when the everyday details of the partnership ran smoothly, practically unnoticeably, under Merry's management. It was weird how something as inconsequential as a cup of coffee could bring back the grief. He hunched his shoulders and sipped the bitter coffee and tried to put the feelings away.

Satoshi loved Stephen Thomas, of course, but living with him the past couple of weeks had not been easy. Satoshi could not figure out why his youngest partner's idiosyncrasies and occasional blithe self-centeredness bothered him more with Victoria away.

"You're mad at me," Stephen Thomas said.

Satoshi took a gulp of coffee. "No, I'm not. Yes, I am. I don't know. It's early and I'm still tired and I just wanted some coffee."

"I offered to make you some."

"You give strangers more respect than you give the people you sleep with."

Stephen Thomas laughed and kissed him. "I respect you in the morning. Except maybe right after you wake up." He left Satoshi sitting in the sunlight, returned to the kitchen nook, and started opening drawers and cupboards looking for something for breakfast.

Satoshi made allowances for Stephen Thomas. He

thought of Victoria as the strongest one in the partnership, and of himself as the calmest in a crisis, and of their younger partner as the most flighty. But only Stephen Thomas had kept his center after the accident. Satoshi doubted the partnership would have survived without him.

He wished he could get coffee to taste right. *Starfarer* was not yet self-sufficient for food; half of what they used they had to import, not from earth, but from the O'Neill colonies. Maybe coffee plants could grow properly only on earth, the way some types of vegetables and fruit grew properly only in certain places. Like Walla Walla onions. No amount of research or experiment ever reproduced that sort of biological synergy.

Satoshi found it some comfort to suspect the existence of unknowable secrets, like perfect coffee, Walla Walla onions, and his younger partner's lab equipment.

He would be glad when Victoria got home. It seemed like forever since they had talked. Before she left they had all agreed to communicate via the web, which was relatively cheap, rather than by voice link from *Starfarer* to earth, which was expensive. What with the eagle eye being kept on campus expenses, everyone was on their best behavior about keeping personal calls on their own accounts.

She'll be back soon, Satoshi reminded himself. She'll even be back in time for the solar sail's first full test.

Stephen Thomas returned from the kitchen nook carrying a bowl of white rice with a raw egg on top, a plate of pickles, and a cup of milky tea. He knew better than to offer any of it to Satoshi.

"I miss her, too," he said.

"Yeah," Satoshi said, then, "Dammit, I wish you wouldn't do that. It bothers me, and it drives Victoria crazy."

Stephen Thomas laughed. "You guys act like I was reading your minds. I don't read minds—"

"Of course not, but you do answer questions before people ask them, and you comment on things people haven't even said yet."

"—I read auras."

Satoshi groaned. He wished Stephen Thomas would stop this silly joke, even if he believed it, because it did nothing either for his credibility or for that of the alien contact team. Stephen Thomas was unusually sensitive to other people's moods and feelings—when he wanted to be. That, Satoshi believed. But he did not believe Stephen Thomas could see something nonexistent.

"Let's splurge and call her," Stephen Thomas said.

Satoshi sipped his coffee, tempted.

"Come on," Stephen Thomas said. "She's on the transport, it won't cost that much."

"Okay."

They connected with Arachne.

Because the hypertext link was on, as usual, the web boxed recent references to Victoria Fraser MacKenzie. The display refreshed, adding a new article about the banquet that British Columbia's premier had hosted in Victoria's honor. Curious, Satoshi brought it up to read.

"Oh, my god," he said.

"What?"

"Look."

"*Dr. Victoria Fraser MacKenzie, when asked whether she could describe the scientific advances we may expect to achieve from the voyage of the* Starfarer, *replied with a single word: 'No.'*

"*Last night, British Columbia's premier hosted Dr. Victoria Fraser MacKenzie, the Canadian physicist-astronaut who heads the deep space expedition's alien contact team, at a formal dinner. This is Fraser MacKenzie's last trip to earth before* Starfarer *departs for an alien star system, overcoming relativity's limits on speed and achieving superluminal tran-*

sition energy via the 'cosmic string' that has moved within range of our solar system during the past decades."

"Cosmic string" and "superluminal transition energy" were highlighted, indicating that the reader could obtain fuller explanations of the terms through the hyper. Satoshi and Stephen Thomas continued reading the main body of the article.

"After dinner, Fraser MacKenzie conversed informally with the premier and others about the expedition. The first question put to her concerned the U.S. proposal that Starfarer be converted into a mini-O'Neill colony, to help relieve earth's population pressure. Fraser MacKenzie acquitted the starship's cause well, pointing out that the O'Neill colonies were constructed not as population valves, but as bases which would create and supply the necessities: food, water, air, and shelter from the vacuum, in order to permit human beings to live in space without draining earth's resources.

" 'Starfarer,' Fraser MacKenzie stated, 'is much smaller than the existing O'Neills, neither of which have made any difference whatever in the population of earth, nor were ever intended to.' She also explained cogently why the starship had to be large enough to sustain its own ecosystem. 'Sending the expedition out in a traditional ship would be extremely costly,' she explained. 'The starship was created out of leftover lunar material from the O'Neills. By living within a functional ecosystem, we can plan to be self-sufficient. Madame Premier, we hope to return within a year or two, but the truth is that we have no idea how long we might be gone. We don't know what we're going to find or how far we're going to have to go to find it. If we set out with nothing but processed stores, we run the risk of running out of everything: food, water, and air. Mechanical recycling, as on a traditional ship, isn't efficient enough.'

"It was at that juncture that the premier asked Fraser MacKenzie for a description of the benefits to be gained

from the expedition, and Fraser MacKenzie declined to offer one.

"The premier, reacting with surprise, pressed her for a more complete reply to her concerns about what the country might expect to gain from our enormous investment.

" 'Madame Premier,' Fraser MacKenzie said, 'I cannot tell you what scientific advances will result from the deep space expedition. If I could, there would be no need for us to go on the voyage at all. I could speculate,' Fraser MacKenzie continued. 'So could anyone with a minimal level of scientific literacy. But speculation is a game. The history of humanity is a record of explorations intended for one purpose that have completely different effects. People didn't walk east across the Bering land bridge, or sail west across the Atlantic, because they expected to find North America. We didn't go to Mars expecting to break through to superconducting bio-electronics.'

"The premier pointed out that we did go to Mars with a purpose in mind. Fraser MacKenzie agreed, and suggested that anyone who wished could access a library database and inspect half a thousand gigabytes of information on the experiments already planned for Starfarer. However, Fraser MacKenzie would not describe any benefits that would surely accrue to society on account of these experiments.

"The head of Starfarer's alien contact team offered two reasons for her refusal. The first was the pure science mode of many of the proposals. 'Science,' she insisted, 'is not meant to create useful applications of scientific knowledge.' Her second reason was more esoteric. 'A proven hypothesis may have useful applications,' Dr. Fraser MacKenzie stated. 'However, a scientist does not do an experiment to prove a hypothesis. A scientist does an experiment to test a hypothesis. You may guess about the answer that nature might give back to you. You may even hope for nature to give you a particular answer. But you can't know what

*answer you'll get until you've performed the experiment.
If you did, or if you thought you did, you'd be back two
thousand years when experimentation was looked upon as
unnecessary and vulgar, or, worse, back a thousand years
when belief was more important than knowledge, and people
who challenged beliefs with knowledge were burned at the
stake.'*

*"The premier observed that the new president of the
United States, Mr. Distler, occasionally behaved as if he
would like to consign research scientists in general and
scientists attached to Starfarer in particular to precisely that
fate. Fraser MacKenzie admitted that she had, on occasion,
felt singed by some of his comments. 'Science involves risks,'
she explained. 'One of the risks involved is that of failure.
President Distler, unfortunately, chooses not to acknowledge
the possibility of risks, or of failure.' Fraser MacKenzie
added that she did not expect the expedition to fail—after
all, her life will be at risk if it does fail. But the risk of
failure is a possibility.*

*"The premier then asked Dr. Fraser MacKenzie if one
risk could be that Canada's investment in the starship might
result in no benefits at all.*

*"Victoria Fraser MacKenzie replied with a single word:
'Yes.' "*

Satoshi read the article, frowning, but Stephen Thomas
laughed with delight.

"About time somebody said straight out that we're
not up here to discover the twenty-first-century version of
Teflon!"

"The Teflon hypothesis slides down more easily."

"No, it'll be great. People love mystery, and that's what
we're heading for."

"I wish you were right," Satoshi said. "But you're not."

"Hey, Satoshi?" Stephen Thomas said.

"Hmm?"

"Does Victoria really talk like that when she's in Canada, or was it just the reporter?"

"A little of both. You've been to Vancouver with Victoria, didn't you notice she uses more Canadian and British speech habits there?"

"I noticed her accent got stronger, but I was putting most of my energy into trying to make friends with her great-grandmother. For all the good it did me."

"Grangrana's okay. She disapproves of the partnership in theory but she likes us as individuals."

"She likes you. She's not so sure about me," Stephen Thomas said, with his usual certainty about the accuracy of his perceptions. "Why did the article keep calling Victoria 'Fraser MacKenzie'?"

"They don't much go for middle names—that's a British tradition, I think. They figure Victoria's got one of those unhyphenated double last names. Like Conan Doyle.

"Wonder what they'd do with my name?"

"Probably figure you didn't have any last name at all."

Stephen Thomas laughed and hit him, light and playful, in the ribs.

The message filter suddenly beeped and started to fill up with call requests, mostly from strangers, mostly from people outside *Starfarer*, and mostly for Victoria. Satoshi sifted through them.

"Good lord," he said. "If we call these people back, we'll use up our communications budget for the next six months."

"Call them collect," Stephen Thomas said. "And tell them Victoria isn't here."

"How to win reporters and influence public opinion, by Stephen Thomas Gregory," Satoshi said.

The message filter in Victoria's cubicle signaled and then sang. Still half-asleep, disoriented by darkness, Victoria tried to sit up. The restraints of her sleeping web held her gently in place and she remembered where she was. A streak of light fell across her; the fabric door did not quite close.

"Answer," she said. "Hello?"

After the short time-delay, Satoshi spoke.

"Love, have you seen the news today?"

"I'm not even awake yet." She was surprised to hear his voice. "I think I slept the clock around. What time is it? Never mind, what's up?" she said quickly, not waiting through the reply delay of *Starfarer* communications laser-to-satellite-to-transport and back. She did not want to waste expensive time on trivialities.

"You have a huge slug of messages from admirers of your interview," Stephen Thomas said.

"I'm not sure you can call them all admirers," Satoshi said.

"What interview?"

"Some are from people up here," Satoshi told her, "but a lot are from earth."

Victoria waited through the delay. She and Satoshi had perfected the technique of holding two simultaneous conversations on the communications laser, letting their comments cross and recross, one exchange being held during the reply delays of the second. To his own irritation, Stephen Thomas had not quite got the hang of it. Keeping him in the discussion, Victoria restricted herself to one line of thought and talk.

"The web's reporting on your banquet," Satoshi said. "And your conversation with the premier. You'd better look at it. They emphasized your not wanting to speculate on what benefits *Starfarer* might bring back."

Victoria felt a hot flush of embarrassment spread across her face.

"I'll read it, of course. I thought I was having a conversation, not doing an interview for the record. Nobody was introduced to me as a reporter, and who ever reports Canadian news, eh?" She sighed. "I never met the premier before. She's honorable, I admire her. I wanted to tell her the truth, so she could understand what it is we're about."

With growing unease, she waited out the delay. Despite her cynical remark about Canadian news, she should have realized that anything the head of *Starfarer*'s alien contact department said to the premier of British Columbia was fair game for reporters.

It was late and I was tired and keyed up, she told herself. And then there were those toasts . . .

But I know better, she thought. I know better than to let my guard down, ever, and still sometimes I do it. What *is* it about people? Why do they prefer it when we claim we know everything? What's wrong with the truth, that not everything's been discovered?

"I understand what you were trying to do," Satoshi said. "But I wonder if there's any way to downplay it after the fact?"

"Oh, bull," Stephen Thomas said. "Don't do that! You said just what needed to be said, Victoria, and anybody who doesn't back you on it has shit for brains."

"I can defend my comments. I can't retract them, Satoshi, not if I was quoted correctly. And it sounds like what I said is what got reported."

Victoria was glad of the privacy scramble that kept inquisitive types with backyard antennae from listening in on the laser calls. She had more or less become accustomed to the casual profanity Stephen Thomas used, but in public it still embarrassed her. And the first time he swore in front of Grangrana . . .

"We just wanted to make sure you'd seen the article," Satoshi said. "So you'd have some warning if people pounce on you about it. We'd better get off the line. I love you. Goodbye."

"Wait," Stephen Thomas said. "Did Sauvage finally show, or not? And I love you too."

"Yes, she's on board. I'll tell you all about that when I get home. It's complicated. I love you both. I wish we had a picture. Bye."

She ended the connection.

Why did I feel so comfortable about telling the premier the cold hard truth about science? Victoria wondered. I was ready to back off if I picked up disapproval, if she wasn't prepared to hear it.

She had not picked up on disapproval because the premier had not shown any. Whatever her reactions to Victoria's comments, she had let Victoria make them. She had listened, and Victoria still believed she had understood.

Victoria closed her eyes, linked with the web, and let it play the article behind her eyes. When it ended, she decided it had been written without malice, but with an eye for the flashy line.

Victoria sighed and unfastened the restraint net. She wished she were already home, in bed with Satoshi and Stephen Thomas. She felt so lonely. She grabbed her shirt and struggled into it and swiped her sleeve across her eyes, pretending her vision had not blurred. Right now Satoshi and Stephen Thomas were almost as far out of her reach as Merry. But she was on her way home.

Chandra left the inn and used the pedestrian tunnel to cross beneath the highway. The cold damp tunnel smelled of cement. On the other side she stepped out into dry hot sunlight. Traffic rushed past on the magnetic road behind her. All last evening the other guests had babbled interminably about the good weather. Chandra, however, felt cheated. She had come to visit a rain forest. She expected rain.

She started recording, waited until the nerve clusters gnarling her face and hands and body started to throb, and stepped beneath the trees. The light dimmed to a weird gold-green, and the temperature dropped from uncomfortably hot to cool. She hurried deeper into the forest, hoping to outdistance the sound of the traffic as well as the next group of visitors. At first she walked gingerly, preparing for pain to catch up to her, waiting for the dullness of too much medication. To her surprise, her body worked fine, swinging along the trail. She had balanced the pills perfectly against the pain, astonishingly intense, of having spent all the previous day on horseback. This morning the muscles of her inner thighs had hurt like hell. Until she took a painkiller she could barely walk.

Time pressed too hard for her to give herself a day off to recover, so she masked injury with drugs and hoped to get the dosage and the mixture right. If she had to wipe any recordings because of distorted body reactions, those images would be lost forever.

Chandra intended never to repeat an experience. She could relive them on recording, if she felt like it, but she wanted every bit of reality to be new.

The nerve clusters that ridged her face felt hot and swollen.

She left the sunlight behind. Inside the forest, the light possessed more dimensions. The trail led through cool green shadows. To her left, dusty gold light hung suspended in a shaft that passed through a rare break in the cover. In every direction, great tree trunks stretched a hundred meters high. Chandra stepped off the path, though she was not supposed to, and spread her arms against a tree she could not begin to span. Three people might have reached halfway around it.

Moss covered the bark. She rubbed her cheek against it. Its softness astonished her. She compared the feel to feathers, to fur, but neither description acknowledged the gentle green irregularity. She looked up. Every branch bore a coat of moss that looked like it had dripped on, then begun to solidify.

The ends of the branches, the new year's growth of intense green needles, had begun to outdistance the relentless creep of the moss. When the branch stopped growing for the season, the moss would catch up. The cycle would continue, another turn.

Some other artist would have watched the tree long enough to detect the growth of the moss. With a few hours' observation, Chandra could have stored enough images for fractal extrapolation. But she had no interest in electronic manipulation of the images she collected. She edited when she wanted to—she despised no-cut purists—but her aim was to collect as many images as she could, as accurately as she could, to preserve every sensation and impression. She rose and walked farther, deeper into the jungly forest.

The sounds of vehicles faded. The tourists passed beyond her hearing while she stood out of sight off the trail. More people would soon follow. She wanted and needed solitude. Not even the Institute had been able to persuade the park service to close the park and the highway for a few hours while she made her recordings. It had been difficult enough to get an entry reservation out of turn. Ordinary people, tourists, signed up two years in advance.

Knowing she would be ejected, perhaps arrested and prosecuted, if anyone detected her presence off the trail, Chandra moved on.

She passed into a different silence than she had ever experienced. It was a cool, damp quiet, far from total. A stream, rushing steep from pool to pool, created a transparent wash of background. The electronic Doppler of a passing mosquito added a bright sharp line. An invisible bird warbled an intermittent curtain of sound. Chandra sat on the bank of the stream and let the smell and sight and sound and feel of the rain forest permeate her body. She gathered in the foaming rush of negative ions. The whole world smelled green.

At the top of the slope, the waterfall split. One rivulet splashed into a bubbling, swirling cauldron of water whitened by the agitation. The other spilled over a curved stone and ran smoothly into a still, clear pool. When she leaned over, her translucent gray eyes peered back at her.

Chandra stripped off her clothes. Naked, she climbed down the bank and slowly thrust herself into the frigid water. The numbing coldness crept up her gnarled feet and along her nerve-streaked legs. The flowing water rose into her pubic hair, lifting it as if with a static charge. She never hesitated when the icy stream touched her powerfully sensitive clitoris. She gasped and sank in deeper. Her nipples were always erect from the extra nerves; now they throbbed and ached as the water caressed her. Her toes dug in among the round, smooth stones.

She let the chill seep into her till all pleasure faded. She shivered uncontrollably, as if the glacier upstream had taken over her whole body. She turned and clambered awkwardly onto the bank, too numb to feel stones or roots, almost too numb to grab them and haul herself from the water.

The stream made a narrow break between the trees. A bit of sunlight crept in through the leaves. Chandra crawled to it and collapsed, exhausted and trembling and elated by what she had captured. As she sprawled in the sunlight, trying to regain the full use of her body, she could not resist replaying the stream's sensations.

When the playback ended and her experiential body rejoined her physical form, she shuddered with the shock of the change from intolerably cold to nearly warm again.

As she rested, seeking the strength to rise and continue, she stretched out to touch everything within her reach. The range of softnesses in the forest amazed her: the green and feathery softness of the moss, the crisp softness of a tiny-leafed vascular plant growing amidst the moss, the unresisting plasticity of a circle of slime mold. The top of a fungal

shelf felt like damp velvet. A slug glistened out from beneath
a fallen branch. It was slick as wet silk, but it left behind a
sticky, insoluble secretion on her ridged fingers.

A mosquito landed on her arm. She watched it dis-
passionately. Unlike a fly, it wasted no time with careful
grooming. It set itself among the fine dark hairs and plunged
its proboscis into her skin. She submitted to the thin, keen
pain. She had read that the insect would bite, drink, and
neutralize its own hemolytic enzymes before it withdrew.

The mosquito had read different texts. It filled itself with
Chandra's blood and whined away; then Chandra watched
the itchy lump of the mosquito bite swell and darken. She
concentrated on the unpleasant sensation.

When she had added the bite to her store, she realized
that the cold of the stream had brought back the ache of her
muscles. She quickly disconnected the recording, grabbed up
her clothes and fumbled through her pockets, took another
pill, and waited for the soreness to dissipate. She reconnected
and got dressed as if nothing had happened.

Chandra climbed the stream bank and entered the trees
again. Ferns grew in clumps and clusters, but the ground
level was surprisingly clear. She had to make her way around
an occasional enormous fallen tree. Whenever a tree fell, it
opened a passage for sunlight and encouraged new growth.
Saplings sprouted on the logs, then grew to full-sized trees,
reaching around and to the ground with long gnarled roots.
Sometimes the nurse log rotted away completely, leaving a
colonnade of six or eight trees rising on roots like bowlegs.

Disconnected from the web, Chandra passed through
the forest in ignorance of the names of most of the plants.
She wanted to make a record of perceptions uncolored by
previous knowledge. Anyone who wanted to use her piece
as a study tape could do so by hooking into the web and
requesting an information hypertext link. Chandra thought
that would be like using a Rembrandt as a color chart.

Ahead, the sun streamed through a break in the upper story of the forest, illuminating a cluster of large, flat leaves that glowed gold-green. Light shimmered over the thick silver hairs covering their stalks. Chandra walked toward the plant, concentrating on its color, on the way the leaves spread themselves to the light, each parallel to all the others, as if the bush were arranged and lighted by some alien attention.

The silvery covering on the stems consisted not of soft hairs, but of sharp, wicked thorns. Chandra touched one with the nerve-thick pad of her forefinger. Like the mosquito, the thorn pierced her skin. The pain of the stab burst into acid agony, and she had to exert her will to keep from snatching her hand away. Her blood welled in a glistening drop around the thorn, spilled thick and warm down her finger, and pooled in her palm.

She expected the pain to fade. Instead, it increased. Her hand burned. Angry at herself, she jerked away from the thorn: too fast. Its tip broke off beneath her skin. She snarled a curse and put her hand to her mouth, trying to suck out the point. Her blood tasted bitter, as if it were poisoned.

Pain and shock separated Chandra from terror. Though her hand felt hot, the rest of her body felt as cold as if she were still in the pool. Chandra stumbled away from the gold-green plant. She had no idea which direction to move to meet the trail. If she kept going she must hit it eventually, for it made a complete circle, and she was inside. Hoping to extricate herself, she kept going as long as she could.

The thornbush disappeared behind and among a thousand tall, straight tree trunks. Chandra sank to the ground. The illusion of softness disappeared when the rotting evergreen needles poked through her clothes and scratched her skin.

She cursed again and sent a Mayday to the web.

She waited.

Pain altered Chandra's perceptions. Time stretched out to such a distance that she feared she would use up all her sensory storage. Yet when she checked the remaining volume, she had filled it only halfway.

She heard the ranger approach; she raised her head slowly. He towered above her, scowling.

"Whatever possessed you to leave the trail?" His face wavered. When it solidified again, it carried an expression mixed of pity and horror. "Good lord! What happened to you?"

She lifted her hand. Blood obscured the swelling. He knelt down and looked carefully at the place where the thorn had penetrated.

"I got a lot of good stuff," she said, to reassure him and herself.

"You stuck yourself with a devil's club thorn," he said, both unimpressed and contemptuous. "But . . ." He touched the other swellings, the ridges of nerves tracing her fingers and palm.

"That isn't part of it," Chandra said. Talking tired her. "I mean, it's part of me." She took a deep and frustrated breath and blew it out again. "Don't you know who I *am?*" Exhaustion tangled her words. "I'm supposed to be like that."

He was staring at her eyes. The biosensors covered her eyes with a film of translucent gray.

"My eyes, too," she said.

The ranger kept his expression neutral as he returned her to the lodge.

Chandra slept for a long time. When she woke, the medication had caused her hand nearly to finish healing. Only a residual swelling remained, but it was enough to squeeze the accessory nerves and disrupt all her finer sensations. As for the pain, it had faded till the persistent ache took more of her attention.

She spun into the web. Her agent and her manager were

fighting with each other, the one urging her to take care of herself, the other urging her to get back to work. Ignoring them both, she called for her schedule to look at which experiences had been arranged, which arrangements were causing problems, and what she might have to rearrange. She resented the delay, but her results would be worth it.

She thought she would still have time for the sea-wilderness visit before catching the spaceplane to *Starfarer*. The starship contained only a ring of ocean, shallow salt marshes, and freshwater lakes. Chandra wanted to collect diving in the deep sea before she left earth. Since she hated to swim, since the whole idea of diving made her claustrophobic, the coming task was a challenge. Ordinarily she preferred to go out on her own, but this once she was glad she would be accompanied by an expert.

Before her schedule appeared, the web displayed a priority message. The ranger had written her a ticket for leaving the trail. The fine was considerable. She could contest it if she wished.

She thought of staying, in order to explain about the results being worth it, but that would mean more delay. She could stay and explain and record, but lots of people made recordings of court cases. Chandra was not interested in repeats.

She signed the ticket so it could subtract the fine from her account.

It was worth it. She had a lot of good stuff.

Victoria and J.D. floated near the transparent wall of the observation room, watching the stars and the distant starship.

"I thought the sky was beautiful from the wilderness," J.D. said. "But this . . ."

Victoria gazed at the region of doubled images created by the local strand of cosmic string.

"Could you see the lens effect from where you were? There it is." She pointed, tracing out the line where the string bent light from the stars behind it.

"I see it," J.D. said. "But you've been out there."

"I've been as close as anyone. Yet." Cosmic string had fascinated Victoria from the time she was a child. It drew her to astronomy, thence to physics.

Cosmic string, a remnant of creation, formed a network through the galaxy. The strings vibrated in a cycle measured in eons, a cycle now taking a strand past the solar system and within reach of earth's current technology.

The cosmic string made *Starfarer* possible. The starship would use the moon's gravity to catapult it toward the string. Then it would grasp the string with powerful magnetic fields, and tap the unlimited power of its strange properties. *Starfarer* would rotate around the strand, building up the transition energy that would squeeze it out of Einsteinian space-time and overwhelm the impossible distances between star systems. When it returned to the starting point of its rotation—

It would not return to its starting point. From the point of view of those left behind, the starship would vanish. It would reappear . . . somewhere else.

That was the theory. Victoria had spent the better part of her career working on that theory.

"It's incredible it could be so close and not affect the solar system," J.D. said.

"We're lucky," Victoria said. "If it came close enough to cut through the sun, then we'd've seen some effects." She touched her thumbs together, and her fingertips, forming a sphere with her hands. "The string distorts space-time so thoroughly that a circle around it is less than three hundred sixty degrees. So if the string passes through a region that's full of mass . . ." She slid the fingers of her right hand beneath the fingers of her left. "Double-density starstuff. Instant nova." She snapped open her hands. "Blooie." She grinned. "But that missing part of the circle gives us an opening out of the solar system."

"What do you think of the idea that the string is a life-line?"

Victoria chuckled. "Thrown to us by a distant civilization? I think it makes a great story."

J.D. smiled, a bit embarrassed. "I find the idea very attractive."

"I'll admit that I do, too—though I might not admit it to anyone else. I'd need some evidence before I got serious about it. And let's face it, a civilization that could directly manipulate cosmic string—they'd think we were pretty small potatoes. Or maybe small bacteria."

"Excuse me . . . You are Victoria MacKenzie, aren't you?"

Victoria glanced around. The youth smiled at her hopefully.

"Yes," Victoria said. "And this is J.D. Sauvage."

"J.D. Sauvage! I'm glad to meet you, too."

"Thank you."

"And you are—?"

"Feral Korzybski." He offered Victoria a card.

"Really—!" She took the card and glanced at the printing: a sketch of a quill pen, his name, his numbers.

"I've seen your articles," Victoria said. "I think you do an excellent job." Victoria had not expected to encounter the public-access journalist here.

He blushed at her exclamation. "I just read your interview," he said, "and I wanted to tell you how much I admire your straightforwardness. I wonder . . . would you like to expand on what you said? I thought your comments made the beginning of a provocative piece."

Despite his name, he looked quite domesticated. Victoria regarded him. He was not at all the way she would have imagined from his name and his articles. He had curly

red-brown hair cut all the same length. In weightlessness it
fluffed out around his head. His eyes were a gentle brown.
His chin was round, his lips mobile and expressive.

"It wasn't exactly an interview, and I think I've said as
much as I need to . . . or want to." Victoria smiled to take
the sting out of turning him down. "I mean . . . I said what
I meant. If I start explaining myself, it would sound like
weaseling."

"When I interview somebody," he said, "they only sound
like they're weaseling if they really *are* weaseling."

"I don't have anything more to say right now. Maybe
the opportunity will come up while you're visiting *Starfarer*,
eh? I'm sure you'll find most people happy to talk to you."

Feral Korzybski wrote about the space program. He
had resisted jumping on the new U.S. president's anti-tech
bandwagon. As far as Victoria knew, all his articles appeared
in public-access, not in sponsored news or feature information services.

"I really would like to talk to both of you about the alien
contact team."

"Have you been in space before?" Victoria said, changing the subject without much subtlety.

"No, first trip. First time I could afford it."

"You've got a sponsor, then. Congratulations."

"Sponsors are nothing but untitled censors!" he said
with startling vehemence. "When you read sponsored stuff,
you're paying extra for the privilege of reading work that's
been gutted to make it acceptable. If I can't make my name
as an independent, I don't want to do it at all."

"How'd you get up here?"

"By saving for a ticket, like any other tourist."

"But tourists can't come onto *Starfarer* anymore. We're
too close to final maneuvers."

"That took a lot of persuasion and a lot of calling
in obligations. Including a few nobody owed me yet." He

looked away, obviously embarrassed by the admission of any flaw in his independence.

"If I can help you find your way around," Victoria said, "I'd be glad to."

He smiled shyly from beneath his heavy eyebrows. "I'd appreciate that. A lot. Will you talk to me off the record? 'Deep background,' we call it in the trade."

"Of course I'll talk to you," Victoria said. "I just like to be warned when somebody's about to start quoting me. All right?"

"Sure. What do you think about the Senate bill to transform *Starfarer* into a military base with remote sensing capabilities?"

"You don't ease into anything, do you?"

"No," he said cheerfully. "The argument is that we need more information about the Mideast Sweep, and more defenses against it."

"I understand the argument, but the proposal has already damaged the expedition. You know about the recalls, I'm sure."

He nodded. "It's last century's space station all over again."

"That's right. We lost a couple of decades' worth of original research and intercultural cooperation right there. Now, as soon as we start to recover, as soon as there's hope for peaceful applications, your country is making the same damned mistake. You contributed more than half the funding and more than half the personnel, so your president thinks he can get away with this bullying."

"He's not *my* president. I didn't vote for him."

Victoria quirked her lips in a sardonic smile. "Nobody did, it seems like. Nevertheless, he is your president and he is bullying us. He's violating several treaties. Unfortunately, your country is still sufficiently powerful that you can tell everybody else to take a high dive if we don't like your plans."

"What about the Mideast Sweep?"

"What about it?"

"Don't you want to keep an eye on them?"

"From here? You *can* do remote sensing from very high orbits, but why would you want to? You might as well use the moon. You don't need something the size of *Starfarer* for spying. You don't even need it for a military base powerful enough to blow the whole world to a cinder. *Starfarer* as a military base—even as a suspected military base—becomes vulnerable. I hope it won't come to that. Look, Feral, your country is trying to make itself so powerful that it's becoming paralyzed. When you rely solely on your weapons, you lose the art of compromise that created the U.S. in the first place. Soon your only choice will be between staying in the corner you've backed into, doing nothing . . . or blasting the whole building down."

"Do you think we can talk the Mideast Sweep around to a reasonable position?"

Victoria had no fondness for the Mideast Sweep. To begin with, there was the sexual and racial discrimination they practiced. If she lived under its domination she would subsist at a level so low that it would barely count as human.

"I don't know how much can be achieved with talk. But I hope—I have to believe—that the United States is a country too ethical to destroy a whole population because it lives under the control of an antagonistic hierarchy."

"Does everybody else on the crew agree with you?"

Victoria chuckled. "Getting everybody to agree on anything is one of our biggest problems. One thing we do agree on, though, is that we aren't 'crew.' "

"What, then?"

"*Starfarer* isn't a military ship—not yet, anyway, and not ever if most of us on board have anything to say about it. It's only a ship in the sense that it can move under its own power. There's a hierarchy of sorts, but it isn't based on a military structure. There's faculty and staff and technical support. It's more like a university. Or a university town. Most of the decisions about how things are run, we try to decide by consensus."

"That sounds awkward," Feral said.

"Only if you hate five-hour meetings," Victoria said, straight-faced.

"Don't you have to be able to react fast out here? If there's an emergency and there's nobody to give the order to do something about it, doesn't that put everyone at risk?"

"*Starfarer* has redundancies of its redundancies. With most emergencies you have plenty of time. As for the others . . . everyone who lives there takes an orientation course that includes possible emergencies and what to do about them. You have to pass it if you expect to stay. That's how fast you'd have to react to an acute emergency—you wouldn't have time to call some general and ask for permission."

"What about sabotage?"

"There's much more reason to sabotage a military installation than a civilian one. And a lot more explosive-type stuff sitting around to use to sabotage it with." Victoria laughed. "Besides, in a group run by consensus, all a saboteur would have to do is come to meetings and block every proposal. That wouldn't stop us cold, but it would slow everything down and drain a lot of energy." She sighed. "Sometimes I think we already have a few saboteurs aboard."

"How would you respond to an attack?"

"We have no response to attack. We're unarmed. We had to fight to remain unarmed, but it's an important part of the philosophy of the mission."

"I meant response to an attack from earth, or on earth. If you were armed—suppose somebody attacked the U.S. or Canada. What could you do?"

"Not much. Even if we were armed, *Starfarer*'s in a

lousy strategic orbit. It's too far from earth to be of use as a defensive *or* offensive outpost. Any of the O'Neill colonies would be more effective. And nobody is talking about making them into military bases."

"Yet," Feral said.

"Yeah," Victoria said. "Yet."

"You're pretty emphatic about *Starfarer* in relation to solving earth's problems. Or not solving them."

Victoria frowned. "I hoped you were on our side."

"I'm not on anybody's side! It's my job to ask questions."

"All right. People want the expedition to promise to go out and find easy, quick solutions. We can't."

"Promise it, or do it?"

"Either. We already know how to solve a lot of our problems. Take food. I don't know the exact numbers— my partner Satoshi could tell you—but if we stopped the expansion of a couple of deserts for one year, we'd gain more arable land than ten *Starfarer*s. If the U.S. hadn't opposed family planning in the 1990s—"

"There's not much we can do about that," Feral said. "After all."

"But don't you see? We act in stupid and shortsighted ways and then we behave as if we didn't have any responsibility for those actions. Somehow that justifies our continuing to behave in the same shortsighted ways. Instead of trying to change, we hope it works better this time."

"Do you see the expedition as a change?"

"Yes. I hope it is."

"You use the word 'hope' a lot," Feral said.

"I guess I do."

"What do you hope for the expedition?"

"I'm the head of the alien contact department," Victoria said. "That should give you an idea of what I hope for."

3

Nearby, a nondescript passenger listened to the unguarded conversation. Griffith, of the General Accounting Office, had hidden himself so deeply within his objectivity that he would not permit the comments of Victoria MacKenzie to anger him. He filed them away, along with the opinions of the journalist, for future reference and use.

He wished he had the observation room to himself, so he could look at the stars in silence and solitude. He envied the early space explorers, who had put their lives on the line. He wished he had been one of the Apollo astronauts. Not the ones who landed on the lunar surface: the one who remained in the capsule, orbiting all alone, completely cut off from every other human being, from every other life form, out of contact even by radio during the transit behind the moon.

But those times were long over. Nowadays, traveling into space meant a few minutes of discomforting acceleration and a few hours or days of weightlessness. He had already heard several people complaining about the trip: complaining of boredom! The journey from low earth orbit to *Starfarer*'s libration point took too much time for them; they were bored and restless and a few even complained about the lack of gravity.

They've seen too many movies, Griffith thought. They don't understand anything about the way things work. Why did they come up here? If they wanted earth-normal gravity, they should have stayed on earth. These are the people who think they know how to use space. Researchers. An old woman. A writer. An alien contact specialist, for God's sake!

In disgust, he left the observation room and floated through the cramped corridors of the transport. If he had anything to say about it, this would be the last transport taking civilian personnel to *Starfarer*.

He wished he had pulled some rank and seniority in order to demand a larger private compartment. But that would have been as suspicious as getting into an argument with MacKenzie and the journalist about the proper function of *Starfarer*. Griffith of the General Accounting Office could reasonably expect only the same sleeping closet as any regular passenger.

He made another circuit of the transport's corridors. Though he tried returning to the observation room, all the conversations he heard angered him with the self-centered shortsightedness of their participants.

Having failed to tire himself, he sought out his cubicle, wrapped himself in the restraint blanket, and made himself fall immediately asleep. He would keep himself asleep until the transport reached the starship.

J.D. sailed slowly through the corridor, trying to keep herself an even distance from all four walls. In some ways free-fall was easier than diving; in some ways more difficult. Everything happened faster, so her reactions needed some retraining.

She passed one of the other passengers, going the other direction.

"Hello," she said.

He passed her without speaking, without acknowledging her presence. The second time they passed, she respected his privacy. After that, he disappeared.

J.D. had begun to reaccustom herself to what she thought of as the real world. She felt both more crowded and lonelier. Since returning from the wilderness, she had touched no one more closely than a handshake. Several times she had to remind herself not to hug someone, or stroke their arm, or pat their shoulder. In this world such behavior was unacceptable. With the divers it was expected. Perhaps it was necessary.

The wilderness had begun to feel like a dream, yet a dream of such intensity that she could bring it back in vivid memory.

Three orcas breached, one after the other, bursting free, turning, splashing hard and disappearing beneath the slate-blue water. A moment later they leaped again, heading the opposite direction. The white spring sunlight glazed their black flanks and the stark white patches on their sides.

Walking down the path to her cabin, J.D. watched the beautiful, elegant creatures, and wondered how she could even consider leaving them.

The three half-grown orcas swam to the mouth of the harbor, cutting the choppy surface with their sharp dorsal fins. They joined a larger group of whales. Without her binoculars, J.D. could no longer tell which three had leaped and played. The whole pod swam toward shore. Five or six divers, sleek in the water, swam with them.

J.D. expected Zev to clamber out and greet her, but orcas and divers-alike swam to where the beach shelved off into deeper water. There, they stopped. One of the divers—she thought it might be Zev—waved and gestured to her.

She sent a signal to her metabolic enhancer and scrambled down the bank. A rush of heat radiated from beneath the small scar on her side. The enhancer kicked her metabolism into high gear. Stripping off her clothes, she left them in a pile on the rocks and waded into the frigid water. She gasped when the water reached the level of her nipples. She hesitated, shivering, then plunged underwater.

When she surfaced, Zev bobbed in front of her. A wave slapped her face, reminding her that she was ·in an alien element. She sputtered and moved past Zev so she could turn her back to the swells.

"We came to talk to you," he said. "Will you come?"

"Of course," she said. "But I have to get my lung."

He swam with her to the anchored platform. The orcas and the other divers accompanied them. The dorsal fins all around reminded her of the trunks of the trees in the center of the forest, primordial and eternal, multiple yet individual. The water transmitted the pressure of the orcas' passing, and the vibrations of the first level of their speech. She could hear them with her body as well as her ears.

At the platform she put on her swim fins and let the artificial lung slide onto her back. Warm, a little slimy, it spread itself across her shoulders. She slipped her mask on. By the time she had cleared it, it had connected with the lung. She breathed in the musky, warm, highly oxygenated air.

J.D. sank beneath the choppy waves. The peacefulness of the sea enfolded her, and the alienness and fear vanished. Here she was at home.

She wondered if space would have surrounded her with the same experience. She supposed she would never find out. She had decided to choose the ocean over space, the divers over the starship.

Zev dove with her. His sleek body and pale hair collected light and bounced it back. Even under the gray surface, he glowed.

J.D. swam farther from shore, till the surf rolling onto the beach faded to a sound like the wind in new spring leaves. The whales encircled her, each great ebony body a shadow in the wavery light, the white patches glowing like Zev. The young diver accompanied her like a puppy, dashing ahead, spiraling around her, falling behind and speeding past.

The change in the current, the drop in water temperature, told her they had left the inlet.

They traveled for a long way. Except for Zev, the other divers formed an outer circle beyond her range of vision.

J.D. swam much more slowly than Zev, never mind the orcas. They moved at quarter speed to accommodate her. Squeaks and clicks flowed through the water and through her body. She recognized the phrases of encouragement to very young whales. She managed to smile. But if she really were a young orca, an adult would be swimming close beside her, drawing her along within the pressure wave formed by its body in the water.

She struggled onward, resolute. Her legs began to ache. She breaststroked for a moment. That slowed her even further. She kicked in the metabolic enhancer again, knowing she would pay for it tomorrow.

She wondered how far they had come, and where they were. Drifting upward, she broke the surface. The offshore fogbank, a pretty white curtain, had moved in with a vengeance. It flowed over the water like a second sea. J.D. could see nothing of the island, nothing but a few meters of ocean, no longer choppy but glassy calm. Even the dorsal fins were dim, imagined shadows in a distance impossible to estimate. A smooth wake of tiny parallel ripples angled across her. One of the orcas swam past, and out of sight.

She trod water. Uneasily, she circled. The view was the same in all directions: flat water, dense fog.

Surfacing had not restored her link with the information web. The contact, which diving always interfered with, refused to re-form. Reflexively she looked up, as if she could see the electromagnetic radiation pouring out of the sky, somehow misdirected, and could call it to her. But the web remained silent.

One of the orcas surfaced beside her and blew, exhaling explosively and drawing in a deep breath. Its dorsal fin cut the fog in swirls. The whale raised its head above water and looked at her. Unlike ordinary humans, the orcas—and the divers—could see equally well in water and in air. It spoke to her in phrases beyond her vocabulary. She could recognize the tone. If she had been a young orca, or a diver child, the tone would have been patient. But she was an outsider, she was an adult, and she was tediously slow.

Orcas were easily bored.

J.D. let herself sink, wishing she had never surfaced. She tried to shake off fright. Nothing could hurt her, for she was with powerful predators who had no enemies. They themselves had no malice; she trusted the orcas. They could injure her or kill her without effort or consequence. For that reason she found herself able to place herself in their power equally without effort or fear.

The divers, however, were more mysterious. Essentially human, they retained human motives, human rationalization.

What if this is a test? she thought. What if they plan to bring me out here and leave me, to see if I can make my way back to shore by myself? Lots of cultures won't accept a new member without proof of the person's competence.

The loss of the link gained a stronger and more sinister significance. With it, she could start from the center of the Pacific, if she liked, and navigate to any shore within a meter's error. Without it, she was helpless and disoriented. Left alone in the fog, she might swim in circles as if she were walking in the desert.

She struck out swimming.

Zev appeared before her and guided her in a slightly different direction. This drained the last of her confidence, because she thought she had resumed swimming in her original direction.

J.D. spoke to Zev, awkwardly, with her arms and her body and vibrations from her throat, a sort of two-toned hum, telling him she was frightened and confused and tired. He encouraged her, and again she found herself surrounded by whale baby-talk. No explanations accompanied the encouragement, which quivered at the edge of impolite urgency.

J.D. swam on. She shivered, oblivious to another jolt from the metabolic enhancer.

The texture of the water changed. Abruptly the opaque depths turned translucent, transparent, as the sea bottom shelved toward land. Wavelets lapped softly at the precipitous rock sides of a tiny island.

The divers and the whales gathered in a sheltered cove. The shore rose gently to tide pools. J.D. stroked gratefully into shallow, warm water. She stood, waist-deep, and pushed her mask to the top of her head. Her legs trembled with fatigue. The lung stopped breathing for her and clung to her back.

Beyond the tide pools, fresh water bubbled from a hot spring. It spilled into the salt water, billowing steam. The hot spring raised the temperature of the shallowest part of the cove. Within the steam, the ghostly shapes of divers lounged and played. The whales remained in the deeper, colder water.

J.D. knew Zev well, and she had spent time with the younger divers, the adventurous adolescents of the family. She had met a few of the standoffish older divers, the adults. The youngest divers, children and babies, stayed close to a parent or to an auntie, whether diver or orca. Now here they all were, two dozen of them, newborns to mature adults, waiting for her.

Zev beckoned. J.D. followed.

"Mother," Zev said, "this is my friend J.D."

J.D. accepted the diver's gesture to join her, and sank onto the rough rock in the warm water.

"My name is Lykos," Zev's mother said.

"I'm honored to meet you," J.D. said.

Zev resembled his mother closely, beyond the genetically engineered changes, common to all divers, of body type, dark skin, and dark, large eyes. Lykos had a square, strong face and deepset eyes of a coppery brown. Her close-cropped curly hair was red-gold, her skin a deep mahogany. The other divers arrayed themselves around and behind her, watching J.D., content for the moment to let Lykos speak for them all. A few drifted with only their heads out of water: intense faces haloed by bright hair of any shade from white through gold and auburn.

"Zev told you of our discussion."

J.D. glanced at Zev, wondering if he knew his mother knew he had spoken to J.D., and if she should admit it. He glanced at her sidelong, embarrassed, yet smiling.

"I could not keep it secret," he said.

"This is a flaw in Zev's character," Lykos said. "However, he is working to improve himself." She eased her criticism with a fond look.

"I didn't tell her—"

"I will tell her the rest," Lykos said, interrupting. "J.D., what Zev told you is true. This family of divers and orcas invites you to join us. Have you considered?"

"Yes," J.D. said. "And decided. But it frightens me. It would be . . ." She searched for words. Unable to think of anything strong enough, she ended up with a comment of complete inconsequentiality. "It will be a big change."

"And it is illegal."

"It is."

"Does this trouble you?" Lykos asked.

"It does," J.D. admitted. She had tried to persuade herself that no one would even notice, unless she went out of her way to make it public. Whether she could publish without declaring what she had done was another matter entirely. J.D. had never deliberately broken a law in her life, even an unnecessarily paternalistic. one. She kept reminding herself that her action would affect no one but herself.

Lykos nodded, more to herself than to J.D. "Zev thought it might. He describes you as an honorable being."

"That's kind of him."

"He is perceptive."

J.D. felt the diver's gaze like a physical touch. Behind her, the orcas hovered at the edge of the shallows. They, too, watched and listened.

"We are also honorable beings, I think," Lykos said. "I must not permit you to accept without telling you everything that is involved."

"What do you mean?"

"Before I speak, I must ask you to promise not to repeat what I say. To anyone."

Her voice and her expression were serious. The other divers waited, listening, intent on J.D.'s reply. Even the orcas stopped spouting and ruffling the water with their flippers and flukes.

J.D. hesitated. She was not in the habit of breaking confidences. But Lykos was so serious.

"I promise," she said. She sounded more confident than she felt. She had thought the decision was hers alone, but the divers could refuse to accept her if they thought she did not trust them, if she made it impossible for them to trust her.

"You are aware of . . . increasing tensions between human countries."

"The permafrost," J.D. said.

"I do not understand—?"

"They used to call it the cold war—hostility, aggression, but no direct physical attack of armies. Now, there still isn't any shooting war, but the hostility is so cold and so hard it never thaws. Permafrost."

Lykos nodded. "I see. It is a good metaphor. But not, perhaps, eternal."

"It's better than the alternative."

"There are two alternatives. The other is peace. You are correct, though, in that the most preferred alternative is the least likely. I think it is possible that the worst possibility may be provoked."

A psychic chill replaced the comfortable warmth that had dispersed the physical chill of J.D.'s body. She waited in silence for Lykos to continue.

"We are in an unusual position with regard to your government," Lykos said. "They do not approve of us, yet they permit us to cross freely over the boundary of their country; they have set aside a portion of wilderness within which no ordinary human may travel without our invitation and permission. They are willing to expend resources to maintain this prohibition. They have expended other resources on us.

"Now," she said, "they claim us as their debtors, and demand repayment."

"Repayment! What do they want?"

"They want us to spy."

"But . . . what about the treaty?"

"They speak of setting it aside."

"Can they do that?"

"Can they be prevented from doing it?"

"I . . . I don't know." J.D. thought: I guess I can't blame the military for wanting help against the Mideast Sweep.

"We are much less detectable than mechanical devices," Lykos said. "We are also more vulnerable. And . . . I think the demands would soon include other tasks than spying."

"What are you going to do?"

"We do not wish to spy."

"I don't blame you. It's terrifying! I wouldn't . . ." She stopped. "But I would have to, wouldn't I? That's why you're telling me this, isn't it? So I'll know what I'll have to do if I accept your invitation." She shivered. J.D. thought of herself as having less than the average amount of bravery, and doubted she would make much success of spying.

"We do not intend to comply with the demands. We will not comply. We do not believe in boundaries, or hostilities between intelligent beings. However, we must take the demands seriously. Your government may rescind our right to live here, they may interfere with our research." Lykos gestured around her, at the beautiful island and the sky and the water. "We have accepted the boundary of the wilderness, though we never learned to like it. We do think of this territory as our home. In order to resolve our problems, we must give it up. We will travel north to Canada. We will not be able to come back. That is what you must know." She paused. "Soon the government will demand that we act—"

Oh, no, J.D. thought. This is all my fault. It's my publications that brought this on the divers! I described their abilities, their incredible stamina and speed, their knowledge of coastal geography . . .

"Lykos, stop it, please! Don't tell me any more. I'm sorry, I didn't realize—I shouldn't have let you tell me this much."

Lykos stopped. Zev splashed to J.D.'s side, distressed by her fear. He stroked her arm.

"J.D., what is wrong? It will be exciting!"

"Zev, I'm sorry . . . Lykos, I said I wouldn't tell, and I'll do my best not to—not to tell anything more about you! But it may be too late. If you resist, there's no telling how our government will react, much less the Sweep. You'll be fugitives, unprotected—you must have some idea of the power you'll be opposing."

"I think we have no choice, J.D. It is true that I cannot see all the implications of our plan. Your knowledge of the land world is one of the reasons—though not the only one— we asked you to join us."

"I can't," J.D. said, her voice flat with pain and disappointment and guilt. "I thought I could, but I can't. I'd be more of a danger to you than a help."

"Yet you know the government will react unfavorably, perhaps even behave badly, if we act."

"But that's obvious," J.D. said. "They wouldn't have any choice."

"It is not obvious to me. Nor is it obvious why the Mideast Sweep would have any interest in us at all."

The chill that centered in J.D.'s spine, just behind her heart, had nothing to do with wind or water or waves. She had to stop talking with Lykos before she found out more things that could injure the divers if she were compelled to say what she knew. But they accepted her, and she admired them, and she wanted to warn them.

"If you said publicly your reasons for rebelling, the Mideast Sweep would see that you *might* be a threat against them. I don't think it would matter that you'd chosen not to be. Maybe you'd change your mind, or maybe you'd be forced to act against them. You wouldn't be safe in the open sea."

Lykos placed her hand flat on the water, swimming webs spread, and thoughtfully watched her hand rise and fall, tilt and rock with the motion of the wavelets. J.D. blinked back sudden tears.

"We understood that we would not be safe if we agreed. No one suggested we would not be safe if we refused."

"I wish I were wrong," J.D. said. "But I don't think I am." She had watched the rising level of paranoia in her own country. She feared it. And she knew that in the Sweep, the third of the world that was closed and suspicious, the paranoia was even stronger.

One of the orcas spouted suddenly behind her. It articulated a train of clicks that she could both hear as sound and feel as vibration. The other divers nodded and murmured.

"You are correct," one of the other divers said. "You have made an observation that is obvious only after it is made."

"It is true," Lykos said. "J.D., please join us. We have the facilities to support your change. You would be welcome with us, and you would be valuable. You might make our survival possible."

J.D. shook her head. "I can't." Water splashed as she rose. "You don't understand, this is all my fault."

Lykos and Zev and the other divers gazed at her, bemused, not yet comprehending.

J.D. was afraid to remain, to see, inevitably, the change in the divers' feelings about her. She was afraid to see the look of pain and betrayal in Zev's face when he understood what she had done. And she was perversely angry at the divers for waiting until a crisis to offer their invitation.

She turned and plunged between two orcas, dragged her mask down over her eyes and nose, and hit the boundary between warm spring and frigid sea. She swam into the tide.

Soon she had left the small harbor behind. Every shadow of a ripple through the water startled her, though she knew that the divers would not force her to return against her will.

As she swam she tried to clear her faceplate. Only after she failed did she realize she was crying. She stopped swimming, let herself rise to the surface, and pulled off the mask. It was hard to tread water while she was crying. She struggled to get herself under control. Blinking away the tears, she ducked her face into the water and shook her head.

The droplets she flung away vanished into the fog that still lay flat on the glassy water.

She tried to link up with the web, but the interference remained. Scared, J.D. looked around, hoping rather than fearing to see one of the divers or one of the whales.

She remained alone.

She had failed to find her bearings while swimming with the divers. This time she could not afford to fail.

If she chose the right direction, she would eventually end up somewhere on the long north coast where her cabin lay. Choosing the right direction was the problem. If she got turned around, no other land lay within her range.

J.D. spat into her mask, swished it around with seawater, emptied it, and put it back on. The air of the artificial lung was the only warmth in the world.

She dove, but remained near the surface. If the fog cleared she wanted to know it immediately.

By the slant of the seafloor and the movement of the water relative to the fog, she chose a direction and set out swimming. Tiny jellyfish passed overhead, bobbing just beneath the interface of air and water.

J.D. swam, refusing to listen to the voice in her mind telling her she needed the web, clear sight, and the help of the divers to find her way anywhere.

Her muscles already ached from the long swim out, from the abuse by enhancer overdose. The lung tired, too, and its air grew cool and thin. She rose to the surface and sidestroked, saving the lung's capacity in case she struck rough water. The darkness of deep water lay beneath her.

The current was a presence that surrounded her. Without a fixed point she could not tell its direction. It might be strong enough to sweep her completely past the island, no matter which direction she swam.

Her breath came in a sob. The metabolic enhancer reached its limit, like the artificial lung. Successive doses did nothing but shoot pain through her exhausted muscles.

When she thought she could not swim another stroke, when she had convinced herself that she was swimming in circles and would never find her way back, her link began faintly to respond. Though its connection was too feeble for any useful information, its return encouraged her to continue.

The link grew stronger.

All at once she burst from the fog into clear skies, clear sea. As if the mist defined the limits of the interference, the link returned full force. The north shore lay a hundred meters away. She recognized a headland a kilometer east of her cabin.

She was afraid she could not cover the distance without a rest, but she was also afraid to stop. She forced herself onward.

She fetched up on the gravelly shore, gasping for breath like a drowning victim, and dragged herself beyond the waterline. If she passed out with the tide coming in, she might wake up in the sea again.

She never quite lost consciousness, though a long time passed before she wanted to move. Exposed to dry air, the artificial lung shrank against her back. All she could do was feel sorry for it.

Warm hands held and rubbed her cold fingers. A soft crooning noise, a double-noted hum, surrounded her.

Zev crouched beside her. He stopped humming, but kept hold of her hand. Even his swimming webs felt warm.

"J.D., J.D., I am sorry. We did not think when we let you leave by yourself. We forgot about the interference and we forgot that you cannot hear the seafloor. We thought only that you wished to be left alone. Then I remembered! How did you find your way?"

"Beats the hell out of me," J.D. said. She could barely speak. Her mouth was dry. This struck her as funny.

"Oh, you would make such a good diver," he said.

J.D. freed her hands from his grasp, pushed herself to her feet, and wobbled back to the water. The idea of diving again nauseated her. She peeled off the lung and immersed it. Its unhealthy drying dark red color bloomed to deep pink.

"Zev, would you do me a favor?"

"Yes."

She looked at him askance. He agreed without hesitation or question, still trusting her despite everything.

"I'm going to walk home," J.D. said. "I'd appreciate it if you'd put the lung in its place underneath the floating dock."

"That is easy," he said, sounding downcast. "Would you not like to swim? We could help you." He gestured: offshore, several of the orcas circled, waiting. "They would even let you ride."

"No. I wouldn't like to swim. Tell them thank you." The orcas did not enjoy letting human beings ride them.

Zev walked down the beach.

"Zev . . . goodbye."

He faced her. " 'Goodbye' means for a long time."

"Yes."

"But you could come with us! Then we'd all be safe!"

"It isn't that easy. You're free out here, but I have connections to the land world, and they could make me come back. Then . . . I might not be able to help putting you all in more danger than I've already done."

"But where will you go?"

"To the starship. If they'll still have me."

"What if they will not?"

"Then . . . I'll have to wing it."

He looked at her. "I did not know you could fly, too."

J.D. laughed.

"I will miss you."

"I'll miss you, too, Zev."

"Come wade in the water."

"Why?"

"So that I can hug you when I say goodbye."

It was too complicated to try to explain why she had told him not to touch her yesterday, but why it would have been all right for him to hug her now. She walked with him into the water until they were knee-deep, and then she hugged him and stroked his curly hair. He spread his fingers against her back, and she felt the silky swimming webs against her skin.

"Goodbye." His breath whispered warm on her breast.

Zev took the lung and slid beneath the surface. J.D. did not see him again.

Floris Brown rested in the soft grip of a zero-g lounge, held gently against it with elastic straps. At first, weightlessness had disoriented her, but by the time the spaceplane docked with the transport she had begun to find it welcome and comforting. It eased the pains of eighty years of fighting gravity, and even the bruises of seven minutes of crushing acceleration.

The braided strands of her hair floated in weightlessness. She let three patches grow long, but shaved the rest of her hair to a soft short fuzz. The shells and beads strung into the braids clinked and rattled softly. The end of the longest braid drifted in the corner of her vision. It was completely white. The central patch was streaked with bright pink, the right-hand strands were green. But she always kept the leftmost long patch the natural color of her hair. She also left her eyes their natural blue, but wore heavy black eye makeup on her upper and lower eyelids and her eyelashes.

She gazed out the wide bubble window. It provided an unending source of interest.

As the transport powered gently out of low earth orbit, it passed within sight of the deserted Soviet space station. To the unaided eye it looked like any other satellite, moving from sunlight to shadow. With binoculars it looked old. Though the vacuum of space protected it from rust or other deterioration, cables dangled and twisted eerily; and the antennae all hung motionless, aimed at nothing.

Floris remembered the vigor and assurance of the Soviet space program, as it outdistanced that of her own country when she was very young. All its promise had been lost, its lunar base abandoned and its Mars expedition never begun, when the Mideast Sweep gained power and eliminated the space program as useless, extravagant, an insult to the face of god, a tool of Satan. It made Floris sad to look at the old space station, drifting dead in its orbit, kept as a monument to the past.

Once they left low earth orbit, her nostalgia dissipated. The transport pilot, showing off the sights, oriented the observation window first toward earth, then toward the moon, then toward the stars. Undimmed by earth's atmosphere, the constellations stunned her. She could imagine the sky a hundred or a thousand or a million years ago, the air free of the pollution of human activities, the galaxy sweeping in a brilliant path from one horizon to the other. Back on earth she had seen the Milky Way as a fuzzy patch of light across the middle sixty degrees of the sky. Out here she knew that if she could see all the way around her, she would see the entire disk of the Milky Way. For the first time she understood why prehistoric people—and even some modern people who ought to know better—could believe that the stars contained esoteric meaning.

Occasionally one or another of the passengers came by and greeted her. She was a curiosity: not the oldest person ever to travel into space, but the oldest to make a first trip, the first member of the Grandparents in Space program.

One of the benefits of her years was that her lifelong difficulty remembering names and faces could now be ascribed to age. She smiled and nodded and said hello and thanked people for their welcome; but after five or ten she gave up trying to remember any individual.

"Ms. Brown?"

She looked around, seeking the voice.

Someone drifted into her vision from above the level of her head, upside down from her orientation.

"Please call me Floris," she said.

"Thank you. I'm Victoria Fraser MacKenzie. I'm on the faculty of *Starfarer*. I just wanted to welcome you into space, and see if you needed anything. I could show you around, or help you to your sleeping net."

"I'm not ready to sleep," Floris replied. She found herself tilting her head to try to get the faculty member's face right side up. "I seldom sleep more than a few hours at night." This was not strictly true, but Floris had occasionally found the claim useful. No one had ever disputed her when she repeated the cliché about old people and sleep. "I'm just going to stay here and watch the stars."

The faculty member smiled. That's interesting, Floris thought, that a smile upside down still looks like a smile, and not like a frown. She had never had occasion to observe this before.

"They're beautiful, aren't they? The whole galaxy as if you could touch it. And in a little while I think Esther is going to orient the transport so we can see *Starfarer*."

"Esther?"

"She pilots this transport."

"Thank you for your welcome." Floris tried to keep her attention on the young woman speaking to her, but it was hard to talk to someone upside down. Besides, her gaze kept returning to the stars.

"If you need anything, just let me know."

"All right."

Victoria hovered solicitously, protectively, near Floris Brown. She wished she had come right out and said that she had been one of the major proponents of the Grandparents in Space program, arguing that the expedition needed a wider age-mix. Perhaps she could work it subtly into a conversation.

Victoria felt comfortable around Floris Brown. She hoped they would be friends. No one could take the place of Victoria's great-grandmother, but Grangrana refused to apply to the expedition. Victoria would not see her again for at least a year. Probably more than a year. Already Victoria missed her.

But she liked to think of Grangrana living comfortably in the house that Merry had arranged for the partnership to buy. On the rare occasion that property came up for sale, corporations bought it, not ordinary people. Victoria had never expected her family to own a house. But there it was. It even had some land of its own, away from the city, on the edge of the Vancouver Island wilderness.

Only yesterday she had run up the front stairs of the house for her last visit with Grangrana before the expedition departed.

The door recognized her. Expecting her, it opened. Inside, the air was hot and dry.

"Grangrana?"

She went upstairs. Soft bright light filled the hallway, spilling through the glass wall separating the corridor from the sun porch. Beyond the windows, Victoria's great-grandmother sat sleeping in her favorite chair.

Victoria entered the room quietly, trying not to wake the eldest member of her extended family. She sat in the other chair and watched Grangrana doze. Heat radiated up at her from the black flagstone tiles. She slid out of her jacket and settled back, content to wait, comfortable despite the oppressive warmth. Grangrana had always welcomed her.

Victoria let her surroundings create another memory to take with her on the long trip. Grangrana wore her hair shorter these days than the way Victoria first remembered, still in an iron-gray Afro, but more subdued and easier to care for. Her black skin was smooth except for the ritual scar on her cheek, obtained on a research trip before Victoria was born. Grangrana could have had the scar removed, but she chose to keep it. She admired the people she had visited; they refused to condescend completely to the modern world. They paid tribute to ancient traditions with a single, elegant facial scar.

Whether they still carried on their new tradition or had been forced to change, Victoria did not know. Their territory had been swallowed up in the chaos of the Mideast Sweep two decades before, almost as an afterthought, a brief southern lunge of the greater wave that overtook the U.S.S.R.

Victoria hoped this house would be a haven for Grangrana, the way Grangrana's small apartment in Vancouver had been a haven for Victoria, for Grangrana's friends and colleagues and former students; even, once in a while, for a member of the group she had lived with in Africa. A few of them had been trapped in the West. They could not legally return to their homes. Victoria's most powerful recollection of them was the dignity with which they bore their grief and displacement.

Gradually they had stopped visiting; gradually even Grangrana lost contact with them all. She believed they had returned home, no matter what they had to do to get there. No matter what happened to them when they arrived.

"Victoria?"

Victoria started awake. Grangrana stood before her, a little stooped, frailer than six months ago.

"I fell asleep," Victoria said, abashed. The heat and the few minutes' sleep made her groggy.

Grangrana smiled. "So did I."

She touched Victoria's hair, brushing her fingertips across the soft, springy surface. Victoria wore her hair shorter than Grangrana used to, longer than her great-grandmother kept hers now.

"I'm so glad to see you," Grangrana said. "I thought I might not again."

"I know," Victoria said. "I was afraid of that, too."

She stood and hugged her great-grandmother and kissed her cheek.

"I'm still afraid of that, Grangrana. We're going to be gone so long . . ."

The house AS rolled into the sunroom.

"Come have tea," Grangrana said.

They sat at the white wrought-iron table in the corner, on spindly white wrought-iron chairs.

"The time will seem longer to you than to me," Grangrana said. "The older I get, the faster time passes. I think we perceive time as a proportion of our lives. A year isn't a large proportion of my life anymore. I think I'll still be here when you get back."

"I hope so. But won't you reconsider coming? Won't you at least apply?"

Grangrana shook her head. "No, I've finished my adventuring. I'll wait here for you to come back to me and tell me all about it. Tell me things now. Are you happy?"

"Worried. Distler has only been in office a couple of months, but he's already started trying to carry out his campaign promises . . ."

"Don't tell me about the United States, don't tell me about sword-rattling. I can hear all that on the news, I can remember it from twenty years ago, forty years ago. It's all cycles. I want to hear about you. Has it been a year, since . . . ?"

"A little more," Victoria said. All the memories surrounding the accident came back to her. Time had begun to dim the pain, but she had to work to keep her voice steady. "Stephen Thomas got through it better than Satoshi and I."

"You're still with them both," Grangrana said hesitantly.

Victoria turned away from the window and toward Grangrana, the relative she loved most in the world. Her vision blurred and she blinked furiously. She had thought and believed she would never hear that particular querulous tone again, and never have to live through this conversation.

"Yes, Grangrana," she said. "I'm still with them. They're still with me. We're a partnership, personal and professional. The accident—Merry's death—changed things. But it didn't end the partnership."

"I thought it would," Grangrana said, softly, as if she were speaking to herself. "When it happened, I was sorry for your grief, but I thought it would release you."

"It isn't like that!" She sat on the floor at Grangrana's feet and clasped one frail hand in both of hers. "I'm not entrapped, I'm not blinded—I never was. It's true that Merry was the catalyst for the family. Merry loved falling in love and being in love and staying in love with a lot of people and managing the partnership. But . . . Why can't I explain it right to you? I love you and I want you to think well of me, I don't want you to be ashamed of me—"

"Ashamed! Victoria, nothing you could ever do could shame me. No, I'm so proud of you, but when you told me about this arrangement, I remembered some of the foolish things I did when I was your age—younger than you."

"But it isn't like that. It isn't a cult, Merry didn't use charisma to keep us as pets, or worshippers, or slaves."

"*Chérie*, you never know it until it's over. It's so easy to persuade yourself to give up yourself for someone. Especially someone you love."

Anger mixed with despair. "I've made myself believe it happened to you, because you say it's so. Why can't I make you believe it isn't happening to me?"

"Because I'm old and stubborn and I love you." She drew Victoria up and embraced her. "I want you to be happy."

"I am, Grangrana." Victoria let her cheek rest against her great-grandmother's shoulder. She breathed the cool cedar scent of Grangrana's perfume, the fragrance of clothing kept in cedar trunks and a huge freestanding cedar-lined cabinet, Victoria's favorite hiding place during childhood games.

"They seem like good men, Satoshi and Stephen Thomas," Grangrana said. "But don't stand for it if they pretend to be better than you. Men like to do that, even when they don't realize it."

Victoria knew the struggle her great-grandmother had had to endure to succeed, in a different time. It seemed, to her, nearly as bizarre and incredible as the lives of Grangrana's great-grandparents, who had escaped to Canada from the United States during the years of slavery. Grangrana's stories of times past had taught Victoria the fragility of freedom.

"They wouldn't, Grangrana," she said. She sat down again in the wrought-iron chair, in the warm sunroom. The rays slanted through the windows, nearly horizontal, casting blacker shadows against the black flagstones. Victoria suddenly chuckled.

"What is it, *chérie*?"

"It's that you think my household is outrageous," Victoria said, "and all my other friends think it's terribly old-fashioned."

4

Next morning, orbital time, Victoria floated into the transport cafeteria. She wanted a cup of strong tea. Stephen Thomas used to tease her about the British influence on her eating habits, but once she persuaded him that a single taste of English breakfast tea with milk and sugar would not kill him, he decided he liked it. He still drank coffee the rest of the day and night, immune to the effects of caffeine, but sometimes he drank tea in the morning. Victoria thought she had done him no favor, for tea was scarcer than coffee outside earth's gravity well, and milk was expensive.

She passed Floris Brown, so far the only member of Grandparents in Space, accompanied by a member of the transport crew.

"Good morning, Ms. Brown." Victoria smiled. "I mean, Floris. How are you enjoying the trip?"

"Oh . . . hello. It's fine, thank you." Nothing in the tone of her frail voice indicated she remembered Victoria from yesterday.

She must be tired from the stress of lift-off, Victoria thought, trying not to be disappointed.

"Victoria!"

J.D. and Feral called to her from across the room. She was impressed that they had both already learned not to make unnecessary gestures in zero-g.

Feral, who looked like he had been up for hours and had already hit his stride, pushed toward her and handed off a hot-pack to her. He kicked against the wall and passed her again going the opposite direction, still facing her.

"Good morning. Docking in an hour."

They both reached J.D. at the same time. Feral grabbed a handhold; Victoria brushed her hand along the bulkhead, using the friction to dissipate her momentum.

Victoria extended the hot-pack's straw and sipped it. Tea, with milk and sugar.

"Thanks," she said to Feral. Most Americans, even if they had noticed how she liked her tea, would have put cream in it. "Have you guys had breakfast already?"

"Just finished," J.D. said. "I wanted to be sure to get a good spot to watch the docking."

"I don't think you'll have any trouble," Victoria said. "Most of the folks on board are old hands. You and our new grandmother are the only new permanent residents, and Feral and that other guy are the only temps."

"What other guy?" Feral asked.

"He was in the observation bubble yesterday morning, but he disappeared and I haven't seen him since."

"I don't remember him."

"He has kind of brown hair, or was it blond—you know, that color that you think is blond but when you really look at it, it's brown. And . . ." She tried to remember what color his eyes were. Her image of him shifted and faded. "Medium height, maybe a little taller." Height was difficult to judge in weightlessness. "Medium build." She searched for a distinguishing characteristic.

"I saw him a couple times in the corridor," J.D. said. "But he didn't say anything."

"I guess I didn't notice him," Feral said, frowning.

"Not much to notice. Anyway, even if he and all of us here and half the crew go to watch the docking, it won't be crowded." She sighed. "This is the first time I've ever taken a transport to *Starfarer* that hasn't been full."

"So Chandra's not on board?" Feral asked.

"Who?"

"The sensory artist. I heard she was leaving earth soon. I thought I might get a chance to interview her."

"Oh, dear," J.D. said. A blush crept up her cheeks.

"What's the matter?"

"I was supposed to take her diving. I completely forgot about it. I just . . . left."

"Didn't she call you?"

"No. Isn't that odd . . . Maybe she forgot our appointment, too," J.D. said hopefully. "Excuse me, I'd better try to reach her and apologize, at least."

Her eyelids flickered closed and she fell silent as she connected with the web.

Letting the hot-pack drift in place, Victoria took a sandwich from a service module, tore off a corner of the wrapper, and pulled off a bite-sized piece of the sandwich. She left the rest inside the paper so it would not shed crumbs. She ate the bite, then ate the corner of the wrapper as well.

Feral watched her with an expression that indicated he thought Victoria was pulling his leg.

"Rice paper," Victoria said. The crinkly film dissolved on her tongue. "We try to make everything we can from renewable resources, and as recyclable as possible." She grinned. "One way or another."

She ate another bite of her sandwich, and another corner of the rice-paper wrapping.

J.D. opened her eyes again. "I left her a message." She sighed. "How could I just forget? I guess I'll have to do some seriously apologetic groveling when she comes on board."

"You folks didn't exactly make it hard for your opponents to take potshots at the expedition," Feral said. "You're taking along artists, and grandparents, and the social structure is a pretty weird mix—"

"Should I take that comment personally?" Victoria asked.

"Only if you want to. You've got to admit that polygamy is unusual."

"But my family isn't polygamous."

"What, then?"

"The technical term is 'family partnership.' It isn't as rigidly defined as polygamy. A family partnership is gender-transparent. It doesn't require a particular mix, like several members of one gender and one member of the other."

"But that's what yours has."

Victoria forced herself to answer without hesitation. "It does right now. But it doesn't have to."

"Can I have an exclusive on your next engagement?"

"I was only speaking theoretically." Victoria tried to smile, but the idea of bringing in another partner hurt too much. It would not be replacing Merit—no one could replace Merit—but it would feel like trying. "Besides, the last time somebody wrote about our personal lives, we got insults from weirdos who think we're reactionary, even stranger messages congratulating us on our traditional values, and a handful of proposals from people who thought they'd fit right in. It takes too long to answer the mail."

"Why'd you choose the arrangement, if I'm not being too nosy? Are you . . . I don't know what the parallel term for 'monogamous' would be for a family partnership, but you know what I mean. Don't you trust the Thanthavong viral depolymerase?"

Victoria found herself more amused than offended by Feral's unapologetic nosiness.

"I admire Professor Thanthavong tremendously. She's the head of the department where my partner Stephen Thomas has tenure, and he's eloquent about her achievements."

"Her work made a big difference," said J.D., who was older than either Victoria or Feral. "It's hard to explain how scared everybody was, to anybody who's too young to remember."

"Then why the partnership?"

"U.S. law provides for it, and it helps ease some of the problems of a multinational family arrangement," Victoria said. "But the real reason is . . . it seemed like a good idea at the time. It still does. But it's a long story. I'll tell it to you someday. I have a couple of things to do before we dock, so I'll meet you both in the observation bubble. All right?"

Feral looked disappointed. Victoria had learned, in their short acquaintance, that Feral would talk about anything for as long as anyone else could stand it.

"I wouldn't mind the condensed version—"

"The orcas have an interesting social structure." J.D. gave Victoria a sympathetic glance as she interrupted Feral without appearing to. "You can draw parallels between it and a family partnership . . ."

Victoria extricated herself gratefully.

She felt a bit guilty about implying that she had some kind of important errand to run before the transport docked. In fact, she wanted to take a shower and change clothes.

Zero-g showers amused her. The water skimmed over her, pulled across her body by a mild suction at one side of the compartment. When she was wet, she turned off the water and lathered herself with soap, scraped off most of the suds with an implement like the sweat-scraper of an ancient Greek athlete—or a racehorse—and turned the water on again till the last of the soap washed away. It felt like standing in a warm windy rain. When she finished, she was covered all over with a thin skin of water. She scraped herself off again, got out of the shower and closed the door, and turned the vacuum on high to vent the last of the water out of the compartment and into the recycler. Her whole body felt tingly and refreshed.

As she dressed in her favorite new fancies, the warning signal sounded softly through the ship. A few minutes later, microgravity replaced zero-g as the transport decelerated.

Victoria hurried to the observation bubble, anxious to be home.

All alone, Zev swam through the cold water toward the harbor. He had come this way by himself a hundred times, maybe a thousand, and he had never felt alone. Before, he always knew he would find J.D. in the cove or on the shore, and his family back in the open water.

The tidal outflow from the harbor, just perceptibly warmed by the sun, flowed over him. He swam between the headlands that protected the beach.

When he reached J.D.'s anchored dock, he stopped and floated beneath its shadow. He could hear the artificial lung respiring in its compartment, waiting and waiting for someone who might never return. It was full of oxygen, ready, with a willingness bred into its cells, to give up the oxygen whenever a human needed it. It had no consciousness, of course, no brain, only the bare minimum of nerve tissue necessary to make it function. Yet Zev had the urge to reach in and stroke it, comfort it, like a pet.

Instead he dove deeper and swam toward shore along the harbor bottom, taking the environment into his memory like a baleen whale scooping up plankton to store up energy before its long migration. He gathered the details of scarlet and yellow and green anemones, great gooseneck barnacles kicking their feet in the water to draw in their food, long strands of kelp reaching up toward sunlight, a pretty little octopus, watching curiously, following him cephalopod-fashion, squirting water and trailing its legs.

Zev's cousins, the orcas, did not forage for plankton. They hunted: they hunted what they found wherever they found themselves.

He had always done the same; he would continue to do the same, despite a changed environment. He kicked hard and burst through the surface, nearly leaving the water before he splashed down again.

A human stood on the beach. He did not mistake this human for J.D., though he had met precious few other true humans in his life. J.D. was gone.

The water became too shallow to swim in. He stood up on the rocky shelf and waded forward.

The human saw him coming and hurried toward him. She was different from J.D., her eyes without pupils and all gray. She wore a wet suit and carried a mask and fins.

"Hello," he said. "I am Zev."

"My name's Chandra. I don't suppose *you* ever heard of me, either. Do you know where J.D. Sauvage is?"

"She left for the starship."

"Oh, great."

He had no idea why her voice held anger, nor why she smelled of fear. Smells carried poorly in air, compared to water, and the wet suit covered all the places that would send off useful odors.

Chandra extended her hand to Zev. Zev slid his fingertips along her knobby fingers, up the back of her hand, and along the wrist. He felt her start to draw away, then relax again.

"Goodbye," he said.

"Wait! Where are you going?"

"To represent the divers on the deep space expedition."

"Hey, great, maybe I'll see you on board. Will I find other divers in the water?"

"Where else?" he asked, amused.

"I mean nearby."

"No," he said.

"Where are they?"

"They have gone somewhere else."

Zev started up the beach.

He heard more humans coming toward the cove. They were still out of sight, beyond the hill and among the Douglas firs. He glanced back at Chandra.

"Are your friends coming to swim with you? I'm sure the orcas would not mind, if you asked, but you are supposed to ask."

"It's just me," she said. "I was supposed to dive with Sauvage, but since she's not here I'm going in anyway."

A group of people, all dressed the same, appeared between the trees. They crashed down the slope, not bothering to be quiet.

"Military exercises, maybe?" Chandra said. "Those folks are in uniform, and they're carrying guns."

Zev hesitated. He was not entirely sure what the military was, but he knew they were responsible for the difficulties his family faced. He did know the meaning of the word "gun." Guns were not permitted in the wilderness.

Zev was fearless, but he was not foolish. If he knew a shark was nearby and he was all alone, he would avoid it if he could. If the family were around, that might be different. But his family was far away.

He walked back down the beach and waded into the water.

"Wait!" Chandra called. "I'll go with you!"

He could tell she knew nothing about swimming as soon as she pushed off into the low waves. Instead of diving into them she tried to rise above them. They splashed her in the face and made her cough and choke and try to find her footing. Instead of turning back, she floundered on toward the dock. Terror poured out of her, the flavor carried strongly by the sea. Zev wondered what frightened her so.

He stroked beside her. "Put on your mask," he said.

She had jumped in so quickly that the mask still dangled from her arm by its strap, further hampering her attempts to swim. Zev moved closer to her, put one arm around her, and held her steady. She pushed the mask over her head. It pressed against the growths on her face. Zev wondered if it hurt. He pulled a few locks of her hair from beneath the edges of the mask, and hoped it would not leak.

The other humans reached the shore. They saw Zev and Chandra in the water. They broke into a run. Their feet made loud noises on the rocks. J.D. sometimes wore shoes, but not great heavy ones. The humans wore thick clothing and wide web straps from which depended chunks of metal and plastic. The smell of oil and fire drifted across the water.

Zev dragged Chandra toward the dock.

"Hold your breath!"

"No—wait—"

She gasped and got a mouthful of water as he pulled her under. She struggled. He let her go and she rose toward the surface. She came up in the airspace beneath the dock, coughing again. Strips of bright sunlight poured through the cracks between the dock's floorboards.

"What's this all about?" she said. Her voice shook, and the water transmitted the trembling of her body. Excitement flushed her face. She had not trained herself to draw the blood from her skin and from her extremities while she swam in cold water.

"I do not know for sure," he said. "But I think they are dangerous to me. Perhaps not to you. I should not have pulled you like that, but you said you wanted to come and I thought you were in distress. Do you want to use the lung, or do you want to go back to shore by yourself?"

"I want the lung," she said.

"Take one deep breath, hold it, and relax." Though his request further intensified her fear, she did as he asked.

Zev pulled her underwater. He freed the lung and urged it toward her. When it touched her she shuddered, but she did not fight. The lung fitted itself against her and extended its processes toward the mask. When it had established itself, when Chandra could breathe its oxygen, Zev towed her deeper underwater and swam away with her, leaving the other, stranger humans behind on the beach.

Satoshi stretched, arching his back and spreading his arms. His research image, displayed above him in the air, cast colored light over him and across half the geography theater. His hands moved through the reflection of delicate lines.

He pressed his head back against the contour couch, tensing all his muscles, then relaxing them. He had barely moved for four hours, as he put all his attention and energy into the map overlays. He kneaded his trapezius muscles.

Stefan Tomas of the world's best back rubs, Satoshi thought, where are you when I need you?

The display was so pretty he hated to put it away, but it took up half the theater. Though it was past eight o'clock, someone else might want to use the theater later on.

"Give me a projection," he said to Arachne. "Hard copy. Then file and store."

A two-dimensional projection of a three-dimensional representation of a four-dimensional problem was little more than a reminder of what he was doing. Nevertheless, he enjoyed the artistic aspects of it. He rolled up the hard copy and slid it into the accordion pocket of his cargo pants.

Twenty minutes to transport docking. Twice as much time as he needed to get to the waiting room, but he was eager to see Victoria. He wanted to be there when she arrived.

Pausing near the only other patch of light in the theater, he regarded the overlays critically.

"What do you think?"

Fox peered out from beneath the display. Its lights striped and shadowed her face.

"Not bad," Satoshi said. He looked at her quizzically. "You don't have to spend twenty-four hours a day in here, you know. I'm already on your side."

"Is that what you think?" she said belligerently. "That I hang around here all the time just to impress my thesis professor? Thanks a lot."

"You're welcome," Satoshi said, nettled. Fox had that effect. She did not want sympathy. She wanted to stay with the expedition.

"Maybe I wanted to get the damned research done before I get kicked out. Maybe I'm trying to age myself six months prematurely so I can get exempted from the stupid rules."

"Maybe you're lucky to be up here at all. I'm surprised your family let you stay this long. How did you arrange that?"

"I do creative hysteria very well," Fox said sulkily.

"I'm sorry," Satoshi said. "I'm afraid you've reached the limits of creative hysteria. Even if your uncle approved—"

"Don't call him that!" She looked around, theatrically. "Jeez, I'll never live it down if people start finding out the president is my uncle!"

"There's nobody else in here. Even if he approved of the expedition, he wouldn't be able to exempt you. He doesn't have the authority, and pulling strings would look bad."

"I don't much care how it would look," Fox said. "All I care about is that I want to go on the expedition, and you won't let me."

"I know you're disappointed," Satoshi said. "But I did all I could. Now I'm leaving. Don't stay too late."

She made a sound of anger and frustration and disappeared beneath the research display.

The conversation had taken up most of Satoshi's extra time. Fortunately, the theater lay at the same end of the cylinder as the docking hatch. He went outside, blinking in the bright daylight.

Satoshi jogged to the end of campus, where the floor of the cylinder blended into the cylinder's conical end, forming a steep slope. He sprinted up the hill. As he climbed, the gravity fell. His strides turned to long leaps. He bounded across a surface nearly perpendicular to the floor of the cylinder.

Satoshi jumped over the transition between the rotating cylinder and the stationary axis, grabbed the rungs of a guide ladder, and drew himself fast through the zero-g environment of the central cylinder. He climbed past the ends of the solar mirrors and ducked through the hatch that led to the docking port. Spotting Stephen Thomas on the other side of the waiting room, he threaded his way among the other people here to greet returning friends. The crowd was much smaller than it would have been a few weeks ago. A lot of people had been recalled. If the United States continued to insist on the conversion of the starship to military purposes, even the Canadians would pull out in protest. Satoshi had no idea what he and Stephen Thomas and Victoria would do then.

Satoshi drifted to a stop. Stephen Thomas, who hated zero-g, waited uneasily with one hand clamped around a grip. He managed to smile when he saw Satoshi. Satoshi floated to his side and put one arm around him. Stephen Thomas hugged him with his free arm, then massaged the junction of Satoshi's neck and shoulder. Satoshi groaned as the tight muscles started to loosen.

"Thanks. That feels great."

A hologram created itself in the center of the waiting room. As the image of the transport approached the image of the cylinder, all the people within the volume of the hologram drifted out of it and surrounded it, watching. The bulky, asymmetrical transport touched the docking port. The faint vibration of its attachment quivered around them.

Victoria had been away for less than two weeks. It felt like months.

Stephen Thomas patted Satoshi's shoulder. "I'll give you a proper massage when we get home."

"It's better already." He let himself drift in the quiet air. Stephen Thomas did his best to appear nonchalant about the lack of gravity.

"When are you going to let me take you out for a spacewalk?" Satoshi said.

Stephen Thomas pushed back his hair with his free hand. As usual, he had come into zero-g with his hair flying loose.

"Probably never."

"You'd like it."

"Probably get sick in my spacesuit," Stephen Thomas said.

Satoshi let the subject drop. He was convinced that Stephen Thomas would learn to like zero-g if he experienced the complete freedom of an untethered spacewalk, but Stephen Thomas grew sullen if he was pushed to do something he preferred to avoid. Gentle encouragement worked better.

The docking port opened and the transport passengers entered *Starfarer*. The more experienced travelers came first. A couple of helpers went in to assist the novices.

Satoshi and Stephen Thomas greeted their friends and acquaintances. The people who had traveled all the way to earth stood out from those who had just visited one of the O'Neill colonies; all the veterans returning from earth wore bright new clothes.

Victoria appeared, wearing a gold scarf around her hair, a matching vest, and a swirly black split skirt. She soared toward him, hand in hand with a plain, heavyset woman who must be J.D. Sauvage, though Sauvage was supposed to be a novice in space. This woman moved with the assurance of a veteran. Behind her she towed a young red-headed man whom Satoshi could not place.

Victoria let go of J.D.'s hand and floated toward Satoshi. They clasped wrists, tumbled one around the other, and drew close enough to embrace. Victoria kissed him.

"Oh, I missed you."

"Me, too," Satoshi said.

Victoria fended off the wall with her foot, and, in doing so, damped most of their spin and changed their direction back toward Stephen Thomas. A second touch stopped them in front of him. He embraced Victoria with his free arm, but kept hold of the grip with his other hand.

"Welcome home."

"Thanks," she whispered, not trusting her voice any louder. After a moment holding them both, she opened the circle to include the two newcomers. "J.D.," she said, "these are my partners, Satoshi Lono and Stephen Thomas Gregory. Guys, J.D. Sauvage, our alien contact specialist. And this is Feral Korzybski, the journalist. He's come to do a story on the expedition."

"Welcome to *Starfarer*."

Stephen Thomas glanced at J.D. quizzically.

"Are you all right?"

"Yes, of course." She stared at Stephen Thomas. "Why do you ask?"

Satoshi hoped Stephen Thomas would leave auras out of the introductions. Sauvage apparently had some reservations about joining the team and the expedition. The last thing they needed was to have her decide Stephen Thomas was too strange to work with, and go straight back to earth on the same transport that had brought her. Never mind talking about auras in front of a reporter.

"Oh—no reason," Stephen Thomas said. "You looked worried, that's all."

"Have you been up here before?" Satoshi said.

"What?" She looked away from Stephen Thomas. "No, never."

"You look like an old hand in zero-g. But everybody knows everybody out here, and I know I've never met you."

"It must be because of diving, though there are a lot of differences. You move a *lot* faster than underwater." She took them all in with her glance. "Thank you for inviting me onto the team. I know I'm going to like it. This feels . . . natural."

"Not to me," Stephen Thomas said plaintively. "Can we get back to solid ground?"

J.D. followed her new teammates from the transport waiting room, anxious for her first view of *Starfarer*.

Stephen Thomas disappeared over the lip of the tunnel entrance, hurrying toward the floor of the cylinder and *Starfarer*'s normal seven-tenths gravity.

J.D. stopped short at the outlet of the tunnel, amazed by *Starfarer*. She sank toward the floor in the low false gravity, at the last moment remembering to get her feet under her.

The sun tubes, reflecting and dispersing sunlight from the solar mirrors, stretched along the axis of the cylinder, from above her to the distant far end. Their heat warmed J.D.'s face and shoulders and their light dazzled her.

Victoria glanced at her from a few meters down the hill.

"J.D., don't stare at the tubes!"

J.D. looked down fast. An abrupt wave of dizziness overtook her as the cylinder rolled back and forth around her. Victoria bounded to her side and grabbed her arm before she lost her balance.

"Stay still. It'll stop in a minute."

"I'm sorry." J.D. felt foolish. "I know better—about looking at the tubes *and* about nodding or shaking my head."

Victoria smiled and patted her shoulder. "It's all right. Everybody 'knows' when they get up here that the light is direct from the sun, and that the inner ear reacts to the spin of the station. But the sun tubes look like great big fluorescent lights, and the acceleration feels just like gravity, so it takes a while to develop the new habits. Have you stopped spinning yet?"

"I think so." The dizziness had begun to disperse. It was a *very* strange sensation, one that would change depending on whether she nodded or shook or tilted her head, and depending on her relative orientation to *Starfarer*'s spin. For the moment she had no wish to experiment with it.

Victoria let go of her elbow. "The light's filtered, so it's safer than looking at the sun, but it can damage your eyes. You have to be more careful in the wild cylinder, if you cross over for a visit. The light's even less filtered there."

"I'll remember." J.D. looked around, her gaze oblique to the sun tubes. "I know *Starfarer* is big—I knew exactly how big it is before I came up here. But I didn't realize how big it would *feel*."

At the foot of the hill, the ground curved upward to her left and to her right. Far overhead, hazed by distance, the sides of the cylinder curved toward each other. The sun tubes obscured the side of the cylinder directly opposite, but the rest lay spread above and around her like a map.

"Almost everybody has that reaction, their first time here."

"Come on, you guys!" Stephen Thomas shouted from halfway down the cylinder's end-hill. Below, the interior of the starship stretched out into the distance. Feral and Satoshi waited, ten meters down the slope. J.D. and Victoria joined them.

Feral squinted past the sun tubes toward the cylinder's far side. "Amazing how the people up there can keep their balance, walking upside down and all."

Victoria glanced sideways at him.

He grinned. "You've heard that one before, huh?"

"It's about the first oldest joke."

"I love your accent, " Feral said.

"What accent?" Victoria said.

"You say 'oot' and 'aboot' instead of 'out' and 'about.' "

"I don't have an accent," she said. "It's all you Americans who talk funny. *Parlez-vous français?*"

"Huh?" Feral said.

"*Un peu,*" J.D. said.

"You do?" Victoria said to J.D., surprised. "I don't remember it from your vita—"

"It isn't academic French," J.D. said. "I picked it up the last few months. Most of the divers speak it."

They reached the bottom of the hill, and joined Stephen Thomas. On solid ground he was at ease, and he moved with grace and certainty. As Victoria and Satoshi came off the hill, Stephen Thomas kissed Victoria intensely, and drew Satoshi into the embrace. J.D. envied them a bit, and she felt glad for them, and a little embarrassed.

"I'll see you all tomorrow," she said. She started away.

"J.D.," Victoria said, "do you know where you're going?"

"Um, no, but I'm sure Arachne will get me to where I'm supposed to stay."

"Don't be silly. We'll show you, and get you settled."

Victoria and Satoshi went with J.D., while Stephen Thomas set off with Feral to show him to the guesthouse.

Thick, weedy grass and flowers covered much of the land of the campus. At first J.D. could not figure out why it looked so familiar to her, until she realized that the ecosystem of *Starfarer*, planned as a natural succession, reproduced the first growth in a forest after a big fire. Of course the campus lacked the black tumble of half-burned trees, snags, uprooted trunks.

They followed a small stream. J.D. tried to trace its course along the inside of the cylinder, but soon lost it among hedgerows. Above, on the other side of the cylinder, a network of silver streams patterned the raw ground and sprouting grass.

The interior radius of one end of *Starfarer*'s cylinder was slightly shorter than that of the other end. The resulting slope formed a gentle gradient of artificial gravity that caused the streams to flow from this end of the cylinder to the other. They erupted at the base of the hill and flowed in spirals around the interior of the campus. Every so often a stream spread out into a clear lake, or a bog or swamp thick with water hyacinths and other cleansing plants. At the far end of the cylinder lay a salt marsh and a ring of ocean, the main buffer of the ecosystem. Evaporation and transpiration and rain recycled some of the water, and some flowed underground through pumps and desalinizers, back to its starting point.

At first Victoria and Satoshi followed a resilient rockfoam path, but after a few hundred meters Victoria turned down a dirt trail that had been worn into the grass.

"Do you have deer on campus?" J.D. asked.

"Not in this cylinder. These are people trails. If one gets awfully popular, we foam it."

J.D. looked around curiously. Along the length of the cylinder she could see clearly only a few hundred meters, because windbreaks of saplings or bushes separated the fields.

She stopped short. "What's that?"

Several dog-sized animals bobbed toward her through the high grass of the next field. Back on the island, a pack of half-wild dogs ran free, far more dangerous than any wolf pack or coyote band.

"That's the horse herd," Satoshi said.

"Horse herd!"

Their tiny hooves tattooed the damp ground, the thick grass. Five miniature horses skidded to a stop in front of J.D., whinnying in high-pitched voices, snorting at each other. A pinto no taller than J.D.'s knee squealed and kicked out at a bay that crowded too close. They whuffled expectantly around her feet.

Victoria reached down and scratched one behind the ears.

"I'm fresh out of carrots," she said. "Satoshi, have you got anything for them?"

He dug around in the side cargo pocket of his pants, underneath a crumpled map printout, and found a few peanuts. He opened them, rubbing the shells to powder between his fingers before letting them fall to the ground. The miniature horses crowded closer. Satoshi gave J.D. the peanuts. The horses lipped them softly from her hands. They nuzzled the backs of her knees, her ankles, and her shoes.

"I didn't know horses liked peanuts," J.D. said.

"They might prefer apples," Satoshi said, "but the trees aren't established yet. Next year we may get some fruit. Sugar's still fairly expensive up here, since we haven't started processing it. Lots of carrots, but peanuts are easier to carry. Drier."

Victoria chuckled. "He left a carrot in his pocket once, for I don't know how long. The laundry sent it back."

"It wasn't *that* bad," Satoshi said to J.D. He shrugged. "It was more or less fossilized before anybody found it."

"Why are they here?"

"The minis, you mean, not the carrots?"

"People do better with pets around," Victoria said. "And they keep the grass from getting completely overgrown."

"I see," J.D. said. "The mini-horses are easier to keep track of than cats or dogs or hamsters—and easier on the ecosystem, too, I suppose." She sat on her heels and rubbed the soft muzzle of a seven-hand Appaloosa.

"Right. Alzena—Alzena Dadkhah, she's the chief ecologist—is trying to get some birds established. A lot of people would like to have dogs or cats—I'd like to have my cat. But I can see her point about predators. And domestic rodents are too adaptable. According to Alzena, once you've got them, you've got them everywhere. So far we haven't had any rats, but it could happen. Then there's the waste problem."

"Sorry, little one, that's the end of the peanuts," J.D. said to the Appaloosa. "I see the point about waste. Herbivore waste isn't quite as unattractive as carnivore waste."

"Easier to compost, too," Satoshi said.

J.D. patted the Appaloosa one last time. She straightened up. The mini tossed its head, looking for another handout. It was a cute little animal.

Something about it made J.D. uncomfortable, and that was exactly the problem: it was cute. In being bred down from magnificence, the horses had been made trivial, converted from strong, powerful animals to lapdogs.

She clapped her hands sharply. The minis snorted and started and galloped away. They scattered, galloping and bucking, and re-formed their herd a hundred meters across the field.

5

J.D. saw her new house for the first time. She had known the houses formed part of the topography, built into hillsides with one wall of windows. But she had not expected hers to be beautiful.

"I love it," J.D. said. "It looks organic, somehow. But why do it like this? Not to conserve energy, surely." While *Starfarer* still flew within the solar system, the sun would provide all the power it could possibly use. Once it clamped itself to the universe's web of cosmic string, the problem would be to keep from being overwhelmed by the energy flux.

"Not here and now," Victoria said. "But we can't know all the conditions we'll face after we leave. The basic reason is aesthetic and ecological. The more plants on the surface, the less ground we cover with buildings and pathways and so forth, the more stable and resilient the ecosystem will be. The plants keep the air fresher, they soak up the runoff from rain—"

J.D. glanced up. *Starfarer* was large enough to have its own weather patterns, including rain. Two different systems of clouds drifted over the land on the other side of the cylinder.

Victoria pointed at the most distant cloud system. "That far-overhead system will be near-overhead in half a rotation.

The ecosystems analysts encourage rain in the cylinders—it's easier and cheaper than air-conditioning. Smells better, too."

"No thunder and lightning, though, I'm sure," J.D. said wistfully. That would be too risky, both because of all the electronics within *Starfarer*, and because of the amount of energy even a small lightning bolt can let loose.

"No, you're right." Victoria laughed. "That, they discourage."

"It's the one thing I missed in the Pacific Northwest," J.D. said. "There was lots of rain, but hardly ever any thunder." She hesitated. She wanted to ask so many questions about *Starfarer* and the alien contact department. But she would have time. "I'll see you tomorrow, right?"

"First thing," Satoshi said.

"We'll come and get you and go watch the solar sail test."

They bid each other good night. J.D. watched Victoria and Satoshi walk away, hand in hand.

Griffith glanced back at earth one last time before leaving the transport. This was his first trip into space. He had known, intellectually, how far he would be from the planet, but the distance struck him emotionally only when he could hold out his hands and cup the world between them.

At this distance, it would take the very best surveillance equipment—perhaps even the next generation of surveillance equipment—to get fine detail from earth. The starship would have to move to a lower orbit.

Griffith hated waste. *Starfarer* should never have been built this far out to begin with. A great deal of time and money and reaction mass had gone into its construction. Even though most of its mass came from cheap lunar material, O'Neill colony leftovers, it had required a significant number of earth-to-orbit payloads.

Griffith moved into the starship, hand over hand along the grips. He was getting the hang of zero-g navigation, but he envied people with the experience to move naturally and gracefully.

He left the docking gate and entered the main body of *Starfarer*. He stopped at the center of the slope where he could look out into the cylinder.

Where earth had been too small to believe, the cylinder was far too large. He was amazed and appalled by the amount of space. From where he held himself, the end of the cylinder appeared to slope up to meet the walls of the cylinder, the living space of *Starfarer*. He knew, though, that when he started to travel along one of the numerous paths leading away from the gate, the apparent gravity would increase. He would perceive himself climbing down to the floor.

Disorientation dizzied him. He closed his eyes, but that only made it worse. Keeping his gaze away from the weird slope and the enormous cylinder, he found the path leading to the proper section. He drew himself onto it and gripped the rail.

Lower on the slope, the artificial gravity held him on the stairs. He released his death grip on the railing. Other people on the path at the level he had reached were leaping up and down the slope like gazelles, like moon-walkers, ignoring the switchbacks, but Griffith moved slowly and steadily and cautiously. He felt dizzy. He supposed it was a psychosomatic reaction that resulted from his knowing that the cylinder was spinning, for he was below the level at which his inner ear ought to be able to detect the spin. The dizziness bothered him, for he was not much given to psychosomatic reactions.

He made some quick calculations about the population density of the starship. Though he knew he had done the calculations correctly—he made a policy of exercising his mind in this way, so as not to become too dependent on

outside databases—the number struck him as so absurdly
low that he sent out a line to the web and had it check his
arithmetic. It was accurate. Then his amazement at the size
of the cylinder—and there were two of them, one completely
uninhabited, designed and intended to remain that way—
changed to resentment and envy. The people who lived here
had all the space in the world . . .

He laughed, a quick sarcastic bark. Back in the world,
there was arable land, there was useless land, there were
restricted wildernesses, and there were cities. Not much space
remained for stretching out. The spoiled academics who lived
up here had no idea how fortunate they were. Or, more
likely, they knew perfectly well. No doubt they had planned
it this way.

They had better enjoy their luxury while it lasted. Soon
everything would change.

The path forked. He let Arachne guide him to the proper
track. Below him, on the slope, the pathways branched and
branched again, like a river splitting and spreading its fingers across a delta. Otherwise the pathways that had begun
so close together, in the center of the cylinder cap, would
end at great distances from each other. By following the
correct branch, Griffith could reach the proper longitude of
the cylinder.

No one had come to meet him, which was as he had
planned. He preferred being left to himself. He would
observe in anonymity and make his recommendations without any fuss.

The departure of several of the associate nations could
only help in the conversion he planned. It could be made
to look as if they were grasping at a convenient excuse and
cutting their losses, finding the starship project to be too big,
too expensive for their budgets. And, who knew? That might
even be true.

A few associates might hold out, but the change had

begun and it could not be stopped. At this point, objecting to the use of the starship as a military base came close to treason. Unfortunately, it would not look good to arrest half the faculty and staff of the expedition even if Griffith found evidence against them. Never mind. Arrests would be unnecessary. By the time he finished his work, the scientists would give up and go home.

Griffith knew there must be people on board who disagreed with the majority view, but who feared to speak up against it. He hoped to discover them.

He took a mental glance at a map of the campus transmitted by the web. His perception of the transmission made it overlap his sight, like the tactical display on the window of a fighter jet. Most people had to close their eyes to receive visually oriented information from the web.

The map led him to the guesthouse. He climbed the path and walked under the hill and through the open doorway. It irked him that he would be forced to stay in an underground room. Back on earth he lived high in a skyscraper, and he had waited a long time—and paid several bribes—to get an apartment looking over the city and the flat stark plains beyond. Having paid the bribes still troubled him.

The lobby was deserted and empty. Not even an AS waited to serve him.

"Hello!"

No one replied. Griffith went behind the desk, intending to go into the back and rout out whoever or whatever was supposed to be in attendance.

A sheet of paper rustled beneath his shoe. He picked it up: a sign, blown to the floor by a breeze. It carried a notice in several languages, beginning with French. He glanced farther down and found the English version.

"We regret that we are not here to aid you. Our government has called us home for consultations."

Griffith snorted at the idea of hotel keepers being called

home for consultations. His briefing had neglected to mention that France held the guesthouse concession and that all its personnel would be gone by the time he arrived.

"Please choose a chamber from our diagram and consider our house yours during your stay. We have no locks so no code is required. Please put soiled linen into the laundry chute. Fresh linen may be retrieved from the armoire in the hallway."

The lack of locks irked him even more than the idea of staying underground. Not that he was stupid enough to bring anything sensitive with him, but if anyone found out who he was they would not know that, and they might search his belongings. Besides, some people would snoop even without suspicions to go on.

Griffith was a very private person.

He glanced at the diagram. Two rooms out of ten had been spoken for. He left signing in till after he had seen what the guesthouse had to offer.

He strode along the ramp leading to a second-story hallway. The interior wall was blank. Doors to the guest apartments opened from the exterior wall. Each end of the hallway led out onto a balcony and exit ramp.

The guesthouse was more pleasant than he expected, and, though it was indeed underground, each room flowed into its own small terrace just beneath the crest of the hill. All the rooms were similar, with one wall of windows. The hillside sloped to a stream and a small grove of trees. The furnishings were Spartan: a futon, a small desk, woven mats on the floor. His shoes crunched on the floor coverings.

To give himself the most privacy, he chose the room next to the most distant exit. He dumped his things, apparently at random, on the futon, then left to take a long exploratory walk.

*   *   *

Floris Brown waited in the transport until someone came along to help her. The excitement of the trip had begun to catch up with her, and she felt tired. She dreaded the return to gravity. Weightlessness was a blessing, easing the aches of lift-off as well as the aches of age that she had suffered for twenty years.

As she waited, she looked out the dorsal port.

The bow of the transport obscured her view of the inhabited cylinder, but the wild cylinder spun slowly in the distance. Even farther away, the furled sail lay waiting for its test deployment. It looked like a huge, tautly twisted silver cable.

A young man dove into the transport, sailed through the aisle, and stopped himself just above her. She smiled at him. Everyone on the transport had been so clean-cut. This was the first person she had seen who dressed in a manner she found familiar and comfortable. He was a big man, with dark skin and hair so black it had blue highlights. He wore ragged blue jeans and a black leather vest; he was clean-shaven but his hair was long, tied back in a ponytail, fanning out behind his head. Despite his youth, sun-squint lines radiated from the corners of his eyes.

"I'm your liaison. Infinity Mendez."

"Hello." She extended her hand. "My name is Floris Brown."

He took her hand and held it rather than shaking it. His hand completely surrounded her skinny, wrinkled fingers. She felt embarrassed by the gnarled blue veins.

"We don't shake hands much in zero-g, Ms. Brown," he said. "One more force to counteract."

"Please call me Floris."

He unfastened her seat belts with deft and impatient movements, then turned his back to her. The fringe on his leather vest dangled raggedly.

"Grab your stuff and grab hold," he said.

The fastenings stuck. She fumbled at the net.

He made a peculiar motion of his hands and shoulders that caused him to rotate toward her. Without comment, he unfastened the net, stuck it under his arm, and presented her with his fringe again. She wound her hands in the cut leather. It felt warm and slippery. He gathered his strength, like an animal about to leap.

She was afraid he would wrench out her arms, but he pushed off carefully and glided with surprising smoothness between the seats of the transport, drawing her after him. They were the last people to leave the passenger compartment. Even the waiting room had cleared out.

"How are you on hills?" Infinity asked.

"Slow," she said.

"Okay." He took her to an elevator. "Hold on, and keep your feet near the floor."

He pointed to one surface, which Floris would not necessarily have chosen as the floor except for the orientation of the grasps and the painted outlines of footprints.

"This'll feel weird. Something to do with the spin. You need a physicist to explain it, but you get used to it. Down," he said to the elevator. It complied.

At first she thought he must have told her the wrong surface to keep her feet near, for she felt a force drawing her toward the surface of the elevator at her back. Gradually, as the elevator slid toward the floor of the cylinder, the force slid, too, pulling from a more and more horizontal orientation till it felt and acted like gravity, staying steady and "down." The elevator stopped.

"Most folks don't come this way," Infinity said. He set off toward the bright end of the tunnel.

Floris stepped out of the elevator. She stumbled. Strange how she could have gotten so used to weightlessness in two days. She steadied herself and followed Infinity Mendez, trying to keep up.

Returning to gravity was not as hard as she had feared. *Starfarer*'s seven-tenths g made walking easier than back on earth.

She stepped cautiously out into the cylinder, into fresh cool air. She looked around, then up. For a moment she shrank back, as if the whole incredible construction might collapse upon her. Pictures failed to reproduce the feeling of observing one's world from the inside, from above. Floris felt as she imagined a fifteenth-century explorer might have, had he crossed the equator and discovered the people on the other side really did walk upside down on the far side of the world. She stepped gingerly out of the tunnel, crossed the semicircle of rock foam at its base, and stood on the new grass.

She glanced at her liaison.

"Why are you looking at me like that?"

"Not many old people on board *Starfarer*," he said. "Not as old as you, anyway. I hardly know anybody who's old."

She tried not to be offended. She wondered how many other people on board *Starfarer* had grown up in space, in a society that was missing the entire eldest generation.

"Don't you have grandparents back on earth?"

"Somewhere. I don't know. Come on." Carrying her things, he strode off across a bright green lawn that lay between rougher fields. His unshod feet barely marked the grass. She followed, wondering if she, too, should take off her shoes. When she glanced back, the tender new blades had sprung back from his tread, but she had left marks on the grass and on the ground.

He had already crossed half the field. She gave up trying to match his speed; it was impossible. Instead, she walked at her own pace. She wondered if the people on board *Starfarer* would be able to accept her limitations.

Her limitations were one of the reasons for her being here: to help people remember the variety of human beings.

Infinity turned and watched her from a distance.

"What's the matter?"

"Nothing," she said.

"Then why are you going so slow?"

"This is as fast as I can go."

"Oh."

She hoped he would come back and help her, but he simply waited, watching with puzzlement rather than impatience. When she reached him, she wrapped her thin fingers around his elbow before he could stride off and outdistance her. Though his forehead furrowed when she took his arm, he tolerated the touch.

Floris found it astonishing to walk inside a starship in the same way she would walk through a meadow. She tried to remember the last time she had walked through a meadow. She had been living in the city for many years.

The starship seemed empty. Occasionally she would see someone at a distance, but Infinity took her to the next meadow, a rougher, wilder one, and after that she saw no other people.

Floris kept up as long as she could. When she was young she loved to take long walks. She hated to admit that even in low gravity she no longer could do it. Finally she let go of Infinity's arm and sank down on a boulder with a sound of distress and exhaustion.

"I'm going to get you a cart."

Floris remained silent until her heartbeat steadied. "You said it wasn't very far. But we're in wilderness! Where are the people?" Above, on the other side of the starship, there were tracks and paths, streams and buildings, and the movement of small spots that she took to be human beings.

"There's lots of open space, but plenty of people live

around here. Some of them have, you know, left, but they'll be back. We're almost there."

She pushed herself to her feet.

They walked through a wide, shallow valley that cut diagonally across the cylinder floor. A creek ran through its center, bubbling over jagged cracked stones to a confluence with a larger stream. Bushes grew in ragged scatters. Straight bare vertical branches crowded together along the creek bank.

"Pretty, huh?" Infinity said.

"It's half-finished. Like everything else I've seen."

He nodded. "Yeah. That's true. You should've seen it before the ground cover sprouted. Mud. What a mess. When the lilacs grow some more, it'll be solid green over there. They've already got buds. And look at the willows. See the pink and red and yellow at the tips? That's where they're growing."

Floris tried to find comfort in the faint haze of color that tipped the bare willow twigs, but the ragged landscape depressed her.

"How do you know so much?" She did not mean her tone to be so sharp.

"I planted most of it," Infinity said mildly. "There's not much call for station builders anymore, but I didn't want to go back to the O'Neills. I like working outdoors. So I transferred to gardening."

She barely heard him. The far curve of the cylinder loomed overhead, and the bright reflected sunlight dazzled her. She wanted to get inside, beneath a roof. She wanted to rest.

"Do you even *have* roofs here?" she said. Her voice was faint.

"Sure," Infinity said. "How else would we keep the rain off?" He stopped. "And here's your roof itself."

Floris stared, appalled. "They promised me a house," she said. She felt near tears.

It looked like pictures she had seen of ancient pueblos, abandoned for centuries. This one had been abandoned so long that even the climate had changed, and the clean dry rock was covered over with dirt and moss and growing things. It was full of windows and doors and pathways and stairs. She knew she would have trouble getting around in it.

"Here you are," he said. He opened a sliding window and led her inside.

"I don't want to live in a cave," she said. "They promised me a house."

"This *is* a house. What's wrong with it? It's as good as anybody's got, and better than most. The chancellor lives down the path a way."

He led her across a treacherous carpeting of slippery woven grass mats to a stone window seat. She sat, gratefully.

"All these mats are gifts," Infinity said. "People on campus made them for you. There's a welcome party for you tomorrow night."

The underground apartment felt dank and cold. Floris shivered.

Hearing footsteps, she glanced up. A tall figure strode past her outer doorway and vanished.

Infinity stared out the window.

"You know who that was?" Awe took his low voice down another half octave.

"I have no idea," Floris said.

"It was Nikolai Petrovich Cherenkov. He lives here, but I've only seen him a couple of times. You know, the Russian—"

"I remember."

Nikolai Petrovich Cherenkov had defected when the

Mideast Sweep recalled the Russian cosmonauts. Now he lived permanently in space. He was nearly Floris's age, and very famous. He could not return to earth because the Sweep had convicted him of treason, in absentia, and sentenced him to death.

"He lives here? In my house?"

"No, sure not. The way it works, it's easier to put together a bunch of houses at a time, then put a hill over top of them. You're in kind of a triplex arrangement, and Cherenkov has the one highest up."

"Who lives in the third part of the triplex?"

"Thanthavong. The geneticist."

Floris frowned. The strange name sounded familiar, but she could not place it.

"They say she came up here because she couldn't get any work done back on earth. She was too famous, and the publicity just kept going on year after year."

"Publicity about what?"

"The anti-virus. She invented it. Before I was even born, but don't you remember?"

"Oh. Yes."

"Ms. Brown—"

"Floris. Florrie."

"—I'm sure they won't bother you. I've been planting here for weeks and this is the first time I've seen Cherenkov. Thanthavong leaves for her lab at dawn and hardly ever comes back before dark. I bet you won't see Thanthavong any more than you see Cherenkov."

"But I want to see people! That's why I came up here! Do you think I want to be all alone?"

She might as well have stayed on earth. Only two things prevented her from demanding that Infinity Mendez take her back to the transport. The first was that she felt so tired. The second was that though the starship would fly into the darkness and disappear, it had a good chance of returning.

Back home, entering the darkness forever was a possibility she had to face every time she worked up the nerve to leave her apartment.

"I didn't mean nobody would talk to you. Sure they will. I meant nobody would bother you if you didn't want to be bothered."

Floris turned away from the window and huddled on the seat. When she applied to the program, it had all sounded wonderful. A house of her own, and people to talk to anytime she wished, and no worry about being sent away. Instead, here she was in an unfurnished concrete apartment, with only two neighbors, both foreigners, both so famous they would probably not even deign to speak to her, and one of them a hermit.

And both of them, she suddenly realized, elderly.

She tried to remain calm.

"You've brought me here and put me in an old people's home," she said.

"What? No, I didn't, I mean, there isn't any such thing on *Starfarer*."

"I don't believe you. My children wanted me to go to an old people's home. I can't. I'll die."

Floris pushed herself to her feet and crossed the slippery mats.

"I don't want to live here anymore," she said, and walked out into the valley.

The net bag full of presents bounced gently against Victoria's side, and the muscles of Satoshi's back moved smoothly beneath her hand. As she walked beside him toward their house, she slid her fingers under the black tank top that showed his shoulders to such good advantage. The heat of his skin made her shiver. He tightened his arm around her waist. Victoria covered his hand with her free hand, and laced her fingers between his.

Everything around her felt and looked and smelled and sounded sharp and clear and vivid, as if happiness had intensified all her perceptions, as if she possessed more than the normal number of senses. For tonight, she would put aside both her desire for some uninterrupted work time, and her worries about the expedition.

The low round hills had gone gray in the shadowless twilight. The sun tubes dimmed nearly to darkness as Victoria and Satoshi turned off the main path and strolled up the gentle slope toward the house. Hills formed the interior topography of both the campus cylinder and the wild cylinder. Hills increased the sense of privacy as well as the usable surface area, but they made Victoria feel closed in. Despite her years in Vancouver, she had spent much of her childhood in and around Winnipeg. She always expected to be able to see long distances to the horizon. *Starfarer* had no horizon.

Dwarf fruit trees lined the approach to the house. Because of her trip, Victoria had missed the peak of *Starfarer*'s first real spring. The cherry blossoms had already fallen. The petals lay in pink and white drifts across the path.

The hillside that covered Victoria's house stretched one long low ridge in a semicircle to form a courtyard in front of the main windows. Victoria and Satoshi rounded the tip of the ridge. They were home.

Victoria stopped. Scattered patches of flowers covered the inner slope of the ridge. In the fading light, the blue-gray foliage lost most of its color, but the petals glowed a brilliant, luminous white.

"They bloomed!"

Satoshi smiled. "I thought you'd be pleased."

When Victoria left for earth, the pinks she had planted had been nothing but hard gray buds. Now they spotted the slope with color and spiced the air with their scent.

Victoria bent down, cupped one of the pinks between her hands, and breathed its carnation fragrance. She left it unplucked, though there must be a thousand flowers on the hillside, white ones, pink ones, white with bright red veining. When they spread and grew together, they would cover the bank with dusty-blue ensiform leaves.

The house was still dark—Stephen Thomas must not be home yet. As Victoria and Satoshi approached, the inside lights came on, casting bright patches across the courtyard. French windows formed the entire exterior wall of the house. They were, as usual, wide open. Only Stephen Thomas insisted on using the front door, which he had chosen. It was solid and opaque, a tall rock-foam slab with a rounded top. Stephen Thomas was an unregenerate fan of J. R. R. Tolkien. Victoria liked to tease him that he was far too tall to live in a hobbit-house. He must be of elfin stock. Sometimes she wondered.

The British countryside had influenced Victoria, too. The grass on the roof grew so long that it drooped, and occasionally Victoria trimmed the edges to resemble the thatched roof of an ancient Devon cottage. The thick shaggy grass made the house look as if it had eyebrows.

Victoria and Satoshi stepped through the open French windows. As Victoria kicked off her shoes, she noticed the contraption of glass and metal tubes that hunkered on the floor.

"I give up," Victoria said. "What is it?"

"It's a still. Stephen Thomas was going to find some-place else to put it. I guess he didn't get around to it."

"What's it *for*?"

"He says that when his vines are established, and after he learns to make wine, he'll be able to distill brandy."

"What happened to the champagne he was going to make?"

Satoshi chuckled.

They circumnavigated the still.

The main room was plainly furnished. Woven mats

covered the solar-fired tiles on the floor; the furniture was of rattan and bamboo. Alzena promised that soon a few trees could be harvested, but for now everyone who wanted furniture made of organic materials had to make do with members of the grass family, fast-growing annuals.

Victoria wanted a rug, but in order to get one she might have to persuade Alzena to approve growing a couple of sheep—it was probably too late to import any from the O'Neills—then raise them and learn to shear and spin and weave the wool herself. Victoria barely had time for her garden, not to mention the problem of persuading Alzena that sheep would not denude the hillsides. As indeed they might: one more factor Victoria would have to research if she proposed the project.

Victoria signaled the interior illumination to dim. As the last sunlight faded and the sun tubes began reflecting starlight, the wall of windows and the skylights filled the room with a soft silver illumination.

"Stephen Thomas?"

No one answered.

"He better come home soon," Victoria said. She let the carrying net slip from her shoulder to the floor, and flung herself onto the folded futon they used for a couch.

Satoshi joined her. Their shoulders touched, and their thighs. Satoshi's kiss left his taste on Victoria's lips.

Victoria heard Stephen Thomas's voice, low and light and cheerful, unmistakable even at a distance. A second voice replied.

Stephen Thomas strode up the path and opened the front door. Kicking off his thongs, he took two long strides and flung himself onto the couch beside his partners.

"Let's go to bed and screw like weasels," he said.

Feral Korzybski, carrying a net bag, followed him into the house.

Completely unembarrassed, Stephen Thomas kissed Victoria and Satoshi and sprawled on the lounge beside them, one arm around Satoshi's shoulders, fingertips brushing the back of Victoria's neck. Of the members of the partnership, he was—at least in public—the most physically demonstrative.

"Uh, hello, Feral," Victoria said. "Was the guesthouse full?"

Victoria felt glad that her dark complexion hid the blush that crept up her face. Stephen Thomas was only voicing the thought all three partners had. One of the things that first attracted Victoria to him was his ability to say exactly what he thought under most circumstances; and his ability to get himself out of the trouble that sometimes caused him. She reached up and touched his cool slender fingers where they rested against the back of her neck.

"There's hardly anybody at the guesthouse," Stephen Thomas said. "Feral checked in, but it's kind of creepy over there. So I invited him to stay with us."

Victoria looked at Stephen Thomas, surprised and unbelieving.

"I really appreciate the hospitality," Feral said. "I don't think I'd get a good feel for what it's like to live here if I had to stay in the hotel."

"But—" Victoria stopped, not wanting to hurt Feral's feelings.

"Let me show you to the spare room," Satoshi said quickly. He got up.

Sometimes his good manners were too good to be believed. This was one of those times.

He took Feral into the back hallway. Stephen Thomas followed.

Disgruntled, Victoria sat with her elbows on her knees and her chin on her fists. After a moment she got up and went unwillingly down the hall.

The corridor was almost dark. Lit only by daylight or starlight shining through roof windows, it ran behind the main room and the bedrooms. The rough rock foam remained unfinished. No one had taken the time to pretty it up. She passed Satoshi's room and Stephen Thomas's room and her own room.

She hesitated outside the fourth bedroom, the room that should have been Merit's. Then she berated herself silently. She would have an excuse for her feelings if anyone had ever used this room, if it had real memories in it. But the accident occurred before they ever even moved here. Overcoming her reluctance to go in, she followed her partners. Overcoming her reluctance to let a stranger use it would be more difficult.

The partnership used the room for nothing, not even storage. Victoria had seldom gone into it. The AS kept it spotless. It remained as impersonal as a hotel, with a futon folded in one corner and no other freestanding furniture, only the built-ins. Stephen Thomas stood just inside the door, suddenly uneasy, and Satoshi stood by the closed window, looking out into the front yard.

"We weren't expecting company," Victoria said.

Feral tossed his duffel bag on the floor.

"No, this is great. I don't need much, and I promise not to get in the way. This will really help. Isolation is no good for getting decent stories."

J.D.'s house was very quiet. The thick rock-foam walls cushioned sound. Woven mats, gifts from co-workers as yet unmet, softened the floor. A futon lay in her bedroom. Victoria had apologized for the sparseness of the furnishings, but after the beach cabin this house of three rooms felt perfectly luxurious.

Still, a lot of work remained before her new place would feel like home.

She ought to try to sleep, but she was still wide awake. The season on *Starfarer* was spring, and the days were lengthening. It lacked at least an hour till darkness.

Her equipment—her books—had not yet arrived from the transport. She could ask Arachne for something to read. Instead, she curled up on her futon and dug her notebook out of the net bag.

She worked for a while on her new novel. She tried to write a little every day, even when she was busy with other projects. Writing helped her to imagine what it could be like if . . . *when*, she told herself . . . the expedition met other intelligent beings.

Her first novel had enjoyed less than magnificent success. Critics complained that it made them feel off balance and confused. Only a few had realized that it was *supposed* to make them feel off balance and confused; of those, all but one had objected to the experience. That one reviewer had done her the courtesy of assuming she had achieved exactly what she intended, and she valued the comments.

She knew that nothing she could imagine could approach the strangeness of the expedition's first contact with non-Terrestrial beings. She could not predict what would happen. It was the sense of immersing herself in strangeness that she sought, knowing she would have to meet the reality with equanimity, and wing it from there.

Her library contained a number of novels and stories about first meetings of humanity and alien beings. Those she reread most, her favorites, embodied that sense of strangeness. But it troubled her considerably to find so many fictions ending in misjudgment, incomprehension, intolerance; in violence and disaster.

J.D.'s stories never ended like that.

She put the novel away, got up, and opened the floor-to-ceiling windows. Outside lay a long, narrow terrace, bright green with a mixture of new grass and wildflowers.

Victoria had said she could do whatever she liked with the terrace—whatever she could find the time to do. J.D. recognized some of the meadow flowers from the wilderness, but she had never done any gardening. She had no idea where to start. She liked the big rock over at one edge. Barefoot, she walked across the delicate new grass and sat on the heat-polished stone. It had been blasted to slag sometime during the creation of *Starfarer*. The melted curves sank gently into the earth. The rock was warm from the heat of the day, but J.D. imagined it remained hot from the blast that had shattered it from its lunar matrix. She imagined heat continuing to radiate from it for eons.

The starship had no sunsets, only a long twilight. Darkness fell, softened by starlight shining on the overhead mirrors. Rectangles of light, other people's uncurtained windows and open doorways, lay scattered across the hillsides. The air quickly cooled, but J.D. remained in her garden, thinking about so suddenly finding herself a member of the alien contact department.

J.D. liked Victoria. She felt grateful that the expedition's original rejection of her application, and her brief rejection of their subsequent invitation, had not destroyed the possibility of friendship. Satoshi and Stephen Thomas she did not know well enough to assess.

J.D. shivered. She thought about kicking in the metabolic enhancer, but decided against it. The rush would remind her of the sea and the whales, and the divers, and Zev.

She might as well let the artificial gland atrophy. She would probably never need it again.

She rose and went inside.

The interior of her house was as cool as the terrace. She had not yet told Arachne her preferences for temperature and humidity and light level and background sounds. If she took off the outer doors and the curtains, as Victoria suggested, to open her house to the artificial outdoors, most of that programming would be superfluous. J.D. thought she would leave the doors and the curtains as they were. After the damp, cold mornings of the cabin, the idea of stepping out of bed onto a warm floor appealed to her.

Flicking her eyelids closed, she scanned the web for mail. Nothing important, nothing personal.

Nothing from Zev.

She could send him a message. But it would be easier for both of them if she left him alone. Best for all concerned if she and Zev never talked again. Her eyes burned. She blinked hard.

She took off her clothes, crawled into bed, ordered the lights off, ordered the curtains open, and lay on her futon gazing into the darkness.

A quick blink of light startled her. She thought it was a flaw in her vision until it happened again, and again. Short, cool, yellow flashes the size of a match head decorated her terrace.

They were fireflies. She had not seen one for a long time. They did not exist on the West Coast. They were even becoming rare in the East, in their home territories, because of the size and effects of the enormous coastal cities. Here they must be part of the ecosystem.

The ecosystem fascinated her. If it contained fireflies, lightning bugs, did it contain other insects? She would like bees—bees must be essential. But what about ladybugs? Surely one could not import ladybugs without importing aphids as well. No one in their right mind would introduce aphids into a closed environment intended to be agriculturally self-sufficient. If no noxious insects existed, but the ecologists were trying to establish songbirds, what did the songbirds eat? Did anything eat the songbirds?

J.D. drifted off into complexity, and sleep.

Victoria tapped lightly on Stephen Thomas's door.

"Come in."

The scent of sandalwood surrounded her. Stephen Thomas often brought incense to campus in his allowance. The incense stick glowed, a speck of pink light moving downward through the darkness. The sliding doors stood open to the courtyard, letting in the breeze and mixing the sandalwood with the spice of carnation. The pale white wash of reflected starlight silvered Stephen Thomas's gold hair and his face in quarter profile. He turned toward her.

"Your hair sparkles," he said.

"And yours glows." She let her kimono fall from her shoulders and slid into bed beside him. He wore nothing but the crystal at his throat, as black as obsidian. He rolled onto his side. The crystal slipped along the line of his collarbone, glinting in scarlet and azure.

"Where's Satoshi?" Stephen Thomas asked. "You guys aren't mad at me, are you? Feral looked so downcast when he saw he'd be practically alone in the guesthouse . . ."

Victoria felt Stephen Thomas shrug in the darkness, beneath her hands.

"Satoshi's in the shower," she said. "He'll be here in a minute. I'm not mad at you, exactly, but, god, Stephen Thomas, your timing is lousy."

She brushed her fingertips down his side and stroked the hard muscles of his thigh and wished Satoshi would hurry up.

Stephen Thomas drew her closer. His soft breath tickled her shoulder.

"I think it's damned nice of us," Victoria said, "to use your room tonight so we don't keep Feral Korzybski awake till morning!"

"What's the matter with my room?" Stephen Thomas said plaintively. His room was a joke among the partnership. He collected *stuff* the way a magnet collects steel shavings. Victoria's room was almost as Spartan as the fourth bedroom, and Satoshi's works in progress were always organized. Stephen Thomas kept a desk full of bits of equipment and printouts, a corner full of potted plants, and he never picked up his clothes until just before he did his laundry.

"Nothing," Victoria said. "I enjoy sleeping in a midden heap. But my room is right next to our guest, and we've never tested the soundproofing."

Satoshi came in, toweling his hair. He launched himself across the room and came down flat on the bed beside Victoria. He smelled of fresh water and mint soap. A few droplets flicked off the ends of his hair and fell across Victoria's face. His skin was cool and just barely damp from the shower.

He leaned over her and kissed her. The cool droplets of water disappeared in the warmth of his lips and his tongue. Satoshi reached past her and took Stephen Thomas's hand. Their fingers intertwined, gold and silver in the dim light. Victoria reached up and joined her hand to theirs, adding ebony to the pattern. She hooked her leg over Satoshi's thighs, and as she turned toward him drew Stephen Thomas with her, closer against her back and side. His breath quickened and his long silky hair slipped across her shoulder. Mint and carnation and sandalwood and arousal surrounded them with a dizzying mix. Victoria and Satoshi and Stephen Thomas surrendered themselves to it, and to each other.

6

Victoria woke when the sun tube spilled light through the open wall of Stephen Thomas's bedroom. Stephen Thomas lay on the far side of the bed, stretched on his side, his hair curling down across his neck and shoulder, one hand draped across Satoshi's back. Satoshi sprawled in the middle of the bed, facedown, arms and legs flung every which way, his hair kinked in a wing from being slept on wet. Victoria watched her partners sleeping, wishing they could stay in bed all morning, in the midst of the comfortable clutter. The scent of sandalwood lingered.

Stephen Thomas yawned and turned over, stretching. He rubbed his eyes and blinked and yawned again, propped himself on his elbow, and looked at her across Satoshi. Satoshi snored softly.

"Good morning," Stephen Thomas whispered.

"Good morning." Victoria, too, kept her voice soft. "Is that how weasels screw?"

He laughed.

"Shh, you'll wake Satoshi."

They got up, creeping quietly away so Satoshi could wake up at his own pace. Stephen Thomas grabbed some clean clothes from the pile in the corner. Victoria had no idea how he always managed to look so good. When she referred to his room as a midden heap, she was only half joking.

* * *

After a shower, Victoria smoothed the new clothes in her closet but resisted the urge to wear them. They were party clothes, inappropriate for work. She put on her usual jeans and shirt and sandals, reflecting that back on earth, on almost any other campus, what she had on would be considered inappropriate for a professor.

Victoria smelled something burning. Something burning? Stephen Thomas's incense—? She hurried into the hallway. She stopped short. The smell of food, cooking, filled the apartment.

None of the three surviving members of the partnership was much of a cook. Merit had known how to cook. These days Victoria and Satoshi and Stephen Thomas ordered meals from the central kitchen when they had time to eat together.

Victoria drew a deep breath. Getting upset because someone had decided to make breakfast was silly. It was just that the homey smell brought back memories.

Satoshi was the best cook among them, but Victoria knew from long acquaintance that Satoshi was not cooking breakfast. If he was even out of bed she would be surprised. That left Stephen Thomas.

"He can burn water" had always been a metaphorical phrase to Victoria, until Stephen Thomas once put water on for coffee, forgot about it, and melted a kettle all over the heating element.

The breakfast smelled much better than burning water or melting kettles. Stephen Thomas was always trying new things; maybe cooking lessons were his newest enthusiasm.

Victoria headed to the main room. At the stove, Feral Korzybski glanced over his shoulder.

"Morning," he said. "I wanted to make myself useful." He gestured to the set table, the skillet. "You folks sure don't have much equipment."

"We don't cook here very much," she said. "No time."

"It's a hobby of mine," he said. "I think this will be edible." He poked the edges of the big omelet, letting the uncooked egg run underneath to sizzle against the hot pan. "Are you ready for tea?"

"Sure."

He poured boiling water into her teapot.

"I talked to the database—"

"Arachne," Victoria said.

"Right, thanks. I talked to Arachne about what was available for people to cook. Strange selection."

"Not if you consider how and where it's produced. We're beginning to grow things ourselves. But a lot of fresh stuff, and most everything that's processed, is from one of the colonies."

Stephen Thomas sauntered barefoot into the main room. He wore orange satin running shorts and a yellow silk tank top. Victoria tried to imagine the combination on anyone else, and failed.

"What's for breakfast?" he said.

Feral dumped the filling into the omelet and folded it expertly. "Let me see if I can remember everything I put in it. The eggs were fresh—that surprised me."

"We grow those here."

"With or without chickens?"

"With." Victoria laughed. "We aren't that high-tech."

"The mushrooms are reconstituted but the green onions and the tomatoes were fresh. I was hoping I could get micrograv vegetables, but Arachne didn't offer them. I've seen them in magazines—perfectly round tomatoes, and spherical carrots, and beans in corkscrews—but I don't know anyone who can afford to cook with them."

"We don't get any of those out here. The colonies export them all to earth. There are problems with growing plants in quantity in micrograv, so whatever you get is labor-intensive. Especially those corkscrew beans."

"I can see where they would be. That's it—except for the cheese. The package said, 'Tillamook Heights.' "

"That's from a colony. The people who run one of the dairies there emigrated from someplace called Tillamook—"

"It's on the West Coast of the United States," Stephen Thomas said to Victoria. "A few hundred kilometers south of Vancouver." He liked to tease her about her Canadian chauvinism, about the way she sometimes pretended to know less about the United States than she really did. He could get away with it.

"—and they wanted to name the dairy after their original place. But 'Tillamook East' or 'Tillamook South' didn't sound right, so: Tillamook Heights."

"I like it." Feral rubbed his upper lip and gazed blankly at the omelet, filing the information away, thinking of how to use it in a story.

"Your omelet's about to burn," Victoria said.

He snatched the pan off the single-burner stove.

"Damn!" He lifted the edge of the omelet. "Just in time. Where's Satoshi?"

"Still asleep, probably."

"Damn," he said again. "I thought you were all up. This is no good cold. I'll go get him."

"Don't, if you value your life," Stephen Thomas said.

"Trust me, he'd much rather eat your omelet cold than have you wake him up. You would, too."

"All right," Feral said, doubtful and disappointed.

The omelet tasted wonderful.

"The coffee's great," Stephen Thomas said. "What did you do to it?"

Victoria took his cup and tried a sip. It was much stronger than she was used to, but tasted less bitter, almost the way coffee smelled.

"I'll show you. It's not hard, but if you boil it you might

as well throw it out and start over. That's what I did with what you had in the pot."

Feral ate part of his omelet, occasionally glancing with some irritation at the warmer where he had left Satoshi's share.

"It isn't the same warmed over," he said. He got up, poured coffee from the thermos into a mug, and disappeared down the corridor.

Victoria and Stephen Thomas looked at each other. Stephen Thomas shrugged.

"It's his hide," he said.

Feral returned unscathed. He got the last quarter of the omelet out of the warmer and put it at Satoshi's place. A minute later Satoshi himself appeared, wearing Victoria's hapi coat, carrying the coffee cup, and apparently wide awake. He joined them at the table.

"Nice morning, isn't it?" He sipped his coffee. "That's very good," he said. He put it down and started eating his omelet.

Victoria watched him, amazed.

"Do you want a job?" Stephen Thomas said to Feral.

"No, thanks. I'm self-employed."

J.D. woke very early in the morning, too early, she thought, to call the other members of the alien contact team. Feeling restless, she went for a walk. She suspected that on board *Starfarer* she would have trouble getting enough exercise, here where she would have neither opportunity nor time to swim several hours each day.

A stream trickled past her house. She followed it. Soon a second stream joined it, and the combined watercourse cut down through the hill. J.D. found herself walking between sheer cliffs.

The cliff must be designed, J.D. thought. There had

been no time for the stream to cut it. *Starfarer*'s interior topography was carefully sculpted. Striped with stone colors, this sculpture looked like a water-eroded cliffside of sedimentary rock.

J.D. rounded a bend and stopped in surprise.

Beside the stream, someone scraped at the bank, probing with a slender trowel. A blanket lay on the ground, covered with bones.

"Hi, good morning," J.D. said. "What are you doing?"

The young digger glanced at her and stood up, stretching her back and her arms. She was small and slight, with a sweatband tied around her forehead. It rumpled her short straight black hair.

"Digging for fossils," she said.

J.D. looked at her askance. "It seems to me," she said, "that if you'd found fossils in lunar rock, the news would be all over the web by now."

"Not digging to take them out," she said. "Digging to put them in."

"You're *making* a fossil bed?"

"That's right."

"Why?"

"Don't you think we deserve some prehistory, too?"

J.D. leaned over the blanket. The relics resembled the exoskeletons of huge insects more than any mammalian bones.

"Whose prehistory· *is* this?" she asked.

"Whoever came before."

"Whoever came before didn't look much like us."

"Of course not."

"What department are you in?"

"Archaeology."

"But—" J.D. stopped. "I think I'm being had."

"I'm Crimson Ng. Art department."

"J.D. Sauvage. Alien contact—"

"You're the new AC specialist! Welcome on board." She stuck out her grubby hand. J.D. shook it.

"But why are you burying fossils of a different species?"

"I'm just one of those crazy artists," Crimson said.

"Come on," J.D. said.

Crimson opened up to J.D.'s interest.

"Every time the argument about evolution comes along again, I start wondering what would happen if it were true that god invented fossils to fool us with. What if god's got a sense of humor? If I were god, I'd plant a few fossils that wouldn't fit into the scheme, just for fun."

"And that's what these are? Does that mean you're playing god?"

"Artists always play god," Crimson said.

"Don't you believe in evolution?"

"That's a tough word, 'believe.' Believing, and knowing what the truth is—you're talking about two different things. Human beings are perfectly capable of believing one thing metaphorically, and accepting evidence for a completely different hypothesis. That's the simplest definition of faith that I know. It's the people who don't have any faith, who can't tell the difference between metaphor and reality, who want to force you to believe one thing only."

"I can't figure out who you're making fun of," J.D. said.

"That's the point," the artist said with perfect seriousness. "Everybody needs to be made fun of once in a while."

"Oh, I don't know," J.D. said. "I can get along without being made fun of for two or three days at a time without permanent damage."

Crimson glanced at her quizzically, then picked up one of the artifacts. The long and delicate claw nestled in her hand. J.D. could imagine an intelligent being with those claws instead of hands, a being as dexterous and precise as any human.

"What happens if everybody forgets you've put these things here," J.D. said, "and then somebody comes along and digs them up?"

"My god, that would be wonderful."

"What will people think?"

"Depends on who they are. And how smart they are. I'm trying to create a consistent prehistory, one that doesn't lead to us. Maybe future archaeologists will figure it out. Maybe they'll realize it's fiction. Maybe they won't. And maybe they'll think it was god playing a joke, and they'll laugh."

"And then they'll figure out that you made the bones."

"Oh, I don't think so," Crimson said. "I grew them very carefully. You shouldn't be able to tell them from real. And I cooked the isotopes, so the dating will be consistent." She grinned. "Got to get back to work."

She returned to her fossil bed.

J.D. watched her for a few minutes, then continued on beside the stream. She smiled to herself. She wished she could tell Zev and the whales about this. They would, she thought, find it very funny.

Though she was curious how J.D. had liked her first night on the starship, though she was eager to get out to the sailhouse for the first full test of *Starfarer*'s solar sail, and though she was anxious to get over to the physics department and get back to work, Victoria also wanted to give Satoshi and Stephen Thomas the presents she had brought from earth. But she wanted to do it when they were alone. As she was thinking up a polite way to ask Feral to leave for a while, Stephen Thomas put one hand on the reporter's shoulder.

"Feral," he said, smiling, "thank you for breakfast. Why don't you go look around, and we'll see you in the sailhouse later."

"Huh? Oh. Okay." He drained his coffee cup. "I'd like to visit the alien contact department," he said to Victoria. "Would that be all right?"

"Sure. This afternoon."

"Thanks." He sauntered cheerfully out of the house.

"How do you get away with that?" Victoria asked.

Stephen Thomas looked at her quizzically. "Get away with what?"

"Never mind." She picked up the carrying net and opened it flat on the table.

"This is for the household," she said. She pulled out a package of smoked salmon.

"We should save this for sometime special," Satoshi said. "Maybe even after we leave."

One thing habitat designers had not figured out was a way to grow anadromous fish in a space colony. The salt marshes and the ocean ring, so important to the ecosystem, could not support deep-water fish.

Victoria handed Stephen Thomas a rectangular gold box. He took it carefully and hefted it gently.

"I know what this is," he said.

"I had my fingers crossed at lift-off," Victoria said. "It survived."

Stephen Thomas grinned, opened the box, and drew out a bottle of French champagne.

"Victoria, this is great, thank you."

She had known he would like it. And she knew why he liked it. Before Stephen Thomas joined the partnership, she had never drunk good champagne. By now she had tasted it several times. Saying that she had drunk it hardly seemed accurate, for each sip flowed over the tongue and vanished in a tickly barrage of minuscule bubbles.

"Something else for a special occasion," Stephen Thomas said. He was never stingy with his things. Whenever he managed to get good champagne to *Starfarer*, he shared it with his partners.

"I bought it in a fit of enlightened self-interest," Victoria said.

She handed Satoshi one of his presents. "Not quite on the same scale, but . . ."

He smiled, carefully unfolding the tissue paper from the package of chili paste. Victoria and Stephen Thomas always brought back chili paste for him. Victoria could not stand the stuff herself. Sometimes she wondered if, in fifty years, Satoshi would confess that forty years before, he had developed a loathing for chili paste, but wanted to spare the feelings of his partners.

"We'll have to get something good to drink with it," he said.

"Oh, no, not my champagne," their younger partner said. "If you're going to blast your taste buds, you can do it with local beer."

Victoria gave Stephen Thomas his second package. This one was as light as the first had been heavy. He untied the scarf that wrapped it. Victoria never wrapped his presents in paper, because wrapping paper was hard to come by in the starship and he always tore it.

She had brought him two of the loose silk shirts he liked. The ones he had now he had worn almost to rags. He still wore them. He lifted the new turquoise one, and saw the bright red one beneath it.

"Victoria, these are incredible!" He put on the turquoise shirt. It intensified the clear blue of his eyes. He stroked the smooth fabric. "How does it look?"

"How do you think?" She put one hand on his shoulder and let her fingers slide down his back. The silk felt soft; his muscles, hard. He met her gaze and reached out, letting his arm match the curve of hers.

"It looks terrific, kid," Satoshi said. "Don't wear it into any dark bars—we'll have to wade in and rescue you."

They all laughed. Victoria wished it were evening; she

wished they were sitting around the dinner table getting silly on champagne. She handed Satoshi his second present.

He unfolded the wrapping, smoothed it, set it aside, and opened the plain white box.

He pushed aside the cushioning and lifted out the white bowl. The sunlight touched it and turned the graceful round shape translucent. Satoshi caught his breath.

"It's absolutely beautiful."

"It rings," she said.

He tapped it with his fingernail. The porcelain gave off a soft, clear tone. Satoshi looked at her. The smile-lines at the corners of his eyes crinkled.

"Thank you."

"When I saw it . . ." Victoria said, "you know, if anyone had told me I'd be moved nearly to tears by a porcelain dish, I'd've told them they were nuts."

Last she gave him the stones she had picked up on the beach after her first meeting with J.D.

"These . . . they aren't really anything, just something I found. I thought you might like them."

They were gnarled and smooth, like wind-blasted trees; some had holes bored straight through them. A few carried holes bored partway through, with the shell of the creature that had made the hole left behind, stuck inside after it bored its way in, and grew. One stone was a mass of holes, till nothing was left but a lacework of edges.

"I kept hoping nobody would pick up my allowance and say, 'What have you got in here, rocks?' If I admitted I was carrying plain rocks out of the gravity well, no telling what Distler would do with that."

Satoshi chuckled. "These aren't just plain rocks." He held one in his hand, rubbing it with his thumb. Victoria recognized it as the one she had kept in her pocket all the way back home; rubbing it had given it a slightly darker color.

Victoria found herself in a mood more suitable for the

end of Christmas morning: glad her partners liked what she had brought for them, but sorry that the occasion had ended.

They spent a few minutes tidying up, giving the dirty dishes to the house AS, then left to meet J.D. and go out to the sailhouse to watch the solar sail's first full deployment.

As Victoria left the house, she saw Satoshi's porcelain bowl in the center of the table. The gnarled sea-worn stones lay artlessly, precisely placed within its smooth white concavity. Victoria gazed at the stones, at the bowl. The arrangement's effect was calming, yet it was also arousing, and in a definitely sexual way. Victoria wondered how Satoshi had managed that.

Griffith woke at the silent arrival of an AS with his breakfast from the communal kitchen. He had slept as he always slept, soundly but responsive to his surroundings, waking once just before dawn when a bird startled him by singing outside his window.

Only one of the other guests had slept in the guesthouse. The other had yet to make an appearance; Griffith would have heard if anyone had come in during the night. No one had taken any notice of Griffith, and his things remained undisturbed.

He wolfed his breakfast, hungry after two days in zero-gravity. Leaving by way of the emergency exit rather than the front door, he set off to continue his exploration.

Griffith had read all the plans, all the speculations, all the reports. He knew why *Starfarer* resembled a habitat instead of a vehicle. He understood the reasons for its size. He even understood the benefits of designing it to be aesthetically pleasing. Nevertheless, both his irritation and his envy increased as he strode along paths that led through what for him was, even in its raw and unfinished form, a paradise. He had no chance at all of living in a similar environment back on earth. He did occasionally work with—more accurately, for—people who were extremely wealthy or extremely wealthy *and* extremely powerful. They owned places like this. But regular scientists, regular administrators, regular government employees, lived in the city and liked it. They figured out ways to like it, because they had no choice.

People who had lived here would never consider going back to the crowds and noise and pollution of earth. Not willingly. Back on earth, Griffith had been skeptical of the suggestion that the personnel of the starship intended to take it away and never bring it back, either turning it into a generation ship and living on it permanently, or seeking a new, unspoiled planet to take over. That suggestion smacked too baldly of conspiracy theories for Griffith. Now, though, he found the idea more reasonable to contemplate.

The contemplation made his analysis easier.

He looked up.

The sun tubes dazzled him. He blinked and held out his hand to block off the most intense part of the light. To either side of the tubes, the cylinder arched overhead, curving all the way around him to meet itself at his feet.

He had seen such views looking *down* from a mountain, during brief training exercises outside the city. Looking up for a view was disorienting. A multiple helix of streams flowed from one end of the campus to the other. Here and there the streams flowed beneath the green-tipped branches of a newly planted strip of trees, or widened and vanished into a bog of lilies and other water-cleansing plants; or widened into silver-blue lakes or marshlands. A wind-surfer skimmed across one of the lakes. The brightly colored sail caught the morning breeze. Small gardens formed square or irregular patches of more intense green in the midst of intermittent blobs of ground cover.

It would all be very pretty when the plants finished growing together over the naked soil. But it was unnecessary.

Machines could clean the water and the air nearly as well as the plants could. Well enough for human use. A ship a fraction this size could store years and years' worth of supplies. Griffith found the claim of the necessity of agriculture to be questionable at best. Wind-surfing was a quaint way of getting exercise, but treadmills and exercise bikes were far more efficient in terms of the space required, not to mention the time. If the scientists had intended to set out on a proper expedition they would have designed a proper ship.

Griffith tried to imagine what the cylinder would look like when all the plants reached their full growth. As yet the intensely green new grass remained thin and tender, brown earth showing between the blades. Other ground cover lay in patches, not yet grown together, and most of the trees were saplings, branchy and brown. Some of the vegetation in the wild cylinder, according to the reports, had been transported from the O'Neills, but most came from single-cell clones engendered on board *Starfarer*. It was far too expensive to import bedding plants or trees all the way from earth. The cell banks of *Starfarer* boasted something like a million different kinds of plants and animals. Griffith thought it extravagance and waste.

He kept walking, following a faint, muddy path worn through new grass. They should at least pave their paths. He saw practically no one. Half the people working on *Starfarer* had been called back by their governments in protest over the changes the United States was proposing in *Starfarer*'s mission.

Griffith had drafted most of the changes.

Now that he was here, he could see even more possibilities. If he had to, he would accede gracefully to the objection that the cylinder was too large to use as a military base. He would turn the objection to his advantage. The body of the cylinder was a treasury of raw materials, minerals, metal ore, even ice from deposits of water that had never thawed since the moon's formation. *Starfarer* could be mined and re-created.

He would rather see it used as an observation platform and staging area. That way its size would be useful. It could be as radical a training ground as Santa Fe, the radiation-ruined city. Griffith had spent a lot of time there, wearing radiation protection, inventing and testing strategies against urban terrorism and tactical weaponry. He imagined working up here under similar conditions. It would be easy to evacuate the air from the cylinders. A spacesuit could hardly be more cumbersome than radiation garb.

He did not see any problem in taking over the starship. Now that Distler had won the election, Griffith's political backing was secure. MacKenzie's ill-considered comments could only speed things along.

When he first started studying the starship, he could not believe it was unarmed, that its naive philosophy allowed it—required it!—to vanish into the unknown without weapons.

Getting weapons on board was Griffith's next priority.

Victoria and Satoshi and Stephen Thomas walked over to J.D.'s house. Victoria wished she had invited her to break-fast. She would have, if she had known that Feral would be around.

None of the paths on board *Starfarer*, even the paved ones, had been designed for three people walking abreast. In this the starship was much like Terrestrial towns. Satoshi was in the middle, so Victoria and Stephen Thomas alternated walking on the verge. Knee-high bushes sprinkled dew against Victoria's legs.

"Hello!"

They paused at the edge of J.D.'s yard. She appeared in the open doorway and beckoned them inside.

"Good morning."

"How did you sleep?"

"Just fine. Sometimes it takes me a few days to get used to a new place, but this feels like home."

They followed her into the main room. Her boxes of books stood in stacks; books from opened boxes stood in stacks. J.D. had set several of the packing boxes together to form makeshift shelves. *Starfarer*'s houses contained few bookshelves, since everyone used the web or temporary hard copy.

"This will have to do till I can get something more substantial. What do I do to requisition some boards?"

"Plant a tree," Stephen Thomas said.

J.D. looked at him curiously.

"Wood is scarce," Victoria explained. "The trees are still growing. What you want is some slabs of rock foam."

Stephen Thomas picked up one of the old books, handling it gingerly, as if it would disintegrate in his hands. As it probably would.

"Why do you have all these?"

"For research. They give me ideas that I try to build on."

"Nothing a human being is going to think of is going to match a real first contact," Stephen Thomas said.

"No," J.D. said. "It's not. But the ideas are for mind-stretching, not script-writing."

She picked a book out of an open box. The cover painting looked like a peeled eyeball.

"Here's one," she said. "It's got a story in it called 'The Big Pat Boom,' by Damon Knight. Aliens visit earth and decide that cowpats are great art. They want to buy them and take them back home—to alien planets. So everybody on earth tries to corner the market in cowpats. What would you do?"

Victoria laughed. "What would I do with a cowpat? Yuck."

"What," Stephen Thomas asked plaintively, "is a cowpat?"

Satoshi explained. Stephen Thomas snorted in disbelief.

"I can't even think how I'd *move* a cowpat," Victoria said.

"I haven't read the story in a long time," J.D. admitted. "I forget the exact details. I think they let the cowpats dry before they try to move them."

"What did they do about the dung beetles and the maggots?" Satoshi asked.

"I don't know," J.D. said. "I didn't know about the dung beetles and the maggots."

"Your science fiction writer must have used some poetic license," Satoshi said.

"How did you get to be such an expert on cowpats?" Victoria asked.

"I'm a font of wisdom," Satoshi said, doing a subtle imitation of Stephen Thomas in his occasional pompous mode. He grinned. "And I used to spend summers on Kauai herding cattle. I saw a lot of cowpats. Or steerpats, as it happens."

"Come on," J.D. said, "what would you do?"

"I'd go looking for some different aliens," Stephen Thomas said.

"I guess I'd let them buy the cowpats," Satoshi said.

"I think we should try to get the cow farmers—"

"Ranchers," Satoshi said.

"Okay, ranchers—to give the aliens the cowpats as a gesture of friendship." Victoria chuckled. "Though I don't know how that would go over with the proponents of free trade."

"That's a good idea," J.D. said. "I hadn't thought of that alternative."

"The government would buy them and form a whole new bureaucracy to decide which aliens to give the shit to," Stephen Thomas said.

Everybody laughed.

"I'd nominate our new chancellor to be the minister of that department," Satoshi said.

J.D. glanced at him quickly, startled. Victoria found it interesting that the chancellor had earned Satoshi's dislike so quickly. Satoshi was notoriously slow to take offense.

"Here's one," J.D. said. "About some kids who smuggle a cat onto a space station."

"Don't show that one to Alzena," Victoria said. "She swore she'd draw and quarter anyone who smuggled a predator on board."

One of the makeshift shelves collapsed. J.D. tried to catch the books as they spilled out in a heap on the floor.

"Oh, this is hopeless," J.D. said. "But it's been so long since I had my books out. I was afraid they'd mildew at the cabin."

Satoshi picked up some of the fallen books and put them back in the box, setting it on its base rather than trying to use it as a shelf.

"I'll walk you through requisition," Victoria said. "The supply department can't be busy these days. . . . You can probably get some real shelves in a day or two."

"All right. Thanks."

"No problem," Victoria said. "Come on, let's go watch the sail test!"

Infinity led Nikolai Petrovich Cherenkov toward the guesthouse, trying to explain the problem about Floris Brown. The trouble was, he felt so intimidated about talking to the cosmonaut that he kept getting tangled in his words.

"I took her to the guesthouse last night. I didn't know what else to do. I couldn't just leave her in the garden. I sleep there sometimes, but you can't let an old person sit out all night in the dew. Do you know what I mean?"

"I do have some experience speaking English."

"I know that, I mean, I didn't mean—"

"I suppose you could not leave her to sit in the garden, but she might have come to her senses and moved back into her house if you had."

"She's pretty stubborn."

Infinity glanced sidelong at Nikolai Petrovich. This was the first time he had talked to the cosmonaut. Physically, Cherenkov was still vigorous. He had been tall for a cosmonaut, nearly two meters. The bone loss of years in space, in zero-g, had given him a pronounced stoop. His posture caused him to peer out at the world from beneath his brows. Exposure to sun and radiation had weathered his skin as severely as if he had spent his life in the desert. His dark brown hair was turning gray in discrete streaks. Gray striped his bushy eyebrows.

He turned his head and caught Infinity looking at him. His gaze locked with Infinity's.

His age was in his eyes. Infinity felt a chill, a prickle of awe.

Nikolai Petrovich smiled.

"Why do you think an old stranger like me would change her mind, when you could not?"

"You can tell her it isn't a nursing home."

"That is what she fears?"

"That's what she said."

"She thinks Thanthavong and I are geriatric cases."

Embarrassed, Infinity tried to think of something to say. "She doesn't understand . . ."

Cherenkov chuckled.

"Where does she wish to live?" the cosmonaut asked.

"She wasn't quite clear on that. It sounded like she wanted to live in her own house by herself, but she also wanted her family around. I guess she couldn't have either one back on earth."

"So she came here. Alone."

"Right. She said they'd put her in a nursing home, and she'd die."

"I see. I remain here . . . for similar reasons."

"I know," Infinity said.

It was not a nursing home that would kill Nikolai Petrovich if he went back to earth. The executioners of the Mideast Sweep did not wait for their victims to turn themselves in.

"Why did you come to me, instead of going to the housing committee?"

That was a good question. Infinity realized that the answer was, he wanted an excuse to meet the cosmonaut face-to-face. He was embarrassed to say so.

"There are lots of empty houses, but they either belong to people or they're just shells. Nothing's been finished in a couple months. There's hardly anybody left on the housing committee to do the finishing. Just a few Americans and a Canadian and a Cuban."

"You are still here. You are Cuban, perhaps?"

"No. I use the U.S. passport mostly, but my father was Japanese and Brazilian and my mother was United Tribes, so depending on what rules I pay attention to, I can claim four citizenships."

"And four political entities can claim your allegiance. Complicated."

"It could be, but political entities don't spend much time claiming allegiance from metalworkers turned gardener."

"More fools they," Nikolai Petrovich said.

"Anyway," Infinity said, "I can't ask the committee to put her in somebody's house, because we're all pretending everything is going to be all right and they're coming back and the expedition will go on the way it's planned."

"Pretending?"

"Yeah," Infinity said. "What else? If the Defense Department decides they want us, they'll have us, just like they get everything else they want."

"You are cynical."

"I know how it works!" Infinity said. He fell silent, wishing he had not spoken with such bluntness.

Nikolai Petrovich walked along beside him in silence for a while. "Your mother . . . she was from the United States? The Southwest?"

Infinity shrugged. It did not mean much to be from one of the Southwest tribes anymore. He wished he had not given Cherenkov the key to his background by bringing up the Department of Defense. They had ripped the Southwest land away from the people who inhabited it, and in doing so they had ripped the heart and soul out of most of the people Infinity had been closest to.

"We will not speak of it further," Nikolai Petrovich said, "and we will continue to pretend. So Ms. Brown has the choice of the guesthouse, or the first level of our hill. You wish me to help you persuade her to live in the hill."

"I thought she'd like it. Especially the garden . . . I think the best I could get for her, for a while, would be a place with no windows yet, and mud puddles outside."

"The garden you made for her is beautiful," Nikolai Petrovich said. "I notice the changes."

"I saw your footprints sometimes, where you stood to look at things. I wondered what you thought about it," Infinity said, feeling unreasonably pleased. "It'll look better when it's finished. When it has time to settle in and grow for a while. The other thing is, there's a welcome party tonight and if it isn't going to be at her hill I need to tell people where to go. Or whether to go at all. Um, are you coming?" The invitation was general, but he had done a special one for Cosmonaut Cherenkov, and left it not only in electronic form on the web but in written form on his doorstep.

"I seldom accept invitations these days," Nikolai Petrovich said in a neutral tone. Infinity did not know if that meant he was going to make an exception, or if he was put out to have been invited. "A party, you say. Is this sort of thing to become a common occurrence?"

"I don't know. Depends on her, I guess."

"Perhaps I should encourage her to stay in the guest-house," the cosmonaut said drily. "I value my privacy."

"Oh," Infinity said. "I didn't . . . I mean—I'm sure it won't get too noisy. I'll tell people to keep it down." He stopped. "I'm sorry."

"*Nichivo,*" Nikolai Petrovich said. "The truth is I am seldom at home and I probably would not notice. I had planned to go away later."

"Then you will talk to her?"

"I am here with you, after all," the cosmonaut said.

Griffith returned to the guesthouse. He had ten kilobytes of notes filed away in the web, scrambled and guarded, and plans for a tour of the infrastructure tomorrow. An inspector for the General Accounting Office had complete freedom, and no one on board to answer to.

In the hall, he hesitated. Beyond the central stairway, one of the occupied rooms stood open. Several people laughed, and someone spoke. Griffith frowned, trying to place the familiar voice.

He strode quietly down the hall.

"You see that I would not be such a disaster as a neighbor."

"No one will come to visit," a second voice said, a voice that was quivery, feathery.

"Give it a chance, ma'am." The third voice belonged to someone who had grown up speaking Spanish and English both, and at least one other language that Griffith, to his annoyance, could not pin down. He walked past the open doorway and glanced inside.

"They will visit if you wish. Believe me. I had to train

them very hard before they gave up and accepted me as a hermit."

Griffith stopped, staring at the man who sat hunched on the window seat. Griffith was more familiar with him as he had looked when he was younger, but age could not distort the wide, high cheekbones, the square line of the jaw. It only intensified the unusual gray streaks in the man's dark hair.

"My god!" Griffith said. "You *are* Cherenkov!"

The younger man jumped to his feet, startled; the elderly woman flinched. The old man turned toward Griffith.

"Yes." His voice was as calm as before. "But I prefer my acquaintances to address me as Kolya. Who are you?"

"Griffith, GAO. I heard your voice, I recognized it. Sir, I just want to express my admiration for your exploits, your bravery—"

"I was very young," Cherenkov said. Suddenly he sounded tired. "Only young people are foolish enough for that kind of bravery. Will you join us? This is Mr. Mendez, who is an artist of the earth. This is Ms. Brown, who has just moved here."

"You frightened me," the old lady said with frail dignity.

"I didn't mean to," Griffith said. He looked her up and down. Grandparents in Space was a program he intended to use against the expedition. With Ms. Brown as the program's first member, he thought his attack would be even more effective.

"Will you have some tea?" Ms. Brown said.

The chance to talk to Cherenkov lured him in.

"Sure."

As Griffith entered the room, Mendez sank down on the edge of the bed. Griffith could feel his attention, his suspicion, his fear. He was a strange-looking character, with long thick black hair tied up on the top of his head. He wore a couple of earrings and a grubby, fringed leather vest. Dirt was ground permanently into the knees of his pants. Pretending to be oblivious to the younger man's discomfort, Griffith sat next to him. Cherenkov had the window seat, and Ms. Brown the only chair. The old woman leaned forward and tremulously poured another cup of tea.

"What is GAO?" Cherenkov asked. "I'm not familiar with that branch of the military."

"GAO's the General Accounting Office, sir," he said. "It isn't military at all. I'm just here to do a few surveys. Check the outlays and so forth."

"Ah. By your carriage, I took you for a military man."

Griffith made himself chuckle. "Well, sir, the drill sergeant would accept that as a compliment. She said I was hopeless. I did my time, General, like everybody else."

"Your sergeant drilled into you too much military courtesy. You must not call me 'general' or 'sir.' If you must use a title, 'tovarishch' will do. I still prefer 'Kolya.' "

"I'll try to remember, sir, er . . . Kolya. It wasn't the sergeant who drilled that into me so much as ten years in government." Cherenkov put him off balance. He sipped his tea to cover his discomfort, to conceal the intensity of his interest. He wondered if he could get Cherenkov to talk about the past without putting his own cover at risk. Griffith glanced at Mendez, sitting beside him and holding a teacup with surprising delicacy. "So you're part of one percent for art," he said.

"I'm a gardener," Mendez said.

"But the general said—"

"It was a joke," Mendez said, looking down, embarrassed.

"A joke!" Cherenkov said. "Hardly. You are an artist, and my admiration is sincere. Floris, did you admire Infinity's work when you walked through the garden?"

"I used to have roses," she said. "But when I moved, there wasn't any room for roses."

"We don't have too many roses up here yet," Infinity said. "We needed ground cover first. Annuals are fastest. Roses take a while to get established, and they need a lot of hand labor."

"Oh." Ms. Brown's voice was small and sad and disappointed.

"I could try to get some, though," Infinity said.

Griffith decided the old woman was self-centered at best and getting on toward senile at worst, and he did not understand what she was doing here. The one percent program was bad enough; who ever heard of an art department on a scientific expedition? But *grandparents*? Next thing, they would be shipping kids up, or having their own. He supposed that if he were planning to create a generation ship he might want to begin with a complete age-mix. He filed the information away for further use.

"Floris," Cherenkov said, "will you consent to be my neighbor for a week? If at the end of that time you prefer to move, Infinity and I will speak to the housing committee on your behalf. We both have some credibility here."

She hesitated, watching him and blinking, like some elderly cold-blooded reptile waiting for the sun to warm her enough that she could move and think.

"They said I had to stay even if I didn't like it," she said. "I had to sign a paper." She waited expectantly.

"Transportation is expensive," Cherenkov said. "But papers can sometimes be changed. This I cannot promise, but if in a week you ask for my help in the respect of returning to earth, I will do what I can."

Though it would be better for Griffith's purposes if Ms. Brown stayed, he thought Cherenkov would be doing the expedition a favor to have the old woman sent home whether she wanted to go or not. He could not imagine anyone refusing a request that Cherenkov made.

"I'd like to go to my house now."

Ms. Brown made Griffith feel creepy, the way she responded to comments without really acknowledging them.

"Excellent," Cherenkov said. "Infinity, I will entrust Floris's comfort to you. I must hurry—I have another obligation."

He left the room. Griffith put his cup down with a clatter and hurried after him.

"Sir! I mean, Kolya—"

He caught up to Cherenkov, who continued without pause. The cosmonaut had a strange, careful way of walking, as if he feared that gravity would trap him forever on the ground.

"You said your name was Griffith," Cherenkov said. "Is that your surname or your given name?"

"Surname."

"And your given name?"

Griffith felt a blush rising. He had not blushed for years. He hoped his tan concealed it; he hoped Cherenkov did not notice. Then Cherenkov glanced at him, and Griffith knew that even if his tan did conceal the blush, Cherenkov noticed it.

"It's Marion, sir."

"It's Kolya, sir," Cherenkov said, mocking him a little.

"I don't use my given name." Griffith tried to keep his reaction cool, his tone cold.

"Everyone uses given names here. The informality is refreshing."

Griffith kept his silence.

"You do not agree."

"I think informality leads to sloppiness. There's no clear chain of command here. I think that's dangerous, especially in an environment as severe as space."

"Spoken like a military man," Cherenkov said, "or a government worker," he added before Griffith could object.

"But you are wrong. In such a self-contained environment, a certain democratic sloppiness can be turned to advantage. Why did you follow me?"

"You said you were going outside. Would you let me tag along?"

"Outside? I think not. That *is* dangerous without training."

"Just to the staging area, I mean."

"You may do that without my permission. The ship is open to inhabitants and visitors alike. You may be required to pass training to engage in certain activities, but no one is denied the opportunity to attempt the training."

Griffith frowned. "That seems awfully loose to me."

"Spoken like a true—government man."

Griffith wondered again if Cherenkov were laughing at him, deep down under the intensity of his gaze. And yet even if the cosmonaut had pegged him as a military observer, what could he do? Exposed, Griffith might expect some uncomfortable moments. The more recalcitrant expedition members might denounce him. It would be verbal, not physical, abuse; of that he was certain. If Cherenkov blew his cover, Griffith would have to return to earth. Having to send another observer could delay Griffith in implementing his plans. On the other hand, he already had most of the information he needed. A few more days . . .

He found it difficult to understand the core of resistance against the changes that had to occur. The deep space expedition was all very well when it was planned, two decades ago in a time of prosperity, civil international relations, and silence from the Mideast Sweep. All of that had changed. *Starfarer* had to change, too.

Griffith's job would have been much easier if he had not had to deal with the researchers, the stubborn, self-centered idealists. As the starship had to change, the people had to change, too.

If Griffith could arrange to antagonize a few more countries into withdrawing from the expedition, the remaining personnel would not be able to continue alone.

He was doing a good job. No one would fault him for giving himself a few minutes. He wanted to get Cherenkov to talk about his experiences, and he knew it would not be easy. The general obviously felt no nostalgia for the past. Griffith held no power over this man; he could not demand a reply. He would have to be patient.

Kolya wished the young officer would follow someone else. It mattered little to him if Griffith were here under false pretenses. Kolya ignored politics with the strength of visceral aversion. He hated politics almost as much as he hated violence.

He also did not like to be followed. Nikolai Petrovich Cherenkov had been followed by people who wanted to kill him and by people who wanted to worship him. The two experiences were not all that different.

He had become more and more private over the past two decades. One morning in the company of Infinity Mendez and Floris Brown tired him to a startling degree. The effort of remaining civil, pleasant, even cheerful, had drained him of the anticipatory energy he experienced before his spacewalks. Human contact affected him with a kind of sensory overload that only the emptiness and completeness of space could overcome.

Kolya entered the elevator to the outside, hoping Griffith would remain at the inner surface.

"It is boring and dark down there," Kolya said. "Unpleasant. Stay in the sunshine."

"It's all right," Marion Griffith said. "I want to see." The officer stayed with him.

Griffith made Kolya uncomfortable. He showed too much interest in Cherenkov's past. But Cherenkov did not exist anymore. Only Kolya existed. Kolya was not a pioneering cosmonaut or a heroic antiterrorist or a terrorist traitor. Kolya was an old man who loved space.

The elevator fell through the inner skin of fertile dirt, through the underground water level, through the massive radiation-stopping shell of lunar rock.

Paying Griffith no more attention, Kolya analyzed his reasons for letting Infinity persuade him to talk to Floris Brown. What did it matter to Kolya if she lived on the bottom level of his hill, or in the guesthouse, or back on earth, or out in the garden in the dew? Thanthavong never bothered him—she was no recluse, but she did spend all her time in the genetics lab. That was what she had come up here for, after all, to escape the demands of achievement and publicity and public adoration, to get on with her work. Like Kolya, but with more meaning to her life.

A lonely old woman living downstairs would demand attention, whether from Kolya or from others who would visit. Kolya could see nothing coming from the change but an invasion of his privacy.

He felt no obligation to offer anything to Floris, but Infinity was different. Kolya thought Infinity was far more admirable than any of the scientists, who worked in their minds, or he himself, who did not work at all anymore, except at tasks he chose, tasks that took him into space. It would have been possible to program an AS to do most of what Kolya chose to do, and an AI to do the rest. But no one had ever succeeded in programming an expert system to replicate a master gardener. To approximate, yes. Not to replicate. There was something about technological complexity, mechanical complexity, that machines could handle, and something about organic and aesthetic complexity that befuddled them. Kolya thought the gardeners, like Infinity, to be the most important people on board the starship.

The elevator stopped. Assuming a strong young military officer would be embarrassed to have his discomfort noticed, Kolya said nothing to explain the strange sensation produced by riding an elevator through a rotating environment. If Griffith had neglected to read his introduction manual on the way to *Starfarer*, that was his problem.

The artificial gravity was perceptibly stronger here, nearly one g. The radius of the cylinder's outer skin was significantly longer than the distance from the axis to the inner surface. The increased radial acceleration increased the sensation of weight.

At the outer surface of the cylinder, the corridors were solid, rough, and ugly. Few people came this far down. If they wanted to spacewalk, they went out at the axis and avoided the rotation. Kolya liked the rotation. He climbed into his pressure suit as Griffith watched.

"That doesn't look too hard," Griffith said, breaking the silence for the first time since they left the inner surface. "How long does the training take?"

Kolya had already drifted into the strange and vulnerable state to which he surrendered in space. Without a word, he stepped into the airlock and sealed it, leaving Griffith behind as abruptly as he had left Floris and Infinity.

The pump drew the air from the lock and back into the ship. Surrounded by vacuum, Kolya opened the outer hatch. He let the radial acceleration press him past the skin of the cylinder and into the harder vacuum of space. With the ease of long practice, he lowered himself onto the narrow framework that crept over the cylinder's surface. He stood in the same orientation as he had inside the cylinder, with his head toward the axis of rotation. The outer skin of the cylinder lay a couple of meters above him. Nothing separated him from space except the cables of the inspection net.

Beneath him, the wild cylinder and the furled sail slipped past. Kolya sank to his knees, then inched flat. He let his arms dangle toward the stars. Someday, he thought, he would let himself slip from the framework and be flung away into space. But not quite yet. He was not quite ready yet.

Rotation took him out from between the cylinders. Before him, the stars made a fine, spangled sheet.

He lay there, still and silent, staring at the galaxy.

7

The transparent skin of the sailhouse placed no barrier between the room, and space and stars and the sail outside. People floated in zero-gravity along one side of the curved glass wall: fewer people than should have gathered to watch the first full test of *Starfarer*'s solar sail.

Satoshi floated farther into the transparent chamber. The sensors surrounded him with melodic chords. Iphigenie DuPre, the sailmaster, drifted with eyes closed, listening to the musical reports, invisibly connected to the computers and control strands of the sail. Her long, lithe, dark limbs reacted with reflexive, minuscule motions as she ordered a strand tightened here, balanced there.

The sail, untwisting from its cable configuration, now appeared as a great sheet of silver, closely pleated.

Victoria and J.D. and Feral joined Satoshi. Still inside the access tunnel, Stephen Thomas hesitated. He pushed off gingerly, awkwardly, with one hand. In the other he carried a sack, which he had avoided explaining.

Satoshi looked around. Almost everyone in the sailhouse was faculty or staff. There were a few sponsored reporters, and Feral, and a number of remotes transmitting the event back to earth, but none of the VIP visitors the expedition had prepared for. Chancellor Blades had chosen not to attend the test, and he had not even sent his usual deputy, Gerald Hemminge, the assistant chancellor.

Feral pushed off and started interviewing people, setting the background for his story. *Starfarer* navigated from one star system to the next via cosmic string. But once it reached a destination, it required other methods of propulsion: primarily the sail. Cosmic string provided macronavigation, the sail, micronavigation, though it sounded strange to apply the term "micro" to distances measured in millions of kilometers.

The sail was slow, but near a star it was steady. It had the great benefit of operating without reaction mass or onboard fuel. It would propel the starship from its entrypoint into the star system to a point from which it could reenter the twisted space-time of a cosmic string. The alien contact team had a small, fast explorer to use in traveling between *Starfarer* and a new system's worlds.

Feral drifted over to the sailmaster.

Iphigenie DuPre's astonishing mathematical ability reached so deep that it appeared instinctual to anyone who overlooked her years of experience and practice. She was one of the first people to build a sail-ship and to sail it in space. She had designed most of the sail systems that racers used down around the O'Neill colonies. Once her sails started winning races, she retired from amateur competition and put her time into developing and marketing. She was probably the wealthiest person on board *Starfarer*, thanks to the popularity of sail-ship racing.

The challenge of a starship's esoteric combination of propulsions had brought her to EarthSpace, and to *Starfarer*.

"Ms. DuPre—" Feral said.

"Hush, now," she said quietly. The tempo of the sensor melodies quickened.

Everyone fell silent, and the change began.

Tension eased at the ends of the pleated surface. The folds turned to close-set ripples.

The sail opened.

Liquid silver spread over blackness, widened, flowed

like a flooding lake across the path of the Milky Way, and cut off the stars. One edge quivered. A vibration shimmered through the satin film. The shivering threatened to twist the surface out of shape, but control strands shifted and tightened and eased away the oscillation.

The sail grew.

Its complex harmonies filled the sailhouse. No one spoke.

The sail shivered with one final ripple, then lay quiet, stretched out across space. Satoshi imagined that he could see a slight curve in the surface, as the sail filled with the invisible solar wind. He imagined he could already feel the acceleration, already detect the most infinitesimal widening of the starship's orbit.

The sensor melody decreased to a whisper.

"Full deployment."

Iphigenie's quiet statement filled the sailhouse like a shout. Her voice held suppressed laughter and excitement. She opened her unusual cinnamon-brown eyes. For a few seconds, no one else made a sound. Satoshi released the breath he had been holding.

"Watch it!"

The shout and an explosive "pop!" broke the silence. It sounded like damage, like decompression, like a breach of the sailhouse wall into the vacuum of space. Satoshi tensed, forcing himself not to jerk toward the noise. Any quick movement in freefall would send him tumbling.

A projectile shot past.

The champagne cork slammed into the transparent wall beyond him. It rebounded nearly as fast, hit the glass on the other side, and bounced again. It narrowly missed Satoshi and several other faculty members.

Somersaulting slowly backward, Stephen Thomas laughed as the cork flung itself around the glass cylinder until it used up its momentum. Champagne pressed itself out of the bottle he held. Without gravity, the bubbles formed on the sides and bottom of the bottle instead of exploding upward; their pressure pushed the champagne out. As Stephen Thomas tumbled he left a liquid rope twisting in his wake. It fizzed softly.

Stephen Thomas looked like the star of some weird zero-gravity sport, celebrating a championship by trying to spray his teammates with champagne, but being defeated by weightlessness.

He'd have to be the star of something yet to be invented, Satoshi thought. He's wrong for the most popular earth sports: too slender for football, not ta¹l enough for basketball, and far too beautiful for hockey.

Stephen Thomas spoiled the effect by bumping into the wall and snatching awkwardly at a glass handhold to stop his tumble. He came to a halt, still laughing, still holding the bottle. The twisting stream of champagne broke itself into spherical globules that drifted among the spectators.

"I was wondering how to split it up," Stephen Thomas said. The pressure of the bubbles slowly pushed the last of the champagne into the air.

The cork tumbled lazily, having lost most of its momentum without hitting anyone in the eye. Everyone was looking at Stephen Thomas rather than at the sail.

He tossed his head. His long blond hair flipped back for a second, then fell forward again to drift in front of his eyes. He tucked it behind one ear.

"Congratulations, Iphigenie," he said.

"Yes," Victoria said. "Iphigenie, the sail's beautiful."

"Thank you." She reached out and waved a rippling sphere of champagne toward her, placed her lips against it, and drank it with a kiss. Unlike most zero-g workers, she kept her hair long, but she wore it in a smooth mass of thin, heavy braids caught up at the back of her neck.

Iphigenie's action broke the tension of waiting for

deployment, and the fright of Stephen Thomas's exploding champagne cork. Everyone clustered around Iphigenie, sphering her with their congratulations, surrounding her like the bubbles surrounding the wine; people caught and drank the fizzing globules of champagne that drifted and trembled in the air currents. Satoshi kissed one and let it flow between his lips. It dissolved against his tongue, dry and gentle and ephemeral.

Nearby, J.D. floated alone, watching the sail, occasionally glancing at the celebration with a slight smile on her lips. Satoshi waved a bubble of champagne in her direction.

"J.D., catch!"

Instead of reaching for the rippling bubble, she pushed her hand toward it to create a counterdraft in Satoshi's direction.

"Thank you," she said. "It's very kind of you, but I don't drink. I quit when I started diving."

Stephen Thomas paddled awkwardly toward them.

"Are you guys playing tennis with my good champagne?" He tried to capture it with the air pressure of a gesture, and succeeded only in breaking it into several smaller drops. Satoshi caught one in his mouth and pushed one toward Stephen Thomas.

"Victoria! Feral!"

They joined him. Together, they drank the last bubbles.

"I knew I'd think of something good to drink this with," Stephen Thomas said.

Satoshi chuckled. Victoria smiled and drifted close enough to brush her lips against his cheek.

In one direction, the sail lay taut. In the other, the twin cylinders of the campus rotated, one clockwise, one counterclockwise, toward each other, and away. Beyond campus, at a great distance, the earth hung in space, one limb bright and the rest of its face dark, a new earth.

* * *

Most of the spectators had left the sailhouse. Stephen Thomas floated near the transparent wall. For once he felt almost comfortable in freefall.

Maybe, he thought, I ought to combine it with champagne more often.

"Are you coming?" Victoria asked.

"I'll be along in a little while."

Satoshi passed the sailmaster. "Thanks for the show, Iphigenie."

"My pleasure," she replied, too experienced in zero-g to disturb her equilibrium by turning.

Stephen Thomas watched his partners glide out of the sailhouse. He envied their grace. He knew he would get the hang of navigating in weightlessness soon enough—it had better be soon, because he hated feeling physically incompetent and off balance, baffled and awkward.

Stephen Thomas was the last spectator. Intent on the sail, Iphigenie paid him no attention.

The sail lay almost motionless in space, but every now and again the silver surface shimmied. When it did that it looked alive, like some huge ether-breathing animal, twitching its flank to drive off a fly.

Stephen Thomas wondered if a space-living creature would have an aura. Idly, he narrowed his eyes and focused his vision beyond the center of the sail. He had never thought of seeking the aura of an inanimate object. The idea amused him. He did not expect to find anything.

He looked.

Gradually, as if the act of searching for it caused it to appear and grow, a pale violet light glimmered along the edges of the sail. It flowed down the feedback lines and crept across the sail's face.

Stephen Thomas gazed at the lavender light until it swept all the way to the sailhouse, surrounded the transparent cylinder, and wrapped it in a transparent gauze of illumination.

Iphigenie did not react to it, though every now and again she glanced out at the sail as if her eyes and her instincts could tell her more than the feedbacks and computers and musical sensors. Stephen Thomas said nothing of the aura. She would probably shrug it off or laugh or refuse to look for it, or all three.

It always amazed him when he saw something so direct, so spectacular, and everyone else was oblivious to it. He could never persuade his partners to try to see what he could see. Victoria, in particular, was so open-minded about other things: she had to be, or she would never have won her job.

The effort of seeing began to tire him. He let his concentration wander. The perception vanished as if he had snapped off the current powering the violet light. The sail billowed silently before him, plain silver again.

Chandra tried to persuade herself that being on the run, hiding out from—who *were* those guys?—in a fishing camp would be good stuff to record, but the truth was that she hated this part of it. The cabin smelled stale and fishy. The bed was both lumpy and too soft. The window which could have looked out on the water, opened onto a grotty gravel driveway sprouting dusty weeds. And the bathroom was really nasty.

The diving sequence would be great. It would reproduce her utter terror at being pulled underwater, her certainty that she was about to drown. But this place would ruin the rest of the experience. It would do nothing for either her reputation or her bank account. It had to go. She had to end the sequence somehow, but she did not see how she would find the time to do any restaging and still make it onto the spaceplane.

"How do the folks who own this place make a living?"

she said. "We're the only ones here. I bet we're the only ones who were *ever* here."

"It is not fishing season," Zev said. "This is a place where humans fish. I mean where they sleep when they are too tired to fish."

"Oh."

"If it had not been here, " the diver said, "you would still be swimming."

"Listen," she said, "that was a great sequence. That was real terror. *Nobody* has ever gotten anything that intense before. They all think their sex scenes are so great. Hah."

The young diver wandered around the wooden cubicle, touching things at random: the rough, threadbare ticking on the mattress, the frame supporting the upper bunk, the planks of the drafty door, the doorknob.

"I don't think that's a good idea," Chandra said.

The diver looked at the handle curiously. "Why? Will it break?"

"I mean I don't think you should go outside. Those guys are probably still looking for you."

"Oh."

"What do they want?"

"All I wanted was to join the deep space expedition."

"Distler hasn't made *that* a criminal offense," Chandra said. "Not the last time I heard, anyway. There must be something else."

The diver took a deep breath and let it out slowly. "They want divers to do things for them that we do not wish to do. I think they would have taken me away and kept me until they made my family come back from Canada."

"They were going to *kidnap* you?"

The diver shrugged and changed the subject. "What is that room?"

"It's the bathroom. Only there isn't any bath. I guess you don't need to take baths out in the ocean."

"We like to rub ourselves on smooth rocks or scrub ourselves with sand."

"Close enough. Turn on the faucets in the sink if you need water. Do you have to stay wet like the guy in that old tv series?"

"No. Do you like that show? I do, too. But divers are not from Atlantis. There is no such place. Divers can live on land. I never have, though. I am not used to it."

Suddenly something protruded from the diver's crotch. Chandra watched, startled, as the male diver, whom she had assumed to be female, extruded his penis and began to pee on the floor.

"Wait! Stop! What are you doing?"

His penis slid back inside. "Peeing," he said, equally startled. He looked down. "I never did it on land before. It is not very aesthetic, is it?"

"No, especially if you do it on the floor!"

"What should I do?"

"Wipe it up, to begin with."

"But I need to pee."

Chandra sighed and showed him the toilet, then fled, embarrassed, when he started to use it in front of her. Very few things embarrassed her, but this sequence of events was getting weird.

He came out of the bathroom, carrying their single ragged towel. "Why did you run away?"

"Because—wait!" she said again. "This isn't a hotel." She snatched the towel, put it back in the bathroom, and threw him a wad of paper tissue. "I don't think we get maid service and clean towels every day with this room."

He wiped the floor, gazed at the sodden paper for a moment, then carried it into the bathroom and got rid of it.

"I didn't run away," Chandra said when he came back. "I left to give you some privacy. It isn't polite to piss in front of other people."

Fine gold hair, nearly transparent, almost invisible except when the light struck it just right, covered his whole body. His pubic hair was slightly thicker, slightly coarser. She stared at the smooth flesh between his legs. She could stare at anyone or anything, anytime she liked, because no one could tell where her eyes were focused.

"It is not considered polite to piss on land, you mean," the diver said. "Divers think nothing of it. I did wonder what that small room in the corner of J.D.'s cabin was. She always kept the door closed."

"J.D! J.D. Sauvage? Do you know her?"

"Yes."

"This is all her fault!"

"I do not believe it," the diver said. "She would not lend herself to this occurrence. Please do not talk of my friend that way."

"She was supposed to *be* there! Where does she get off, forgetting our appointment?"

"She left for the starship," the diver said. "And if she had not, she would be hiding along with us."

"Yeah. Maybe." Chandra scowled. The nerve ridges on her forehead twisted. "Serve her right."

"She would probably know what to do," he said.

Chandra glared at him, but the silver-gray nerve tissue that hid her eyes and allowed her to stare also prevented her from glowering effectively.

Zev changed the subject. "Are you allowed to eat in front of each other?"

"Of course. What a dumb question."

"Why 'dumb'? You do not pee in front of each other. I do not understand why eating is so different. I have spent time on land with only one ordinary human. J.D. is almost a diver herself. I cannot compare her customs with yours."

"Okay, I see your point. Are you a guy, or are all divers built like you?" Chandra said.

"I am male, if that is what your question means. I am physiologically mature, though I have not yet fathered anyone."

"You mean you're a virgin?" Then she had to explain "virgin." The diver laughed.

"No—how foolish. We don't even have a word for that. We play all the time—whenever we meet another family. J.D. says regular humans don't do that. And she said regular humans have to learn how not to be fertile. You have to concentrate on it. Divers have to learn how not to be sterile."

"Why?"

"Because that's how we designed ourselves. External genitals would cause hydrodynamic drag."

Chandra waited for him to continue, but he seemed to think that told her all she needed to know.

"Nobody ever put it quite like that to me before," she said. "Which is probably a good thing, since I haven't got the faintest idea what you're talking about."

"Male humans have to learn to raise their temperature in order to become sterile—you know this?"

"Sure."

"I had to learn to extend my scrotum—do you understand? And when I father someone, when a diver from another family chooses me, I will have to leave it extended long enough to overcome the sterility my body temperature causes."

"Sounds dangerous, if a hungry shark comes along . . ."

"If a hungry shark came along, I think I would not mind putting off parenthood a few more weeks in order to withdraw myself." Zev grinned.

"What about women?"

"Women who are divers learn to ovulate, and do so only when they choose someone to conceive with."

"How did we get off on this subject?"

Zev looked hurt. "You expressed interest."

"I guess so. But I'm a lot more interested in how we ended up being here."

"That does not interest me anymore. I am interested in how to get out."

"Me, too."

"Excuse me a moment," Zev said. "I must tell my mother where I am." His eyelids flickered.

"Wait!" Chandra grabbed him and shook him roughly before he could hook into the web.

He opened his eyes again. "What is wrong?"

"The web's probably being monitored!"

"Oh. I did not know that was allowed."

"Maybe not, not usually, but I bet they're doing it."

"Lykos will be worried."

"She'll be a lot more worried if they catch you!"

"That is true," Zev said.

Kolya came in from outside, drugged with dizziness and wonder. The path of stars lay before him, a web passing across his image of reality. The vision would remain for a while; then, as it faded, he would be drawn to the stars again.

He opened the fastenings of his spacesuit.

He had watched the sail unfurl. He hated it. It cut off a significant portion of the sky. But he loved it, too, because every increment of time added another increment of velocity to the ship's speed, pulling it toward the stars. Soon—

"General Cherenkov? Is everything all right?"

Kolya started violently and stumbled in the awkward half-removed suit. Marion Griffith lunged forward, caught him, and held him on his feet.

"*Bojemoi*," Kolya said, "don't you know it's dangerous to startle a—someone with a background like mine? Have you been waiting all this time?"

"Yessir. My apologies, sir, I didn't mean to scare you. I thought you saw me . . . and then I couldn't tell."

"Several hours outside will affect the vision. Why are you still here?"

"I wanted to talk to you, and since you said I couldn't go outside, I decided to wait."

"If I reward your preposterous devotion, will I encourage its continuation?"

"I don't understand what you mean, sir."

"I mean that I like my privacy. I have not made that sufficiently clear to you. What do you want?"

"Only to hear what it was like in the early days, in space. When you didn't have all this. When it was tough, and dangerous. About the years when you went back to earth. And about coming back up here, when you knew you'd never be able to leave again."

"I believe that the expedition will be both tough and dangerous. More than we can conceive. As for the rest— all that is in the archives. I sat for the cameras answering questions for . . . far too long."

"I know," Griffith said. "I saw you. I watched the tapes. But it isn't all, there's nothing about the years when you disappeared. And it isn't the same as hearing it straight, being able to ask questions . . ."

"The years when I . . . disappeared . . . are not fit stories for civilized people. Are you civilized, Marion?"

"I . . . I think so."

"I'm going to walk back to my house," Kolya said. "If you wish, you may walk with me, and I will answer what questions I choose. In return you must promise not to trouble me again."

Griffith hesitated.

"It is that, or nothing," Kolya said.

"All right," Griffith said. "Deal."

Victoria returned to campus feeling a little drunk, more from excitement than from champagne.

"That was something, wasn't it?" She giggled.

"It was," J.D. said. "It was. I guess . . . we're really on our way."

"We are." Victoria turned down the path toward Physics Hill. "Come on, I want to show you your office."

"I don't really need an office," J.D. said. "I've never had one—I won't know what to do with it."

"First rule of academic life," Victoria said. "Never turn down the perks."

They reached a long low barrow with strips of windows that squinted out along the bushy slopes. The hallway behind the offices was cool and dank, a tunnel lined with gray rock foam. On the left, doors opened into offices. Someone had made an attempt to brighten the hallway with photos of particle interactions, abstract art of lines and curves and collisions, and fractal movies.

"Nobody *needs* offices anymore," Victoria said. "But if we did all our communicating through Arachne, we'd never get out of bed. Here's my office." She opened a door. Few of the doors in the main cylinder of *Starfarer* opened automatically. The simpler things were, the less there would be to fix, light-years out in interstellar space.

"We're old-fashioned here in Physics Hill," she said. "We even have a conference room, down at the end of the hall. I know lots of people who claim they can do conferences by link, but I like being face-to-face."

J.D. followed Victoria into her office. The entire exterior wall was a window, open from waist height to ceiling. The hillside dropped away steeply, ten meters to the ground below. Victoria's desk was an extruded slab of rock foam; the chair was bamboo and rattan.

A display hovered in the corner. Victoria glanced at it. Numbers and symbols crept across it, a new one every few seconds.

"Still working," Victoria said.

"What is it?"

"Cosmic string calculations. For navigating, once we reach transition energy. It's ferociously complicated to figure out where you're going once you grab a piece of cosmic string, and even harder to figure out a reasonable way back."

"But those calculations are already done. Aren't they?"

"The set for our first trip, sure. But I've been spending a lot of time working out better methods of doing the calculations."

"How long before it's finished?"

"Don't know. No way to tell. This is a new symbolic manipulation routine. Solving cylindrical stress-energy tensors is tough. This one's been running for two weeks already, but that's nothing. The shortest solution so far took fifty-three days."

She watched the display for a few seconds, then blew out her breath and turned away. "I never let Arachne send this stuff straight into my head. It's hypnotic."

Suddenly she stared at the display again. "Except . . ." She fell silent for so long that J.D. grew concerned.

"Victoria?" she said softly.

"What? Oh, sorry." She squeezed her eyes shut and opened them again. "I have an idea. I think it might speed things up some more. Solve the problem more elegantly . . ."

"Go ahead and work on it. The office can wait."

She was tempted. "No, it's okay—your office will only take a minute."

Victoria led J.D. to her office, two doors down, and tried to open it. It remained closed.

"It's supposed to have been cleared by now," she said.

"Maybe it's fixed on me. Open my office, please, Arachne," J.D. said. She echoed the request over her link. Nothing happened. Then she remembered it was a simple mechanical door. She tried the door handle. Nothing happened.

"I'll be damned," Victoria said. She described a query path to J.D, who followed it into Arachne's web.

The bursar had not yet assigned her any office space. Nor had the chancellor accepted her appointment as alien contact specialist.

"This is outrageous," Victoria said. "It's my decision to invite you onto the team. Accepting your appointment is nothing but a formality!"

"The rules must have changed," J.D. said.

"A lot of things are changing around here."

"This is scary, Victoria."

"It's ridiculous, that's what it is. Damn! Come on, you can use Nakamura's office till we get things straightened out. I know I have access to it."

"I don't know . . . I'd hate to invade his privacy."

"He didn't leave anything behind to invade. He's not coming back. He quit."

"For good? Are you sure? *Why* did he quit?"

"I'm not sure I can tell you."

"Is it a secret?"

"No. It's just that it's hard to explain why someone quits when they're brought up to be infinitely polite and never mention when something is wrong or tell you what it is. I don't even know that anything *was* wrong. Except it must have been, or why would he have quit? He wasn't recalled. Maybe he decided we don't have a chance to get out of orbit. He might have decided to cut his losses."

"Maybe he read the article about the selection process. Maybe he felt humiliated."

"That article was all speculation," Victoria said.

"Was it?"

Victoria hesitated. The article had claimed that the selection of *Starfarer*'s personnel depended more on political considerations than academic qualifications.

"I don't like to think so," Victoria said. "I like to think my family's application blew all the other possibilities out of contention. But I'll never know if a bunch of politicians got together and looked at the candidates and said, Say, we need more Canadians to make Ottawa happy, and never mind the qualifications. I decided to stop worrying about it."

J.D. followed Victoria uncertainly to another office.

It, too, refused to open.

"This is embarrassing," Victoria said. "I am *angry*."

"Victoria, please don't go to any trouble for me. I have more than enough room in my house, and that's where all my books are. I'll see you later, okay? What should I wear to the party?"

"The party? Oh, anything you like. It's informal, and you dress better than most of us."

J.D. smiled. "It will take a while before I fit in with the *Starfarer* look," she said. "Most everything I brought with me is new." She shrugged. "Oh well. I never was in the height of fashion."

"Don't worry. I usually don't dress up, but I might tonight because I haven't had a chance to wear my new clothes. Stephen Thomas always dresses up, and Satoshi never dresses up."

"You have an interesting family."

"That's sure true," Victoria said. "What's your family like? Do you have any sisters and brothers?"

J.D. giggled.

"Wrong question?"

"No, not at all," J.D. said. "But it's complicated."

"Tell me," Victoria said, intrigued.

"Okay, you asked for it. My mom was fifty, when she and my dad got together. I have a half-brother and a half-sister from her previous biological family. Her partner in an intermediate relational family brought along his daughter. He and Mom didn't have any children with each other, but his daughter is also my half-sister."

"You lost me there," Victoria said.

J.D. grinned. "That's where I lose everybody. What happened was, my dad didn't want to father children. Chemical toxin exposure. He worried about gene defects."

"Couldn't he get them fixed?"

"That was expensive and chancy. It was another few years before the technology was perfected. Anyway, when my folks decided they did want to raise a kid together, my dad's full sister donated an ovum and my mom's previous partner donated the sperm."

"So your dad is your half-father and your mother isn't genetically related to you."

"No, it's more complicated than that. My mom is my nuclear mother—induced meiosis and nuclear body transplant into my aunt's ovum."

"And you're related to your father through mitochondrial inheritance."

"Right, even though I got the mitochondrial DNA from his sister. But those are maternally inherited, so Dad's and his sister's are identical."

Victoria whistled. "That's as complicated a personal pedigree as I ever heard. You have four biological parents?"

"Five, since they decided to use a surrogate."

"Truly impressive. Family reunions must be interesting."

"We've never had one," J.D. said. "We get along all right, but we aren't particularly close. Cool but cordial."

"What did they say when you joined the expedition?"

" 'Congratulations, dear. Have a good time.' "

"Hm." Victoria contrasted that reaction with the reactions she and her partners had received. Grangrana was quietly and fiercely proud, Stephen Thomas's father disbelieving, and Satoshi's folks ecstatic for him and for them all. Practically the whole range, Victoria thought.

After J.D. left, Victoria hurried back to her own office, sat at her desk, and composed herself outwardly. She cooled her anger, persuading herself that the mix-up about J.D.'s office must be just that, a mix-up. Reacting uncivilly would not help. It might even slow up a correction.

The research display kept catching at the corner of her vision. All she really wanted to do right now was work on her new approach. Instead, she put in a call to the chancellor's office.

J.D.'s remarkably calm about this, Victoria thought. She hasn't spent enough time in the academic world.

The office was only part of the problem. Until all J.D.'s paperwork went through processing, the bursar would not activate her salary. Victoria had been handling the partnership's accounts since Merry's death. She suspected life could quickly become difficult in the face of a financial setback.

Chancellor Blades had arrived on the transport incoming that Victoria had taken, outgoing, back to earth. She had never spoken to him or met him and she knew very little about him. She wanted to be fair to him. But he was from the U.S., so she found it hard not to suspect that he was purely a political appointment.

She supposed he would be at the welcome party tonight. The rest of the faculty and staff would use the opportunity to welcome him, since he had pled the press of work and declined to have a party of his own. Perhaps it would have been better to wait till then to talk to him . . .

"Chancellor Blades's office." Chancellor Blades's AI answered the call. It possessed a deliberate, soothing voice, a display pattern of pastel colors.

"Victoria Fraser MacKenzie. Director Blades, please."

"The director cannot speak in person at this time," the AI said. "Would you leave a message, please?"

"Yes. Chancellor, there's been an unfortunate oversight. J.D. Sauvage's appointment hasn't been formally accepted. Her office is locked. This is awkward. And I'm concerned that her salary not be delayed."

"The message has been placed on his register," the AI said. "Thank you."

The voice and the pattern faded.

Victoria swore softly.

Trying to think of some other way of solving J.D.'s problem, Victoria glanced at the research display. Its moving background figures took her in. Soon another display formed before her. Her thoughts began to manipulate its space. She forgot everything else.

Victoria hurried through the courtyard and into the house.

"I'm late," she said to Satoshi, "I know it, sorry, but I *had* to get that new manipulation up and running. I think it's a real breakthrough! I'll be dressed in a minute—damn!"

"Victoria, relax. What's wrong?"

"I want to take Ms. Brown some carnations. It won't take long to dig them—" She opened the storage cupboard and rummaged around for the rock-foam pot she knew was in there somewhere.

Satoshi came up behind her and put his arms around her.

"I'm all ready. I'll dig them for you." He was wearing his usual cargo pants and tank top.

"Would you? That would be great."

"You've got plenty of time. Stephen Thomas just got home, too."

Victoria took a quick shower and stood in front of her closet for a minute, deciding what to wear. Finally she chose her suede pants and the new lace shirt. She liked the way the lace felt, softly scratchy against her skin.

Stephen Thomas finished dressing just when she did. They returned to the main room together. J.D. had already arrived.

"You all look wonderful!" she said. She looked as if she had tried to dress up, but did not quite know how.

Stephen Thomas wore his turquoise shirt for the first time. Instead of his usual plain gold stud, he wore an earring Satoshi had given him on his last birthday. It twisted up behind his ear and drooped forward again, dangling small emerald crystals all the way to his shoulder. A second loop of crystals branched off from the back and draped across his long blond hair and over his other shoulder.

Satoshi handed Victoria the newly potted carnation, and they set out for the party.

Victoria walked with Stephen Thomas, J.D. with Satoshi. J.D. evened out the group and made walking on the narrow pathways less awkward, though of course not the same as before, walking with Merit. It surprised Victoria to find herself thinking of before with only a dull ache, instead of a deep hard pain. Maybe she was beginning to heal. Finally. She shook herself out of that train of thought, knowing how fast the depression could hit her.

Satoshi and J.D. chatted as they walked ahead. J.D. was beginning to relax with her new teammates. Victoria enjoyed talking with her. If someone had told her that discussing the plots of old short stories would be fun, she would not have believed them.

The discussion brought the team members as well as the members of her partnership into closer contact. Victoria had never known of Satoshi's summer herding cattle.

Victoria shifted the flowerpot from one hand to the other. She stroked the gray-green leaves and separated the blossoms. The scent of carnations rose around her and she smiled. She hoped *Starfarer*'s first grandparent in space would like her gift.

Stephen Thomas reached out and took her hand in a companionable way.

"You're pretty excited," he said.

"More mind reading?"

"Hardly necessary."

"I think I worked out something qualitatively different this afternoon," Victoria said. "A real 'a-hah!' experience. I'm ready for a party! I'm so glad Ms. Brown is here—It isn't the same as if Grangrana had agreed to come. But I'm glad she's on board all the same."

"I don't understand why they picked *her*," Stephen Thomas said. "She's not a colleague. Even if she wasn't past retirement, she was never a scientist. She doesn't have a proper vita. I don't even know what to call her."

"By her name, probably."

"You don't need to be sarcastic. I'm just saying I have some doubts about the grandparents program." Stephen Thomas grimaced.

"I thought you were neutral on the subject of age-mix. I didn't realize you were opposed."

"I can't help it if my personal landscape is different on that subject than yours. And, look, if we get into a bad spot, we'll have to worry about her."

"Why? How will worrying help? She knows the risks as well as any of us. And she's just as capable of making an informed decision."

"There's no more excuse for bringing elders up here than for bringing kids."

"No excuse—! I never heard you talk about Thanthavong or Cherenkov like this, by the way."

"They're different."

"Not in terms of their ability to decide whether to join the expedition."

"That isn't what I meant. I meant they both have reasons to be up here. They have things to do."

"Stephen Thomas, next you're going to try to tell me that Nikolai Cherenkov was a hero of the Soviet Union for making scientific discoveries."

Stephen Thomas blushed.

"I admire him, too," Victoria said. "But let's face it, holding the time-in-space record doesn't mean much nowadays. There must be a couple of hundred people who can measure their experience in decades."

"Okay, I'll grant that Cherenkov is here because he wants to be and because a lot of us admire him. And maybe because he's the only person in existence who'll be safer on the expedition than he would be anywhere in the solar system. That doesn't change anything. I still don't see any reason to bring a grandmother up here just *because* she's a grandmother. Besides, if she's such a great grandmother, why isn't she grandmothering her own grandchildren?"

"Maybe for the same reason we aren't parenting any children," Victoria said.

"That isn't fair!"

"Sure it is. We chose to put off having children so we could join the expedition. Maybe her grandchildren are grown up. Maybe she decided we needed her more than they did. Maybe she didn't feel needed back on earth at all. Maybe she has a spirit of adventure."

"What's going to happen if we do meet aliens—"

"When," Victoria said.

"Whatever, and they see her and say, 'Why in the world did you bring *her* along?' "

"What would happen when we meet aliens if they didn't

see her and they said, 'Where are your elders? How can we talk to people who cut themselves off from their wisest individuals?' Stephen Thomas, your argument has been used against every minority in history. 'You can't represent us, because you'd be talking to people who think you're less than human. For the sake of getting along, we're going to pretend to agree.' "

"I didn't mean it that way."

"Then don't suggest we deform our society to try to please some other culture. They're going to have to take us as we come."

"If you take that argument as far as it can go, we ought to bring kids along."

"There's a case to be made for that suggestion," Victoria said. "Maybe you should bring it up at the next meeting."

"Maybe this is a dumb argument. The age-mix decision's made now, we have one grandparent in space and maybe more to come. That's that."

"You're awfully passionate about it, now that it's too late. Why didn't you say anything at the committee meeting when we talked about age-mix in the first place?"

"Native shyness."

Victoria laughed.

Stephen Thomas gave a small and self-deprecating shrug. "Everybody sounded so enthusiastic. I didn't want to break consensus."

"If you weren't concerned enough about the subject to talk about it at the meetings, I don't think you should second-guess it now."

"I'm not going to embarrass you at the party, if that's what you mean."

"You haven't had good experiences with grandparents. Give Floris Brown a chance before you convince yourself she's going to be more of the same."

"I wish you wouldn't psychoanalyze me."

"And I wish you wouldn't read my aura, but that doesn't stop you."

Quite a way ahead, Satoshi turned back and beckoned to them.

"Come on, we're going to be late!"

He and J.D. waited till Victoria and Stephen Thomas caught up. Various tributaries had brought other people to the path. They passed the fossil bed, which was much farther along than the last time Victoria had seen it. She wondered if Crimson Ng intended to leave even a bit of bone showing, to indicate the bed's presence, or if hiding it completely was part of its aesthetics.

The party was going great. Infinity had never run a big party before. Small ones, a few friends and strangers, sure, but nothing on the scale of an open invitation to everyone left on campus. If Florrie and J.D. Sauvage had arrived a few transports before, it would have been much larger, but as far as Infinity was concerned it was plenty big enough. Guests crowded the main room, listening to Florrie tell stories in her feathery voice; other folks had spilled out into the garden. Professor Thanthavong, the geneticist, and Alzena Dadkhah, the head ecologist, stood in the garden drinking fruit juice and chatting. Even the new chancellor had made an appearance, though he had already left. Infinity had hoped Kolya Cherenkov might come, but maybe that was too much to ask.

An hour before, Infinity had watched a cloud form diagonally far-overhead, close to the spiral path that would bring it over the hill garden just as the party was about to start. Rain had not been predicted anywhere on campus till later tonight, but even inside a starship, weather remained wild and free. Inside a starship it was only gently wild, but a drizzle would dampen a party as badly as a downpour.

The cloud drifted by, shadowing the garden. Infinity stood outside, watching it and talking to it in an undertone. Perhaps it listened. As its edge trailed past, it sprinkled a few drops onto the hill, leaving the air fresh and the flowers sparkling and the grass barely damp. Infinity thanked the cloud.

Arachne had arranged to leave bright one section of the sun tubes. A great shaft of sunlight washed down over the hill, keeping the garden full day while the rest of the campus lay dark, spangled here and there with light. Infinity would have preferred lanterns, strung light bulbs, even darkness and fireflies, but the attention, the trouble someone had gone to—even if the someone was a computer—clearly thrilled Florrie.

Infinity took a glass of fruit juice and wandered out into the garden. The area around the hill lay in bright sunshine. Sunshine on campus was always noon in direction; only its intensity varied as the day progressed. Darkness encircled the pool of light.

Most everybody stood in clusters more or less on the paths, either because of the dampness or because they understood that the grass needed a few more weeks of growth in which to become established. Wildflowers glowed with jeweled colors. They had bloomed just in time, and Infinity felt pleased.

As far as Infinity could tell from the conversations he overheard, the guests had made a tacit agreement, just for tonight, not to discuss the troubles facing the expedition. They sounded more cheerful and relaxed than almost everyone had been for a long time.

He had worried that the guests might be bored with nothing but snacks and fruit juice, but no one appeared to mind the lack of mood-altering refreshments. The campus kitchen would supply food and drink for any reasonable gathering, but did not consider beer or wine to be nutritional necessities.

Infinity found alcohol uninteresting as a recreational drug, so he had never bothered to learn to make either beer or wine, nor had he gone out of his way to make friends with anyone who did. As for importing anything stronger from the O'Neills, that was out of the question on his salary even if he had had time to arrange it. The expedition paid him better than any job he could get on earth, but nothing like what it cost to import luxuries.

He sipped his fruit juice and sidled through the flower garden till he stood among the cactuses, in the penumbra between light and dark. He hoped people could see well enough out here; pulling cactus spines out of somebody's hand, or their butt, was no picnic.

Voices approached, disembodied by the darkness. A group of four people appeared out of the shadows. The alien contact team stood at the edge of the garden, still chatting with each other as they blinked and squinted and waited for their eyes to accustom themselves to the illumination. Infinity knew Stephen Thomas slightly; the geneticist had asked him for advice on planting grapevines. J.D. Sauvage was an unknown, and Satoshi and Victoria he had barely met. The personnel of the expedition liked to believe they avoided dividing themselves along class lines, but gardeners and scientists had very little to do with one another.

The team members strolled through the garden toward Florrie's house. Victoria carried a carnation plant, Satoshi a reed mat, Stephen Thomas a paper scroll.

Infinity took note of the alien contact specialist. She was plain and heavyset, pleasant enough but unmemorable. He wondered what alien contact specialists *did*.

The three old hands took J.D. through the garden, introducing her to everyone they passed. People greeted her and welcomed her and gave her small gifts.

"Victoria!" Someone Infinity did not know loped across the yard toward the team.

"Hi, Feral. Enjoy your first day on *Starfarer*?"

"It's fantastic—!"

Kolya Cherenkov's voice spun toward Infinity out of the darkness, that odd, low, powerful voice. Kolya, too, paused at the edge of the light to let his eyes adjust. He continued talking, though he stared straight ahead and never glanced toward his companion.

Griffith stepped into the light and stopped beside Cherenkov.

Griffith gave Infinity the weirdest feeling. An easygoing man, Infinity seldom took an immediate dislike to anyone. In Griffith's case, he was willing to make an exception. He disliked his pushiness, he disliked his rudeness and his disrespect toward Florrie. Infinity admired Cherenkov, too, but Griffith's reaction bordered on worship. Such intensity in any area of life struck Infinity as dangerous.

Infinity had been on campus since before there *was* a campus, and had never met Cherenkov before today; Griffith, having just arrived, had spent the whole day with the cosmonaut. Disgusted with himself for feeling jealous, Infinity turned away from the pair and headed for the house to make sure everything was going smoothly.

Florrie sat in the window seat with her guests arrayed in concentric circles around her. She wore black pants, and red ankle boots over them, a long fringed black tunic, and black eye makeup.

The alien contact team approached her. J.D. turned aside to put the awkward handful of presents people had given her in a neat stack in the corner.

Victoria handed Florrie the carnations.

"I hope you're getting settled in," she said. "I hope you like *Starfarer*."

"Yes . . ." Florrie said. "I'm sorry, I don't know your name—?"

"Victoria—from the transport?"

"Oh . . . of course." Florrie bent down to sniff the carnations.

Looking puzzled, Victoria stepped back.

Satoshi handed her the mat.

"It's not the same as having a rug," he said apologetically. "The mats last for quite a while, though."

"Thank you. You made this yourself?"

"Yes, ma'am."

Stephen Thomas knelt formally at her feet. Bowing slightly, he offered her a scroll that he held in both hands.

She untied the ribbon, unrolled the paper, and read it. Perplexed, she looked up at him. "A tea ceremony? I don't think I . . ."

"I'm trying to add the cultural roots of my family to my own personal landscape," he said. "Tea ceremony is an ancient Japanese custom. I'm learning it, and I'd like to do it for you sometime."

"Are you . . . Japanese?"

"No, but that's part of Satoshi's background. I keep trying to get him to study it, too, but he doesn't want to."

"My family is pretty well Americanized," Satoshi said.

"And I'm trying to trace Victoria's family so I know what to study from Africa."

"Dream on," Victoria said, in a tone that sounded to Infinity just a shade bitter. "It would make more sense to study some Canadian customs, eh?"

"I would," Stephen Thomas said, "but I don't like beer."

Victoria and Satoshi laughed.

"You are all three in the same family?" Florrie asked.

"Right, a family partnership."

Infinity thought the family partnership was a fairly weird arrangement. No necessity existed anymore to promise sexual fidelity to one person or to a group. He wondered if J.D. Sauvage had to join the partnership in order to become a member of the alien contact team.

Florrie smiled, accepting the old-fashioned system.

"Goodness," she said, "I had no idea young people did that anymore. I was born in a commune. Sit here near me. I'm sorry I don't have any chairs."

Stephen Thomas continued to kneel at her feet, like the hero of a martial-arts interactive, attending the dowager empress of Japan. Stephen Thomas looked pretty good, sitting *seiza*, Infinity thought, though he ducked his head too far when he bowed.

Satoshi sat on the floor cross-legged, shifting uncomfortably now and then. At a little distance, Victoria drew her knees up under her chin and wrapped her arms around her legs. J.D. sat beside her, arms folded on her chest, her legs outstretched and crossed at the ankles.

Infinity listened contentedly as Florrie recounted her parents' story, in which a group of people tried to form their own rural tribe, despite being culturally maladapted to communal living and inexperienced at subsisting off the land. Of course it ended badly, when Florrie was very young, but Infinity had a high aesthetic appreciation for well-meaning tragedies.

Suddenly the atmosphere changed. Infinity felt it as surely as a change in temperature or a sudden wind. Stephen Thomas turned. Infinity looked toward the door. Kolya entered, carrying a small package.

Griffith paused in shadows, right behind him.

Infinity moved to one side of the room, farther from Griffith, trying to act natural rather than surreptitious about his desire to get as far away from the other man as possible. Without meaning to he glanced back, and found Griffith gazing after him, the complete, deliberate neutrality of his expression more frightening than any degree of emotion. Anger, or hatred, or contempt, Infinity might have confronted. The neutrality could not even be commented upon, though Infinity knew, and Griffith knew, that it meant: I notice you. I'll watch you, if it pleases me.

Someone toward the front of the room noticed Kolya. Florrie continued to tell her story, but people were distracted by the unexpected appearance of the cosmonaut. They began nudging each other, glancing back, exclaiming softly in surprise.

As far as Infinity could tell, no one else paid the least attention to Griffith.

Kolya acted as if he never noticed that anyone had noticed him. He hunkered down in a clear space and listened. Infinity wondered if Kolya found it amusing to hear Florrie's tale of a failed fling with communism in the mid-twentieth-century United States. If he did, he was too well mannered to laugh in any of the wrong places.

When Florrie finished, her audience applauded and Kolya unfolded to his feet. People made way for him. He stopped beside Stephen Thomas, who still knelt in front of Florrie.

"I brought you both small gifts of welcome," he said to Florrie and to J.D. He handed Florrie the package. "It is rather delicate."

As she opened it, her fingers trembled. Infinity was afraid she would slip and drop it, whatever it was, but the wrapping unfolded and floated to the floor, leaving a delicate, intricately painted eggshell in her hands.

"A souvenir," Kolya said. "I believe that they do not make them in my country anymore. Or, if they do, they do not export them."

"Why, thank you, Mr. Cherenkov," Florrie said.

Kolya handed J.D. a slip of paper. J.D. unfolded it, read it, and looked up.

"Thank you," she said softly, and buttoned the slip of paper into her shirt pocket.

Florrie held the eggshell up and looked at it against the light. Infinity wondered if she understood what giving gifts meant here. Gifts were, more often than not, nonphysical: offers of help or time or the gift of a skill. The kind of thing Kolya, apparently, had offered to J.D. People did not have many things to give, up here. Kolya probably had fewer than most. He had not, as far as Infinity knew, been back to earth in two decades. Other people returned to earth on leave and came home with full allowances; Kolya lacked this luxury. Perhaps he had brought the egg into space with him on an early trip, or the last one.

Florrie looked around. "I don't know where to put this," she said. "If I were back home I'd put it on the mantelpiece, but I have none here."

"There is a thread strung through it, to make it easy to hang up."

"In the window, then."

"Oh—" Kolya stopped. He looked uncomfortable, unhappy, but he said nothing more. Infinity had no idea what troubled him.

Florrie rose and turned toward the window, looking for a place to hang the egg. Before she found one, Griffith appeared. Infinity had not even noticed him move. Griffith took the egg from her hand.

Florrie reacted to Griffith even more negatively, more noticeably, than Infinity had. She drew back; the egg would have fallen and shattered if Griffith had not taken it carefully from her hand. He was more concerned about the eggshell than he was about Florrie, for he showed no reaction to her fright.

"Sunlight will fade it," Griffith said. He took the eggshell to the corner farthest from the window, stretched up, and hung it from a hook set into the ceiling.

Florrie's aesthetic sense was better than Griffith's. The eggshell looked odd and lonely high up in the corner, where it was safe. It would have looked fine in the window, but not at the expense of its existence. Infinity could see that someone would have to build Florrie a table or a stand or a little cabinet for the egg, maybe with a bit of mirror behind it.

"Well!" Defending herself with indignation, Florrie sat stiff and straight on the window seat.

Both relieved and embarrassed, Kolya offered Florrie a small bow.

"I hope you will be happy on our expedition," he said. "I hope you will be happy, too, J.D."

"Thank you, Kolya," J.D. Sauvage said.

In a moment the cosmonaut was gone.

Though the party inside took a little while to ease again, the party outside had loosened up considerably. As the light faded to dusk, people put lines out to Arachne for music. Couples and groups danced on the grass, unsynchronized, each to a different interior melody. Infinity would have to reseed the center of the yard, after all. He did not mind too much.

He kept an eye on Griffith, trying to figure out what bothered him about the man. After Kolya left, Griffith acted like everyone else, mingling, chatting. But every so often, when Infinity glanced around, he found Griffith gazing at him with that scary neutral expression.

Infinity went inside. Florrie sipped lemonade. Stephen Thomas still knelt at her feet—as far as Infinity could tell, he had not moved. They chatted.

Infinity admired Stephen Thomas's new earring. He wondered who had made it and whether they would make a similar one for him, only with synthetic rubies instead of emeralds.

He joined Florrie and Stephen Thomas.

"You let me know if you get tired, Florrie," Infinity said, "and I'll chase all these folks home."

She peered out the French doors. "Who *is* that man?"

Griffith stood alone on the porch.

"He said he's with the GAO," Infinity said.

"The GAO!" Victoria frowned, doubtful. "What's he doing, auditing our books?"

"Could be, I guess."

"He's a narc," Florrie said.

"What?"

"A narc."

"I heard you, I just don't know what that means."

"Is the government going through anti-drug hysteria again?" she asked. "I gave up reading local news years ago."

"The main tantrum the U.S. is going through right now is about *Starfarer* and the expedition," Infinity said. "Florrie, please, what's a narc?"

"Be careful around him," she said. "If you use any kind of drugs, he'll put you in jail."

Infinity and Stephen Thomas looked at each other, confused. What kind of drugs could get you put in jail? Most recreational substances were designed so their effects wore off quickly, and anyone who chose something more powerful ought to have the sense to check out their tolerance for it and make adjustments. Infinity had known people who too frequently sought out effects that were too strong—watching them was one of the reasons he did not drink—but he could not imagine involving the law in the problem. A supervisor, or a doctor, sure. Even the community council. But the law?

"You don't know much history, do you?" Florrie said.

"Not enough, I guess," Stephen Thomas said politely.

"You be careful. If you do anything they don't like, if you make trouble, they'll accuse you of using drugs and they'll ruin you. They take a real problem and they pervert the solution to it to increase their power over you. They'll take your job away. That happened to a friend of mine, and he didn't even use alcohol, much less something illegal. But he was a troublemaker! And they destroyed him for it!"

"I don't think you need to worry," Victoria said, keeping her voice gentle, neutral, almost as neutral as Griffith's expression. "We're all troublemakers up here, in one way or another. They can't get us all."

"Don't patronize me, young lady!" Florrie snapped, with a spark of real anger. "If you ignore me because you think I'm a senile old coot, you'll be sorry!"

"I don't think—it wasn't my intention—" Victoria's voice broke. She stopped. Her dark skin flushed. "—to patronize you."

Infinity suddenly shivered. He looked out the window at Griffith, wondering if Florrie was worried over the wrong details, but for the right reason.

When he glanced back toward Florrie and the alien contact team, Victoria had disappeared.

Victoria hurried to the edge of the garden, out of the light. She felt as if someone had punched her in the stomach. Not someone. Floris Brown.

"Victoria?"

J.D. crossed the shadows and stopped beside her.

"What's wrong?"

"I don't know. It's just . . ." She fell silent. "She had a perfect right to react that way, I *was* being patronizing."

"There's a difference between being patronizing and being reassuring. I thought her reaction was kind of extreme."

Victoria shrugged.

"Why did what she said hurt you so much?" J.D. asked.

Victoria told J.D. about her own great-grandmother.

"I tried to get Grangrana to apply to the expedition, but she wouldn't. She's older than Ms. Brown, quite a lot. She's frailer. She traveled all over when she was younger, and now . . . she's tired. I'm worried about her. I don't want to leave her behind. I miss her, J.D., I miss her so much."

Victoria smiled. "Grangrana can give you what-for, but she wouldn't ever slap you down."

"You wanted Ms. Brown to like you, didn't you?"

"I did. I think she's admirable, to apply for the program and come all this way. I thought she did like me. On the transport. But tonight she didn't even remember me."

"I'm sorry."

"Isn't it strange," Victoria said, "how somebody can say a couple of words to you, and make you feel like a four-year-old?"

"No," J.D. said. "Not strange at all. Especially when it's somebody you want to make a connection with."

Victoria squeezed J.D.'s hand. "Thanks. For talking. For . . . noticing." She still felt shaken, as much by surprise at the intensity of her reaction as by Ms. Brown's words. She made herself smile. "What did Cherenkov give you?"

"Hey, Victoria!" Satoshi joined them. He carried J.D.'s presents in the crook of his arm. "J.D., you forgot these."

"Oh. Sorry. Thank you." She took them from him. "Kolya invited me to lunch," she said to Victoria. "He offered to make piroshki. I don't know what piroshki is, but I'm looking forward to finding out."

"Piroshki are the Russian version of fried dumplings or pasties or ravioli," Satoshi said.

Satoshi put his arm around Victoria's shoulders. His bare skin touched hers through the open lace of her shirt. She put her arm around his waist, glad of his warmth.

"He doesn't spend time with people very often," Victoria said. "He's given you a unique gift."

"What's wrong?" Satoshi asked her. "The way you rushed out . . ."

"I'm okay now, but I'm going home."

"Wait just a minute and we'll all go."

"There's no reason for you to leave, too—"

"Stephen Thomas is already making our excuses. It's getting late. There he is."

Stephen Thomas walked toward them, staring at the ground. When he reached them he stopped and looked up. His fair skin was pale, his blue eyes dark-circled.

"Stephen Thomas—?"

"Let's go," he said shortly, and strode into the darkness.

People began drifting home soon after the light faded. Infinity was spared having to urge anyone to go, since everyone had to work the next day. Stephen Thomas surprised him by leaving so early—he could usually be counted on to close out any gathering, no matter how late it ran. He had bid good night to Florrie, then he had risen from his kneeling position as smoothly as if he had knelt at her feet only for a moment. Infinity wondered how he kept his feet from going to sleep.

The AS from the campus kitchen had already collected the bento boxes and taken them away. The housekeeper rolled about, looking for other things to do. As usual after parties on campus, no litter remained. Disposable eating utensils and suchlike did not exist out here. The AS carefully placed crumpled wrapping paper in a stack by Infinity's feet. Infinity smoothed the sheets out and folded them.

"You should keep this, too, Florrie," he said. "It's as much a gift as anything else you got tonight. Nobody manufactures wrapping paper out here."

She hardly heard him. She had not calmed down from her reaction to Griffith. Though she trembled with weariness, excitement and fear brightened her eyes.

"You will watch him, won't you?" she said. "Whatever he's about, you'll find out and make him stop."

"I can't do that," Infinity said. "How could I make him stop anything? He's a government representative, I'm a gardener."

"You've got to, that's all. You've got to."

"Please try to be easy. There's nothing I can do, and if there were I couldn't do it tonight. And, look, if he is a spy or something, maybe you ought to be careful what you say about him, or anyway who you say it to. It might get back to him."

She glanced at Infinity, quickly, sidelong, and immediately fell silent.

"I don't mean *me*," Infinity said. "I don't like him either." He stopped, wishing he had kept that admission to himself. "Florrie, do you need any help, or shall I leave you alone?"

"I don't need help."

"Okay, then, I just live over the next hill if you want to call me."

"But . . . you could brush my hair."

"All right," he said uncertainly. "Sure."

Except for the three long locks, she kept her hair cropped so close that he worried about scratching her scalp with the well-worn bristles of her brush. Her papery skin felt fragile. The brush made a soft, whispery noise, like her voice. A bristle caught against one of the unshorn and braided patches. He disentangled it. The shells and small pierced stones rattled together.

"Go ahead and take those out," she said.

Three diamond-shaped patches of hair lay in a diagonal line across the back of her head. There, her hair was heavy and thick. She had divided each section into two hanks and braided them with a soft leather thong from which dangled the shells and stones. He laid the thongs on the counter and brushed the long sections. She let herself relax into the chair; she pushed her foot against the floor, just once, then stopped trying to rock a chair that had no rockers.

Infinity found it pleasant to brush her hair. He had never done that for anyone before. After a while he thought Florrie had gone to sleep. He stopped brushing. He would have to wake her—

"Thank you," she said. She opened her eyes. "Maybe I'll see you tomorrow."

"Sure," Infinity said. He put the brush beside the shells and stones and left her alone.

He walked home across the darkened campus, thinking about the strange day. Once he heard a noise: he stopped short and spun toward it, expecting to see Griffith gazing expressionlessly at him half-hidden by shadows.

The miniature horse herd's miniature stallion stamped the ground with its miniature hoof, snorted at him, and reared and whinnied. A moment later the whole herd galloped away into the darkness, making a noise like rain. Infinity smiled. When he got home, he took a blanket into his own garden, to sleep in the reflected starlight.

Griffith returned to the guesthouse in the dark, knowing he could walk safely anywhere and anytime up here, yet unable to shake off a practiced tension. His aggressive swagger let potential assailants know he was no easy target. Here he tried to tone it down, for it did not fit the character of Griffith of GAO. On the other hand, he was not willing to be accosted even for the sake of his assignment.

He had complied with the rules of campus—of all the orbital habitations—to the extent of going unarmed. Even Griffith of GAO would never do that in the city. Being unarmed made him uncomfortable, and he wished he had at least tried to circumvent the laws.

He went to bed in his silent room. Lying on the thin hard futon, he listened. He heard nothing, no sign of the other guest, only the evening breeze brushing through the open windows.

Cherenkov had talked to him.

Griffith's thoughts kept returning to the question of how

to persuade the cosmonaut to continue talking to him, to continue answering his questions. Griffith's mission to *Starfarer* seemed inconsequential in comparison to his need to learn everything he could about Nikolai Cherenkov. Today was the first time in a long time that he had felt the drive to know everything about anything or anyone. At the party, Griffith had felt as if he wore his nerves outside his skin, sensitive to every stimulus that passed. He gathered everything in: observations of Cherenkov and information about the rest of the faculty and staff of the expedition as well, the kind of indiscriminate data that would collect in the back of his mind, work like fermenting beer, and help him discover a way to complete his mission. But after Cherenkov left, the party bored him, the interactions between the people bored him; their negative opinions about the new administration bored him.

The agreement he had made with Cherenkov must not stop him. As Griffith lay in bed, he let the prospect of the quest excite him. It pushed away the depression that had settled when he could no longer keep Cherenkov in sight. It recharged him.

In the darkness, he drafted a quick memo to his superiors. Before he ever came here he had tried to tell them that directly co-opting the personnel would be hopeless. Now he could demonstrate it. The hope had been a foolish one to begin with. The crew of *Starfarer*, the faculty and staff, as they referred to themselves, would all have to be recalled in one way or another. Then the starship could be converted.

Griffith encrypted his message, sent it back to earth, and fell asleep. He dreamed all night.

Kolya wanted to go outside again, but he knew that Arachne, fussing over his radiation exposure, would go so far as to call out human help to persuade him to stay inside.

Since he recognized his desire as a selfish one, he refrained from indulging in it. The only result would be that someone would be fetched, probably out of a warm bed, to come and talk to him.

He feared he had made a tactical error in conversing with Marion Griffith. The intensity of the officer's questions troubled him. He should have seen the problem coming when the fellow waited in the access tunnels for him. Even before that. Kolya tried to excuse himself on the grounds of having been spared the more obvious forms of hero worship during the past few years.

The person he looked forward to talking to was the alien contact specialist. J.D. Sauvage and her profession fascinated him. He thought that if he were younger, if he had a different background, he might have tried to go into her field himself.

Since yesterday, he said to himself, you've added a party and a lunch date to your socializing. Soon your reputation as a hermit will be ruined.

Do you even remember how to make piroshki?

J.D. enjoyed working at night; she enjoyed the solitude and the long uninterrupted hours of quiet thought. She might have to change her schedule around, though, in order to spend time with the rest of the alien contact team. Victoria and Satoshi and Stephen Thomas kept awfully normal hours.

She liked them all, which surprised her a bit. She liked Victoria in particular. The team leader sparked off ideas like phosphorescent waves. Satoshi was quieter, but what he said usually counted. As for Stephen Thomas . . .

She decided not to think about Stephen Thomas for a while.

She stayed awake for a long time after the party, reading, gazing out into the dark courtyard. Once she got up and rearranged the new woven mats on her floor. For all their homemade roughness, they made her happy, and a little scared. The gifts represented a welcome that made her believe she had found a place where she might be at home. This disturbed her, because she had always believed that being an alien contact specialist meant remaining an outsider in her own culture—not just the culture of her country, but the culture of humanity as a whole.

J.D. took Kolya Cherenkov's note from her pocket and smoothed it out. He had given her, as Victoria said, a unique gift. She did not understand why he had given it to her, but she knew it was not to be trifled with or abused. In some ways, his was the welcome that meant the most to her.

Before she finally went to sleep, she checked her mail: the usual tsunami of junk, most of which she filtered out without even scanning; scientific journals; magazines of experimental fiction (interior landscapes, mostly; deliberately, stolidly human, but every now and again a story she could savor, save, and think about); no personal mail. Nothing from Zev. She scanned the news summary, lingering just perceptibly over the Pacific Northwest.

The divers, as usual, received no mention.

Victoria propped herself on her elbow next to Satoshi, who lay in the middle of his bed with Stephen Thomas on his other side. Stephen Thomas lay flat on his back, staring at the ceiling, his arms crossed on his chest.

"Do you think J.D. had a good time?" Victoria asked Satoshi.

"She seemed to."

"I wasn't about to say anything in front of her, but I'm so mad at the chancellor I could spit—he came early, he left early, he was too rude to stay and welcome her to campus! Gerald was there—did he even speak to her?" She

tried to remember seeing the assistant chancellor anywhere
near J.D.

"I don't think so," Satoshi said. "We can't take this stuff
personally, Victoria. It's all politics."

"They mean it personally and I take it personally, politics or not."

They heard a noise from the front of the house, sharp
and loud, quickly stilled. Victoria sat up.

"What was that?" She started to rise. "Oh—Feral coming in." They listened as he tiptoed down the hall to the
end room.

Concerned by Stephen Thomas's uncharacteristic silence, Victoria glanced over at him. The crystal lay dull
and black in the hollow of his throat. He had taken off his
sexy emerald jewelry, but he had not replaced the regular
gold stud.

"The hole in your ear is going to close up," Victoria
said.

He shrugged.

Victoria slid out of bed and went into Stephen Thomas's
room. His jewelry hung in a tangle on a rock-foam stand
that someone in the materials lab had made for him. The
gold stud was nowhere she could see it, so she picked out
a little platinum ring and returned to Satoshi's bedroom.
She stepped over both her partners, sat cross-legged beside
Stephen Thomas, and smoothed his hair away from his ear.
In the darkness, she had trouble finding the hole to put the
earring in.

"Ouch, shit, that hurt!"

Victoria leaned down and kissed his ear. "Better?"

"Give it here, I'll put it in." He took the earring from
her and put it on. Victoria lay down beside him and put one
hand on his hip.

"I'm glad to know you can still talk," Satoshi said.
"You've been awfully quiet since we left the party."

"You remember that conversation we had with Florrie?" Stephen Thomas asked.

Victoria said nothing, wishing Stephen Thomas had not reminded her about talking with Ms. Brown.

"You hit it off pretty well with her, didn't you?" Satoshi said.

"Yeah, I did. I like her. I thought she'd be reactionary, but she's more open-minded than half the people up here."

"You just like her because she approves of our sleeping arrangements," Victoria said.

"That doesn't hurt. And you don't have to be careful of every word you say to her. But she goes off at a different angle, sometimes."

"What do you mean?" Satoshi said.

"What she said about Griffith."

"He was on the transport," Victoria said. "But I hardly ever saw him. I almost forgot about him."

"He's *weird*. When Florrie said he was a narc—after she told me what a narc was—I tried to shrug it off." Stephen Thomas shifted uneasily. "But I think we ought to pay attention to her intuition."

"Oh, no, not another aura reader!" Victoria flopped forward and hid her face in Stephen Thomas's pillow.

"I don't know whether *she* is or not, but *I* looked at him. Dammit, that guy doesn't *have* an aura."

"Wouldn't that mean he's dead?" Satoshi asked.

"I don't know what it means," Stephen Thomas said. "Since he obviously isn't dead."

Victoria raised herself from the pillows and propped her chin on her fists. "Maybe they've been improving robot technology in secret—"

"Laugh if you want. He said he's with the GAO—that may be worse than being a narc. I think he's trouble. Even if he's just an ordinary government accountant."

"There's not much we can do about him that I can see."

"There's got to be something." Stephen Thomas lay back and stared at the ceiling with his arms crossed over his chest, as if he intended to try to think of something right now, and stay where he was until he succeeded.

8

The solar sail drew *Starfarer* beyond the orbit of the moon.

During its construction, the starship held steady in the libration point leading the moon. With the sail deployed, *Starfarer* accelerated out of its placid orbit. Each imperceptible increment of velocity widened and altered its path.

Because the starship took longer to circle the earth in its wider orbit, the moon began to catch up to it. Soon it would pass beneath *Starfarer*, and the ship would use the lunar passage to tilt its course into a new plane.

As the orbit increased in complexity, the logistics of transport to *Starfarer* would become more difficult and more expensive.

In the middle of *Starfarer's* night, Iphigenie DuPre set in motion the interactions of gravity and magnetic field and solar wind to tilt the starship out of the plane of the lunar orbit.

The angle would grow steeper and the spiral wider: the sail plus the effect of traveling past the earth and the moon would soon drive the ship toward a mysterious remnant of the creation of the universe, a strand of cosmic string that would provide *Starfarer* with superluminal transition energy.

Starfarer prepared for lunar passage. Afterward, it would be well and truly on its way.

*   *   *

Grangrana was making breakfast. Victoria could smell biscuits, eggs, a rice curry. Coffee.

Coffee? In Grangrana's house?

Victoria woke from the dream. She was on board *Starfarer*; Grangrana remained on earth. The straight up-and-down sunlight of morning, noon, and evening reflected from the porch. Nevertheless, she smelled breakfast.

Satoshi, beside her, half opened his eyes.

"Is that coffee?"

"Uh-huh."

"Your friend Feral can stay if he wants," Satoshi said, and went back to sleep.

Victoria smiled, kissed the curve of his shoulder, tucked the blanket around him, and slid out of his bed.

In cutoffs and one of Satoshi's sleeveless shirts, Victoria went out to the main room. Stephen Thomas was up and dressed, in flowered cotton Bermuda shorts and a purple silk shirt. Victoria remembered rising partway out of sleep in the middle of the night when he left Satoshi's room and returned to his own.

Victoria dodged around Stephen Thomas's still.

"Good morning."

"Hi." The circles beneath his eyes had faded. He looked better this morning, not as shaken as after the party. But if he had thought of what to do about Griffith, he made no mention of his plans.

"Morning." Feral set a pot of tea in front of Victoria as she sat down.

"This is a real treat for us, Feral," Victoria said. "But you don't have to make breakfast every morning." The pleasure of having breakfast cooked and waiting gave her mixed emotions. She missed having a family manager, but it seemed disloyal to enjoy it when someone else did the tasks Merit had always smoothly, almost invisibly, taken care of.

"I know. I like to cook." He grinned. He had mobile, expressive lips that exposed his even white teeth when he smiled. "And everything I made this morning will reheat. Satoshi can sleep in if he wants to."

"Speak of the devil," Stephen Thomas said.

Satoshi arrived wrapped in his threadbare bathrobe, his wet hair dripping down his neck.

"Stephen Thomas, there's no clean laundry," he said in a neutral tone. "And you used the last towel."

"Uh-oh," Stephen Thomas said.

"You might at least have hung it up so I could use it."

"It was *wet*," Stephen Thomas said.

"Yeah, well, so am I." Satoshi accepted a cup of coffee. "Thanks, Feral."

Victoria sometimes wished Satoshi would simply blow his stack. He hardly ever did.

Stephen Thomas sighed. "I'll do some laundry. Today. A little later. Okay?"

Satoshi did not answer him.

"Want some curry?" Feral said.

"Sure." Satoshi wiped the sides of his face and his neck where water had dripped from his hair. His elbow stuck through a hole in the blue terry cloth. He had gotten away with bringing the robe to *Starfarer* by using it as packing material when they first moved here. He needed a new one, but terry cloth was far too heavy and bulky for an ordinary allowance.

Satoshi dug around in the cupboard among his collection of condiments. There was a hole in the back of the robe, too, just below his left hip. His tawny skin showed through it. Victoria was glad he hated sewing and would probably never darn the battered fabric.

Feral brought breakfast to the table. Satoshi opened the new hot chili paste.

"I'm looking forward to trying this stuff."

Feral laughed. "Don't tell me they import *that* here."

"Victoria brought it up in her allowance. What's life without red chili paste?"

"Quieter," Victoria said, and Satoshi smiled.

"This is pretty hot already." Feral offered Satoshi the curry.

"Good."

Feral passed the food around and sat across from Satoshi. As she watched Satoshi put chili sauce on his curry and on his eggs, Victoria hoped he and Feral would not get into a competition of who could eat the hottest food. Despite long acquaintance with Satoshi, Victoria had never understood the lure of the more violent forms of Cajun, Chinese, or Mexican cooking. Even from a distance, the volatile oils were enough to make her eyes water.

Feral tasted the curry. "You're right, it isn't hot enough. Steve, would you pass the chili sauce?"

"Please don't call me Steve," Stephen Thomas said.

Feral looked up, surprised by the sudden change in tone of Stephen Thomas's voice.

"Stephen Thomas has this phobia about nicknames," Satoshi said.

Stephen Thomas scowled at Satoshi. "Do I have to let everybody call me anything they want? Maybe I should make up a nickname for Feral? In the North American style, Ferrie. Or the Japanese style, Feral-chan. Maybe the Russian style, Ferushkabababushka."

"Dammit, Stephen Thomas!"

Feral started to laugh. "It's okay, Satoshi," he said. "I can do without the Russian style, but I kind of like 'Feral-chan.' Stephen Thomas, I apologize. I won't try to change your name again. After all, if you've got three first names, it only makes sense to use at least two of them."

Stephen Thomas scowled, unwilling to be placated. "I

don't have *any* first names," he said. "They're all last names."

"Will you accept my apology anyway? *And* pass the chili sauce?"

Stephen Thomas tossed the jar across the table. Satoshi winced and grabbed for it, but Feral caught it easily.

"You're really acting like an adolescent," Satoshi said to Stephen Thomas. "And I wish you'd quit."

"I thought I was performing a public service," Stephen Thomas said. "That's one of the problems with this campus— no kids live here."

Victoria went straight to her office. She had some more ideas about the cosmic string problem. Four different displays, each working on a separate manipulation, hovered in the corner. She glanced at them, though it was too soon to expect results.

One had stopped.

"I'll be damned!" Victoria said.

Her "a-hah!" equation had produced a solution. Already. The quickest one yet, by several orders of magnitude. *If* it was correct. She looked it over. She felt like a bottle of Stephen Thomas's champagne, with the strange invigorated lightness that the joy of discovery always gave her. The solution *felt* right, as the problem had felt right when she chose it to work on.

"I'll be damned," she said again. And then she thought, if I hadn't had to go back to earth, I would have finished the algorithm a couple of weeks ago. We would have had plenty of time for Iphigenie to recalculate the orbit for the cosmic string encounter. We could have substituted this approach to the string for the first one we chose.

The approach promised a faster, more direct route to their destination. And it hinted at a safer and more usable way home from Tau Ceti, but Victoria could not yet prove that. Nevertheless, she was outrageously pleased with her success. Victoria collected the arrival coordinates and set the return calculations going. At the same time she packaged up the string solution.

As she was about to tell Arachne to send the information to EarthSpace for archiving, she thought better of it.

Then she did something that abashed her. But she did it anyway.

She made a copy of the solution and slipped the copy into the pocket of her cutoffs and took the results out of the web altogether.

Stephen Thomas sat sipping his coffee until Feral and Victoria and Satoshi had left the house. He hated it when Satoshi got so annoyed about trivial things like laundry, and then would not even admit he was mad.

All three members of the family had begun to deal with the grief of losing their eldest partner, but that did not resolve the problem of being without a manager. The strain was showing as plainly as the holes in Satoshi's robe. Stephen Thomas knew what needed to be done, but he did not know how to make Satoshi and Victoria admit that they needed a manager. He had even tried to figure out how to make the family finances stretch to hiring someone. It might have been possible back on earth; it might even have been possible on *Starfarer* if they were not buying the house. As things stood, that solution was out of the question.

Maybe Victoria, having finally begun to accept Merit's death, was also beginning to accept the need for other changes. She had, after all, started the connection with Feral. She made no objection when Stephen Thomas invited him to stay. Stephen Thomas found Feral attractive, and he believed Victoria did, too, though he could not be certain she had admitted it to herself. And then there was the interesting fact that for a houseguest, Feral was making himself spectacularly useful.

I probably shouldn't have snapped at him about calling me "Steve," Stephen Thomas thought.

He finished his coffee. In no hurry, he left his bike on the porch and walked on over to the genetics department. He enjoyed watching the changes in the landscape he passed every day. When he first arrived, the naked earth-colored hillocks sent off rivulets of eroded mud with every rain shower. Puddles on the path turned red or yellow or blue with clay or white with sand: stark pure colors unleavened by organic content. Slowly the grasses and succulents, the bushes and bamboo, sprouted into pale green lace covering the new land. The erosion slowed; now it had nearly stopped, and the vegetation covered the ground as if it had always been here. In many spots the gardeners had planted sapling trees, species either naturally fast-maturing or genetically altered to grow at enhanced speed. The primary colors of the soil had begun to dull into fertile shades of brown as the plants and the bacteria and the earthworms worked them.

According to Infinity Mendez, most of the wild cylinder would be permitted to grow and change by normal processes of succession, until in a hundred or five hundred years it would contain mature climax forests of several climates. The plan presented difficulties—never mind that no one expected *Starfarer's* first expedition to last more than a few years; the starship itself should be essentially immortal. But many types of forest required periodic fires to maintain their health, and that of course could not be permitted within the confines, however large, of a starship. Other methods, mechanical and bacterial and labor-intensive human work, would have to substitute. Some of them had only been tried briefly and experimentally. This both troubled Stephen Thomas and excited his appreciation of the unknown.

He strolled through the stand of smoke bamboo growing

above the genetics department and walked down the out-
door ramp to the main level. As he headed for his lab, he
brought his current project to the front of his perceptions and
immersed himself in it.

He passed the conference room, the first door after
the entrance, so engrossed in his thoughts that he was five
paces past it before he noticed the yelling. He stopped and
went back.

"Wretched fucking government plots—" Anger and profanity sounded particularly odd in the beautiful faint accent
Professor Thanthavong retained from her childhood in South-
east Asia.

Gerald Hemminge replied in a cool voice. "I came all
the way across campus to give you this news in person. I
didn't expect to be abused for my courtesy."

"But it's outrageous!" Thanthavong exclaimed, unre-
lenting. "How did you expect me to react?"

"Oh, come now, it's simply your Congress on one of
its toots. They haven't passed their budget, or appropriations
bill, or somesuch. Then all you Americans rush about pretending that the government is packing up and going home.
American congressional shenanigans give the rest of us enormous entertainment."

Stephen Thomas had never been able to tell if Gerald pa-
tronized his colleagues deliberately, or if it was just the effect
of his upper-class British background and accent. Stephen
Thomas ignored academic hierarchies on principle, but even
he thought it was not a survival characteristic for an assistant
chancellor to patronize a Nobel laureate. Beyond that, he felt
an enormous respect for Dr. Thanthavong, and he felt himself
fortunate to work with her. Gerald's attitude annoyed him.

"I think I can tell the difference between a normal governmental screwup and a conspiracy!" Thanthavong exclaimed.

"I'm always astonished when you criticize your adopted
country with such severity," Gerald said.

"It's bad enough when other Americans expect blind loyalty, but—"

"What's the matter?" Stephen Thomas said, before Thanthavong could finish. Having found a topic that could ruffle Thanthavong's usual restraint, Gerald managed to bring it into conversation whenever possible.

Stephen Thomas joined them. Thanthavong glared at Gerald for another moment, then broke away and turned toward Stephen Thomas. The tension eased just perceptibly.

"You haven't heard." Thanthavong blew out her breath in annoyance. "No, I suppose not. Gerald came over to be sure I got the news in person, as he's been so kind to point out."

"All I've heard this morning is that the moon's going to pass without crashing into us."

"Distler has impounded the United States' share of *Starfarer's* operating funds."

"Maybe it was the only way your president could think of to get your attention," Gerald said.

Stephen Thomas looked at him with disbelief. When the expedition first came together, Gerald had been as enthusiastic as anyone, as convinced of *Starfarer's* necessity. His attitude had changed recently, with the arrival of the new chancellor. He had not quite said out loud that he agreed with the idea of sending *Starfarer* into lower orbit, or even dismantling the ship. Stephen Thomas had given up arguing with him, because the arguments never went anywhere. Since Gerald never acknowledged anyone else's points, discussions began and ended in the same place. Besides, Stephen Thomas had finally realized that Gerald liked to argue, and would do it for fun. Arguing was not Stephen Thomas's idea of a good time.

"How can you be surprised?" Thanthavong asked Stephen Thomas. "Didn't you see it coming?"

"No. I didn't. The idea never crossed my mind."

"Something like this," Thanthavong said. "It had to happen."

"This isn't 'congressional shenanigans,' Gerald," Stephen Thomas said. "This is a serious attack."

"Yes, in the most vulnerable American area—the pocketbook."

Stephen Thomas let the jab fly past.

"It would be easier to prepare the expedition without any money than to continue without half our personnel," Thanthavong said.

Stephen Thomas frowned, trying to put a hopeful spin on the news. "Maybe it's not as bad as it looks. We're supposed to be self-sufficient eventually . . ."

"He's suspended the salaries of all U.S. citizens," Thanthavong said. "They'll send out enough transports to pick people up, but they won't send supplies beyond what are already in preparation."

"That isn't quite true," Gerald said. "We can have anything we want, as long as we pay for it ourselves."

"Does he think he can starve us out?" Stephen Thomas said. "How long can it take to grow, I don't know, potatoes?"

"Somehow," Gerald said, "I cannot see you holding out for long on a diet of potatoes. You're looking at the situation from a far too personal point of view. Our civilization is faced with problems much bigger than ours—"

"And the problems of one starship don't amount to a hill of beans," Stephen Thomas said.

"This isn't funny, Stephen Thomas," Thanthavong said.

"Yeah. I know."

"Putting off the expedition for two or three years," Gerald said, "might make the difference between survival and destruction."

"*Starfarer* cannot fill the new role the president suggests," Thanthavong said. "If the ship moves to a lower orbit, it will never leave the solar system. And I believe you know it."

She left the conference room.

"The same thing could happen to Europe and Britain as happened to half of Asia and Africa," Gerald said. "Perhaps it can't happen in North America—note that I place emphasis on 'perhaps.' I don't expect any native-born Americans to have a conception of what that means, but surely a natural-ized citizen—"

Stephen Thomas remembered some of the stories Victo-ria's great-grandmother told about her friends and the Mideast Sweep. He felt distressed and off balance, unable to counter Gerald's arguments.

"Gerald," Stephen Thomas said, though it was hardly a survival characteristic for a professor to antagonize an assistant chancellor, "shut up." He followed Thanthavong out of the main room and went to his lab.

"Stephen Thomas!" His two grad students and his post-doc converged on him.

"Give me a few minutes," he said. He went into his office and shut the door.

Stephen Thomas came out of his office and into the deserted lab. He wondered where everyone had got to. He wanted to talk to them; he had spent the whole morning with Arachne, and he thought he had figured out a way to keep the lab going. At least for a while.

The president's announcement had completely disrupted everything he had planned for today. In addition, the staff and faculty had put in enough recommendations to schedule a general meeting. Even Stephen Thomas had joined in that proposal, though he hated meetings. It would eat up the evening.

Stephen Thomas left the genetics building and headed for the park. As he walked, he set up another problem for

Arachne to work on. Every twenty paces or so, his stride faltered as he rejected the results, changed a variable, and started another report cycle.

He barely noticed the blossoms that had opened since his last visit to the park. A kitchen AS stood next to a round table, waiting patiently with lunch. Otherwise, the meadow was deserted. In normal times every picnic table by the stream would be in use.

Stephen Thomas waited for Victoria and Satoshi. He pillowed his head on his arms. The bento boxes breathed a warm smell, but Stephen Thomas had no appetite. He was still linked up with Arachne, juggling numbers and trying not to see the pattern they insisted on producing.

"Stephen Thomas."

Stephen Thomas started when Satoshi touched his shoulder.

"Sorry."

"I was thinking."

"Yeah."

Victoria joined them. They embraced. Victoria and Satoshi looked as somber as Stephen Thomas felt. They had probably been doing the same calculations as he had.

Satoshi set the bento boxes out on the stone table, then sat on the rock-foam bench beside his partners.

"So," Victoria said.

"They've really done it this time," Stephen Thomas said.

"How many graduate students are you losing?" Satoshi said.

"No one has bailed out yet," Stephen Thomas said, adding, to himself, As far as I know.

"All mine are Canadian," Victoria said. "The temps plan to stay as long as they can be sure of a transport home. But with the supply runs curtailed, my kids are scared."

Most of the researchers on board had several graduate

students and post-doctoral students: till now, at least, it was considered quite a coup to win a position helping prepare the expedition. Most of the students were temps, permitted to stay only while the starship remained in range of the transports. Some had applied for positions on the expedition itself: the ultimate make-or-break dissertation project.

"Leaving now sounds kind of shortsighted to me," Stephen Thomas said. "They wouldn't lose that much—unless somebody raised grad salaries when I wasn't looking." He tried to grin.

"What have you been *doing* all morning?" Victoria snapped.

"What? What are you mad about?"

"Didn't you even read the new rules?"

"I got as far as 'Salaries and grants are suspended until further notice,' and I spent the rest of the morning figuring out how to keep the lab together."

"The new rules are that American grad students who quit now and go home still get their trips free. If they stay and change their minds later they have to pay for it themselves."

"Oh."

"Oh," Victoria said.

"Come on, Victoria, this wasn't my idea, don't take it out on me. And the money's only been impounded for a couple of hours. Distler will get overruled, or whatever they do. Won't he?"

"I hope so, for you guys' sakes." Victoria turned to Satoshi. "What about your students?" ·

"Fox volunteered to stay on," he said drily.

Victoria laughed despite herself.

"I'm glad to hear somebody's expecting to come out ahead in this," Stephen Thomas said sourly. He opened his lunch, closed it again, and stared at the variations in the table's surface.

Satoshi rubbed his shoulder gently. Stephen Thomas looked at his partners and took Satoshi's hand. Victoria reached across the table to him, her irritation dissolving into sympathy.

"Have you talked to your father yet?"

Stephen Thomas shook his head—and immediately regretted it. The interaction of the cylinder's rotation with his inner ear made his field of vision twist and tilt. He squeezed his eyes shut and waited for the weird sensation to stop.

"Oh, shit!" By now he should have got over the habit of shaking his head or nodding, or adapted to the weirdness.

He opened his eyes hesitantly. The world steadied. Satoshi put a cold glass in his hand. Stephen Thomas rubbed the side of the glass against one temple, then sipped the iced tea.

"Thanks."

"You okay?" Satoshi said.

"Yeah," Stephen Thomas replied, without nodding. "No, I haven't talked to my father. Yeah, I'm going to have to. And I don't think I can get away with text only."

"No, of course not," Victoria said. "It's all right, don't worry. Go ahead and call him direct. We'll manage."

"What are you going to tell him?"

"It beats the hell out of me," Stephen Thomas said. He felt not only embarrassed but humiliated. The feeling would only get worse when he called his father.

"Stephen Thomas—" Satoshi said, speaking tentatively.

"Satoshi—" Victoria said.

"We've got to work out something fair."

"I know it! But with only my salary, we're going to be lucky if we can keep the house. If we lose it, that's five years of work and all Merit's planning down the drain. Grangrana will have to move back to the city . . ."

"I'll work something out with Greg myself!" Stephen Thomas surprised himself with his own vehemence. "And it won't be at the expense of Grangrana or the house. Dammit, I've never pulled my financial weight in the partnership, I'm not going to start being a drain on it, too!"

"Maybe Greg will reconsider moving to Canada," Victoria said.

Stephen Thomas flinched. "I don't think that's within the range of possible solutions." He tried not to sound defensive, but failed. That made him feel guilty and angry, for he knew Victoria was not leading up to a lecture on the best ways to save money. Her family had worked hard and long to pull itself into the middle class, but she seldom talked about their history. What few details Stephen Thomas knew, he knew from Satoshi. Stephen Thomas came from a family that had been middle or upper middle class since before Victoria's ancestors escaped to Canada. It was his father's own fault—perhaps not so much fault as bad luck—that had pushed him down to an income that did not meet subsistence without his son's help.

Victoria, reacting to his defensive tone, withdrew from the conversation, turning aside and gazing across the park.

"If you thought my financial responsibilities were such a drawback, why did you invite me into this partnership in the first place?"

Victoria's shoulders stiffened, but she neither spoke nor turned toward him.

Stephen Thomas stared at her, stunned.

"We invited you because we love you," Satoshi said.

"Merry did. Maybe you do. But dammit, Victoria, sometimes I wonder—!" Stephen Thomas rose and started away.

"Stephen Thomas—" Satoshi called after him.

Stephen Thomas flung his hand to the side, a gesture of anger and denial, warning Satoshi off.

Stephen Thomas crossed the park. He jammed his hands

into his pockets and hunched his shoulders. He felt hurt and confused by Victoria's reaction. He could not think of a way to explain the sudden change to his father.

Back at the park table, Victoria opened her bento box and stared at her lunch. She no longer felt like eating, either.

"How could he *say* that to me?" she cried.

"All he wanted was a little reassurance," Satoshi said. "He can't face this alone, Victoria."

"His father isn't our only responsibility."

"But his father is one of our responsibilities. Stephen Thomas was open with us about it."

"He was. You're right. *He's* right." She sighed. "It's just that I get so tired of Stephen Thomas and Greg playing out the archetypal American father-son relationship. And I still don't see how we're going to be able to juggle fast enough to keep everything in the air on one salary."

"They can't impound the money for long—I'm sure Stephen Thomas is right about that."

"Satoshi, love, you and our partner are brilliant scientists. You are ethical people. Stephen Thomas is charmingly neurotic and too spiritual for his own good—"

"Be fair."

"—and you are both great in bed. But between you, you have the political sense of the average nudibranch. This could take months to get resolved, and it will drain the expedition's energy the whole time. Don't hold your breath waiting for your next pay deposit."

Satoshi had not even opened his lunch. He looked down at his hands, flexed and spread his fingers, turned them over, and stared at his palms.

"I won't," he said. "And I don't see how we're going to keep everything in the air on one salary, either. If we help Greg out—" He hesitated, but Victoria knew as well as he did that they had a responsibility to the elder Gregory. Stephen Thomas had already made the commitment when they invited him into the partnership. "If we help Greg out, the house . . ."

Victoria, scowling, rested her chin on her fists. "Let's not talk about losing the house until we have to."

"Maybe it was a dream all along."

"It was—but it was working, dammit!"

Under ordinary circumstances, they would never have had a hope of buying their house. Nobody living on ordinary incomes—even three ordinary incomes—could afford to buy property. But several years on the expedition, with no living expenses, gave them the chance to put most of their income against the price while they were gone. It was Merit's idea and Merit's plan. Merit even, somehow, found a decent house that a real estate corporation was willing to sell.

"If one of us went back to earth for a few days . . ."

"They will have to send wild horses up here on a transport to get me off *Starfarer*!" Victoria said. "This is exactly what they're hoping will happen, and it's only taken us three hours to start thinking about leaving. If they shoot down our morale, we'll argue, we'll abandon the expedition, we'll go groundside and get new jobs. I wouldn't go back even to lobby for us—they want us out of the sky, no matter what. They're collecting excuses. They have the associates' withdrawal to hold against us already. If the rest of us leave, they'll just come in and claim salvage—"

"I wasn't talking about leaving permanently."

"Let's not talk about leaving at all. If we lose our house, we lose our house. If we lose the expedition . . ."

"You're right," he said. "Of course you're right."

"Besides," Victoria said, trying to smile, "if we lose the expedition we can't afford a house anyway."

They hugged each other, then packed the bento boxes into the AS and sent it home to put the food away for dinner. Victoria wondered if anyone would be hungry then, either.

"The meeting tonight is going to be something," she said.

His graduate students had reappeared by the time Stephen Thomas got back to the lab. He wanted to talk to them, but the tension of having to explain things to his father would emotionally distort everything he said to them. He reached his office. When he touched the door, it crashed open without his meaning to slam it. He hesitated, then turned. All three students stared at him, startled.

"Don't anybody go anywhere," he muttered. "I'll be back in a couple of minutes."

In his office, Stephen Thomas asked Arachne to connect him to earth, and his father. The conversation would be awkward, because of the distance of *Starfarer* from earth and the resulting time delay. His father was no more proficient at holding two simultaneous conversations than was Stephen Thomas.

"Steve? I didn't expect to hear from you."

"How are you, Greg?" Stephen Thomas said. "My partners send their regards."

"Oh. Well. You say hi to Vicky and Satoshi for me."

Stephen Thomas could not help but smile. His father was the only person in the world who called him "Steve"; his father was probably the only person in the world dense enough to keep calling Victoria by a diminutive. He was sure Greg would have shortened Satoshi's name if he could have figured out how to do it.

"Long time," Greg said. "What's the occasion? Have you settled the plans for your visit?"

"That's part of why I called," Stephen Thomas said. "I don't think I'm going to be able to get back to earth again."

"What? Why not? You didn't make it over here the last time you were on earth. You said—"

"I thought you understood about the conference. And how hard it is to reschedule transport trips—"

"What's the problem now? Have you—"

"Greg, have you heard any news today?" Stephen Thomas spoke before his father finished his question.

After the two-second delay, his father replied. "I never pay any attention to the news."

"There's a problem with the starship's operating funds," Stephen Thomas said. "Will you be all right if the next deposit is late?"

This time the delay was more than the two-second light-speed lag.

"What's happened? You're overextended?"

"I'm not! It hasn't anything to do with me directly, but it makes a personal trip out of the question. The money's held up in Washington. I don't know when I'll get paid next."

Again he waited, hoping for nonchalance, reassurance.

"This is cutting pretty close to the bone, Steve," Greg said.

"I'm sorry. I don't have any control . . . I can't . . ." While he was still trying to think of how to explain, the lag began and ended.

"Is it all up to you? In my day, when you got married, you didn't just marry your wife, you married her whole family, too."

"We're members of each other's families, Greg," Stephen Thomas said. "And Satoshi's got the same problem. Everybody up here who's from the U.S. has had their funding impounded."

Greg had taken a while to accept Victoria and Satoshi as individuals; accepting them as partners, and lovers, of his son was taking a good bit longer. Stephen Thomas wondered how Satoshi would react to being referred to as a wife, not to mention how Victoria would react.

"If you'd given me a little notice that you intended to cut me off—"

"Greg, that isn't fair!"

"—I'd've tried to make some other plans."

"That isn't fair," Stephen Thomas said again. Something else Stephen Thomas disliked about voice communication over this distance was that it was impossible to interrupt anyone, impossible to head them off from saying something they might regret, impossible to keep from hearing something he would regret. Stephen Thomas could not even react with anger, because he understood Greg's fear. He had hoped for some understanding, some encouragement, even just a little slack; and he knew he should have known better. All he could do was pretend not to be hurt.

"You don't even have any expenses up there," Greg said. "At least that's what you told me. Haven't you put anything away in all the time since you got out of school?"

"The family's finances are too complicated to explain on long-distance transmission," Stephen Thomas said. "With the impoundment, we aren't going to have much extra."

"It's none of my business, you mean," Greg said.

"That isn't what I said. That isn't even *close*."

"I'll have to move," Greg said. "It will take me a while to find a cheaper place."

"Don't do that!" Stephen Thomas said. "It will cost you more short-term than you can possibly save, and with any luck this will just be a short-term problem. I wouldn't even have bothered you with it except I thought you should hear about the problem from me. I thought you'd be worried."

"I am worried. There's no way I can keep up the rent on this place. I never should have taken it to begin with. I wouldn't have, if you—"

"If you're set on moving, move to Canada!"

Stephen Thomas stopped. He could not even afford an argument right now. Though his hands were steady, he felt as if he were trembling. The trembling began in his center and spread outward, a reaction not of anger or fear but of disappointment and hurt, guilt that he felt though he did not believe he deserved it, and a wish to make everything all right.

"Canada? Forget it. I'm not moving to the ass-end of nowhere just to make things easier on you. If that means—"

"Greg, I'll do what I can, but I just can't manage as much as before. For a while. That's the best I can do."

"And I don't have any choice, do I?"

The web signaled that the communications link had been broken from the other end.

Stephen Thomas hunched down in his chair. When he started getting an ulcer in grad school, he had studied a number of relaxation techniques, ways to control stress, methods of releasing anger and pain. Today none of them worked. The shaking had reached his hands. His chin quivered as he clenched his teeth and tightened his throat and squeezed his eyes shut. He felt like a forlorn child. He despised himself for his reaction. He clenched his fists and jammed them between his knees. Soundlessly he began to cry. Hot fat tears forced themselves out from beneath his eyelids. His nose began to run.

Stephen Thomas thought of himself as an emotional person, a person with open feelings. But he did not often cry. He knew it was supposed to make him feel better, to release endorphins or hormones or enzymes or some damned thing—he knew what he could make all those biochemicals do in his experiments; he did not need to know what they did inside him. But crying never did make him feel better. It made him feel sick and slack and stupid, and he hated it. Other people's crying made him neither uncomfortable nor impatient. The partnership had seen a lot of crying over the past year. Stephen Thomas thought it was probably a good thing that after the accident, one member of the partnership grieved inwardly and alone. Victoria and Satoshi had both needed someone they did not have to comfort.

Stephen Thomas still grieved for Merry, the member of the partnership he had always been closest to, the first of the three he had met. When Merit first took him home to meet Victoria and Satoshi, the experience was disturbingly like being taken home to meet a date's parents for the first time. Never mind that Merry was considerably older than Victoria and Satoshi, who were both older than Stephen Thomas.

It was a long time before he could think fondly of the awkwardness of that first afternoon.

"Are you done now?" he muttered. "Enough maudlin reminiscences?" The tears dried into salty tracks, stinging his skin.

Once in a while one of his students came into his office and cried. For those times, Stephen Thomas kept a couple of clean scraps of silk, remnants of a worn-out shirt. He dug around until he found one, then scrubbed at his face. He wished he could splash cold water over his head without having to see anyone first. But that was impossible.

Now that he had stopped crying he could bring the relaxation techniques into play. He practiced until he felt certain he would not break down again.

He returned to the lab. His students worked steadily, pretending he had not been upset when he arrived and disappeared, pretending not to notice his reappearance.

He crossed to the water fountain, bent down for a drink, and let the stream of water splash over his face. As he straightened, he ducked his head to wipe the droplets away on the shoulder of his shirt. The water plastered a cold patch of thin silk to his skin.

Now everybody in the lab was looking at him.

"They've given us some new problems from ground-side," he said, as he should have said that morning. "We'd better sit down and talk about them."

* * *

Griffith wandered through the places aboard *Starfarer* where people congregated. Everyone expressed complaints and outrage; gossip not only flowered, but formed seeds and dispersed them to sprout anew. Ignored in his guise of Griffith of GAO, Griffith traveled among the members of the expedition, pleased with himself for the chaos his minor suggestion had already caused. Yet the chaos bothered him, too, a little: finally he realized he was disappointed in the reactions he saw. He had assumed everyone would react this way; he had assured his superiors they would. But somewhere he held a suspicion—or had it been a hope?—that they might not.

Without meaning to, he found himself near the hill where Brown and Cherenkov and Thanthavong lived. He walked into the garden. He could always claim to have come by to pay his respects to Ms. Brown. She had acted weird at her party. Maybe she was tired. Maybe she was crazy. Maybe she was senile. She must have taken health exams to be allowed to join the expedition, but maybe the stress of the trip from earth had affected her. Or maybe the exams had made a mistake in passing her. Maybe Griffith could find a use for that.

"Did you need something?"

Griffith leaped around, startled, crouching, ready to react. Immediately he knew he had threatened his cover. He pretended to stumble, catching himself awkwardly.

"Good god, you scared me," he said, forcing a petulant tone into his voice.

"Didn't mean to."

Infinity Mendez stood, brushing the dirt from his ragged kneepads. The rosebush at his feet had laid thin red scratches across his hands and wrists. He avoided looking into Griffith's eyes, and this made Griffith suspect that he had not fooled the gardener in the least. He scared Infinity far more than Infinity scared him, and he knew that if he decided to, he could terrorize the gardener into keeping secrets for him. Maybe even into working on his behalf. Griffith preferred to work alone, and though he would use a terrified ally, he would never trust one.

"I just thought I'd stop by and say hello to Ms. Brown."

"There's some folks already visiting her."

Griffith could not tell if he was being invited in or warned away. He looked toward the hill-house, over Infinity's shoulder, seeking even a glimpse of Cherenkov.

"And Kolya's out," Infinity said in a flat, neutral tone.

"Kolya? You mean General Cherenkov?" He feigned disinterest.

"What are you doing up here?"

Griffith frowned at Infinity Mendez. He was not accustomed to being questioned by gardeners. Come to think of it, he was not accustomed to going to parties to which the gardeners were invited, either. It occurred to him that the starship's extreme democracy had probably gone too far. The word "anarchy" came to mind, and gave him another opening against the expedition.

"What business is it of yours?" Griffith said sharply.

"Sorry," Infinity said, confused and scared. "Just a friendly question."

Griffith thought of saying that he was interested in more important things than whether the service staff put in all their time, but decided to withhold even that much reassurance. Sending somebody all the way to lunar orbit to check on trivia was exactly the sort of thing one of EarthSpace's associates might decide to do.

He gave Infinity a cold, wordless glance and walked away.

Victoria crossed the courtyard and headed toward the cool main room of her house. She hesitated on the threshold, narrowing her eyes with a twinge of annoyance. In the low light, the distillation equipment hunkered on the mats like a giant spider.

She found Stephen Thomas, bare to the waist, sitting crosslegged on the floor in a tumble of silk shirts, carefully picking each one out of the pile, smoothing it, and folding it. He lifted the last one, the turquoise one Victoria had just given him. He stroked his fingertips across the fabric, changing the patterns of reflected light. He folded it fast, tossed it on the stack, picked the stack up and stuffed it into a cloth bag.

All Victoria's annoyance at him evaporated.

"Stephen Thomas."

He jerked the ties shut and knotted them, stood up, and threw the bag in the corner.

"No point in wearing everything out before we even go," he said. "Who knows how long it will be until I can get any more—before we come back, I mean."

What he meant was that he could no longer afford to buy new clothes. No one in the family could, but the restriction would hit Stephen Thomas worst. He looked upon clothing as decoration. It troubled Victoria to see him packing away his pretty shirts. She wished she had something to say to encourage him.

He had on regulation pants, gray twill with a *Starfarer* patch on the front of the thigh. EarthSpace maintained the tradition of its predecessors in designing a patch for each new space mission. *Starfarer*'s was a fractal swirl, flaring wide at its horizontal points, with the EarthSpace logo above and the starship's name below. Stephen Thomas picked up a gray t-shirt from his rumpled bed and dragged it on over his head. It carried the *Starfarer* logo across the chest.

On board the starship, a few people wore the patch, but only newcomers wore the t-shirt. She was surprised to see Stephen Thomas in it because he had been annoyed by it: the design was all right, he said, but who wanted to wear a gray t-shirt?

The real benefit of regulation clothing was that it was free.

"Stephen Thomas," she said. "About this afternoon—"

He interrupted her. "What I said was inexcusable." He reached out to her; Victoria took his hand.

"I love you," she said. "Maybe I don't say so often enough."

"You do," he said. "You tell me, you show me ... But sometimes I can't hear it and I can't see it and I can't believe it."

He put his arms around her and leaned his forehead on her shoulder. She spread her fingers against his back and patted him gently.

When she stepped back, she appraised him. "I must say, you look all right in mufti."

"This isn't mufti—"

"It is for you," she said. "Who's going to recognize you, out of uniform?"

At that, he smiled.

J.D. sat in Nakamura's office, which Victoria had somehow contrived to have opened for her. She tried to work on her novel, but mostly she worried. Too many things had happened too fast; most of them scared and depressed her. She knew too much about the perversion of technology to be confident that the expedition would fend off this assault. She wished she had half Victoria's courage or Stephen Thomas's outrage or Satoshi's calm.

She leaned back and closed her notebook. Her shoulders hurt from leaning over it. The office had no desk, only mats and cushions. If she got her own office, she would ask for one with a desk.

Because of the shortage of wood and the absence of

plastics, the furniture on campus looked odd to newcomers. If she got an office with a desk, the desk would be made of rock foam, a built-in extrusion of floor or wall. The fabric sculpture that served as a chair was far too soft to sit in for long. At first it was comfortable, cushiony; then her back started to hurt. She supposed she could requisition a bamboo chair like the ones in the main room of Victoria's house. Or maybe she would have to make it herself.

She had no reason to have office furniture, because she had no reason to have an office. Her work required no lab or special equipment; she could even get along without Arachne if she had to. She was attached only to the alien contact team, unlike her teammates, who also held departmental positions: Victoria in physics, Satoshi in geography, and Stephen Thomas in genetics.

J.D. had asked to be in the literature department, which could have used a few more members. Like the art department, it was far too small to represent the cultural diversity of earth.

Her request had been turned down. An alien contact specialist did not qualify to be a professor of literature. What she did was too much like science fiction.

J.D. existed in limbo as far as the academic hierarchy of the campus was concerned. None of that bothered her. No matter how democratically the expedition tried to run itself, every department would have its office politics. She felt herself well out of them.

The chancellor had not yet accepted her credentials. J.D. wondered if that was campus politics, or something bigger; or an oversight: nothing at all.

J.D. had to admit that she liked having a place of her own where she could go out and talk to other people if she wanted; and right down the hallway from Victoria's lab, too.

She had no office hours because she had no graduate

students, not even students of Nakamura's to take over. It had been decided, somewhere in the planning of the expedition, that it would be premature to train more alien contact specialists before anyone knew if any aliens existed to be contacted. Even the half-dozen specialists left out of the expedition, back on earth, had—like J.D. herself—begun to diversify.

Her stream of consciousness brought her, as it often did, to the divers. She closed her eyes and asked Arachne for an update.

The news sent her bolting awkwardly from the low, soft chair. She stood in the middle of her bare office, her eyes open, the line to the web broken, but the information still hanging before her like the afterimage of a fire.

9

J.D. sank into the chair, pillowed her head on her crossed arms, and demanded that Arachne make a full search on the subject of the disappearance of the Northwest divers.

She was still there, shivering, when Victoria came looking for her.

"J.D.? A bunch of us are getting together to talk—J.D.? What's wrong?"

"It's the divers . . . They've moved out of their reserve." She managed to smile. "To Canada."

Victoria smiled back. "That's a fine old tradition for political exiles—but why the divers? What's political about living with a pod of porpoises?"

"Orcas," J.D. said. "Nothing, from their point of view . . . Oh, Victoria, I can't talk about this. Maybe Lykos will make some kind of statement, but unless she explains in public—I promised."

"This is why you almost didn't accept my offer to join the team, isn't it?" Victoria said suddenly.

"It was involved." She chuckled sadly. "It's an involved story. It's rococo. One might almost say Byzantine."

Victoria patted her arm. "They made it to Canada, eh? Then they'll be all right. Don't worry about them."

"It's hard not to. They're wonderful, Victoria. They're so completely innocent. I mean that in a good sense. They're untouched by fears that twist us up, they've learned from the orcas what it means to live without hating anyone. But when they come in contact with our world, the innocence turns to naivete."

Victoria let herself rock back so she was sitting on the floor beside J.D.'s chair.

"That could get dangerous."

"I know it. Oh, I *hope* they're all right."

"Tell me about them."

"Most of them are shy—much shyer than the orcas. I got to know one of them well—that was Zev—and I met nearly everyone in his extended family. Zev is different from the others. He's much more extroverted. He used to visit me at my cabin. He likes ice cream. Victoria, I'm making him sound like a pet, and that isn't right at all. He's smart and well educated in the things that matter to the divers. He's the diver I told you about, who wants to travel into space. I miss him . . . At one point we talked about his applying to the expedition."

"But he didn't."

"No. I advised him against it. There isn't enough ocean up here. I think he would have been miserably unhappy. The divers need their freedom. They travel a long way every day. I couldn't keep up unless they chose to let me. No ordinary human can."

"Did you ever think what it would be like to be one of them?"

J.D. hesitated. "All the time. But it's illegal."

"In the States, it's illegal." Victoria gazed at her quizzically.

J.D. wanted to tell her more, but held her silence instead.

"Did your friend apply to *Starfarer*?"

"I'm sure he would have called me if he decided to. He must have left with his family." She sighed. "It's just as well, I guess."

"It would have been interesting to have a diver along with us," Victoria said. "I wish he'd thought of it earlier. And done it."

"He wouldn't have liked it."

"Maybe some of us won't like it. But we'll be here."

"I hope so."

"Do you want to come along to this meeting?"

"I guess so," J.D. said doubtfully.

She pushed herself out of the chair and followed Victoria into the hallway.

"I still can't get through to the chancellor," Victoria said. "It irks me not to be able to get you into your own office."

"The one I have will do fine," J.D. said, following Victoria's lead in making conversation. "Except the furniture. Is it all standard, or can I get something different? Should I build it myself?"

"You can if you like. If you know how. Or call the maintenance department. They'll furnish your office for you." She paused. "Or they would until yesterday. Who knows what today's rule is?"

They left Physics Hill and headed down a flagstone path, side by side.

"I expected the starship to be more automated than it is," J.D. said.

"With things like robotic furniture factories?"

"Yes."

"*Starfarer* isn't big enough. We're planning to take along quite a few spare parts, for the ASes and so on. But we won't have the capability of building them from scratch. With an automated factory you need another whole level of maintenance, either human or machine, to fix it when it goes wrong. No matter how advanced your robotics, human beings are more flexible. A lot of people who aren't scientists wanted to be involved in the expedition. The planning took that into account." She grinned. "Besides, can you imagine how boring it would be if nobody was on board but scientists?"

J.D. made a noncommittal noise. It would be bad manners to point out that most of the scientists on board associated mostly with other scientists.

Victoria stopped short. "A moment—" Her eyes went out of focus and her face relaxed into a blank expression.

Her attention returned. "Damn!" she whispered. She looked shaken. "Come on, let's go!" She sprinted across the grass, ignoring the path.

J.D. pounded along beside her. "What's wrong?"

"I set Arachne to signal me if we got any more orders. The chancellor has forbidden gatherings of more than three people. This is outrageous!" She slowed so J.D. could keep up.

Like most people, J.D. needed to stand still and focus her attention inside her mind in order to communicate with Arachne. She would have to wait till they reached her destination to read the orders.

She had never noticed before that swimming and running used muscles differently, and she was used to swimming. She induced a pulse of the metabolic enhancer and gasped for extra air as the adrenaline hit.

"It really burns me," Victoria said, sounding not the least out of breath. "The U.S. demanded that we run the expedition under your constitution, and now it's breaking its own articles left and right. Who do they think they are?"

At the large hummock that covered the genetics department, she slowed and stopped. J.D. stopped beside her, still breathing heavily, her heart pounding from the enhancer. When she had caught her breath, she straightened up.

"We think we're powerful and rich, I'm afraid," she said. She felt both attacked and embarrassed because she had no defense. "It's an old habit."

Victoria looked abashed. "I shouldn't jump down your throat about it," she said.

They hurried into Stephen Thomas's office. Satoshi and Feral Korzybski had already arrived. Professor Thanthavong stood by the window, staring out, her arms folded. Iphigenie DuPre let herself gently into a worn bamboo chair, moving with caution outside zero-g.

Stephen Thomas stomped in. He stripped off his gray *Starfarer* t-shirt and attacked it with a pair of dissecting scissors. Like Zev, he had fine gold hair on his chest and his forearms.

"There's not a goddamned decent pair of scissors in the place," he said. He sawed at the neckband of the t-shirt. The crystal at the hollow of his throat changed from black to red to blue.

"What are you doing?" J.D. said.

"Complying with regulations." He ripped away the last few inches of the neckband and set to work on the sleeves.

J.D. closed her eyes and read the new orders. First, the prohibition against meetings. Second: "Starting immediately, personnel of *Starfarer* will wear standard-issue clothing. Only regulation apparel will be tolerated." Third: "All faculty members will immediately suspend current research and prepare detailed papers describing the defense applications and implication of their work."

"You'd better shut the door," Victoria said bitterly.

"I think we should leave the damned door open," Stephen Thomas said.

"I think we're in for a fight," Satoshi said. "The clothing rule is trivial—"

"Speak for yourself," Stephen Thomas said.

"—but forbidding public assembly, and suspending research . . . This is serious."

J.D. sank down on the thick windowsill, her shoulders slumping. "I don't know what to do," she said. "My work doesn't *have* any defense applications, and nobody issued me any standard clothes. I didn't know there was such a thing."

"Don't worry about it, J.D.," Stephen Thomas said. "The orders are obviously illegal." He put on the shredded t-shirt, inside out. The printed emblem showed faintly through the wrong side of the fabric. "How do you like my 'regulation apparel'?"

Thanthavong turned away from the window. She was wearing a gray jumpsuit with *Starfarer*'s insignia on the left chest.

"The orders may be judged illegal." She spoke in a calm and reasoned tone. "But defying them, especially publicly, could cause us a great deal of trouble before we ever get to court, much less win."

"Professor, don't you think they're just trying to provoke us?" Victoria said. "Neither Chancellor Blades nor EarthSpace has any authority to tell us who we can talk to or what research we're allowed, never mind what we wear!"

"Victoria, have you read your contract?"

"Sure," Victoria said. "I mean I skimmed it when it arrived. It was about a hundred megabytes of legalese, who ever reads that stuff? EarthSpace said do you want to go on the expedition? and I said sure and they said sign here, so I did." She stopped, abashed by the admission, then looked around and realized that no one else, except Thanthavong, had read the contract through.

"The standard contract gives them a certain authority over you and your actions."

"The authority only extends as far as they can get somebody to enforce it," Stephen Thomas said.

"You can be as flippant as you like, Stephen Thomas," Thanthavong said. "But EarthSpace can ask any of the primary governmental associates to declare martial law."

The comment astonished everyone but Feral.

Thanthavong continued. "If they declare martial law and send troops—"

"Troops!" Satoshi said. "Good lord—!"

"—to enforce it, I think that our chances of continuing with the expedition are vanishingly small."

"You mean we're screwed," Stephen Thomas said.

"Well put."

"You aren't exaggerating, are you?" Iphigenie said. "You believe they may send armed forces to take us over."

"I think the possibility is measurable."

For a few moments, no one could think of anything else to say.

"I don't understand why the chancellor decided these orders were necessary in the first place," Satoshi said. "Never mind whether he'll get away with them."

"It's the meeting tonight," Victoria said. "They don't want us to hold it. The other stuff is just for distraction."

"It's more than the meeting," Feral said.

"What can you tell us about this, Mr. Korzybski?" Thanthavong asked.

"It begins with the divers."

J.D. started. "What do the divers have to do with anything?"

"They applied for political asylum in Canada—"

"I know, but—"

"That's an embarrassment to the U.S. government. Which doesn't want to be embarrassed twice in a row. So *you* get the flak—more restrictions. I can't tell you where I heard this. I haven't been able to confirm it, but it feels right. The rumor is that the divers fled because if they stayed they'd be coerced into spying."

Victoria turned to J.D. "Did you know about this?"

J.D. stared at the floor. "If Lykos makes a public statement about why the divers left, I can talk about what I know. Otherwise, I can't. Victoria, it doesn't matter—whether I knew or not, I wouldn't have made this connection. I should have, but . . ."

"We're a resource," Victoria said. "We are. The starship is. The divers were a resource. Governments can tolerate unexploited resources. But not lost ones. Somebody has decided that letting the expedition proceed is equivalent to losing *Starfarer*."

"So now they don't intend to allow us to proceed," Iphigenie said.

"I don't think so."

"But—" J.D. heard someone in the hall. As if she were a conspirator, as if she were breaking a reasonable law by sitting in a room and talking with her co-workers, she fell silent and glanced toward the doorway. Her reaction caused everyone else to look in the same direction.

And so Gerald Hemminge appeared in a moment of quiet during which they were all staring at the doorway, during which it looked as if everyone, not just J.D., felt frightened and guilty.

"Perhaps you haven't heard the new rules," Gerald said. "Dr. Thanthavong, I'm sorry to come twice in one day bearing unwelcome news—"

"We heard the damned rules, Gerald—ow!" Stephen Thomas winced when Victoria elbowed him, too late to shut him up.

Gerald scowled. "Haven't you any loyalty to anything? You've all put me in an unpleasant position."

"I've about had it with you accusing me of treason every time I disagree with you!" Stephen Thomas said.

He rose, but Victoria put one hand gently on his arm and drew him down again.

Gerald backed one fast step into the hall. "I can hardly pretend I never saw you."

"You could," Stephen Thomas said, sounding calmer than he looked. "But you won't."

"Bloody right," Gerald said. "You have a great deal to learn about conspiracy. Perhaps you might close the door next time." He hurried away.

"As laws of conspiracy go," Feral said, "closing the door is a good one to start with."

Victoria buried her face in her hands, laughing. Satoshi started to chuckle, too, and soon everyone but J.D. was laughing. J.D. saw nothing funny about being reported to whoever represented the law on *Starfarer*.

"What's he going to do?" J.D. asked.

"Write a memo," Stephen Thomas said.

"You aren't taking this very seriously."

"Bloody right," Stephen Thomas said in exactly the same tone of voice Gerald had used.

"You could have let him lecture us, Stephen Thomas, instead of insulting him," Thanthavong said. "We could have thanked him sincerely for correcting us. That way we would have a few more hours before it became obvious that we intend to defy the orders."

Stephen Thomas looked abashed. Then he smiled, and J.D. wondered how anyone could see that smile and not let him get away with anything he wanted.

"I'm sorry," he said. "It's just that Gerald *asks* for it, and I can't resist."

"It is not necessary," Thanthavong said, unmoved, "to take advantage of *every* opportunity with which one is presented."

"*Do* we intend to defy the order?" J.D. wished her voice did not sound so thin and scared.

They looked at each other.

"You are all young," Thanthavong said. "You have your achievements ahead of you. If we defy the order and fail, you will find that you have made life difficult for yourselves. No one could blame you if you acceded to what may become inevitable."

"Is that what you plan to do?" Victoria sounded shocked.

"No," Thanthavong said. "On *Starfarer*, I have been able to work—to do real work, the work I spent my life preparing for—for the first time in many years. I cannot go back to notoriety and promoting good causes. Nor will I pervert my science to war. My cause is the expedition."

"You aren't alone," Victoria said.

"No," Satoshi said. "You're not." A display formed over the desk. "J.D. had a great idea. There's my report."

He had sent a single sentence to Arachne:

"My research has no defense applications."

Despite their defiance, the group in Stephen Thomas's office could not help but be affected by the orders. They left the genetics building one by one: Thanthavong, then Satoshi, looking overly casual; Iphigenie, and Victoria close behind her. Feral hesitated by the doorway, both anxious and excited.

As the office emptied, J.D. contacted Arachne for an update on the divers. Nothing further had appeared on the public news services: no statement by Lykos, no confirmation of the rumors Feral had heard, no message from Zev. Until the divers spoke out, J.D. felt she should remain silent about what she knew. She wished she had remained silent about them from the beginning. Then none of this would have happened.

She should have seen this coming. It was her job to make connections between apparently disparate events. She should have realized, as Feral had, that the effect of the divers' flight could spread to the expedition.

I let myself get too close, J.D. thought. I got sidetracked into . . . personal considerations.

As she was about to break the link, Arachne signaled her with a message.

It was from Lykos.

J.D. hesitated before accepting it.

Why am I so frightened? she thought. They got away, they're safe, and I said nothing that could have put them in more danger.

She traced her reaction deeper: she was afraid some observer might violate privacy laws, record her communication with the divers, and brand her a troublemaker.

But she had already crossed that line.

J.D. accepted the communication.

"J.D. Sauvage: where is Zev? His family has had no word from him since he stayed behind to join your expedition. We are concerned."

The message ended. J.D. looked up blankly. Nearby, Stephen Thomas and Feral talked together. Feral glanced across at her and grinned.

"I think it's safe out there," he said. "Everybody else has slunk off like spies."

Stephen Thomas looked over his shoulder, also smiling, but his smile vanished as soon as he saw her.

"Good god, J.D., what's the matter?"

"A friend of mine has disappeared."

Searching for the connections she had failed to see earlier, she told Stephen Thomas and Feral what had happened.

"I don't see that there's anything to be worried about," Stephen Thomas said. "So he went off by himself and didn't tell his mother. How old is he?"

"Eighteen."

Stephen Thomas shrugged. "Sounds normal to me. He's growing up."

"But that isn't how divers act."

"That isn't how most divers act. But you've just said most of the divers went to Canada. He stayed behind. So he isn't 'most divers.' Q.E.D."

"He wouldn't scare Lykos."

"Not deliberately. Maybe he forgot."

"I guess it's possible . . ." But she did not believe it. She could not *make* herself believe that Zev forgot to tell Lykos he was all right, forgot to ask if his family had made it to Canada, forgot to tell J.D. he was going to try to join the expedition, even forgot to check his mail.

"No," she said. "It sounds perfectly sensible when you say it, but it couldn't have happened that way."

"If he tried to apply to the expedition, and he's only eighteen, they turned him down," Stephen Thomas said. "So he's probably on his way to join his family."

J.D. made connections she wished she could have overlooked. "Or he applied, and they realized if they kept him, they'd have a hold on the other divers. And what about Chandra?"

"The artist? What does she have to do with this?"

"She disappeared too. At the same time. She was supposed to meet me at my cabin, but I'd already left. Feral, you remember, you reminded me about her on the transport the other day. I tried to call her, I left a message. She never replied, but I didn't think anything of it. Now . . ."

"We've got enough to worry about without adding conspiracy theories!"

"If the diver is being held," Feral said, "if Chandra saw something she wasn't supposed to . . ."

"Where *are* they?" J.D. cried. "How am I going to find them?"

"If your friend wanted to join the expedition," Stephen Thomas said, "why the hell didn't he wait till he got asylum in Canada, and apply from there?"

"I don't know. He probably didn't realize there was any danger. It's a long swim to Canada, and he was probably in a hurry. Maybe he came ashore to catch the bus into town! And somebody was waiting for him."

She looked at Feral for confirmation. He shrugged unhappily.

"It could have happened that way."

J.D. rose.

"What are you going to do?"

"Find him, of course. Feral, will you help me?"

"I'll try," he said. He looked troubled.

"What?"

"Nothing. Nothing that hasn't happened before. But never on this scale."

"*What?*"

"My communication budget is running low."

"You can use my credit. Come on."

"You're going to try to find this guy from way out here?" Stephen Thomas said.

"From way down there, if necessary."

J.D. left the office.

Stephen Thomas followed. "J.D.! If you go to earth now, you might not be able to get back!"

"I know it. I can't help it."

"But—"

She swung angrily around. He stopped short.

"If he's in trouble, it's my fault! If he's in trouble and Lykos finds out where he is before I do, she and the other divers will leave whatever haven they've found to go and get him."

"Why?" His voice was full of skepticism and amazed disbelief.

"Because he's part of their family. Because that's how divers are."

The derision vanished from his expression. "I wish—" he said. "Never mind. But if there's any way I can help you, I will."

"Thank you," she said, startled into curtness.

"Iphigenie!"

The sailmaster turned and waited for Victoria.

"Are you going back out?"

"Mm-hmm. I feel more comfortable watching the sail."

"Would you take a look at this?" Victoria handed Iphigenie the copy of her new string calculations.

"What is it?"

"Results out of a new symbolic manipulation. Usable results."

"Why do you want me to look at them?" she said. "I'm in charge of intrasystem navigation. Not transition."

"I ran some other numbers. If you use the sail during lunar passage, we could take this approach . . ."

Iphigenie looked at Victoria, looked at the copy, and gave it back.

"That isn't a good idea," she said.

"But it's faster, more efficient, and . . . sooner." The copy lay cool in Victoria's hand. "Just take a look. Please."

"But transition's already planned! And I'm not finished testing the sails." Iphigenie did not take the copy. "It's too risky!"

Victoria laughed. "Riskier than what we're already planning?"

"I suppose not," Iphigenie said, nonplussed. "But why do you want to change things?"

"Have you figured out whether *Starfarer* can outrun a transport if it has to?"

"No."

"It can't," Victoria said. "And we won't be out of range for weeks."

"Of course not. We planned it that way. We have a lot of supplies still to take on."

"So if . . . what Professor Thanthavong said, happens, we'd have no way to stop it, eh?"

Iphigenie pushed her hands across the tight braids of her black hair.

"It won't come to that. It *can't*."

"Don't be naive."

"Victoria, if we're called back, I'm the one who has to take the order. I'm the one who has to reverse the sail and decelerate . . . I don't want to do that."

"I know you don't. But everything that's happened makes me think that's what's next. No matter what we do."

Iphigenie pointed with her chin toward Victoria's hand, toward the copy of the new calculations.

"Sooner, you said?"

"Much sooner. The string section we're aiming for now is way to hell and gone out by the orbit of Mars. If you change the sails as we go around the moon, if we use the new solution . . . we'd only need one pass around the moon."

"One!"

"Yes. We'd be aiming for the nearest point on the string."

Iphigenie frowned. Victoria could imagine her setting up the problem in her mind, solving it. The sailmaster rocked back on her heels, astonished.

"Tomorrow! We'd encounter the string late tomorrow! But we're not ready. We're not supplied, half our people are gone."

"We're being set up to be stopped!"

"What about the people who are *planning* to stay behind? What about the rest of us? Everyone has agreed to a certain plan. If we do this secretly, the expedition members will be people who have been lied to and abducted. They'd rebel, and I couldn't blame them."

"I don't intend to do this in secret. A transport docks tomorrow, just before lunar passage." Victoria discussed outrageous possibility with deliberate calm. "After passage it can leave again, right on schedule. Anybody who wants to can go."

Iphigenie gazed blankly through her.

"The alternative," Victoria said, "is getting slapped down to low earth orbit."

"Are you sure of your solution?"

"Yes."

Victoria held out her hand and opened her fingers. As if in slow motion, Iphigenie reached out and took the copy.

"That is," Victoria said, "I'm as sure of those numbers as I was of the others."

Iphigenie snorted. She, like everyone on board, was aware of the inherent uncertainty in cosmic string solutions. The uncertainty was small . . . but it existed.

"I'll look at it," Iphigenie said.

"Thank you."

Iphigenie started away. A few paces on, she turned back.

"You know, Victoria, if I agree to this, we'll be at Tau Ceti without a complete test of the sails. Navigating will depend on a propulsion system that's nearly experimental."

"But you built them. You're the best."

"Yes. Except once you get beyond a certain size, solar sails are all different. You cannot know for sure how they'll behave." She tossed the copy in the air and caught it.

"That's the only copy of those numbers," Victoria said.

Iphigenie caught the copy and lowered it carefully. Hard copies were abuse-resistant, but they had limits.

"I didn't have to join this expedition, you know," she said grumpily. "I could have stayed home and spent my money."

"I know. Why did you join?"

"Because just building the sails wasn't enough. Nor was spending money." She put the copy in her pocket and patted it. "I make no promises."

* * *

J.D. gave Feral access to her credit account so he could get in touch with his mysterious sources. J.D. herself made a call she wished she could put off.

She expected to have to leave a message for Lykos through the web. Instead, she reached the diver quickly, voice and screen both. Lykos looked strange with her pale hair dry and standing out in loose ringlets, instead of soaked with seawater, slicked against her skull.

"You haven't heard from him, have you?"

J.D. waited through the annoying, awkward pause.

"No," Lykos said. "I would have let you know. I have been searching."

"Lykos, I think it's possible that he's been kidnapped."

When J.D.'s message reached Lykos, the expression on the diver's narrow, wild face changed from distraught to confused to angry.

"Only one entity would do such a thing, and 'kidnapped' is not the proper word for it. Let us speak plainly, J.D. Because of his family's actions, he has been taken into custody, arrested—he is under restraint."

"It's possible—but if they offer to trade his freedom for your return, you've got to say no and you've got to make it public. You've got to make everything public."

"At the risk of Zev's life?"

"The one thing they can't afford is to hurt him! If we can get any proof—even any evidence—that he's under arrest, they'll have to let him go. He hasn't done anything!"

"He has refused to spy for them."

"He's got no obligation to spy for them, and they have no authority to make him. Oh, Lykos, don't let them use your loyalties against you."

The diver spread her fingers and smoothed her springy hair with the translucent swimming webs. J.D. had seen divers on their return from weeks-long trips with the whales, and she had never seen anyone as drained with exhaustion as Lykos.

"We cannot abandon him, J.D."

"I know it. I do know it. I can't either. I promise you—"

"No more promises! I am finished with humans' promises." Lykos cut the connection. Her image faded.

J.D. collected herself. She could not blame Lykos for her reaction, but it upset her nonetheless. She glanced over at Feral. He had only been working for a few minutes. Nevertheless, J.D. wanted to ask if he had found anything yet. She knew he would tell her when he did. If he did.

J.D. spent the afternoon running up a large debit against her account, trying to track Zev down. She was afraid to spend too much. If she went back to earth, she would have to pay for the trip herself.

After several hours' useless work, she canceled all the communications and cut herself off from Arachne. She looked over at Feral, who had barely moved in an hour. His eyelids flickered. He was lost in the web, lost in a fugue of communication.

Infinity sat cross-legged under a spindly aspen sapling. The light faded around him as the sun tubes changed from daytime orientation to night.

He felt discouraged. Maybe nothing would have been settled at the meeting tonight, or maybe everyone would have agreed that *Starfarer* should be given over to the military. But at least they would have come to some resolution if there had *been* a meeting.

He smelled smoke. Burning was dangerous on the starship, so he followed the smell. The scent was vaguely familiar, but not a grass fire.

Kolya Cherenkov sat on a boulder beneath the overhanging branch of a magnolia tree. He held a thin burning black stick cupped in his hand. As Infinity watched, Kolya tapped the cigarette on a projection of the boulder, adding a few feathery flakes to a small pile of ashes. Infinity watched, fascinated, as Kolya lifted the cigarette to his lips and drew smoke into his mouth, into his lungs.

Infinity had found other tiny scatterings of ashes and, now and then, smelled a wisp of smoke. But he had never actually seen anyone smoke a cigarette, not for real, only in very old, unedited movies. Back in Brazil, when he was a child, his adult relatives had passed around a pipe of tobacco on rare occasion. The smoke made them act as if they were mildly drunk. He wondered if Kolya would act drunk; he could hardly imagine it.

Kolya breathed curls of smoke from his mouth and nose.

The smell was unpleasant, much harsher and stronger than what Infinity recalled of the pipe smoke. He wondered why people in old movies blew smoke at each other. He would not like it if a lover blew this smell into his face. Suddenly he sneezed.

Startled, Kolya turned. He closed his cupped fingers around the cigarette. He let his hand hang idly down. He blushed.

"I didn't mean to scare you," Infinity said. "I just . . ." It was all too obvious that Kolya preferred no one to know about his cigarette.

The cosmonaut brought the cigarette back into view.

"I suppose I had to be discovered eventually, but I hope you won't say anything about my . . . vice."

"Everybody has vices." Infinity believed in leaving people alone. Nevertheless, he was shocked to see Kolya doing something as dangerous as smoking. You could get cured of the damage nowadays, but the damage was unpleasant, as was the cure. So was the cause, as far as Infinity was concerned. Nobody had ever succeeded in removing all the factors that caused lung damage and still ending up with something anyone wanted to smoke.

Kolya drew in one last lungful of smoke, then stubbed the half-smoked cigarette out against the black lunar stone. He put the cigarette away.

"I only have a few of these left," he said wistfully, "and then I'll have to stop, for I won't be able to get any more. And I'm an old man. I doubt I'll come back from our trip."

Not meaning to, not wanting to, Infinity felt a sudden anger at the cosmonaut. Kolya never participated in campus meetings, never made his preferences public, never criticized the attacks on *Starfarer*. He did not care that tonight's meeting had been canceled, that meetings had been forbidden. He probably did not even know. He would not have come to the meeting if it had been held.

"Maybe there won't *be* any trip!" Infinity exclaimed.

"What? Why?"

"Don't you know? How can you not know they want to turn us into a warship? How can you spend all your time with that Griffith guy and not know he's trouble? Florrie took one look at him and knew he was after us!"

"Ah. I did wonder why he was here . . . But all he seemed interested in was plunging me into nostalgia." He rubbed his fingertips across a smooth place on the rock; he raised his head and gazed across the cylinder, past the dimming sun tubes. Far-overhead lakes, ruffled by a breeze, sparkled gray with the last light.

"If you want this expedition to happen," Infinity said, "you've got to help us. Only I don't know how you can. Maybe it's too late."

Kolya made a low, inarticulate sound of understanding, perhaps of acceptance.

"Infinity," he said kindly, "you are making it most difficult for me to retire as a hermit."

Infinity said nothing.

"There is a meeting tonight?"

"There *was*. It's illegal, now."

"Truly? I have not done anything seriously illegal in many years. Shall we attend this meeting?"

He rose and headed for the amphitheater. After a moment, Infinity shrugged and followed him.

10

"Feral!"

J.D. shook the reporter's shoulder.

"Feral! Come out of it!"

Hooked deep into Arachne's web, he jerked upright as if awakened from a deep sleep.

"What?"

"You're going to have to stop."

"Why? No, J.D., I've got some good leads. A little more time—"

"I'm sorry. It's impossible. This is costing too much, and it isn't doing any good. I'm reserving a place on the next transport to earth. They won't sell me a ticket if I've run my credit past its limit."

"But Stephen Thomas said—"

"And I said I have to go!"

"Okay."

Dejected, they stared at each other.

"You like him, don't you?" Feral said suddenly.

"What? Who?" J.D. was confused by the abrupt change of subject.

Feral grinned. "Stephen Thomas. You like him."

"I like almost everybody I've met up here so far."

"That isn't what I meant."

J.D. shrugged, uncomfortable. "I think he's a very attractive man. What has that got to do with anything?"

"Are you going to do anything about it?"

"Don't be ridiculous." J.D. felt herself blushing. "What kind of a question is that? Are you a stringer for gossip magazines, too?"

Feral laughed. "No. I was just curious."

"I have more important things to think about!"

Feral grinned at her, unabashed. "I think he's beautiful, myself." He jumped to his feet. "I'm starving! What time is it?"

"It's almost eight. The time the meeting would have started, if we were still having a meeting." Just in case, she checked to see if the new rule had been reversed. It had not.

"I didn't get any lunch," Feral said. "I'm going to go find something to eat. Want to come along?"

"No, thanks. I'm not hungry."

"Don't give up, J.D. I put out a lot of feelers. Some of them might touch something."

"I hope so." He regarded the search for Zev as a game to be won, and no great tragedy if he lost it; nevertheless, J.D. appreciated his help. "Thank you, Feral. Whatever happens."

"See you later."

He can go on to the next story, J.D. thought. But I can't.

She rose and paced back and forth. She wished she were near the ocean, where she could swim until she was exhausted. Sometimes exhaustion helped clarify her thoughts: it left her with no energy for confusion or extraneous information.

She made contact with Arachne again and requested a place on tomorrow's transport. It was full. Almost empty coming in, full going out. Under any other circumstances she would have taken the news with resignation and waited for the next ship. This time, she used her status, demanded a place, and got it.

She smiled bitterly. The chancellor's refusal to accept her credentials had worked to her benefit, if being helped to leave *Starfarer* was a benefit. As far as the records were concerned, she was still attached to the State Department, still an associate ambassador.

She had nothing to do now except wait, and worry. She tried to put Zev out of her mind.

She could not help but think about what Feral had said. She wondered if she were as transparent to anyone besides the reporter. Another blush crept up her neck and face. If Victoria had noticed, or Satoshi . . . they must have thought her reaction to Stephen Thomas terribly amusing. She did not worry particularly that Stephen Thomas had noticed. Extremely beautiful people learned to blank it out when ordinary people found them attractive. J.D. supposed it was the only way they could manage.

She would have to get over his extraordinary physical beauty. He was a real person, not some entertainment star she would never have to worry about meeting.

Maybe it won't matter, she thought, downcast again. I have to go to earth. I may never make it back into space; I may never see Stephen Thomas, or Victoria, or Satoshi, again after tomorrow.

"J.D.!" Victoria said.

J.D. jumped.

"Hi, sorry, didn't mean to scare you," Victoria said. "Do you want to come to the meeting with me?"

"I thought there wasn't going to be one."

"There isn't supposed to be one. But everybody I've talked to is going anyway."

"I don't know . . . are you sure—? I mean—damn!" She stopped and blew out her breath. "All right." What else can they do to me, she thought, even if they do decide I'm a troublemaker?

"Did you find your friend?"

"No." J.D. started to tell Victoria that she was leaving in the morning, to find Zev and try to free him, but she could not bring herself to say it.

They crossed the campus. As they walked up the last small hill before the amphitheater, they heard voices welling up and tumbling past like water.

"Maybe we should outlaw meetings more often," Victoria said drily. "Usually we only take up the first few rows of seats."

J.D. followed her along a path cut around the hillside. The daylight was slowly fading.

"Couldn't you run the meeting electronically, rather than having to get everybody together, having to build a place— and what do you do if it rains?"

"If it rains, we usually postpone the meeting. If it rains tonight, I suspect we'll all sit here and put up with getting wet. Every hill had to be sculpted; we designed one as an amphitheater. Sometimes people put on plays. As for meeting electronically . . . you haven't been to a lot of electronic meetings, have you?"

J.D. remembered in time not to shake her head. "A few. They worked all right."

"Small groups?"

"Five or six people."

"That's about the limit. Somehow it's easier to interrupt somebody's image than to interrupt them face-to-face." She gestured at the flat crown of the next hill, coming into sight as they circled the smaller rise. "Besides, if people have to put in some physical effort to attend, the ones who come are more committed. The meetings are smaller, and believe me that makes a difference."

"Not tonight, though."

"No. Not tonight. Satoshi! Stephen Thomas!"

Victoria's partners, twenty meters ahead, stopped and waited for Victoria and J.D. to catch up.

The path brought them to the foot of a circular slope, grass-covered, shaped like an ancient crater. Trails led up its sides to tunnel openings, where a couple of dozen people milled around on the hillside.

"What are they doing?" J.D. asked.

"Beats me," Satoshi said. "I thought it was the custom to go inside and *then* mill around."

About half the people already there wore either standard-issue jumpsuits or t-shirts and reg pants. J.D. wished she had taken Thanthavong's advice and found some regulation clothing to put on, but the whole subject had vanished from her mind while she searched for Zev.

Neither Victoria nor Satoshi had changed: Victoria wore a tank top and shorts that had started out as reg pants but were no longer recognizable; Satoshi had on baggy cammies with all the pockets, and another, or the same, sleeveless black t-shirt. Stephen Thomas wore his formerly regulation clothes as an insult to the orders. Though he had turned the t-shirt right side out, he had obliterated "EarthSpace," and he had painted designs on the legs of his trousers as well.

They joined the group outside the entrance to the amphitheater.

"What's the matter?" Victoria asked Crimson Ng.

"Look." The artist nodded toward the opening of the entry tunnel.

A piece of string blocked the amphitheater.

"All the entrances are like that."

Whoever had put up the string had chosen a symbol far more powerful than any gate or lock, a symbol for the fragile rule of law.

Victoria pulled down the string. One part of her tried to justify her actions, but another knew she had passed a boundary she had never wanted to cross. She felt neither anger nor triumph, only sadness.

She walked into the amphitheater. Satoshi and Stephen Thomas and the others followed.

Victoria had never been the first person inside the amphitheater. It felt bigger than usual. The sound of her sandals scraping the ramp echoed in the silence.

The amphitheater, completely circular with rising ranks of terraces all around, contained only a small platform in its center. All the plays presented here had a limited number of cast members.

Victoria headed toward the left entrance and Stephen Thomas went to the right. Satoshi loped down the ramp, across the stage, and up the other side to the opposite entrance.

On a hillside facing the amphitheater, Griffith watched Satoshi Lono of the alien contact team pull the string barricade away from one of the entrances.

Griffith had decided not to attend the meeting. Though he could not listen in, in real-time, since there would be no voice link for a meeting that was not supposed to exist, he would be able to watch the recording. He would do nothing to interfere with the meeting or to alter its course. He would not inject the presence of a stranger.

Then he saw Nikolai Cherenkov climbing the hill.

Griffith bolted to his feet and stood poised between duty and desire. For one of the few times in his life, the desire won out.

When Griffith reached the amphitheater, he could not find Cherenkov in the crowd. Disappointed, he stood in the shadows and watched.

Victoria hurried through the far tunnel. Outside the fourth entrance, her colleagues watched as she pulled down the barrier and wrapped the string around her wrist.

"Is the prohibition off?"

"No." She went back inside.

Ordinarily she and Satoshi and Stephen Thomas remained apart at meetings, preferring to speak and act as individuals. Tonight they made an exception, sitting together as the alien contact team. She rejoined her partners and J.D. Stephen Thomas lounged on the wide seat, stretching his long legs.

"I didn't think there were this many of us left on campus," Victoria said as the seats began to fill.

People gathered in clusters to argue and talk.

"Why isn't anyone standing on the platform?" J.D. asked Victoria.

Victoria glanced down the slope. "Nobody ever stands on the platform."

"Isn't it for whoever's speaking? Whoever runs the meeting?"

"No. We don't work that way, with one person trying to direct the rest, or only one person allowed to talk at a time." She smiled. "Though you have to be willing to face disapproval if you interrupt someone who's interesting, and somebody eventually talks to anybody who interrupts a lot."

The amphitheater filled quickly. Infinity Mendez, passing the team, did a double take.

"What's that?" he said to Stephen Thomas, with a gesture of the chin toward the decorations on his pants. "War paint?"

"In a manner of speaking," Stephen Thomas said. "Any suggestions?"

"Wrong tribe," Infinity said, and found himself a seat.

"Did he mean he's from the wrong tribe to ask, or I picked the wrong tribe to use symbols from?" Stephen Thomas said, bemused.

"You're the cultural expert in this family, my dear," Satoshi said.

Stephen Thomas grinned. "Maybe I should look up some samurai symbols."

"Maybe I should get you an ostrich feather headdress," Victoria said.

"From Africa?"

"Of course not. I wouldn't know which band to choose. I meant from the Queen's Guards."

"Hey," he said, "if you're really going to go ethnic on me, get me—" Without any signal, the amphitheater fell silent around him. Stephen Thomas lowered his voice to a whisper. "Get me a red Mountie jacket."

The lower third of the amphitheater had filled; another hundred or so people sat scattered around the remaining two-thirds of the terraces. It was a less colorful group than usual: people of all shapes and colors would ordinarily have been wearing clothes of all designs and colors. Victoria felt comforted and strengthened by the number of her colleagues who complied with the trivial rule, but broke the important one.

By a couple of minutes after the scheduled beginning of the original meeting, all the participants sat together silently in the dusk.

Suddenly a wide patch of bright sunlight illuminated the meeting. The sun tubes spotlighted the amphitheater and left the rest of the campus dark.

Victoria took a deep breath and ignored the warning of the light.

"Victoria Fraser MacKenzie," she said. She remained sitting; though she projected her voice, she spoke in a normal tone. After a pause of a few seconds, she continued. "Today's changes, particularly the impoundment of funds, affect my family and my work just as they affect everyone on the expedition, whether or not they're citizens of the United States. I'm angry, and I'm frightened by what the actions imply. I think we're expected to panic. I think we must not. I think we must continue as if nothing had happened.

And I think it would be polite to send a message to the United States, expressing our regret that they are no longer financially able to participate in the expedition."

Victoria kept her tone serious and solemn, and did not react to the murmur of appreciative laughter.

Other members of the expedition said their names and aired their frustration and anger.

Some of the Americans defended their government and some apologized for it; some of the non-Americans excoriated it; several people explained, unnecessarily, the political situation that had caused the trouble. Some defended the right of any associate to withhold funds, to which the response was that no one questioned the new U.S. president's right to act as he had. It was his good sense they wondered about.

"Infinity Mendez." He paused after saying his name. "I think it's true that we can't panic. But if we pretend nothing's happened, if we don't fight back, they'll take more and more and more until they leave us nothing." The intensity of his soft voice left the amphitheater in absolute silence. He raised his head and glanced around. "I think . . ." Tension grabbed his shoulders; something more than shyness silenced him. He ducked his head. "I have nothing more to say."

"My name is Thanthavong." The geneticist paused. "We have a guest."

Thanthavong drew the attention of the meeting to Griffith, standing in the shadows at the entrance of a tunnel. For a moment he looked as if he might try to fade into the shadows completely. Instead, he moved forward and took a stance both belligerent and defensive.

"I have a right to be here," he said. "More right than you do. I'm a representative of the U.S. government, and this ship was built with U.S. funds."

"Partially," Thanthavong said. "But this starship is a public institution of the world, and by law and custom our meetings are open. No one has suggested that you have no right to attend. But you are not a member of the expedition and I am inviting you to introduce yourself."

"My name is Griffith. I'm from the GAO."

"You are welcome to sit down, Griffith . . . if you wish to observe more closely."

He sat, reluctantly, on the top terrace, as near to the exit as he could be. He must have heard the soft, irritable mutter that rose when he announced his occupation. Gradually the complaints fell to silence.

"Satoshi Lono." Satoshi paused. "If we fight—what form of action will we take? Legal battles? Public relations? If we consider physical resistance, where do we set the limits?"

The silence that answered the words "physical resistance" lasted some time. Then, inevitably, people began to look toward Infinity, the first person to mention fighting. Uncomfortable at the focus of the attention, he glanced up the slope toward Griffith.

"I can't say," Infinity said. "I don't know."

"Satoshi, what do you mean when you say 'physical resistance'?" Thanthavong opened her strong, square hands. "Bare hands against military weapons?"

"I had in mind civil disobedience, nonviolent resistance, like this meeting, but—we do need to consider what we'd do if . . ." He let his sentence trail off, unwilling to complete the comment.

"If we were invaded?" Thanthavong said.

"Gerald Hemminge." Unlike the other speakers, he leaped to his feet, and he barely paused. "You have gone from attending an illegal meeting to a discussion of fighting and invasions! Invasions? You are all conspiring against our own sponsors! Satoshi, who do you believe you're speaking to, revolutionaries and terrorists?"

At that, several people tried to speak at once.

Satoshi rose, folded his arms, and stood quietly looking

at Gerald until the commotion died down. Beside him, Victoria prepared herself.

"I see nothing revolutionary," Satoshi said, "about wanting to do the job we were sent up here for."

"Even if a more important job has developed back home? We're needed. The ship is needed. None of you is willing to admit it, and I'm sick of you all. You forget—'The price of liberty is eternal vigilance.' "

"I'm sick of hearing that quote abused," Satoshi said. "Jefferson wasn't talking about the danger of foreign powers—even King George and the whole British Empire. He was talking about the danger of handing over our freedoms to a despot of our own!"

Gerald picked out Griffith at the top of the amphitheater. "Did you hear that? He's called your president a despot!"

Griffith glanced around uncomfortably. "I'm just an accountant," he said.

Gerald made a noise of disgust. "The chancellor sent me here in the hopes of talking sense into you all. I see that I've wasted my time." He stalked out of the amphitheater.

"Nikolai Petrovich Cherenkov," the cosmonaut said in the formal way of the meeting. He was only a few rows away from Griffith, who could not understand how he had missed him till now.

"I am your guest," Cherenkov said. "You have given me your hospitality and asked nothing in return. But now I must behave as a guest should not, and assume privileges that a guest does not possess. Your governments tell you that if you give up your ambitions and turn this starship into a watching and listening post, you will be benefiting the security of your countries and of the world. They tell you that if you accede to these demands, you will be helping my country return to itself." He paused.

Griffith tried to calm his own rapid heartbeat, but his usual control deserted him. He anticipated what Cherenkov would say. The cosmonaut would accept this chance to work against the people who had overwhelmed his country and sentenced him to death. He would speak to the meeting; he would bring everyone together in an agreement to evacuate the starship without resistance.

Cherenkov and his wisdom and his patriotism would give Griffith a spectacularly successful completion to his task.

"What your governments have told you is a lie," Cherenkov said. "Whether it is deliberate falsehood or ignorance, I will not speculate. But I tell you that outside the Mideast Sweep, nothing anyone can do will help anyone within it."

Griffith clenched his fingers around the edge of the stone bench. He was shaking.

"The changes are coming," Cherenkov said. "But they must come from within, they must evolve. Evolution requires patience. The changes gather slowly, until they reach a level that cannot be held back. I tell you that if the rulers perceive danger from outside, they will find scapegoats within their own territory. You will only visit more death and more pain upon innocents. The changes will be eliminated and the evolution will cease."

He waited to be questioned. No one spoke.

"Thank you for permitting a guest to speak," he said. He slowly climbed the stairs. When he reached Griffith, he stopped.

Griffith gazed up at him, stunned and confused. The expression on Cherenkov's face, full of memories and grief, broke his heart.

"Come with me, Marion," Kolya said. "Neither of us has a place in this decision."

Griffith had to push himself to his feet. Kolya took his elbow and helped him. They walked out of the tunnel. The darkness closed in around Griffith like an attack.

Griffith swung toward Cherenkov, his shoulders hunched and his fists clenched.

"How could you say that? I thought you, at least, would understand!" He fought to keep his voice steady. "Do you want to go on the expedition so much that you can throw away your patriotism? Is your brain so burned by cosmic rays that you've forgotten what the Sweep did to you back there, what they did to your family—"

"I do not permit anyone to speak of my family," Cherenkov said in a quiet voice that stopped Griffith short. "And my memory of what happened to me is clear."

"I'm sorry," Griffith said. He could not recall the last time he had apologized to someone and meant it. "But this is a chance to stop them!"

"It is not. I said what I said because it is true."

"But—"

"Why are you so concerned, Marion, if you are nothing but an accountant?"

"I—" At the last moment he caught himself and kept himself from admitting his purpose. He turned away. "I admire you," he whispered. "I thought you'd want this to happen."

"No," Cherenkov said gently. "There's too much blood already, on the land I came from. Blood is too expensive to use as fertilizer."

Griffith glanced back at him. Cherenkov smiled, but it was a strained and shaky smile, and after a moment it vanished.

"But freedom—"

Cherenkov made a noise of pure despair. "You cannot get freedom by shedding more blood in my country! You can only get more blood!"

"Then what *should* we do?"

"I told you. You should do nothing." He took Griffith

by the shoulders. "Your meddling helped create the problem in the first place. So did our own. We cannot pretend otherwise. We cannot continue to meddle, as if we never did any damage." His fingers tightened, as if he wanted to shake Griffith hard. Instead, he let him go. "I am wrong, of course. You can still do that."

Griffith felt as if he had plunged into an icy sea. He shook from the inside out, with a deep, cold tremble. He knew that if he tried to speak, he would be breathless.

"You have always done that," Kolya said. "You probably always will do that."

He walked away.

Cherenkov departed. Everyone understood the effort it had taken for the cosmonaut to speak. Beside Victoria, Stephen Thomas sat slumped with his elbows on his knees, no longer sprawling relaxed and cheerful on the amphitheater bench. He had watched Kolya closely, and Victoria recognized the intensely focused expression: Stephen Thomas sought his aura. Though Victoria did not believe in auras, she knew that Stephen Thomas could be preternaturally sensitive to other people's feelings, that he could imagine and experience Kolya's grief and desperation.

Victoria felt the chill of frightening truth: what happened to the expedition, to *Starfarer*, would affect far more than the people on board.

She searched the meeting for Iphigenie DuPre. She found her. The sailmaker was watching her. Iphigenie inclined her head slowly, carefully, down, then up.

"Crimson Ng." The small, compact artist leaned forward and gestured toward Victoria. Red river-valley clay was ground permanently into the knuckles of her delicate hands. "What did you mean when you said we ought to go on as if nothing had happened? How far do you think we should take it?"

Victoria spoke carefully, deliberately. "I think," she said, "that we should take it as far as it can go."

She imagined that she could feel the stream of tension and excitement, anger and fear, coalescing into a powerful tide of resolution.

"We now have even more reason to continue the expedition as if nothing had happened."

"That's easy to say, Victoria, but it's hardly a plan of action. How do you propose to continue if we're put under martial law and under guard? We're risking that already just by meeting."

"We were already at risk of that. We mustn't let it happen."

"Have you joined Satoshi and Infinity in wanting to fight?"

"I never said I *wanted* to fight," Satoshi said. "I said I was afraid we might have no alternative."

"Satoshi is right," Infinity said. "We'll have no choice, and what we want doesn't matter."

"We do have a choice," Victoria said. "We can choose not to be here if they try to take over."

"Great. So, we abandon ship? How is that going to—" Crimson cut her words short. "That isn't what you mean, is it?"

"No. I mean move *Starfarer*. Use a different approach to the cosmic string. A much closer one. One that takes us to transition tomorrow night."

J.D. gasped.

The meeting's order slipped abruptly into chaos.

Despite the confusion, Victoria felt the meeting flow in the direction she had chosen. She felt opinions and decisions gather together like the individual streams of a watershed, from a state of unfocused, chaotic indecision and rage, toward a cohesive opinion flowing like a river.

She waited until her voice could be heard.

"The expedition members must agree to the change," she said. "There will be time—not much, but enough—for anyone who wants to return to earth to leave by the last transport."

"We aren't fully provisioned," Thanthavong said. "Half our equipment hasn't arrived—"

"And half our faculty and staff has left! I can't help it. If we want the expedition to exist, this is our only chance."

"We'd be trying to outrun a—a cheetah with an elephant."

"The elephant has a big head start," Victoria said drily, keeping up her bravado. The others were less successful; their response was a feeble, frightened laugh.

"Christ on a mongoose, Victoria," Stephen Thomas said. "You want to steal the starship."

11

Stephen Thomas's comment, thoughtless and casual, threw Victoria off center and broke her influence. The gathering's flow toward agreement, toward decision, splashed up against a dam of doubt and fear.

"I can't believe you said that," Satoshi muttered.

"Steal it!" Victoria said. "That's ridiculous."

"But I think it's a great idea!" Stephen Thomas said. "I'll vote for it."

No one else spoke. Victoria stood alone in the silence. Stephen Thomas and Satoshi stood up beside her. J.D. remained in her place, fidgeting. She looked at Victoria, stricken, then plunged to her feet. Victoria took her hand and held it.

They waited.

Scientists, researchers, modern middle-class people, had no experience with taking such risks. Intellectual risks, yes, sometimes; even risks to the reputation, if the subject was large enough, the potential great enough. But this kind of risk . . .

"You're asking us to become lawbreakers," said a senior member of the geology department. "Renegades."

"We did that just by coming into the amphitheater tonight," Satoshi said drily.

"I'm suggesting that we change the schedule," Victoria said. "We've always left the possibility open."

"Don't downplay the seriousness of what you suggest," Thanthavong said sharply. "If we adopt your plan, we'll be going against powerful forces—"

"I thought you agreed with me!"

"I do. But we cannot go into this lighthearted or light-headed. Everyone who chooses to go should know the consequences. Everyone who isn't sure should leave the expedition."

"Wait a minute," Crimson said. "You're talking as if we've already agreed to this—we haven't! And it sounds like if we do . . . we can never come home."

"We'd have to face the consequences when we did come back," Victoria said.

"You're asking us to give up our families, our friends . . ."

"Crimson, those risks aren't new. They have nothing to do with the question we have to decide right now."

"Hey," Stephen Thomas said, "if we come back at all, we'll bring enough with us for the politicians to overlook our misbehavior."

"Victoria herself said we might not find anything!"

"What do I have to do to live that down?" Victoria said, an edge in her voice. "I wasn't trying to predict the future, I was trying to explain what science is about and how you conduct it! But I wouldn't be here if I thought the expedition was for nothing, and nor would you."

Alzena spoke. "I cannot agree to risk ecological stability by leaving our support systems prematurely. It could mean disaster."

Infinity spoke again. "I tell you that if this starship is held back from its journey for one year, for three years, it will never recover. It will never leave orbit. It won't *have* an ecosystem."

They had all seen films of the central plaza of Santa Fe, blasted into rubble, poisoned, destroyed.

No one disputed what Infinity said. But Alzena's warning could not be shrugged off.

"Despite the dangers, I propose that we accelerate the mission's departure to Tau Ceti," Thanthavong said, as if it were the most ordinary thing in the world. "I propose that we take advantage of Victoria's new transition solution." She rose to her feet.

Victoria waited.

By ones, by twos, by small groups, the members of the deep space expedition rose to signify their agreement.

On the way home, Victoria felt simultaneously elated, frightened, and drained. She walked with Stephen Thomas; J.D. and Satoshi followed close behind.

"Say, Victoria . . ." J.D. said.

"Victoria, you did it!" Stephen Thomas said at the same time.

"No thanks to you," Victoria said.

"Now you're mad at me. Shit, I couldn't resist the line. And after all, it's true."

"It is not, and even if you had to say it, you should have realized what lousy timing it was."

"Come on, now," Satoshi said mildly. "It turned out all right."

"Maybe. We still have a long way to go."

Victoria fell silent, knowing that the argument embarrassed Satoshi, especially since J.D. was with them. She wished she could get into a straight-ahead fight with Stephen Thomas. It seemed as if ever since she got home, every other conversation she had with him deteriorated into bickering. She could not understand why. Maybe they just needed to clear the air.

"J.D., what were you going to say a minute ago?"

"I . . . this is hard—"

They heard footsteps approaching at a run.

"Hey, wait for me!"

Feral rushed up, panting.

"Somebody said you had the meeting! Why didn't you tell me? What happened? Damn!"

"You should have been there," Stephen Thomas said. "You missed the creation of—"

"Stephen Thomas!" Victoria said sharply.

"What?"

"I think we have to start being careful what we discuss in front of Feral."

"He was in my office while we were 'conspiring,' for god's sake," Stephen Thomas said. "You didn't object then."

"I didn't think of it then. So shoot me."

"Don't you trust me to tell your story straight?" Feral exclaimed.

"Your interests can't always coincide with ours."

"Maybe we could tell him what happened, off the record," J.D. said hesitantly.

"This is bullshit," Stephen Thomas said. "We made the decision in a goddamned public meeting. It's to our advantage if Feral tells our side. Otherwise it'll all come from the chancellor—or the GAO. Feral, Victoria's research produced a second transition solution. Faster, shorter, better. And sooner. At the meeting we agreed to move the schedule up."

"And I missed it—? Damn! I obviously haven't cultivated my sources properly."

"It's been a tough day," Satoshi said. "We didn't exclude you on purpose—"

"Never mind the apologies. Tell me everything that happened. How soon—?"

Victoria walked ahead, angry at Stephen Thomas more because he was right than because he was telling Feral everything. J.D. hurried to keep up with her.

"Victoria, I have to go back to earth."

Completely shocked, Victoria stopped short and faced J.D.

"What?"

"It's Zev. The diver. He's disappeared. This is hard to explain, but I have to help him—"

"Help him! What about us? My god, J.D., this expedition *exists* to support you! You can't leave it now."

"I have to. I have responsibilities—"

"What about your responsibility to us? You let us put ourselves on the line without telling us what you'd decided, you stood with us for the change—how could you do this?"

"I'm sorry," she said, unable to meet Victoria's gaze, staring at her feet like an embarrassed child. "I tried, but . . . The expedition isn't only for me, that's silly—"

"If you think it's silly, then maybe you'd *better* leave."

"But—"

They reached the turnoff to J.D.'s house. J.D. stopped; Victoria continued, into the darkness.

"Um, maybe I'll see you tomorrow?" J.D. said.

Victoria could not trust herself to speak. Satoshi, Stephen Thomas, and Feral, unaware of what J.D. had decided, paused long enough to say good night to her; their voices, the words indistinct, faded behind Victoria.

"Victoria, wait!"

She broke into a run.

The courtyard surrounded her with a soft carnation scent. The lights glowed on in the main room of the house, responding to her approach. At the open French windows, Victoria kicked off her shoes and stepped inside, onto the cool, rustling reed mats. Their texture usually pleased her. Her vision blurred. Stephen Thomas's complicated distillation equipment hunkered on the floor like some misbegotten creature in a cheap special-effects movie.

Opening the door, Stephen Thomas came in and stood beside her, just gazing at her.

Victoria walked across the reed mats, passing the still.

"I wish you'd move that thing," she said. "Good night."

Stephen Thomas watched as she vanished into the back corridor. Satoshi and Feral came in behind him.

"Is she all right?"

Stephen Thomas shrugged, mystified and upset.

"Maybe I'd better go stay at the visitor's house," Feral said. "I've really thrown a monkey wrench into this . . ."

"No," Satoshi said. "You're our guest. Victoria and Stephen Thomas and I obviously have some misunderstandings to clear up between us, but we shouldn't inflict them on you."

"Come sit down," Stephen Thomas said. "I want to tell you about the meeting."

Feral hesitated, tempted.

"Go ahead," Satoshi said. "I'll talk to Victoria."

In her bed, Victoria curled around her pillow and thought about going back into the main room, behaving the way Stephen Thomas always did, acting as though she had said nothing for which she needed to apologize. But she did need to apologize. And she could not quite face it tonight.

"Victoria?"

Satoshi tapped lightly on her door. Victoria remained silent. He slid the door a handsbreadth open. He knew she was awake; she never went to sleep this fast, even when she was exhausted. Especially when she was exhausted.

"Can I come in?"

"Yes."

He slid into bed beside her, kissed her on the forehead, and held her till she fell asleep.

J.D. lay in bed in the darkness, unable to relax.

I might as well have stayed with the divers and never

even come to *Starfarer*, she thought. Damn! Why is this happening?

Staying with the expedition tempted her with such force that she had to stop thinking about the possibility, the good reasons, the rationalizations. She would return to earth with the reputation of being a troublemaker. She might be barred from her adopted profession. She might fail to find Zev; she might be arrested and put in jail as soon as she touched down. If she stayed here, she would be an alien contact specialist. And Victoria would not be angry with her . . .

She put aside the tempting thoughts and tried to sleep.

When she left, everyone would think she was running away, afraid to continue on the expedition. But for once in her life she was *not* running away.

Trying to sleep was hopeless. She took her notebook and pen into bed with her, and tried and failed to work on her novel.

At least I won't have to get used to writing electronically,. she thought. Now I *will* be able to just go out and buy another notebook.

The thought gave her no comfort.

As he often did, Infinity went into the garden to sleep. Carrying his blanket past the rosebush, he smelled the smoke of a cigarette near the battered lunar rock where Kolya liked to sit. The cosmonaut was nowhere to be seen; his footprints led away across dewy grass.

Infinity went farther around the edge of the garden, beyond the lingering cigarette smoke. He spread his blanket between some juniper bushes, where the smell was clean and pungent. He wrapped himself up in the peace of the garden.

He did not mind the chill. Dewdrops formed on his blanket, glowing silver on the black leaves of the rosebush, which had hardly wilted despite being transplanted when it was wide awake. Though it would have been better to wait till *Starfarer's* mild winter, during the bush's dormant season, Infinity had decided to risk the rose rather than risking Florrie's age. He had wanted her to have her roses.

But of course she would leave the expedition now—she would have to. She had nothing to do with Infinity and the other renegades, and she would not want to remain on board *Starfarer* now that everything had changed.

Though the meeting had chosen the path he desired, he still felt uncomfortable with his part in it. He was not used to speaking up, using the force of his past to influence events. The expedition had to make the change. Without it, they were lost.

But if they failed in their attempt . . .

Hearing footsteps, he rolled onto his chest. The silence of the garden amplified the stealthy sound.

Griffith walked into the garden and stood in the starlight, looking up at the hill. Looking for Kolya. But the cosmonaut had walked away in the other direction.

You don't need to worry about Kolya, Infinity thought. Even if Griffith stops us, he can't have Kolya Cherenkov taken off *Starfarer*.

Or can he?

For anyone else up here, the plan's failure would mean the loss of job and ambitions and hope. It might even mean prison. But if Kolya went back to earth, it would mean his life.

Infinity lay without moving for an hour, watching Griffith watch and wait, wondering what he could do, how he could guard against the danger his outburst had caused.

After Griffith cursed softly to the night and walked away, Infinity lay thinking and worrying for a long time.

Victoria woke alone. She lay in bed, trying to enjoy the sunlight streaming through her open, uncurtained window.

For someone who achieved the impossible last night, she said to herself, you are surely in a terrible mood.

She had to apologize to Stephen Thomas for snapping at him. Maybe she should also apologize to J.D., but that was harder. She understood prior commitments and responsibilities . . . it would be difficult to tell Grangrana that she might have to leave the house, and Greg was sure to grind Stephen Thomas through another emotional wringer. But the expedition members were putting their commitment to *Starfarer* first.

Victoria did not feel up to talking to J.D. Sauvage just now. Every way she imagined the conversation, she ended up angrier than before, and J.D. ended up hurt and confused.

She burrowed deep under the covers and tried to go back to sleep.

Arachne's signal chilled her fully awake. She sat up and let the web display *Starfarer*'s new orders.

When she finished reading the display, she gasped. She had been holding her breath with disbelief. She threw off her blankets and ran into the main room.

Stephen Thomas lounged in the sunlight like a cat. He rose abruptly when Victoria stormed in.

"Victoria, good lord, if you're still mad—!"

"Look at this." She formed a display so they could look at it together.

Stephen Thomas read the message, frowning. "Jesus H. Christ."

Satoshi wandered in, blinking, blank with sleep. "If you've got to fight, why don't you fight quietly?"

"We aren't fighting. Look at this."

He, too, read the message.

It woke him up even better than coffee.

Griffith sat on the balcony of his room in the empty guesthouse. Small puffy clouds drifted between him and the sun tubes. He was as oblivious to the shadows they cast over him as he had been to the bright sunlight shining on him a few minutes before. He had not slept, he had not eaten. All he had done, all he could do, was think about Nikolai Petrovich Cherenkov, and the Mideast Sweep, and the plans he himself had so carefully brought into being.

"Marion."

Griffith froze. He would not have believed anyone could come up behind him without his knowledge. He was fast and he was well trained, but he knew Cherenkov would be more than ready for anything he tried.

Maybe he deserved whatever Cherenkov chose for him.

"Are you responsible for the new order?"

"It was perfect," Griffith said. "It would alienate the EarthSpace associates and convert the ship to military purposes, all at the same time."

"You are such a fool."

Griffith turned, carefully, slowly. Cherenkov faced him, empty-handed.

"All I ever wanted was to be like you," Griffith said. "As good as you—"

"You prove me right," Cherenkov said. "As good as me? My country was destroyed! I had no little part in its enslavement. Is that what you want for yourself?"

"That isn't what I meant. I didn't know . . . I didn't think . . ."

"No. Of course not. We old men send you young men out to do our dirty work, and we teach you not to think. Start thinking now! Is there any way to turn the weapons carrier back? Any way to stop this abomination?"

Griffith shook his head. The interaction dizzied him. He flinched down, cursing, and closed his eyes till his balance steadied.

"No," he said. "It's out of my control. If I were back on earth they might listen to me. Probably not, though. This is what they want to do. I just helped find a way to do it.

If I changed my mind, they'd think you'd found a way to force me."

"And here I believed," Cherenkov said wryly, "that you were not permitted any weaknesses we might make use of."

"I'm not a robot!" Griffith glared at him. "I'm getting married next month! But when I'm . . . working . . . I don't let myself think . . ."

"Yes. That is the problem, isn't it?"

"That isn't what I meant, either, and you know it! What do you want me to say? That I'm sorry? I am, for all the good it will do!"

Cherenkov's expression was mild. "I didn't think you could surprise me, Marion, but you have." He sat on the wall of the balcony and let himself lean back over the ten-meter drop. "Several times over."

"Don't do that," Griffith said.

After a few moments, Cherenkov pushed himself forward again. He sat slumped, his hands hanging limp. His heavy, streaky hair shadowed his face.

"Have you any idea," he said, "how the leaders of the Sweep will react to *Starfarer* looming over them, after you have supplied it with nuclear missiles?"

Infinity entered his dim front room and brushed his fingertips through the cornmeal in the small pot by the door. He tossed his blanket toward a chair.

"Oh!"

"Florrie!" Infinity hurried forward to take the blanket from her lap where it had fallen. "I didn't see you, I'm sorry. What are you doing here? What's the matter?"

She wore her multilayered black clothes and the shells and beads in the long patches of her hair. Her gray eyes looked very pale within their circles of dark kohl. Infinity wondered if the administrators had really thought they could bully her into wearing regulation clothing.

"I've been trying and trying to get you," she said.

"Why didn't you call me on the direct web? You could have said it was urgent."

"I don't know, I didn't want to, I thought you might be asleep."

He guessed that all her contradictions meant that she, like a lot of others, felt uncomfortable using the direct link.

"Okay, I'm here now. What's wrong?" He had seen her a couple of times since the party; she always had people with her, come to talk with her or help her, eat with her or cook for her. Her presence was a tremendous success. At least one thing had been going right, among so much else going wrong.

It was too bad she would be leaving. She ought to be home packing. The EarthSpace transport a few hours ahead of the armed military carrier would be the last civilian vessel to approach until *Starfarer*'s situation was resolved one way or another. EarthSpace had already sent out orders for no one to disembark, but it had no way of enforcing the demand or calling the transport back. The transport had to pick up more reaction mass from *Starfarer*. Otherwise it would have to power itself home with only emergency reserves: a tricky, risky maneuver.

"He was there again last night. He's always there. Can't I make him stop?"

"You mean Griffith?"

She nodded.

"I don't know. You could report him to the chancellor for harassing you."

"I'm sure he's figured out something to report *me* to the chancellor for, and you know who'd be believed."

"I know he scares you. But, Florrie, you know, he isn't really interested in you or me or anybody except Kolya. That's why he's always in your garden at night."

"He hasn't actually *done* anything . . ."

"Isn't it kind of pointless to worry? You'll be going back to earth on the transport. I guess he will be, too, but once you're home you'll probably never see him again. Are you packed? There isn't that much time. You do understand that it's the last chance to leave?"

She sagged in his chair as if she had suddenly reached the limit of her energy.

"Are they sending me away?" she said, so faint he could hardly hear her.

"No, not sending you, exactly . . ."

"Why should I have to go, when I didn't even have anything to do with the meeting? Nobody even told me it was happening!"

"Don't you want to go home?"

"This is my home now! I came all the way out here— why do you think I'd want to leave again?"

"Because everything's changed," Infinity said.

"Not for me," Florrie said.

One of *Starfarer*'s telescopes trained itself on the military carrier as it accelerated toward the starship. It hung in the center of the screen, apparently unmoving, but pushing forward at twice the delta-vee of a regular transport.

Victoria found her gaze and her attention drawn to the image no matter how hard she tried to concentrate on all the other things she had to think about.

The prospect of nuclear weapons on board *Starfarer* angered and distressed and saddened her more than any other element of the attempted takeover, even, strangely enough, the possibility that the starship would be turned into a low-orbit watchpost. The battle against arming the starship was the hardest fight the alien contact team had taken on. Victoria still sometimes felt astonished that they had won it.

The one good thing the approaching military carrier had

done was unify the faculty and staff. There were plenty of members who believed the expedition could present itself as peaceful while carrying defensive weapons, but even they were angered by the means being taken to arm the ship.

Victoria stared at the screen, at the dark ungainly carrier with its exterior cargo of shrouded missiles.

"They've been planning this for a long time," Stephen Thomas said. "They must have. They can't have gotten it all in place and made the decision just since our meeting." He glanced at the image on the screen.

Feral stood beside him. They both looked at the carrier.

"I'm not so sure," Feral said. "I think they realized they had to work fast. I think I would have heard something, rumors . . ."

"Like about the meeting?" Stephen Thomas said.

"Thanks very much," Feral said. "Rub it in. Wait till I get my sources lined up, there won't be anything on this ship I don't know about."

"Sounds intriguing."

"And see if I tell you any good gossip."

Victoria pulled her attention away from the image of the carrier.

"Stephen Thomas, please, I can't stand that. Will you turn it off? Or let me use the screen for a few minutes, then I'll go somewhere else and you can watch some more."

"Sure."

Stephen Thomas and Feral stood aside for her.

"Is this private?" Feral asked.

"I'm calling my great-grandmother. She'll have heard what's happening, she'll be worried."

Stephen Thomas glanced away, his expression frozen. He had to make a call to earth, too . . .

"What's the carrier's latest ETA?" Feral asked. "Will it get to us before we reach transition point?"

For a second Victoria could not figure out why Feral would ask Stephen Thomas a question to which he already knew the answer.

"We can't tell," Stephen Thomas said. "It depends on how efficient Iphigenie's orbit is and how much extra acceleration the carrier's got—which is classified information."

Some animation returned to his face and entered his voice. Feral had asked just the right question to distract him, and he had given him an opportunity to lecture a little.

As Victoria requested an earth connection through the web, she wondered if Feral knew about Stephen Thomas's rocky interactions with his father, or if he had simply noticed his unease. Stephen Thomas did not often open up to anyone on such short acquaintance. She wondered, absently, if Stephen Thomas and Feral had slept together last night. Probably not: no one in the partnership found much attraction in one-night stands. It would be uncharacteristic of Stephen Thomas to start something that would have to end so soon, with Feral leaving on the transport.

"The satellite relay is currently overloaded. Please wait, then try again."

Impatiently, Victoria complied with the unusual request.

"We'll get to the cosmic string before the carrier gets to us," Feral said.

"How the hell do you know that?" Stephen Thomas said.

"Because it wouldn't be aesthetically pleasing the other way around," Feral replied. "And besides, if the carrier gets here before we hit the string . . . I won't be allowed to report the story."

"Feral," Victoria said, "do you know the old joke where the punch line is 'What do you mean "we," white man?' "

"You're right," Feral said, grinning, "That *is* an old joke."

"So, what *do* you mean, 'we'?"

"You don't think I could leave now, do you? This is the best story I'll ever get the chance to cover! I'm one of you."

"You can't sign on at the last minute—"

"The last minute! I only applied about eight hundred times!"

"And you were turned down. I'm sorry, but—"

Feral laughed. Stephen Thomas started to chuckle.

"It isn't funny!"

"But it is, love. I'm sorry, it is."

"You're trying to pull off the biggest theft in the history of humanity," Feral said, "and you want me to worry about application rules?"

That brought her up short.

"Yes," she said. "I do. Maybe it sounds nuts, but if we use this rebellion as an excuse to throw out our laws and customs, we'll be in worse trouble than if we'd let *Starfarer* be taken over."

Returning to Arachne, she tried once more to make the connection. Once more she received the "All lines busy" message.

Stephen Thomas and Feral, both made somber by her comment, looked over her shoulder.

"What's going on?"

"Everybody calling out, just like me. Explaining why they're going. Or why they'll be back sooner than they expected."

All the members of the team, and everyone else on the faculty, had spent the whole morning making sure that everyone knew that they had to decide, immediately, whether to go or stay. Satoshi was off trying to reason with his graduate student, Fox, who had to leave and did not want to.

It was only a few hours till lunar transit, a few more hours till intersection with the cosmic string . . . or takeover by the military carrier.

Victoria made a third attempt to connect with the web.

"Your communication request is in the queue. Please be patient."

Victoria frowned. "This is weird, eh?"

"Yeah," Stephen Thomas said. "Even if everybody up here called at the same time, Arachne's got plenty of channels."

They looked at each other.

"We're being cut off," Feral said.

"I don't . . ." Victoria let her voice trail away.

"It's easy. Just interfere with our access to the relay satellite. Damn! I got two stories out, but the third—and the one I haven't done yet, the live report on reaching transition . . ." He tangled his fingers in his thick hair and turned away with a shout of anguish.

Victoria stared at the blank screen. Not to be able to talk to Grangrana, maybe ever again . . . She slumped on the bench.

Stephen Thomas knelt behind her, put his arms around her, and enfolded her.

"She'll understand," he whispered. "She'll know you tried. *She'll* understand."

Victoria put her hands over his and held him tight. A tear splashed down and caught where their fingers meshed, between his fair skin, her dark skin.

12

Victoria kicked off from the mouth of the entry tunnel and swam into the sailhouse. Iphigenie, entranced in Arachne's web, drifted in the center of the crystalline cylinder, in the midst of the eerie harmonies of the sail's controls. Only a few other people floated, scattered, within the sailhouse. This should have been a celebration. The changes made a celebration impossible.

The moon's shadow sped toward *Starfarer* as the moon caught up with the starship. With *Starfarer*'s orbit widening, the moon would pass below. By then the enormous solar sail would have deflected the starship from its original course, setting it to skim the surface of the moon and arc out of the plane of the solar system, straight to the nearest point of the local strand of cosmic string.

Observers on earth saw the full moon about to occlude a bright new star.

Victoria waited in silence until Iphigenie's eyelids fluttered. The sailmaster gazed around, disoriented.

"Victoria . . ."

"All set?"

Iphigenie's mouth quirked up at one corner, a wry smile. "I sure wish I had some ground support."

"You can do it without."

"Of course I can," Iphigenie said.

She let herself spin, visually checking the starship cylinders, the sail, the moon, and beautiful blue-white earth in
the distance.

"I keep imagining I can see the carrier already," Iphigenie
said. "And the bombs . . ."

"Soon."

"Too soon. It's going to be close. And the transport,
Victoria—the pilot's got to take on reaction mass and undock
as soon as she can. Otherwise we'll have a civilian transport
along for the ride. The last thing we need is a ship full
of kidnapping victims." She pressed her hands against her
tight, smooth braids. "Can we even communicate with the
transport? Or are their systems 'overloaded,' too?"

"We're realigning an antenna," Victoria said. "The transport will hear us. We might get one voice link to earth. But
that's it."

"I wanted a test," Iphigenie said. Her eyelids fluttered.
"How close do we have to cut things?"

"I won't know until after lunar passage. We won't have
more than a couple of hours. Everybody who's leaving is
going to have to cram themselves onto the transport fast. Are
there a lot?"

"Not as many as I was afraid there would be."

"They'll all fit on one transport?"

"It will be crowded." Victoria shrugged. "They'll manage." She did not want to think about who *was* leaving. It
made her too unhappy, too angry.

"I've got to concentrate," Iphigenie said. "Do you want
to link in?"

"Yes!"

She slipped into Iphigenie's multidimensional mathematical space. Images poured through her connection with
Arachne. *Starfarer* fell behind the moon.

Iphigenie drifted in her accustomed position, all her

senses focused on the sail and the connection between Arachne and the sail, measuring control in micrometers.

The craters and maria on the sunlit limb of the moon vanished abruptly into darkness at the terminator.

The sun disappeared behind the earth; the earth disappeared behind the dark limb of the moon. Darkness overtook the starship. The bright sail dimmed. In starlight, it began to collapse. In the illumination of Iphigenie's instructions, Victoria felt the slackening sail's control strands tighten and shift and move.

The dark moon looked huge, a great black shadow in space. *Starfarer* plunged toward it.

Then the ship passed over it, as if over the dark depths of a sea. For a strange, unsettling time Victoria felt as if she were traversing the airless surface in a hot-air balloon, impossibly high.

As Victoria's eyes grew accustomed to the change in contrast, she saw features in the shadows, faintly illuminated by starlight.

Suddenly Iphigenie shouted in anger and in pain. An instant later Arachne jerked the web's connections from Victoria, flinging her into darkness and emptiness. Victoria gasped for breath and fought for consciousness.

The light was very dim. Far beyond the spinning cylinders of the starship, the moon lay shadowed with starlight, craters black at the rim, fuliginous inside. On the other side of the sailhouse, Victoria could see the sail only as a shadow against the starfield. But she knew that without Iphigenie's control, without the solar wind to stabilize it, it would collapse, tangle, destroy itself.

The starship plunged toward the surface of the moon. The illusion of stillness changed abruptly into the reality of tremendous velocity.

The harmony of the control chords collapsed into dissonance. Victoria heard the other people in the sailhouse, all shadows, shouting in confusion, moaning in pain. They, too, had been hooked in.

Awkward with shock, she dog-paddled toward Iphigenie, who tumbled, rigid and quivering, through the air.

"Iphigenie!"

She had a pulse, but she did not respond to Victoria's voice or touch. She had taken the brunt of Arachne's abrupt withdrawal. Outside, the sail began to collapse upon itself. Iphigenie's eyelids flickered.

"Hard connection . . ." the sailmaster murmured.

Victoria grabbed her shirt and towed her toward the backup console at the edge of the sailhouse. She had never seen anyone use it, for the interface with Arachne made it obsolete. Unthinking, Victoria sent Arachne a signal to enliven the console. Of course nothing happened. Victoria felt foolish, and crippled. Losing her connection with the webworks was like losing a limb. Its phantom remained, perceptible but useless.

Victoria slapped the controls of the console. It registered activity. It connected with the starship's computer. Victoria let out her breath. If it had been Arachne itself that was damaged, rather than the computer's connections to the outside world, the expedition would have ended right there.

"Iphigenie, are you all right? It's on, it's here, what should I do?"

"Just . . . feed in the numbers . . ."

Iphigenie reached for the interface, but her long slender hands trembled. Her eyes rolled back and she fainted.

"Iphigenie!"

First Victoria had to remember her password, which she had not used in months. With the direct connection, the web recognized the pattern of her brain waves. At the first try she mistyped it. Whoever had to type anything anymore? Victoria never typed. On the second desperate try she got it right.

Then she had to search for the files in which she had so easily immersed herself under the sailmaster's tutelage. All Victoria could do was change *Starfarer*'s path by rote, without the minute alterations Iphigenie would have made as she flew.

The other people in the sailhouse, recovering, paddled toward her through the dissonant notes of chaos.

"What happened? Is she all right?"

"I hope so," Victoria said. "She talked. Get her to the health center. Anne, please, would you log in and try to keep the tension even on the lines? Maybe there's a control program here somewhere, I don't know."

She heard at the edge of her hearing and saw at the corners of her vision that others were helping, working, taking Iphigenie to aid. Letting them go, she disappeared into the mathematical space that controlled the starship, seeing only the strange dimensions and hearing only a cacophony that she urged toward harmony.

The moon's gravity drew the starship out of the plane of the moon's orbit. In the original plan, *Starfarer* spent the next six months in a shakedown cruise. The alternate path drove the ship immediately to the nearer but more complex transition point.

If the new plan succeeded, *Starfarer* would escape before the military carrier arrived with its nuclear arms.

The tones blended. To Victoria's ear the music lacked the simple beauty of Iphigenie's solutions.

The moon passed beneath the starship. The moon's sunlit limb changed from a bright flaring line, to a bow, to a crescent: dark of the moon to new moon to half-moon in the space of a few minutes.

The sail caught the sunlight again, silver, shimmering. The wrinkled center filled; the edges straightened.

Starfarer passed beyond the moon.

* * *

Within the cylinder, J.D. paused when the moon's shadow cut off the light to the sun tubes. She looked out the window of her house to watch the eerie midday eclipse pass over the land. It lasted too brief a time for the auxiliary power to kick in and illuminate the campus.

The light returned. Everything had, J.D. assumed, gone smoothly.

She glanced around the main room of her house. Mats given to her at the welcoming party remained rolled up and stacked. She had put off laying them out till she finished building her shelves. Slabs of rock foam lay just inside the door, unused, perhaps never to be used. Her books remained in their boxes. She could not take them back with her, for the transport would be too crowded. Many of the people leaving felt like refugees, forced to abandon everything. J.D. had heard the sadness and distress and anger in their voices. She sympathized with them, and knew she should feel lucky, if she had to leave, to be leaving before she could put her roots down very far.

Nevertheless, she felt uprooted.

Though the transport would not dock for an hour, J.D. left her house, empty-handed, and trudged down the path toward the cylinder's end.

Victoria crept silently into Iphigenie's room in the health center. The sailmaster lay bundled in a blanket with the edge pulled close around her face. Victoria sat nearby, prepared for a long wait.

"What happened?" Iphigenie whispered.

"Somebody crashed the web. Turned off the safeguards and crashed it. It was deliberate. It . . ." About to say that it blasted the web to shreds, she stopped herself. It scared her to think what the crash might have done to Iphigenie. "It caused a lot of disruption. But things are getting back together. How are you feeling?"

"I mean the orbit."

"It's pretty close to what you planned. But without any refinements."

"Did it work, Victoria? I want to know if it worked."

Victoria drew in a long breath and let it out. "I don't know yet. We won't know till we outrun the carrier . . . or get caught."

Iphigenie moved weakly, rising from the bed, wrapping the blanket around herself.

"I'm going back out."

"Do you feel up to it?"

"I don't like being in gravity, I've got to get out of here."

Though everyone else in the sailhouse had been hooked into Arachne through Iphigenie, and had felt the web's disintegration only secondhand, many other members of the faculty and staff had been routinely hooked in on the web during the crash. The overworked health center staff were treating everything from headache and nausea to coma. No one even noticed when Iphigenie and Victoria left.

Victoria helped Iphigenie out of the center. The sailmaster looked gray beneath her dark skin, and her hands were cold and clammy. But if she could improve the course by a fraction of a percent, it might make the difference between the continuation of the expedition, and its complete, permanent failure. They had gone too far now to back off from risk.

Once more in the crystal bubble of the sailhouse, Iphigenie glanced at the sail, at the moon, the earth, the sun, as if she could plot out the best course without any technical support at all. She gazed across at the hard-link, warily.

"Is Arachne back yet?" she asked.

A strange question; easy enough to check for herself.

Victoria had been querying every couple of minutes, to no avail.

"No. No answer yet."

Iphigenie pushed herself toward the console. Drifting in weightlessness with the blue blanket wrapped around her, she looked like a forlorn baby-blue ghost. She reached the console and worked over it for a few minutes, every so often reaching up to pull a drifting corner of the blanket closer.

"That's it," Iphigenie said. "That's as good as it gets. You did well, Victoria. Thank you."

Returning, exhausted, from the sailhouse, Victoria realized that it lacked only a few minutes till the transport's departure. She had vowed not to go to the waiting room, not to bid goodbye to anyone who chose to leave the expedition.

But when she reached the corridor that led to the transport access, she realized her vow was a cruel and petty one.

She pushed off toward the waiting room.

Ten meters ahead, someone wearing long black garments pulled herself doggedly forward, trying to maneuver with one hand while using the other to hold the excess fabric of her long, drifting skirt. Each time she let it go, the skirt crept up around her knees.

Such heavy clothing was rare on board the starship, and Victoria could not think who might be wearing it. She caught up and glanced curiously sideways.

"Alzena!"

The chief ecologist continued without pausing. Her *chador* covered everything except her hands and her face.

"Where are you going? Why are you dressed like that?"

"I'm going back to earth. I can take only one set of clothes."

"But you can't leave!"

"I must. If I remain, illegally, my family will be shamed."

"What about your work? The ecosystem depends on your knowledge. The whole expedition could succeed or fail—"

"You don't understand, Victoria. You can't. All the branches of your family are Western. My family is different. I have obligations that have nothing to do with my work."

"So you're going to wrap yourself up in mourning—"

"It is not mourning, and you know it. It is traditional, and I must be wearing it when I reach earth. It's one thing to adopt Western dress up here, in private, quite another to appear in public—there will be cameras . . . My family will see me. I cannot embarrass them."

Victoria looked away. This was a facet of Alzena she had never known about. She would rather not have met the Alzena who would abandon a position of respect, authority, accomplishment, and freedom, in order to return to a cir- cumscribed existence and submit herself to rule by accident of birth.

The ecologist was correct. Victoria did not understand. She could not understand actions that seemed to her more alien than anything she could imagine encountering in a distant star system.

"I'm sorry," she said. "I'm sorry for your decision. I'm sorry things worked out this way."

"So am I," Alzena said.

Distressed, Victoria hurried on, leaving the ecologist behind.

J.D. let herself hover by the wall of the transport waiting room. She felt limp and distressed; if there had been any gravity at all here she would have been sitting slumped in a chair. Other soon-to-be-ex-expedition members filled the room. The noise level was high and harsh, but the talk and argument and recriminations and last-minute goodbyes often fell into the middle of strange abrupt silences.

As the transport approached, the public address speaker broadcast the conversation between its pilot and *Starfarer*'s traffic controller. They had a direct radio link, independent of communications satellites. They exchanged information in a sort of technological ritual, just the same as always, as if nothing had happened.

J.D. knew about the attempted sabotage of *Starfarer* by the disruption of the web. The web had safeguards, to protect people hooked in during crashes. Someone had deliberately overridden them. J.D. could not understand the mind of someone who would hurt people on purpose. Worst of all, it had to be someone on board *Starfarer*.

The sabotage had angered a number of people to the point of changing their minds about leaving. J.D. would have been among them if she had been departing for any reason but the divers.

She shivered, closed her eyes, and extended a tentative tendril toward Arachne. If the web was re-formed, if the connection to the satellite had been restored, she could ask once more if Zev had been found.

No reply.

She was about to go looking for a hard-link to the computer when Victoria entered the waiting room. She paused in the hatchway and looked around. J.D. averted her gaze, wishing Victoria were seeking someone else, but knowing why she must be here.

The transport docked with a faint low-frequency thud, a faint vibration of the walls.

Even without looking, J.D. knew it when Victoria touched the wall nearby and brought herself to a halt at J.D.'s side.

"Hi."

"Hi."

Victoria took J.D.'s hand. J.D. flinched, startled by her touch.

"Please," she said. "Victoria, I'm sorry. I have to leave. I can't—" Her throat tightened. If she kept speaking she would break down.

"I know," Victoria said. "I know it. That's why I came. To tell you that I do understand. I'm furious, but not at you. I think you're an admirable person. I wouldn't have the courage to do what you're doing."

"Thank you for trying to make me feel better . . ." Her smile felt shaky. "It isn't working."

The hatch door opened and people came out. A crowd had already formed around the hatchway. The last transport would be packed. Half its incoming passengers were refusing to disembark. J.D. could not blame them, and besides, as Satoshi said, anyone who could be talked out of being on the expedition for any reason probably should not have joined it in the first place.

Though J.D. was one of the passengers who actually held a confirmed reservation, she did not expect to claim her couch. The transport could accommodate all its passengers only because freefall gave them three dimensions rather than two in which to place themselves.

"I hope you find your friend," Victoria said.

"Thank you."

The last few people straggled out of the hatchway. Hardly noticing them, J.D. hugged Victoria, who embraced her tightly. Finally they drifted away from each other, still holding hands.

"I guess . . ."

J.D. noticed a pair of youths, strangely familiar, moving through the waiting room, among the other new people. She lost sight of them.

"I guess I'd better go." Everyone else had already crowded into the transport.

Victoria put one hand on either side of J.D.'s face, leaned forward, and kissed her lips. J.D. felt herself blushing, but did not pull away.

Victoria let her hands slip away from J.D.'s face. Reluctantly, J.D. pushed off from the wall, moving backward through the hatchway.

"Goodbye."

The doors began to close.

"Goodbye."

Beyond Victoria, the strange youths headed for the exterior hatch. One, awkward in weightlessness, pushed off too hard. She tumbled toward a group of equally inexperienced people. The other youth, of indeterminate gender, wearing an incongruous baggy business suit and an even more incongruous hat, swam after her, caught her, and steadied her. This youth was an old hand up here, swimming in the air like water—

Even as J.D. thought, It couldn't be! she lurched forward through the last crack between the closing doors. They slammed open, then shut again as she barreled back into the waiting room.

"Zev!"

The youth in the business suit spun toward her—and continued turning. He pulled off his hat, freeing his astonishing pale hair, and flung the hat hard in the opposite direction of the spin. His rotation slowed. He touched the wall and launched himself toward J.D.

"J.D.! I did not see you—how did you know I was coming? We thought we kept it a secret. I have a different name now. And I am Chandra's assistant."

J.D. looked at him, baffled. He dodged around her, skimming past her, very close, never touching her.

Chandra made her way to them, hand over hand along the transport wall. "Thanks for leaving me hanging like that. Is that your idea of gratitude?"

"This is Chandra. Chandra, I forgot my new name."

"It doesn't matter. You can go back to being Zev."

"What happened?" J.D. cried. "I don't understand any of this!"

Zev laughed and hovered above them. "What does it matter? We're here now."

Chandra answered her. "It's like Zev said. He's my grad student in the art department. My agent got him a temporary new identity."

"Your agent must be pretty extraordinary."

Zev swooped between them, pushed off gently from the surface beyond their feet, and passed behind J.D.

"She is. She knows some amazing people. She even knows people who can make publishers pay them their royalties on time."

"That *is* amazing. Zev, stop, slow down!"

"I cannot help it, this is exciting."

She took his wrist as he passed, and drew him toward her. She had forgotten how warm his skin always felt. In the sea, heat radiated from him, perceptible a handsbreadth away.

"Come here, let me hug you."

"But you said, about being on land—"

"Never mind what I said. For a minute, we can be divers again."

Zev smiled his luminous smile and pulled himself to her and hugged her tight. He hid his face against her neck. His breath whispered against her collarbone. J.D. felt as if she had been dying of starvation and thirst and loneliness without knowing it, until this moment, and now it did not matter because she was no longer dying.

Victoria hovered nearby while J.D. and Zev hugged each other, floating upside down in relation to Victoria's orientation.

The artist grabbed onto a handhold. She clung tight, her

eyes shut, the weird swellings on her face and hands dark with increased circulation.

She opened her eyes. They were a dull silver-gray. She seemed to look directly at Victoria.

"I have to hook into the computer!" she said. She thrust her chin toward Victoria, arrogant, desperate. "Otherwise I'm going to start losing stuff. Why isn't it responding?"

"The web's been disrupted," Victoria said. "We're in a lot of trouble here—are you sure you want to stay?"

"Of course. How long before you've got a functional web?"

"I don't know."

"I can't afford to wait—do you have portables? Backups? A hard-link?"

Victoria almost snapped at her, almost said, I have better things to do than worry about art.

But the truth was that she did *not* have anything better to do, with Iphigenie capable of watching the course, and also being watched over to be sure she did not slip into shock. Victoria had nothing better to do than worry. She might as well worry about *something*.

"*Where* did you get that suit?" J.D. was asking.

"Chandra had it made for me."

"It fit him better," Chandra said, "before he decided he ought to be able to swim in it."

"She says it should fit more closely, but I like it this way. Is it good space clothes?"

"It's unique," J.D. said. "And so are you."

Victoria smiled. "Come on," she said to Chandra. "I'll get you to a link." She reached out to lead the artist, who ignored her hand and pushed off past her, dog-paddling.

"I'm not blind, you know."

Victoria kicked off after her, nonplussed, but relieved to know that Chandra had not chosen some form of altered sight, even blindness, in pursuit of her art.

Instead of ricocheting toward the hatchway, Victoria grabbed a handhold and stopped herself, her attention caught by a change in the familiar tones of the conversation between the transport pilot and *Starfarer's* traffic controller. Chandra reached the hatch, turned to look for Victoria, scowled, and dog-paddled back toward her.

"*Starfarer* control, no go, repeat, no go. Abort undocking procedure."

"What's the trouble, transport? Your pattern's normal."

"EarthSpace orders. The transport isn't to disengage from the starship."

Victoria cursed softly. If the pilot followed orders, if the transport remained with *Starfarer*, the expedition would have the choice of aborting transition, or vanishing with a transport full of people who did not want to go. At worst, hostages, kidnapping victims; at best, a bunch of very hostile individuals.

Chandra reached Victoria, still dog-paddling, slow but steady. She clutched Victoria's arm and pulled. They tumbled until Victoria grabbed the wall and stopped them.

"Come *on!*" Chandra sounded as desperate as a child who badly needed a bathroom. For all Victoria knew, the sensation of full sensory recorders was the same as full bladder and bowels.

"Just a second, this is serious."

The discussion between pilot and controller frayed around the edges, the pilot's voice losing some of its good-old-boy, feminine version, self-confidence, while the controller held desperately to the precise, rigorously unaccented EarthSpace communications English.

"Transport, you are cutting your window very thin. *Starfarer* will not, repeat not, approach another before transition. You will be at risk of needing a tow."

A transport pilot would never live down making a mistake that required a tow, but this pilot's actions were deliberate.

"Hurry!" Chandra wailed.

"Shut *up!*" Victoria whispered, out of practice with doing the math in her head, hampered by being cut off from Arachne. Just how long did *Starfarer* have, to persuade the pilot to change her mind and disobey EarthSpace orders? If Chandra felt uncomfortably full, Victoria felt desperately empty.

J.D. and Zev swam over to her, Zev already smooth and graceful in freefall. He had taken off the suit coat, but still gave the impression of swimming within his clothing.

"Will they be stranded?" J.D. asked. "If they undock late—will anyone rescue them?"

"They're probably coordinated with the carrier, hoping to stop us. The real question is, what if they don't undock? I don't want to go into this as kidnappers."

"That's what they're counting on," J.D. said. "It must be."

"No!" the pilot shouted at the controller. Her angry voice sounded even more startling coming through a speaker which ordinarily transmitted the most civilized of exchanges. "I've got my orders. We're staying."

The controller replied. "I hope you are all prepared for a very long trip."

Abandoning the sensory artist, Victoria headed for traffic control.

Griffith retraced the route he had followed with Nikolai Cherenkov, to the outer skin of the starship's campus cylinder. He had no need of Arachne's guidance, for he never permitted a computer hookup to substitute for his acute memory. He moved with quick caution. Everyone still on board must have plenty of things to worry about, but he did not trust their preoccupation to protect him from their anger. He doubted he would have time to explain if he were cornered by an infuriated mob; he doubted anyone would believe him anyway.

He wished he had made time to go through spacewalk orientation. A line through to Arachne would have helped make up for that deficiency, but the web was still down. He wondered who had crashed it, and why he had not been told of an ally on board the starship.

The tunnels grew increasingly dim, increasingly rough. He reached the turnoff to the airlock.

A dozen spacesuits hung in the access room. He touched Cherenkov's, but left it in its place. Even if it might have fit him, he lacked the gall to wear it.

I've lost a lot of gall in the last couple of days, he thought. Maybe now is where I get it back.

He picked a suit from its hanger and inspected it carefully, checking how the fittings worked. It was no more complicated than a radiation suit. He climbed into it.

"*Strasvuitye.*"

Griffith turned, disbelieving. From the doorway, Cherenkov regarded him with an expression as matter-of-fact as his voice.

"My faith in human nature is obviously at a low ebb," Cherenkov said. "Otherwise I might have expected to see you here. You did understand what I said to you, didn't you?"

Griffith could not trust himself to answer the question. "I didn't expect to see you," he said. "This is the last place I expected to see you. What are you doing down here?"

"The same as you. Trying to save the expedition. Acting an old part, the part of an unregenerate hero." He spoke drily, self-deprecatingly.

"You can go back up, then," Griffith said. "There's no need for you to leave the expedition."

"You said you wanted to be like me, and I said you were a fool for it. You're still a fool."

"Thanks a lot," Griffith said. "What do I have to do, to make you—" He stopped.

"If you jump out into space and call for the carrier to

rescue you, it won't turn aside from its prey. Its masters will not permit it."

"I think I know them better than you do, and you're wrong."

"I will not let you enter the airlock, Marion," Cherenkov said.

"How are you going to stop me?"

"I may be out of practice, but one does not forget certain survival techniques." He smiled. "Especially when one performs them against an opponent handicapped by spacesuit legs halfway down around his ankles."

"Don't laugh at me!" Griffith jerked the bottom of the spacesuit straight so he was no longer hobbled by the legs. The back hung down behind him like an enormous tail. Cherenkov was right about his being handicapped, less by the suit than by his desperate wish not to fight with the cosmonaut.

"You can't seriously think I'd let you jump out instead!"

"That would be the more rational course," Cherenkov said.

"Because you're sure they *will* turn around to go get you? That's fucking egotistical."

"I'm not sure. But I am sure that I have the better chance of slowing them long enough for *Starfarer* to reach transition."

"Maybe we ought to both jump out," Griffith said sarcastically.

"All right," Cherenkov said. "That would be an acceptable compromise."

Griffith hesitated.

"No," he said. "I can't allow it."

Curious, Cherenkov cocked his head. "But why? I'm sorry if I hurt your pride, believing your superiors will not stop to rescue you. Is that any reason to abandon a version of the plan that would work?"

"It's too risky." Griffith hesitated. "If they won't stop for me . . . maybe they won't stop for you, either."

"I see." Cherenkov let his long legs fold up; he sat on the stone floor and gazed at Griffith.

"You don't want to fight me, either," Griffith said. "I'll take that as a compliment." He managed to smile. "Checkmate."

"Not yet," Cherenkov said. "Only check."

J.D. watched Victoria soar away without a backward look. She hesitated, tempted to follow. But surely Victoria would have asked for her help if she had wanted it. Besides, J.D. did not want to leave Zev.

"Just tell me where there's a link!" Chandra said. "God forbid I should use any of your precious time."

"I'm sorry," J.D. said. "Things are a little complicated up here right now. Come on, I'll find you a place to transfer your information."

She and Zev towed the artist out of the waiting room, past the people listening, fascinated and appalled, to the conversation between *Starfarer* traffic control and the transport pilot.

"Zev, where were you all this time? Lykos has been worried, and I was just about to go back and help look for you."

"It was exciting. We almost got arrested."

" 'We'? You and the other divers? I thought—"

" 'We,' him and me," Chandra said. "I almost let them. I've never been arrested, it would have been good stuff to collect. But they didn't look like regular police, and I was afraid it would take too long to get out."

"I suspect that's an understatement," J.D. said.

She led them down the corridor toward one of the auxiliary equipment rooms.

"Do both of you realize that we're headed for transition

right now? That if you stay, you'll be on the starship permanently? The expedition may be longer than we planned . . . we've gotten ourselves in a lot of trouble."

Chandra laughed. "You think *I* was making an understatement?"

"There's still time to get on the transport."

"J.D.," Zev said, "it would be silly to get on the transport. It is not going anywhere." He loosened his tie and pulled it off.

"I hope they change their minds about that, because *Starfarer* isn't about to change course."

"We can't go back," Chandra said. "By now they'll have figured out that my assistant doesn't exist, and maybe they'll have figured out who he really is. Besides, I'm in the art department, I signed on for the trip."

"Me, too," Zev said cheerfully. He pulled the shirttail out of his trousers and unbuttoned his shirt so it flapped behind him.

"All right . . . Whoa, stop."

They turned in at the equipment room.

"There's a link."

Chandra dove toward it. She would have piled headfirst into the wall if J.D. had not grabbed her as she passed. She had nothing to hold on to, to stop her, but their combined mass slowed them so they drifted to a halt before the console. Chandra did not notice. She hooked in with Arachne, fitting the direct sensors over her head.

The rhythm of her breathing changed: long deep breaths changed to quick hard gasps. Her body quivered, and the skin over the nerve clusters grew livid. She moaned. It embarrassed J.D. to watch her. She turned away and pushed off, letting herself drift toward the other side of the room.

"I'm glad you're here," she said to Zev.

"I, too." He glanced at her from beneath his arm. He hung sideways in the air in relation to J.D., with his knees pulled close to his chest so he could reach his feet. He was untying his shoes.

"Your mother must be glad you're all right."

"Did you call her already? When?"

"No, I haven't called her. Haven't you called her?"

"I could not. Chandra said they would know who I was if I did that."

"She was probably right. Poor Lykos!"

"May we call her now?"

"We can try."

Leaving Chandra, J.D. led Zev to another equipment room and another hard-link.

But they could not get through to Lykos.

The transport pilot, having run out of arguments, turned recalcitrant, then surly. It was a quarter of an hour since she had replied to anyone.

Victoria took a second to check the position of the carrier. It was only a few thousand kilometers away, a hairsbreadth in astronomical terms, and its relative speed was fast enough that as she watched, it came perceptibly nearer.

"They're close," she said. "They're really close."

"Not close enough," the traffic controller said. "They can't accelerate enough to catch us and still have time to decelerate enough not to crash."

"First good news I've heard all day."

Dr. Thanthavong arrived at traffic control.

"Can I be of any help?" she asked Victoria.

"Please," Victoria said with relief. "Surely she'll listen to you." She moved aside so the world-renowned geneticist could come within reach of the sound pickup.

"Esther, my name is Thanthavong."

There was a long silence.

"What?" the transport pilot said.

"My name is Thanthavong."

"So? Am I supposed to know you?"

Dr. Thanthavong drew her eyebrows together in surprise.

"I am Miensaem Thanthavong, the geneticist. I developed viral depolymerase. I want to try to persuade you not to interfere with the expedition."

"I never heard of you and I don't want to talk to any geneticist. What happened to Victoria?"

Thanthavong spread her hands, defeated, embarrassed, and yet drily amused. "And here I thought I was a universal historical figure." She returned the controller's sound pickup to Victoria.

Victoria gathered her thoughts and tried again.

"Esther, you don't want to be responsible for the first hijacking in space, do you? You've got a duty to your passengers."

"The first hijacking!" the pilot said angrily. "You're a good one to talk about hijacking!"

"We've all agreed what to do. Everybody on the transport has chosen to return—and everyone who chose to return is on the transport. *Starfarer* isn't going to change course. There isn't much time. If you stay docked . . ."

"I don't believe you'll kidnap us," Esther said.

Victoria backed out of the pickup's range.

"I don't know what to say to her."

"Is there anyone on board she might respond to?"

Victoria could not think of anyone. She felt as if her thoughts were doing nothing but going around in confused little circles.

"Sure!" the controller said suddenly. "She's a pilot. Get Cherenkov."

"Of course," Thanthavong said.

"Where is he?"

They both glanced at the controller, as if he could divine the cosmonaut's whereabouts.

He shrugged. "No idea."

Victoria reached for the web, but found only the empty blankness of the blasted connections.

"Maybe we could go look . . . ?"

But there were too many places to look, and too short a time left in which to look for him.

The traffic controller groaned. "Oh, shit. Listen."

The voice on the speaker changed.

"*Starfarer*, this is the carrier *Hector*. Reverse your sail immediately. The starship must begin to decelerate immediately or we'll be forced to take drastic action."

Kolya grabbed Marion Griffith and kept him from crashing to the floor. Kolya knew many ways of killing a human being, but very few ways of taking a person's consciousness without causing damage.

He hoped Griffith would be all right. The young officer lay unconscious, but his pulse was strong, his breathing regular, and his larynx uncrushed.

Kolya could not have overcome Griffith by a direct attack. Instead he had let Griffith believe he saw an opening. When Griffith came at him, determined to overwhelm him, Kolya gained the advantage by knowing what he planned.

Kolya considered fitting Griffith into a spacesuit and taking him along. In the end, he decided against the plan. It was too dangerous. Griffith might be right to fear that the carrier would not pause to rescue one human being, or even two.

You will not thank me, I suppose, Kolya thought. But you are fortunate. You will continue with the expedition, while I must stay behind.

Victoria wanted to be in the sailhouse, in the observatory, anywhere but here. She wanted to be watching as *Starfarer*'s magnetic claws grabbed the cosmic string; she wanted to be in the center of everything that happened.

"If you do not reverse the sail, *Hector* will shoot to cripple your ship."

"They can't be serious!" Victoria cried.

"Wait a minute!" the transport pilot shouted. She began to curse at the carrier.

Stephen Thomas shivered.

"I don't know about you, Fox, but I'm getting cold."

He did know about her. She was sitting on a washing-machine-sized ultra-centrifuge, and her teeth were chattering.

"You could've picked a warmer place to hide. A nice meadow in the wild cylinder, maybe."

"You have to sign in," she said. "You would have known where to look."

"Through all sixty square kilometers?"

"Go ahead, make fun of me. I'm not getting on the transport."

"I really appreciate this," Stephen Thomas said. "When we get back, we all get to go straight to jail for kidnapping a minor. A minor president's niece, at that."

"Look on the bright side, Stephen Thomas," Fox said. "You'll get a lot longer sentence for helping steal *Starfarer*. Besides, maybe we won't *get* back." She sniffled. "It isn't fair!"

"I'm sorry. It *isn't* fair. But you still have to get on the transport and go home."

"I thought you were my friend!"

"Stephen Thomas?"

Stephen Thomas glanced over his shoulder. "In here, Satoshi. I found her."

Satoshi came into the cold room.

"Hello, Fox."

"Hello, Lono."

"This is not a great place to hide."

"I didn't think anybody would look here." She glanced at the rock in her hand. "You know . . . if you tried to force me out, and I busted a few things in here, I might infect the whole ship with . . . with . . ." She searched for a suitably horrible possibility. "With black plague."

"Forget it," Stephen Thomas said. "We don't keep pathogens on board except in transcribed form. You might as well try to infect somebody with a book."

"I bet I could do some damage to the gene stocks."

"You're a good geographer," Satoshi said, "but you haven't done any homework on genetics—or on the expedition's backups."

"Says who?"

"Says me," Stephen Thomas said. "Dr. Thanthavong doesn't take chances. We keep backups of everything at the other end of the building."

"Oh, yeah? Then how come you guys don't drag me up to the transport?"

"I don't believe in physical violence."

"I don't either," Stephen Thomas said, "but I'm beginning to understand its attraction."

The final countdown to transition began. As the carrier sped toward *Starfarer*, the starship's sail changed. Not reversing, as the carrier commanded, but withdrawing entirely. In the sunless, starless place they would soon enter, no solar wind existed to fill it and keep it untangled.

"Redeploy the sail," the voice of the carrier commanded. "You will not be permitted to draw in the sail. You must reverse it."

"The starship won't go into transition!" the transport pilot shouted. "I know these people, they won't—"

"Esther, undock *now*, dammit!" Victoria cried.

Victoria let her breath out hard. She wished she were with Stephen Thomas and Satoshi. She wished they were all with Iphigenie in the sailhouse. The halyards drew in the great silver sheet, stretching and compressing it into taut folds, gently twisting it into a cable kilometers long, but only a few meters in diameter.

"Magnetic fields at full strength," Arachne said through the speaker of the nearby hard-link. "Magnetic fields engaged."

"Shit!" Esther shouted. "Undock!"

"It's too late!"

"Undock, dammit!"

"Encounter," Arachne said, in its completely matter-of-fact computer voice.

The magnetic claws engaged with the cosmic string, transformed an infinitesimal percent of its unlimited energy, and began to build transition energy.

The countdown reversed, leading toward transition. Victoria imagined she could feel the increase of the starship's potential.

They can't stop us, she thought. No matter how fast the carrier moves, it can't catch us, it can't follow us, it can't stop *Starfarer*.

Ecstatic, she shouted in triumph and flung her arms around Thanthavong.

The voice of the carrier spoke.

"Fire."

A point of light detached itself from the carrier and accelerated at terrifying speed toward the starship.

The missile hit.

13

Starfarer shuddered.

Victoria gasped. She held Thanthavong tighter, as if she could protect her if the starship collapsed around them.

Drifting free, Victoria saw the ship vibrating, and felt the trembling of the heavy, oppressive air. The rumble of the attack pressed against her hearing, a drumming of such low frequency that she felt it in her bones.

"Esther!" The traffic controller's voice rose as he tried to reach the transport pilot.

J.D. and Zev propelled themselves into the traffic control cubicle, J.D. pale with shock, Zev excited.

"What happened?"

"The missile," Thanthavong said. "Was it armed?"

"It can't have exploded," Victoria said. "We'd . . . we'd know." She dove for the hard-link and desperately demanded real-time information on *Starfarer*'s status.

Arachne responded sluggishly, but it did respond. The campus and the wild side both maintained their air pressure: neither cylinder had been seriously breached. They had been built well, to retain their integrity under the stress of the spin, the pull of the solar sail, the unknown changes of transition.

Equally important, the starship remained magnetically bound to the cosmic string, gathering energy.

"We're still docked!" The transport pilot's voice sounded

hollow and feverish. "I don't believe they—I'm going to—"

If the transport undocked now, *Starfarer* would pull it into transition, like a rowboat caught in the wake of a cruiser. But the transport possessed insufficient mass to survive transition alone.

"Don't let them loose!" Victoria shouted to the controller.

"What? Why?"

"It's too late—we're too near transition! Get everybody back inside!"

The controller locked the transport into the docking module. The pilot swore at him, swore at their pursuers, swore at EarthSpace and *Starfarer* and scientists.

But at the same time she understood what was happening; she understood the danger. No one knew for certain what the conditions might be outside the starship between the point when it vanished from space-time and the moment of its reappearance. Esther slammed the transport's hatch open, and, still cursing, ordered her passengers back into *Starfarer*.

Victoria searched the display. Arachne sent confused and erratic signals.

"The missile must have hit us a glancing blow," Victoria said.

"They can't have planned to do this," J.D. said. "How could they . . . ?"

"They are very determined to get what they want." Zev did not sound like the innocent J.D. had described.

Thanthavong hovered beside Victoria.

"Arachne's called in the damage control team," Victoria said. "But the cylinder's not seriously breached and the missile didn't detonate. Maybe it wasn't armed. Maybe it was only meant to cripple us. At least we're still on course. I hope there isn't an eight-point-five earthquake zone right over where it hit . . ."

Staring at the display, Thanthavong suddenly gripped Victoria's shoulder.

"It hit us directly beneath the genetics department," she said. "The gene stocks . . . sensitizing viruses . . ." She drew back, turned, and pushed off toward the exit. "I've got to get down there—"

Victoria went with her. J.D. and Zev followed close behind. They passed the transport waiting room, where the outbound passengers milled around in anger and outrage and despair.

They reached the hill leading to the floor of the cylinder. At first everything appeared normal in the interior of the starship.

Victoria saw the destruction around the genetics building.

It was as if someone had placed a circle of land on a plate, and tossed it, so it fell back almost into place, but collapsed and jumbled. The earth, so recently covered with the lacy green of new grass, broke open to reveal streaks of harsh red clay. Saplings and bushes lay uprooted, flung against each other, in irregular concentric circles leading outward from the point of damage.

The cracks in the earth cut across a hill, the hill that housed the genetics department.

Victoria plunged down the slope at a dangerous speed, leaving the other three behind. First she pulled herself along the handholds, nearly in freefall, then she took great leaping strides through microgravity, and then she ran, toward the earthquake zone, toward the broken streaks of earth.

The impact flung Kolya against the wall of the tunnel. He slid toward the floor, half-stunned. The body of the starship moaned around him, the bonded rocks grinding together beneath the stress—of transition? Or had Iphigenie been forced to reverse the sail? He did not know whether to feel joy or grief. He turned on the radio in his spacesuit, but heard only confused fragments of talk. The web remained useless.

Kolya heard the faint high hiss of escaping air.

Startled, he flanged his helmet shut and hurried to Griffith, who lay half in, half out of his spacesuit. Kolya struggled, but soon realized he had no chance of getting Griffith into the suit. He grabbed a survival pouch from the emergency rack, dragged Griffith free, and manhandled him into the sphere. He sealed it and activated the oxygen reserve. The government agent remained unconscious.

I did far too expert a job on him, Kolya thought.

He tried to drag Griffith in his silver sphere all the way to an elevator, so they both could escape to the surface. After ten meters he knew it was hopeless. Griffith, though not a large man, made a heavy, awkward weight in the full gravity of the starship's lowest level.

The sound of escaping air grew fainter as the atmospheric pressure fell.

Kolya felt a low, grinding vibration. The baffles were sliding shut. The elevator was already closed off. With one final burst of exertion, Kolya dragged Griffith beyond the moving baffle. He did not want to leave him, but he could do him no good if they both were trapped between airtight doors. Kolya plunged through the narrowing space and ran toward the airlock. Behind him, the misaligned panels shrieked in their tracks with a high-pitched squeal that traveled through the ground, vibrated into his body, and pierced his hearing.

I'll have to travel around the outside of the ship, Kolya thought, and find an undamaged entrance—or go all the way to the axis, if need be—and bring help. From outside, I might detect the position of the air leak, the extent of the damage.

He hoped he would be able to tell what had happened, what caused the impact.

Am I still willing, he wondered, to fling myself into the void and hope our pursuers will stop to rescue me? I will probably never know the answer to that question. By now our escape or capture must be sealed.

Kolya entered the airlock and started its sequence. The inner door slid shut, but refused to close the final few centimeters. Kolya shoved it until it caught, then waited impatiently while the airlock cycled. He held tight to the grips, afraid the lock might open prematurely and fling him out into space with the last of the air. It evacuated properly. At his feet, the hatch leading onto the outer skin of the starship opened halfway and stuck. He climbed down and squeezed through, no easy matter in the bulky pressure suit.

He lowered himself onto the inspection cables and headed for the next nearest of the access hatches that dotted the ship's exterior. With the outer surface of the starship at his back, he crawled rapidly over the cables like a four-legged spider. Only the cables lay between him and space.

The spin took him in view of the sailhouse, the furled silver sail, and the magnetic claws that reached to the cosmic string. Both claws and string should have been invisible: the claws, an energy field, had no substance, while the cosmic string had enormous mass but only the single dimension of length. Yet Kolya perceived an odd, pointillist image: two flexing arms like tentacles, grasping a distant, slender thread. He could only see it when he observed it from the corner of his vision. Perhaps he imagined it all; perhaps he saw some perfectly natural phenomenon. Could Hawking radiation appear in the visible spectrum? Kolya did not pretend to understand cosmic string, or Hawking radiation for that matter.

The starship spun him past the magnetic claws and into the canyon between *Starfarer*'s two cylinders.

He continued to crawl. He had nearly reached the next hatch.

But he had also moved into a region where the starship's smooth rock surface became cracked and jumbled.

Kolya raised his head. The ship curved gradually upward, forming a close horizon.

The cosmonaut stopped, horrified, disbelieving. He had come upon the cause of the impact and the damage.

Far from striking a glancing blow, then tumbling off harmlessly into space, the missile had plunged itself into the starship. It was lodged a meter deep in *Starfarer*'s skin.

When the earthquake hit, Infinity *knew* what had happened. He never doubted the accuracy of his perception.

"What was that?" Florrie jerked her head up, and the small shells in her hair rattled. In the corner of her main room, the painted egg snapped from its thread. It fell, bounced on a woven mat, rolled in a half-circle, and stopped. It lay miraculously unbroken.

Infinity picked it up gently and handed it to Floris. He watched himself perform such an ordinary gesture, astounded. He was in shock, he knew he was in shock. But he was powerless to shake away the stunned certainty that *Starfarer*'s pursuers had behaved every bit as badly as he had feared they might. No: not *quite* as badly. They must not have used a nuclear warhead, or *Starfarer* would be dead.

Arachne's web remained silent. Infinity activated the console in the corner of Florrie's main room and used the hard-link to find the location of the damage and the condition of the ship. One of the few people left on board with hard-vacuum construction experience, he was part of the damage control team. He would have to go below immediately. *Starfarer* possessed self-healing capabilities, but it had limits.

"What happened?" Florrie demanded.

Despite everything, the ship remained on course. Infinity was amazed.

"We've encountered the string!" He gave her the good

news and kept the bad to himself. "I have to go for a while, Florrie. I'm sorry. Will you be okay?"

"Yes." Her smile was quiet, relieved, joyful. "Yes, I'll be fine. They can't make me leave now, can they?"

Despite everything, Infinity grinned. "They sure can't."

He left her sitting in her window seat, cupping the fragile egg in both hands.

Victoria broke into a run. Other people joined her, disoriented, shocked, appalled. She reached the edge of the tumbled earth. The genetics building looked like it had been shaken until it broke. She climbed across the rough ground. She was the first to reach the entrance. The doorway had partially collapsed. Someone was trying to crawl between its crushed supports. Victoria grabbed the clutching hand.

"Help . . ."

"It's all right," Victoria said. "You'll be out in a minute, it's all right."

The green scent of crushed grass mixed with the dry tang of mineral dust and the meaty, organic smell of spilled nutrient medium. Broken rock scraped Victoria's legs and sides, and dirt from the sagging hill's turf sifted onto her. In the dimness of the destroyed building, Victoria could see Fox, Satoshi's recalcitrant graduate student. Fox gripped desperately at her hand.

"Hang on. Can you get a foothold? Pull yourself up, there's more room above you."

With Victoria's help, Fox scrambled higher. Panting, nearly sobbing, she dragged herself out of the rubble. Beyond her it was dark except for the light that reflected from a pillowy cloud of fog: evaporating liquid nitrogen.

"Is anybody else still in there?"

Fox gasped for air. "Satoshi, and Stephen Thomas, in the cold room . . ."

Victoria pushed past her and dove through the opening.

Sliding over the destruction and into the dark corridor, she sprawled on the floor within a layer of cold vapor. She stumbled to her feet. The nitrogen fog flowed across her shoulders and swirled around her legs. Above it, she could breathe. Emergency lights glowed faintly, but the dense mist concealed the floor. She had to feel her way along. Was the cold room the third door of the back side of the hall, or the fourth?

"Satoshi! Stephen Thomas!"

"Victoria, down here!"

Satoshi's voice: Victoria caught her breath with relief. Resisting the urge to try to hurry, she moved cautiously through the dimness. Tendrils of freezing mist, so thick and cohesive they looked like a liquid, swirled around her hips.

Infinity struggled with an access hatch that led into *Starfarer*'s underground. It opened about a handsbreadth, then stuck. Though the worst of the missile's impact had hit the genetics department, a couple of hundred meters away, the earthquake had jammed this hatch as well. He tried again to move it, not wanting to backtrack to a more distant entrance.

"Let me help."

J.D. Sauvage squatted beside him, grabbed the edge of the hatch cover, and settled herself.

Infinity nodded.

They both pulled. The alien contact specialist was a big woman. She powered her effort with her legs, not just her back.

The hatch gave, springing open and slamming out of their grasp. They jumped away. It thudded onto the ground, bounced, and settled.

"Thanks."

"Do you need help?" J.D. said. "Should I come with you?"

"I might have to go outside," he said.

He plunged through the hatchway.

Infinity Mendez disappeared into *Starfarer*'s underground tunnels without really answering J.D.'s question. He was so shy and quiet that J.D. could not be sure whether he had been trying to ask her for help, or trying to tell her to stay behind. But he was all alone, and she could see that whatever the problem was at the genetics department, Victoria already had as much help as she needed. Maybe more help than she needed.

J.D. climbed into the tunnel.

She could not be sure which way Infinity had gone, so she kept going down whenever she could.

She entered a region in which the effects of the impact became evident. An automatic baffle-door creaked open ahead of her. She stopped, scared: if the baffles malfunctioned they might blast her out into space.

Nothing happened: no wind, no shocking cold, no vacuum drawing the air out of her lungs. The door had closed in response to the impact, but the ship's systems opened it again when they detected no difference in the air pressure on either side.

Nevertheless, she accepted the warning. As soon as she reached an airlock's access room, she climbed into a pressure suit.

"—Cherenkov. Can anyone—".

The sound startled her. The disembodied voice emanated from the suit radio. She pulled the helmet shut. The transmission faded, then returned clearly.

"This is Nikolai Petrovich. *Starfarer* has been hit with a missile, which has penetrated approximately one meter into the surface. I cannot move it myself. I need help, tools, a radiation gauge. Can anyone hear me?"

"Kolya?"

"Yes! I am here, who is it?"

"J.D."

"J.D., I do not suppose you have space construction experience?"

"No."

"I must have help."

"I'll go get somebody."

"There may not be time. Will you risk it?"

"I've never been outside in space! I wouldn't know what to do!"

"This is not a complex job," he said. "But I need more strength. More strength than I have."

By his voice, she knew he was tiring. J.D. looked around, hoping to see Infinity or some other damage crew member. But she was alone.

"All right. I'll try."

She entered the airlock. The controls were all too simple. The cycle began. The lock pumped away the air and opened the exterior hatch.

J.D. looked down. The stars streaked past beneath her feet. The only point of stability was the end of the exit ladder. She gripped her end of the ladder and lowered herself hesitantly. The starship loomed above her. Space lay below and all around, separated from her by nothing but the fragile web of cables.

The suit's airgun hung against her leg, useless. If she lost her grip, the cylinder's spin would fling her out into space. No airgun could power her back.

"Kolya?"

"I am still here. It is still stuck. Hurry, please."

"Where *are* you?"

"Orient yourself in the same direction as the spin. I am just over your horizon."

She did as he asked, clutching the cables. She knelt there, balancing precariously. It was as if she were being flung headlong into the Milky Way. She squeezed her eyes shut and took a deep breath.

"J.D.!"

She opened her eyes again. "Yes," she said. "I'm coming."

She had watched recordings of spacewalks; she had even experienced several direct sensory recordings. In every one, the effect had been of floating weightless in silent gentle space, with the stars a motionless background.

This was entirely different. She crawled across the cables with the stars blazing past beneath her. The spin gave her the perception that gravity was pulling her downward into an unending fall.

Her breath sounded harsh and sweat ran down her sides, more from fear than from exertion.

J.D. searched the upward-curving surface of the starship. The cables shuddered beneath her hands and knees, loosened by the impact of the missile. In places the smooth stone surface had cracked, and broken rock projected toward her from above. One slab shifted and scraped against her back, startling her with its touch and vibration. She shrank down, gripping the cables.

After a moment she pushed herself up again and crawled forward.

And then she saw the missile, a sleek shape designed for space-to-air flight, wedged in the cracked surface of the starship. His legs twined in the cables, Kolya struggled to loosen the missile. His perilous position terrified J.D. She hurried on.

"Kolya! Wait—"

"J.D.! *Bojemoi*, I'm glad to see you."

She reached Kolya's side. The cosmonaut touched the flank of the missile and drew his gloved hand along its side. It shifted slightly, vibrating against the cables so they quivered in J.D.'s hands.

"Be careful."

"An elegant bit of warfare, this," Kolya said. "Go around to the other side, and brace yourself. Hook up your work line."

"Can it detonate?" J.D. asked.

"That I do not know."

"They couldn't have used an armed missile!"

"J.D., of course they could. Perhaps they thought that the threat alone would stop us. But I am not willing to bet the life of the starship on it."

J.D. saw what Kolya planned. She moved into place and hooked up her work line.

"I'm ready."

Suddenly the starship shuddered. The spinning stars wavered and brightened and disappeared. J.D. was surrounded by a multicolored, speckled, streaming haze. She gasped in wonder.

The starship had entered transition.

J.D. wanted nothing more than to lose herself in the sight of it. It flung itself toward her, upward, in an optical illusion of continuous approach that never came near. She shivered.

The cables flexed beneath her. She forced her attention away from transition, back to the missile and Kolya. But the cosmonaut, too, gazed downward past the cables, past the end of the missile, into transition.

"Kolya," J.D. whispered. "Kolya, we've got to get rid of this thing!"

"So I felt . . ." Kolya did not look up. "But do we have the right to loose it in this unknown place?"

She wanted to follow his gaze. Instead, she reached out and touched his arm.

"Kolya," she said respectfully, without any irony or sarcasm, "Comrade Cherenkov, this missile could destroy *Starfarer* and all our friends."

Kolya looked at her. The faraway expression slowly faded from his face.

"Yes," he said finally. "You're right. Of course you're right."

Victoria slid between the crushed interior walls of the hill.

It was freezing. The cold fog of evaporating liquid nitrogen flowed past her feet. The smell was intense, of yeast and agar plates and nutrient medium.

"Over here. He's bleeding, I can't get it stopped."

She found Satoshi, awkwardly trying to hold Stephen Thomas above the unbreathable vapor, at the same time trying to stanch a bleeding head cut. There was blood all over, spattering Satoshi's hands and arms, covering Stephen Thomas's face, leaking between Satoshi's fingers.

Victoria pushed away bits of broken equipment, fragmented glass, crumbled rock foam. She reached Satoshi's side.

"What happened?"

"I don't know. He was bleeding, but he said it was just a scrape. We were on our way out, and he keeled over."

Stephen Thomas was heavily unconscious. His hand was cold, his pulse weak and fast. He must be badly wounded, there was so much blood, it covered his face and sprayed the front of his battered t-shirt and pasted his pale hair against his skin.

Rock foam panels grated together, rasping each other to dust that sifted down in the dim light. The nitrogen fog crept to Victoria's waist.

Stephen Thomas might have a concussion, or even a fractured skull. Victoria knew they should not move him, but she was afraid not to.

"Let's get him out of here."

They lifted Stephen Thomas and dragged and carried

him into the corridor. Satoshi tried to keep pressure on the
head wound. A bright light glimmered along the top of the
fog. It flashed in Victoria's eyes, dazzling her.

Zev appeared silently before them, carrying a flashlight.
He glanced at Stephen Thomas.

"Let me see." He moved Satoshi's hand. Blood pulsed
from Stephen Thomas's forehead.

"Zev, don't, he'll bleed to death!"

Victoria and Satoshi both tried to reapply pressure to
the wound, but Zev pushed between them and leaned over
their partner.

Victoria watched, shocked and appalled, as Zev bent
down and placed his lips against the cut on Stephen Thomas's
forehead. Before she could protest or push him away, he
straightened up. Blood covered his mouth and his chin.
Satoshi reached out to put pressure on the wound again,
but Zev stopped him.

"Leave it be."

"What did you do?"

Victoria's horrified expression amused him. "I stopped
the bleeding—what did you think?"

"I thought you were drinking his blood!"

Zev grimaced. "Do I look like a lamprey? Why didn't
you—oh. This must be a difference between divers and
people."

He pushed bloody, sticky blond hair away from the
wound.

The cut had stopped bleeding.

"He is lucky," Zev said.

"Lucky!"

"This is not a serious wound—not on land. Divers fear
head cuts because they bleed so, even a scratch like this one.
Sometimes you can't stop them before the sharks smell the
blood from far away, and come to eat you. But here there
are no sharks."

Stephen Thomas groaned. He opened his eyes, then closed them again.

"What—?"

"It's okay," Satoshi said. "We'll be out of here in a minute."

"This place looks so weird . . ." he muttered.

"Yeah, it's falling down around us. Let's go."

In the uncertain light of Zev's flash, they helped Stephen Thomas to the entrance, boosted him out of the ruins of Genetics Hill, and climbed after him.

As Victoria emerged from the frigid darkness of the ruined genetics building, the light from the sun tube abruptly faded.

Victoria looked up, as startled as a creature beneath a total solar eclipse.

She let out a cry half triumph, half sob.

Starfarer had reached transition.

Out of reach of its pursuers, the ship progressed toward an alien star system. Victoria had made its escape possible.

And right now, instead of feeling triumph, she asked herself if it was worth it.

Light, strange and watery, rose again as the starship drew energy from the magnetic claws and fed it into the tubes.

People surrounded her, some in protective suits, some carrying tanks of liquid nitrogen, some with isolation canisters. ASes and AIs also congregated around the entrance. Professor Thanthavong stood in the middle of it all, coordinating the beginnings of a salvage operation. As soon as she saw Stephen Thomas, she called a paramedic over to help him.

Stephen Thomas stumbled and opened his eyes. Their blue was startling in the mask of drying blood. He looked around groggily.

"What did you do to the light?" he said. He sank to the ground. "Why does everything look so weird?"

Victoria looked around. The campus was different, alien and frightening, in the light of transition.

"You've got blood in your eyes," Thanthavong said.

"Oh, yeah, I'm a real blue-blood . . ."

"Be quiet and sit still for a minute," the paramedic said.

Victoria knelt beside Stephen Thomas, concerned. At first she had thought she understood what he was talking about, but now she could not make sense of what he was saying. Beside her, Satoshi rested his head on his knees, breathing deeply.

"You're going to have one hell of a black eye," the paramedic said to Stephen Thomas.

"A black eye!" Victoria exclaimed. "He was unconscious!"

"There's no serious trauma."

"Then why—"

Stephen Thomas laid his hand on her arm.

"I'm okay," he said. "I am. Honest. I fainted." He looked away, embarrassed. "I can't stand the sight of blood."

Relief made Victoria shiver, and then she started to laugh. When Stephen Thomas glared at her, she hugged him.

Thanthavong hurried over, trailed by Fox and a couple of ASes. Machines had begun to work to clear the entryway of the genetics department.

"Did you see anyone else inside?"

"There's no one," Satoshi said.

"You're sure?" Thanthavong gazed at the ruined hill, her expression unreadable.

"Yes. I passed every lab and every office, from the top down, looking for Fox. There wasn't anybody."

"Yes. All right. Good . . ." Her voice trailed off.

Dr. Thanthavong, whose surface so seldom even ruffled, suddenly cried out in anger and in pain.

Victoria jumped to her feet, startled and scared. Then she went to Thanthavong and embraced her. "I'm so sorry," she said. "All your work—"

"It isn't that," Thanthavong wailed. "It's—" She sobbed and struggled for control. "It is that. But in forty years my labs never had a serious accident. And now, my god, look what they've done!"

J.D. and Kolya strained to move the missile. J.D. could feel the metabolic enhancer pumping inside her, but it was useless. It helped her endurance. What she needed right now was brute strength. Brute strength and the will to keep her attention away from the weird effects of transition.

Suddenly the missile shifted in its crater. The squeal of metal on stone vibrated through the skin of *Starfarer*, through J.D.'s suit, to her ears. It was the only sound except her breathing, her pulse.

Suddenly, unexpectedly, the missile slipped free.

"Hold it!" Kolya shouted. "Keep hold of it!"

J.D. almost let it go. That was what they had been struggling for—! But the desperation in Kolya's voice stopped her.

She clamped her arms around the missile. It moved like a live thing. It escaped Kolya and wriggled half a meter downward through J.D.'s grasp. Nothing but J.D.'s safety line and her feet hooked around the cables held it.

The spin had brought them into the canyon between the two cylinders. If J.D. let the missile go, it would ricochet against the wild cylinder.

Her feet slipped, inexorably. Kolya grabbed her and the missile. She could see the sweat on the cosmonaut's face. Sweat poured down her own face, down her body. Her arms shook with strain. She feared the warhead might detonate at any second, but she could not let it go. The spin, which had felt so fast a few minutes before, now slowed in her perception to a crawl.

Her feet sprang free of the cables. She gasped as her safety line snapped taut. It vibrated in the bass range like a huge alien instrument. Kolya shouted as the missile slid through his grasp. J.D. held it tighter. Kolya tried to pull her back, but all he could do was keep himself twined in the cables and clutch J.D.'s ankle.

Something changed.

She emerged from the canyon. Space opened out around her.

"Now!" Kolya said.

She released the missile. *Starfarer*'s spin flung it away, away from the starship, toward the constellations barely skewed by the vast distance the ship had traveled.

Kolya dragged J.D. to safety.

J.D. tried to speak. Her mouth was too dry.

"Come on," Kolya said. "Hurry."

As quickly as J.D. could move, they made their way to the hatch and into the airlock. As soon as the inner door opened, Kolya grabbed her arm and rushed her deeper into the ship, through the suit room and up, without even pausing to open his face mask.

"What's wrong?" J.D. said. "We got rid of it!"

Kolya finally slowed and stopped. He took off his helmet.

"We should be safe here. I wanted to be sure—"

He cut himself off. The ship trembled with a faint vibration. J.D. looked down, toward the outer surface, as if she could see the missile through the floor.

Outside, the warhead detonated, sending out a wave of debris and radiation that blasted against the starship's thick skin of lunar rock.

Water slicked and darkened the floor of the lowest tunnel. Infinity kept watch for the leak. He could hear no rush of water, so the sealers must be working. He hoped the

attack had not breached the main flow systems and let any
significant amount of water escape into space.

It hurt him to see so much damage to the structure he
had helped to build. Making *Starfarer* whole again would
take more than letting the self-sealers creep into the cracks
and cement the broken bits. That would be like letting a
smashed bone heal without setting it.

Infinity hurried along the upcurving corridor. It truncat-
ed abruptly in a closed baffle.

As a precaution, he fastened the helmet of his pressure
suit. Getting outside might be quicker and easier through
another hatch, but that would be a ten minute walk, and more
than that much again to return along the outside of the ship.
He felt a certain urgency. He kept expecting to encounter other members of damage control, but so far he had seen no one.

He read the display on the baffle. It showed normal air
pressure on the far side. He cautiously opened the door with
the manual controls, stepped through into the next compartment, and closed the baffle behind him.

Soon he faced another airtight baffle. This display
showed very low air pressure on the far side, a few millimeters
of mercury, nowhere near enough to breathe.

Infinity paused, listening carefully. The rhythmic, muffled pounding was real, not his imagination. It came from
beyond the closed door.

The pounding stopped. Infinity hit the baffle with the
side of his fist. Nothing happened. Perhaps the pounding was
nothing but a mechanical malfunction, or perhaps whoever
was on the other side of the baffle could not hear or feel the
vibrations of his fist. He stamped his foot.

One loud "thud!" answered him.

Infinity stamped again. Another "thud!" replied.

He emptied the air from the compartment he was in.
When the pressure equalized, the baffle allowed itself to be
unlocked, but Infinity had to force it open.

A burst of ice crystals exploded through the doorway, scattering like tiny needles against Infinity's suit. Ice crystals and snowflakes filled the chamber with sparkling white light, then fell straight to the floor and melted in the thin layer of water. At the same time, the temperature of the room fell abruptly and the floor froze in a slow wave. Infinity moved forward, his boots crackling on the ice.

Snow blanketed the room, covering a large lump in the middle of the floor. The lump lurched as whoever was within it pounded on the floor. The snow sifted off the silver emergency pouch and fell into small drifts.

Infinity turned the pouch to see its transparent panel.

Curled up like the worm in a jumping bean, Griffith glared out. He said something, angrily, but of course Infinity could not hear him. Instead of turning on his suit radio, Infinity grabbed the handles of the pouch and dragged Griffith back into the second chamber.

He left him lying there, helpless—he had no choice about that—while he closed the baffle. He moved some air into the chamber.

He was laughing uncontrollably.

By the time the chamber held enough air to carry sounds, he managed to stop laughing. He took off the suit helmet and wiped his eyes.

The survival pouch writhed against the floor.

"Get me *out* of here!"

Infinity unsealed the pouch. Griffith scrambled up and kicked away the emergency sphere.

"Damn! What's going on? Where's Cherenkov?"

Infinity did not know the answers, so he did not reply. He settled back on his heels. Griffith strode angrily away, but the closed baffle stopped him.

"How the hell do I get out of here?"

"Open the door."

Griffith fumbled at the controls. The baffle creaked. Radiating anger and impatience, Griffith waited. But when the door had finally slid aside for him to pass, he swung around and glared at Infinity.

"Don't you ever—*ever*—tell anyone about this!"

A day ago, an hour ago, Griffith would have terrified Infinity Mendez to silence with such a command. Now, Infinity regarded him quizzically. Griffith no longer held any power to frighten him.

"I'll tell anybody I want, anything I want. Don't you even have the guts to say thank you?"

And then—he tried not to, but could not help himself—he started to laugh again.

A microsecond's blast of bright white light spread through the interior of the starship, a flash almost too brief to perceive before the filters damped and darkened it. Stephen Thomas cried out and turned away, flinging his arms across his face. *Starfarer* plunged into dusk.

"That wasn't what I had in mind," Stephen Thomas said, his voice muffled, his eyes still covered, "when I said I didn't like the light."

The whole cylinder trembled faintly.

The sun tubes slowly brightened, radiating a more normal light. Victoria knew what must have happened. There was only one explanation for that kind of intense actinic blast. The missile had followed the starship through transition. And it had detonated. Yet it was free of the starship, distant enough for *Starfarer* to survive the explosion. She started to shake. Satoshi knelt beside her and held her, and they drew Stephen Thomas into the embrace. Zev sat on his heels nearby, watching them.

"We made it," Victoria whispered. "We're out of transition." Suddenly she caught her breath. "If the missile *did* detonate—Iphigenie is in the sailhouse! Is she—?"

Professor Thanthavong switched frequencies on her AS controller and opened a voice link to the sailhouse.

"Iphigenie, this is Thanthavong. Can you reply?"

"Are you all right?" Victoria said.

"Yes." Her voice was a whisper. "It's been . . . quite exciting out here."

"The shielding—?"

"It held. Victoria, I saw transition . . . And we are in the Tau Ceti system."

"It's incredible, Victoria!" The second voice from the sailhouse belonged to Feral. "God, I think I'll change myself to be a sensory recorder like Chandra!"

"Don't do that." Victoria struggled to her feet, pulling Satoshi and Stephen Thomas with her. "We ought to be in the explorer," she said. "We're supposed to be continuing the expedition as if nothing had happened."

She reached for the web, expecting emptiness. To her surprise she touched a fragile strand, a tangle of thread tossed over the surface of the massed databases. Though Arachne would not reply, Victoria felt it growing and spreading, interconnecting, compelled to regain its multidimensionality.

"Stephen Thomas, do you feel up to going out?"

"I told you I'm all right! But . . ." He stared at the rubble of Genetics Hill.

"There's nothing you can do," Professor Thanthavong said. "No more people are going in there till the AIs and the ASes have been through it." She spoke to all of them. "You aren't in danger of illness—we store no pathogens. But I want blood samples. I may have to mix you a depolymerase if you were exposed to sensitizing virus. It isn't something you want permanently floating around in your system." An AS buzzed up to her and offered her a half-dozen sampling kits. She took blood from Victoria and Satoshi and Zev and Fox, then came toward Stephen Thomas.

"You can have my shirt," he said hopefully.

"Very funny."

As the kit pulled ten centiliters of blood out of him, Stephen Thomas paled. Victoria was afraid he would faint again, but he averted his gaze and collected himself.

"Where is J.D.?" Zev said.

"I don't know." Victoria looked around. "I thought she was right behind us."

"She does not like to run," Zev said. "She likes to swim."

Automatically, Victoria queried the web, but it was completely involved with its own reconstruction.

"I'm going to the explorer," Victoria said. "That's where I'm supposed to be, and that's where I'm going." She felt near to screaming with frustration. "J.D. knows where it is—maybe she'll meet us there."

They crossed the fields to return to the axis and the explorer dock. Zev tagged along. Victoria walked on one side of Stephen Thomas and Satoshi on the other, just in case.

"I really am okay," Stephen Thomas said. "But I'm going home for a few minutes." He turned toward Victoria, defensive, expecting her to object. "We're all a mess—"

"You're right," she said. They all looked a wreck, particularly Stephen Thomas. Victoria grinned. "We can't go exploring like this. Remember what your mother always told you about clean underwear."

Stephen Thomas said, "No, what?"

"What is underwear?" Zev asked.

The mini-horses pounded past, running, as horses run, in response to fright, their ears back, slick with sweat. Victoria smelled their fear.

On a hillock near the path, Kolya Cherenkov raised himself out of an access tunnel and climbed to ground level. He reached down and gave a hand to Infinity Mendez, then to J.D., and finally to the accountant from the GAO.

Zev ran toward J.D. and hugged her and swung around

with her. She gathered him in and kissed his hair, his cheek, his lips, murmuring to him, telling him what had happened.

For a few minutes it seemed as if everyone tried to talk at the same time, explaining, questioning. Only Griffith stood apart. Victoria did not quite turn her back on him—she distrusted him too much for that—but she would not look directly at him; she could neither meet his gaze nor bring herself to speak to him.

"We had a plan to stop the takeover, Griffith and I," Kolya said. "A very foolhardy plan . . . it might have worked. But then the missile hit, and things became more complicated. Then we entered transition."

"You saw it? What did you see? Tell me!"

Kolya's expression sobered. "I . . . I cannot describe it. I am sorry."

Envious and jealous and angry, Victoria looked for Griffith. She did not know what she wanted to say to him. Perhaps nothing. Perhaps she only wanted to glare.

"I didn't see it at all," he said. He turned around and strode away.

"He has . . . things to think about," Kolya said apologetically.

"No kidding," Victoria said.

As soon as she and her partners had cleaned up, Victoria led the way up the hill to *Starfarer*'s axis, where the team's explorer waited in its dock on the hub.

"Victoria!" J.D. sounded breathless. "Touch the web. The explorer—"

It took Victoria a moment to make her way through the reconnecting pathways.

Her steps faltered.

"Holy shit," Stephen Thomas said. Satoshi looked stunned. Zev reacted with a smile.

The explorer was receiving a transmission: a strong,

regular signal of precise frequency. From outside *Starfarer*. From within the Tau Ceti system.

"Let's *go*!"

Victoria broke into a run. She leaped through the gravity gradient, skimmed across the microgravity, and entered the zero-g core.

The team members sailed weightless through the hallways. They had to pass the transport to reach the next dock, where their explorer waited. Victoria glanced through the transparent partition into the transport's waiting room.

Though the transport passengers had disembarked, most of them remained at the starship's axis, as if they had been delayed by some minor mechanical glitch and would soon return to their places and fly home. Alzena, in her black clothes, huddled in a corner staring at the wall.

Gerald Hemminge saw Victoria. He launched himself toward the doorway, grabbed the doorframe to change his vector, and plunged down the hallway after her.

"Victoria!"

"I can't talk to you now." She kept going.

"But we've still a chance to recover from this awful mistake."

"Did your boss send you out to tell us that?" She was too excited to be bitter, but not too distracted for a little sarcasm. "I didn't see him—does he have his own private waiting room?"

"The chancellor wasn't on the transport," Gerald said. "He accepted the leadership of this expedition, and he determined to remain."

"Nobody cares now, Gerald," Satoshi said. "Leave us alone."

Gerald saw Stephen Thomas. As the paramedic promised, he was developing a spectacular black eye.

"Good god! What happened to you?"

"We nearly got squashed when your damned missile—"

"*My* missile! It belonged to *your* government—"

Stephen Thomas lunged awkwardly toward Gerald and grabbed him by the leg. Both men tumbled, bouncing from one wall to the other.

"Let go!"

Ignoring Gerald's protest, and his kicking, Stephen Thomas climbed up him until they were face to face.

"As far as I'm concerned, that fucking missile belongs to all the jerks who wanted to stop the expedition, and you're one of them!" He shouted, furious; he shoved Gerald away. The reaction knocked Stephen Thomas against a wall. He had to scramble to get his balance. Gerald, more experienced in weightlessness, caught himself with his feet and pushed off again, still following Victoria.

"Victoria!"

"I told you I can't talk to you now. Gerald—we've got a signal. From the Tau Ceti system."

"But—that's wonderful!"

Victoria reached the explorer's hatch.

"I'm glad you understand. Now let us get to work, eh?"

"I do understand! This changes everything. If we go home now, with this evidence, we can start with a clean slate. Repairs, provisions, all our personnel—and then we can come back . . ."

His voice trailed off. All four members of the alien contact team stared at him, unbelieving. Victoria felt completely unable to come up with a sufficient response to what he had said.

When Zev followed J.D. into the explorer, Victoria neither objected nor tried to stop him. The alternative was to leave him out in the hall with Gerald.

Victoria headed for her couch. Before she relaxed into it, before the safety straps eased around her, she had already begun the explorer's system checks.

As the systems signaled green and ready, the sensory overload of the last few chaotic hours flowed away, leaving Victoria physically drained but mentally hypersensitive.

Satoshi and Stephen Thomas and J.D. settled into their places in the circle. Zev drew himself into one of the places reserved for auxiliary, temporary members of the alien contact team, a place next to J.D.

Victoria glanced at each of her teammates in turn.

"Ready?"

"Let's go."

At Victoria's signal, the observation ports cleared and the explorer moved smoothly out of its dock. *Starfarer* fell away, its sail illuminated and filled by the new starlight.

They all gazed at their first close-up view of an alien star system.

A display formed, mimicking the system but exaggerating the planets so they would appear larger than pinpoints. Victoria compared the display to the system before them and showed her teammates the tiny disks of the planets, one half-full, and the other, closer one a slender crescent accompanied by the smaller crescent of its satellite.

"Christ on a unicorn," Stephen Thomas said.

"I'm recording now," Victoria said, "and transmitting back to *Starfarer*. We have not one but two terrestrial worlds—the second and third planets of the system—orbiting Tau Ceti. *Starfarer* entered the system midway between the two orbits. A large moon, approaching lunar proportions, circles the inner terrestrial planet. The signal we are receiving emanates from that inner planet."

"From its moon," J.D. said hesitantly.

"You're right," Victoria said, surprised.

Arachne's web remained unstable, inconsistent. Victoria created a display and routed the signal into it. A holographic image formed at the center of their circle.

"This beacon wasn't meant to reach outside the system," Victoria said. "It's too weak. It was waiting. Waiting for us."

J.D. suddenly giggled. "Look at that."

Acting as a two-dimensional screen, the hologram laid out the transmission a single picture element at a time, in a Sagan frame one prime number of pixels wide by a second, different prime number of pixels high. A handsbreadth of the image was already visible, some structure already detectable.

"This is incredible," Victoria said. "We're getting it right the first time."

"It'll be a map," Satoshi said with a smile.

"Genetic structure," Stephen Thomas said, joining in the game they had often played, of trying to decide how one alien intelligence would attempt its first communication with another.

"Uh-uh," Victoria said. "Electron orbitals."

"It won't be any of those things," J.D. said. "I don't know what it will be, but it will be something different."

"How will you reply?" Satoshi asked.

"Good question," Stephen Thomas said. "We've got a little explaining to do."

They watched as the beacon built up another scan line of black or white dots. Victoria began to think she could make out the pattern that was forming to greet her.

"What can you say to an alien being," she said, "after you've announced yourself with a thermonuclear explosion?"

"I don't know yet." Joy and excitement filled J.D.'s voice. "I guess I'll just have to wing it."

ABOUT THE AUTHOR

VONDA N. MCINTYRE has been writing and publishing science fiction since she was twenty. Her novels include *Dreamsnake* (winner of the Hugo Award, presented at the World Science Fiction Convention, and the Nebula Award, presented by the Science Fiction Writers of America), *The Exile Waiting*, and *Superluminal*. She has written one children's book, *Barbary*. Her books and short stories have been translated into more than a dozen languages. The Starfarers series includes the national bestsellers *Starfarers*, *Transition*, *Metaphase*, and *Nautilus*, a series that has the distinction of having had a fan club before the first novel was written. She is also the author of Bantam's next Star Wars novel, *The Crystal Star*.

"The most important series in science fiction"* concludes in the spectacular final chapter of the *Starfarers* saga!

NAUTILUS

by Vonda N. McIntyre

The *Starfarer* had traveled farther than any human expedition in Earth history, only to encounter alien beings and a galactic civilization stranger than they ever could have imagined. Now, as the galactic string that is the ship's only means to travel back to Earth recedes from its reach, the crew must make the choice between withholding the one secret that could ensure its survival and its entrance into Civilization, or turn back before they're trapped forever, far from home in the company of a society ready to turn on them at a moment's notice!

❑ **Nautilus** (56026-3 * $5.99/$7.99 Canada)

Don't miss the first three books in the *Starfarers* saga:
❑ **Starfarers** (56341-6 * $5.99/$7.50 Canada)
❑ **Metaphase** (29223-4 * $5.99/$7.50 Canada)
❑ **Transition** (28850-4 * $5.99/$7.50 Canada)

And be sure to look for Vonda N. McIntyre's Hugo and Nebula Award-winning novel of one young healer's quest to replace the alien snake with healing powers so vital to her life and her people.
❑ **Dreamsnake** (29659-0 * $5.99/$7.50 Canada)

*Ursula K. LeGuin

Look for all of Vonda N. McIntyre's science fiction, on sale now wherever Bantam Spectra Books are sold, or use this page for ordering:

Send to: Bantam Books, Dept. SF 253
          2451 S. Wolf Road
          Des Plaines, IL 60018

Please send me the items I have checked above. I am enclosing
$_____ (please add $2.50 to cover postage and handling). Send check or money order, no cash or C.O.D.'s, please.

Mr./Ms._____

Address_____

City/State_____Zip_____
Please allow four to six weeks for delivery.
Prices and availability subject to change without notice.   SF 253 10/94